The Watchers
on the
Longships

The Watchers
on the
Longships

A tale of Cornwall in the Last Century

by

James F Cobb

The Watchers on the Longships

Published in 2005 by
Crimond House Publications
"Crimond House"
48 Frances Street
Newtownards
Co. Down
N. Ireland
BT23 7DN
www.crimondhouse.com

ISBN 0 9549 9220 2

Cover Photograph by Peter Puddiphatt Photography

Printed by J.C. Print Ltd., Belfast
Tel: 07860 205 333 Fax: 028 90790420

Introduction

Having heard of this book for many years, and had several friends talk about it, we finally located a second-hand copy. We found it to be as moving and engaging as described, and vowed to have it re-published if ever the opportunity arose. Coming from a fishing family, and after spending many holidays in lovely Cornwall, we could identify with the fibre of this book.

You would enjoy a visit to this part of the world and discover places like Billy Bray's Three Eyes Chapel and Zennor Village with its remarkable museum. Linger at Sennen Cove on a summer's night and watch the beautiful sunset, and visit the Methodist Chapel featured in this book.

We decided to reprint the book unedited, in its original language, thus retaining the character of the times.

This is our first venture into publishing as Crimond House Publications, and we feel honoured to make this particular book available to you.

Richard and Elizabeth McCoubrey. September 2005.

Acknowledgements

We would like to acknowledge the help of Lyla Montgomery, who first introduced us to this book and for proof-reading the text. Also, Carol MacPherson, Elizabeth Birnie and Nannie McKee for their help in proof-reading. Also the late James Thompson, Comber, who so highly recommended the book to us.

Preface

It may be of some interest to the readers of the following tale to know that many of the incidents related in it, highly improbable as they may seem, are strictly founded upon fact. The light was first exhibited in the Longships on the 29th September 1795, as related in the story. That one of the keepers of early days, who was left alone there, and had not been informed previously of the horrible noise caused by the pent-up air in the cavern below, because so terrified that his hair turned white in a single night, is a well-known fact. All the circumstances, also, relating to the little girl who was left alone in the lighthouse – her father, the keeper, having been purposely kidnapped and confined by wreckers – and who was reluctantly obliged to stand on the Family Bible to light the lamps, are perfectly authentic.

The noble and heroic exploits of the young clergyman, related towards the close of the story, is so far true, that the incident really occurred at, or near the spot described. The hero, however, was not a parson, but a schoolmaster.

It is, perhaps, as well to mention that the term "Methodist" was in former days used, not so much to denote any particular sect, but applied indiscriminately in a term of reproach to all earnestly religious people, whether Churchmen or Dissenters. It is in this sense that it is so frequently employed in our story.

Torquay, February 1876

Contents

1

A Death-Bed
And A Darkened Home

"The tongues of dying men
Enforce attention like deep harmony;
Where words are scarce, they are seldom spent in vain,
For they breathe truth, that breathe their words in pain.
He, that no more must say, is listened more
Than they, whom youth and ease have taught to glose;
More are men's ends marked than their lives before:
The setting sun, and music at the close,
At the last taste of sweets, is sweetest last;
Writ in remembrance, more than things long past."

- Shakespeare, Richard III

On a slightly rising ground to the west of the little village of Sennen Cove, near the Land's End, there stood, towards the close of the last century, a small cottage, roughly built of granite blocks, with a thatched roof, on which rested several huge stones. Its situation exposed it to the violence of all the gales which swept over the Atlantic; the winds, from whatever point of the compass they blew, howled and whistled round its walls; the noise of the breakers, as they dashed on the iron-bound coast below, was ever present to the ears of its inhabitants, who had grown so accustomed to their dull, monotonous roar, that they would almost have been startled by its absence. A neat little garden surrounded the cottage; here, in spring and summer, a few hardy flowers might be seen, but it was for the most part planted with potatoes and turnips. Not a tree or a shrub grew anywhere near, but several immense granite boulders were strewn here and there on the ground, within a short distance of the humble dwelling.

It was a wild and tempestuous night at the beginning of November. With more than usual fierceness did the wind roar round the cottage walls. Rain and spray beat against the windows, which shook and rattled with every fresh gust. There was no moon, and not a star was to be seen in the cloudy sky. The scene within the cottage was in complete harmony with the gloom without. On a bed in the corner of a small and neatly-furnished room a poor woman is lying. Her faced is pale, wan, and wasted; it is evident that her last hour is approaching; her thin hands are clasped over her breast, and her eyes wander with sad but affectionate gaze from one to the other of the three remaining occupants of the room, from whom she knows she must so soon be parted. These are a tall, weather-beaten man of sailor-like appearance, between forty and fifty years of age, who is standing close to the head of the bed, and, evidently, is the husband of the dying woman. Every now and then he bends over her with loving tenderness; with his rough hand he smooths her pillow, raises her head that he may put some refreshing drink to her parched lips, while all the time the tears roll down his cheeks. On the other side of the bed stands a little girl, whose acute grief is plainly depicted in her countenance; she from time to time takes her mother's hand and kisses it, covering it with her tears. At the foot of the bed a young lad, of about fifteen, is kneeling; his whole frame is convulsed with sorrow, his face cannot be seen, for it is buried in his hands; but his deep sobs, which he is utterly unable to suppress, may be heard amid the howling of the wind, and the splashing of the rain and spray against the windows.

"Owen," said the dying woman, in a very faint voice, "Owen, the end is near now, I feel sure. I am so weak and faint. I must say farewell to you and little Mary and poor Philip. May God bless you and keep you all when I am gone."

The husband bent over and kissed her forehead, but he could not say a word; fresh sobs and bursts of tears proceeded from the son and daughter.

"Owen," she began again, "you have been a good, kind husband to me, and now we must part; but I have one thing to say before I go."

"Mother! Mother! Will you really leave us?" sobbed the little girl.

"Yes,, my child; it is God's will. Owen," she said, in a still fainter voice, looking lovingly up into her husband's face, "For my sake, when I am gone, don't be led astray again – do not join those bad men – do not go down to the grave with"-

"Stop, Ellen, dearest," exclaimed the man, trying to master his grief, "do not let such thoughts trouble you now. No, no, I promise you, solemnly I promise you, I will never join the wreckers again. I have seen enough of their wicked, murderous ways. O Ellen! You know it was not of my own will. I was to blame, indeed, for I was easy and weak – but I was drawn into it. I have not led a wrecker's life. Only twice"-

"Alas! Owen, yes. I know you are too easily persuaded. You say only twice, but even then, you may have helped to cause the death of some poor fellow-creature just within sight of home. Oh! that wild, wicked way of life – the curse of this land!"

"O Ellen, Ellen! forgive me," sobbed the man; "be assured it will never happen again. You know how sorry I was afterwards; and then we were so poor at that time, and you looked so pale and ill after nursing Philip in the fever."

"Owen! Owen! Money earned in such a way can only bring a curse."

"I know that," said the husband; "may God forgive me the wickedness I joined in then. They shall never force me to go with them any more – they may kill me first."

"Don't be over-confident, Owen. Yet I feel happier now; I know you won't deceive me, nor forget your promise to your dying wife; but pray God to give you strength to resist temptation if it comes."

"I will, indeed, Ellen – I will, indeed," he said earnestly.

"Mary, dearest child," said the poor mother, "I am going to leave you. Try and be a comfort to your poor father when I am gone. He will have troubles enough – don't add to them. And Philip, dear, come and give me a last kiss too." The lad got up and bent over his mother to kiss her. Thick and fast did his tears fall upon her pale face. "Poor boy," she said, "you have been a good son to me. May God bless and protect you. Help your father; don't have him to run away to sea, as many do; and read your Bible, Phil, and go to church on Sundays regular, and go on teaching Mary as I used to do."

"Yes, mother, I'll try and do all you wish; but what shall we do without you?"

"God will take care of you, my boy. May He guide you to do what is right," said the mother.

Philip could not utter a word. In a paroxysm of grief he threw himself on the bed and buried his head in his hands.

The little girl held her mother's cold hand in hers, and gazed lovingly into her face; she did not speak, for she could not, but the tears streamed down her cheeks.

The husband put his head down on the pillow close to his wife's face, and she whispered to him a few words of affectionate farewell. She was rapidly sinking. The silence in the room seemed only intensified by the roar of the tempest without.

All at once voices were heard outside the cottage. Wild shouts of "Come on, men! come on, a wreck! a wreck!" Lights passed the window, and there was a clatter of many feet along the path close by.

The dying woman shuddered, an expression of horror passed over her face, and she looked up at her husband.

"Never, Ellen, never again," he said, firmly and solemnly. "I would rather starve than do it."

"Thank God for those words. Alas! Owen, that I should hear such sounds now!" whispered his wife.

The wreckers, hastening to their wicked work, had just passed by.

"They are gone now, mother," said the little girl. "They won't come back till the morning; do not think about them."

"No, my child … I am trying to think of the blessed place above to which may God bring you all at last, when the wicked cease from troubling" –

She said no more, she was quite exhausted. A few minutes after the good wife and mother breathed her last, and Owen Tresilian was alone with his son and little daughter.

The good couple were humble fisher folk, who had lived a simple life in that remote nook of old England. They had been married well night twenty years, and in that period had experienced as much of the joys and sorrows of life, as is the ordinary lot of most mortals in their lowly spheres. Owen, a native of Sennen, had, when quite a boy, gone to sea, joined his Majesty's navy, and after some ten years' service, returned to, and settled down in, his old home. He married Ellen whom he had known and loved since they were children together, and, taking up abode in the little cottage above the Cove, Owen gained his livelihood principally by fishing, but he also made some profits by cultivating a bit of ground which he rented a sort distance from his cottage. Ellen was skilful at her needle, and worked for the squire's family, and for some of the more well-to-do among the villagers. They had five children; of these the boy and girl above-mentioned were the only ones that remained to them. Two had died, when infants; one boy had been drowned at sea, - a calamity from which his mother never recovered.

The inhabitants of the few scattered cottages on the seashore, which formed the hamlet of Sennen Cove, were in those days a rude, and almost savage, set of people. They professed, indeed, to gain their livelihood by fishing, but in reality smuggling and wrecking were their chief employments. The wreckers of Cornwall have gained an unenviable notoriety. The men of Sennen had, owing to the fringe of rocks which surrounded their coast, to the violence of the tempests which raged there, and to the absence, in those days, of any lighthouses or light-ships on the shore, full opportunity for carrying on their cruel and nefarious occupation. Many a gallant ship, when within sight of home, was, by false lights and signals, ensnared into the very midst of that maze of rocks which bristle round the Land's End, there to be dashed to pieces, while its crew found a watery grave in the angry surf, or more luckless still, succeeded in reaching land, only to be put to death by the inhuman hands of those, who should have been the first to rescue them.

It was but natural that men who were accustomed to partake in such deeds of infamy, should be little removed from barbarians, and that any among them who tried to lead a more humane or respectable life, should be exposed to jeers, mockery, or even persecution.

Such was the case with Owen Tresilian. He had served many years in the fleet, had seen much hard service, and been engaged in several naval battles with the French; he held very different ideas of honour and honesty from those entertained by his fellow villagers. He was a brave man, who would not suffer any act of cruelty or meanness to be done in his presence; his undaunted pluck was recognised by all. Bad as the Sennen men were, yet the better ones could not but respect Owen, while the worst feared him. Still there had, alas! been occasions when even so upright a man as Tresilian had yielded to temptation, and joined in that which in his inmost soul he abhorred.

Twice, indeed, when his wife's health had been failing, when his children had been crying for bread, when fishing had failed, and there seemed no means to provide for the wants of his family, Owen, unknown to his wife, had joined in the plunder of vessels, which foundered on the rocks close by. He had shared in no attempt on either occasion to lure these ships to destruction, in fact, there was considerable doubt, whether the Sennen people had caused these wrecks, and Owen had been persuaded to go down late at night, and help to pick up the plunder which was washed on the shore, by one of his companions, to whom he had shown considerable kindness, and who was in many respects superior to the rest of the villagers, but not above joining occasionally in their dishonest enterprises.

It was only by increased comforts that his wife discovered what Owen had done, and very bitter was her grief. She implored him with tears never to act thus again. She knew it had been done for her sake, which almost made her feel as if she had been an accessory in this sin. It was the remembrance of this which had made her so anxious, during her last hours, to induce her husband to promise her never to consort with wreckers again.

Ellen Tresilian was a good woman, living up to the light she possessed. The last century was notoriously dark and profane. Religion was openly disregarded by all classes. There never was a period in England of lower morality. All vices abounded, drinking to excess, profligacy, riot, cruelty, neglect of the poor, oppression of the weak. But there were, as always, even in the darkest ages of the Church, exceptions to this rule; bright spots here and there; men and women sometimes in obscure towns and villages, sometimes amid all the vice of the great metropolis, might be found leading a holy and a godly life, shining forth like stars on this dark night of iniquity. Though the Church of England was almost lifeless, her clergy for the most part idle or devoted to pleasure, neglecting their holy functions, and only performing those duties which the law demanded of them, yet there were exceptions also among them. Good men and true, who led lives of holy self-denial and earnest prayer, who were not content with preaching to their flocks every Sunday, a mere dry morality; but who in burning words placed before them the old, old story of the Gospel, and pointed to the cross of Jesus, as the only refuge for the weary and sin-burdened soul.

Not many years before our story commences, the great apostle of the eighteenth century, the saintly John Wesley, had made England ring, from north to south and from east to west, with the glorious sound of the gospel of Christ, proclaimed in such a way as that age had never heard before. The holy man had passed into Cornwall; he had gathered around him the rough miners of the interior, and the wild fishermen and wreckers of the coast. In spite of every opposition he preached to them of Jesus. He told them that God loved them, steeped in every crime as many of them were; he assured them that God was their Father, and they His children, far as they had wandered from His fold. Many hearts were touched by his earnest words, tears trickled down hard and weather-beaten faces which had never been moistened by a tear before, and hands, once stained in crime, were now uplifted in prayer. In no part of England was the preaching of John Wesley more crowned with success than in Cornwall; men who had been eminent for fighting, drinking, and all manner of wickedness, now became eminent for sobriety, piety, and all manner of goodness. The wreckers,, who had become such a scandal to humanity, and given the country so evil a repute, were everywhere now on the decrease; only the worst characters indulged in this cruel business; neither was smuggling so universal as before.

Ellen Tresilian was only a child when she first heard Mr. Wesley preach at St. Sennen. His words sank deep into her heart, the impression they made was never effaced. Owen's mother was also among the number of those whose hearts and lives were changed by listening to the gospel message so plainly delivered, and it was owing to her earnest admonitions, and to the good seed which she planted early in her son's heart, that though he was not what in those days was called a Methodist, yet he was honest, upright and well-conducted, in comparison to most of the men in the village.

At that period neither national or Sunday schools existed. Only here and there could a man or woman be found, who was able to read, and no shame was felt on account of such ignorance. Children were allowed to grow up without any education, except what their parents were able to give them, or what they learned from dames, who in some villages set up schools on their own account. To teach reading was generally the extent of their knowledge. Those who were able to write and cypher, were regarded as very learned and superior persons.

It is not to be wondered at, therefore, that Owen Tresilian could neither read nor write. Ellen had learned to read out of an old Family bible, which was an heirloom in the family. Her father, who was a clever man in his way, for he not only could read but write a little too, and taught her in his leisure hours. She was his only child; so when he died, very soon after her marriage, she inherited the old Bible; every evening she would read out of it to her husband, who listened reverently and attentively to the sacred words. And when her children grew up, she taught them to read too. Little Mary would often sit before the fire with the large volume on a chair beside her, poring over the pages; sometimes she would read stories from it aloud, while her mother worked, and her father and brother mended their nets. Thus the whole family were quite familiar with sacred history – perhaps more so than poor folk are in our own days – for the Bible, a Prayerbook, and a selection of Wesley's hymns, were the only books they possessed, and over and over again was the sacred volume, and especially the Gospels, read through.

Ellen Tresilian, never strong, had sunk into a consumption, which had carried her off rapidly at the last, leaving her husband and children overwhelmed with grief in their cheerless and desolate abode.

The body of the good wife and mother was committed to the grave in the little churchyard at St. Sennen, a bleak, dreary spot indeed, very different from the neat, well-kept churchyards nowadays happily so common. In those times a cross was never seen above a grave; at St. Sennen the headstones were mostly of the coarse granite peculiar to the district.. Here and there an urn or a broken column surmounted a tomb, but these belonged to the more wealthy of the parishioners. The churchyard was as ill-kept and untended as the church, presenting no symbol of hope or comfort to mourning hearts. But the beautiful and cheering words of the service, with which, in sure and certain hope of the blessed resurrection, the Church of England commits her children to the earth, then, as now, spoke of peace and joy, and of a happy life beyond the grave.

The three mourners had returned to their cottage. They sat silently round the fire. Owen's head rested on his hand; his eyes stared vacantly before him. Philip was mending a net in a very mechanical way; his hands moved, but his heart was not in his work. He was thinking of his loved and lost mother. Little Mary had reached down the big Bible from its shelf, and was poring with tearful eyes over its sacred pages.

The father was the first to break the silence.

"We have a hard life before us, children," he said; "it has been bad enough indeed hitherto, but now without your good mother, who helped and cheered us so, it's a sorry look out for us all."

"Yes, father," said little Mary, "but mother used often to say when she was ill, and knew that she was going to die, that we were not to fret when she was gone, but do all we could to cheer and help one another."

"I know she did, child, but how can we help fretting? How can I alone do everything for you both? and what's to become of you, Molly, when Philip and I are out fishing all day, and sometimes of a night too? You can't be left all alone here; you would be frightened, I know; and who's to get your meals for you?"

"Oh, never mind about me, father!" said Mary. "I'm not afraid to be alone, neither by day nor by night; there's no one would do me any harm, I'm sure. Mother taught me how to sweep out the room, and showed me how to cook the dinner for you and Phil, so don't trouble yourself about me, father."

"Yes, child, but there are other things to think of. Your mother used to earn a good bit of money with her needle. Often when fishing failed, and I could make nothing either by that or by the garden, she would scrape enough together to keep us honestly afloat. Now she's taken, and there's only Phil and me to depend on. Why, we may be nigh starving before long, Molly, and I don't see who's to help us."

"I do, father," said Mary, firmly. "God will. Mother often told me so. Our Heavenly Father feels the fowls of the air, and He loves us better than them. It's here, in the Bible. I'll find it for you," and then she read the whole passage from the sixth chapter of St. Matthew.

"You are a good girl, Molly, and take after your mother," said the poor man sorrowfully. "That's all true, I know, and I'll try and trust God to provide for our wants, but it's hard to do so at times like these, when all seems to go against one."

"Yes, father," remarked Philip, "and with winter coming on too; if it had only been spring, instead of November, it wouldn't be so bad."

"But it's all the same to God, Phil," said Mary, solemnly.

"You teach us both a lesson, my child," said Owen, as he got up and bent over his little daughter to kiss her. "You have done me good already, and I know your mother is gone to a happier place, and that I ought not to grieve for her. She often said that God would never forsake her motherless children, so I shall try and trust Him, and do the best I can for you myself, as well."

"And I'll work hard, that I will, father," said Philip. "I'll dig at our piece of ground, and plant the potatoes for you, and try and get a job now and then up at the squire's."

They all seemed a little more cheerful now, and were able to talk more calmly about the future – desolate as it appeared to them.

Owen tried all he could to persuade his little daughter to let him send her for a year or two to her aunt at Truro. He said she was too young to live without womanly care, and he could not bear the thought of her being left alone, as she often would be, for days, and perhaps at nights, in that lonely cottage, but he soon saw that it would well nigh break the child's heart to be separated from him and her brother. She implored him to let her stay. Philip, too, espoused her cause, so that the father at last yielded, and consented that she should remain.

2

The Squire And His Son

"Oh, it is hard to work for God,
To rise and take His part
Upon this battle-field of earth,
And not sometimes lose heart.

"Thrice blest is he to whom is given
The instinct that can tell
That God is on the field, when He
Is most invisible.

"Blest, too, is he who can divine
Where real right doth lie,
And dares to take the side that seems
Wrong to man's blindfold eye.

"Then learn to scorn the praise of men,
And learn to lose with God;
For Jesus won the world through shame,
And beckons thee His road."

- Faber

The Lord of the manor, or squire of the district, lived at an old house between St. Sennen and the next village of St. Buryan. It was a rambling building, half castle, half manor house, standing in extensive grounds, in which the trees and shrubs were stunted and dwarfed by the cold winds of that exposed country. The garden was desolate and ill-kept, productive of more weeds than flowers. The proprietor cared only for hunting by day, and drinking by night. He was a fair specimen of the landlords of those times, neither better nor worse than most of them. In his temper he was fitful and uncertain; he had been known to do kind actions sometimes to those in distress, but he could act harshly and unjust too. He was not altogether innocent of the crime of encouraging the wicked system of wrecking. It was said that in his younger days he had warmly joined in it, and made large sums of money by the barbarous trade. Though occasionally seen in church, he laughed at religion, and if there was one thing he hated above all others, it was a Methodist; any one, man, woman, or child, it mattered not which, who was a follower of the abhorred John Wesley, and professed to live a strictly religious life, as that holy man enjoined, was obnoxious to him. But, like most men, however hardened and vicious they may be, he had one tender point in his heart, and that was his love for his only son. His wife had died soon after he was born, and from his infancy the father had devoted himself to this boy, his darling, his heir. No expense or trouble did he spare to provide him with all that could give him pleasure. The servants were ordered to obey, and even to anticipate, his wishes. Hew as a bold, high-spirited lad, loving to roam as a child over the wild, breezy heaths which surrounded his birthplace, to scramble down the granite cliffs on to the sea-shore, to watch the boats tossing on the fierce waves, and the rolling breakers as they dashed in clouds of feathery spray against the rocks. An old servant of his father's, one Roger Barlow, was intrusted with the charge of young Master Arthur Pendrean; from him he learned all the wild legends of the country, and became familiar with the stories of wrecks and wreckers told by the dwellers on the desolate coast. There was not a mine in the neighbourhood whose deepest shaft he had not gone down; he had been out with the fishermen in their boats from Sennen Cove; had been present at hurling and wrestling matches; in fact, the lad was thoroughly Cornish to the backbone. When he grew older he was sent to school at Truro, where he distinguished himself as a clever scholar, and as a thorough athlete. He had been known to thrash a boy nearly twice as big as himself, the occasion of the quarrel being that the great boy had cruelly treated a very little boy whom Arthur had taken under his protection. He was the first in every game of strength and skill, but he was noble and generous, even taking the side of the weak, and never tolerating injustice or oppression.

During one of his vacations, while riding through a village in the neighbourhood of his home, he came suddenly upon a large crowd. An elderly man of venerable aspect, with long silvery locks, was earnestly addressing a number of rough miners, fishermen, and farm-labourers, together with a multitude of women and children who were eagerly drinking in his words. Arthur listened. He had heard his father very often speak about John Wesley and the Methodists, cursing and swearing as he mentioned them; so the young fellow naturally imagined them to be a very evil and mischievous set of people, whose object was to stir up sedition and trouble in the country. He did not guess, therefore, the object of the meeting and when he was told that the speaker was John Wesley, and that this was an assemblage of Methodists, he was not a little shocked to find himself in such company. However, as he was here, he thought he might as well stop and listen to what the man had to say; he could tell his father all about it at dinner; he thought it might amuse him, and possibly raise a laugh. Arthur's religious opinions were of the crudest character. He had been taught his Catechism at school, he heard the Bible read at church whenever he went there; but as to listening to the sermon, he always followed the example of his father, and some of the small congregation, by composing himself to sleep when it began. It was literally now for the first time that he listened to the story of the cross, as it fell in plain, yet eloquent, accents from that old man's lips. He preached of repentance, of the world to come; he told them of the love of Jesus towards mankind, how He had left His Father's throne to come and dwell on earth, and then asked them to give their hearts to Him Who had died on the cross to save them.

All this was new to Arthur; he might indeed have heard it before, but it had made no impression upon him. He was riveted to the spot, he was obliged to remain till the sermon was over.

The preacher had met with attention, on the whole, though there had been some slight interruption from a group of rude, savage-looking miners, not far from where Arthur was standing. As the old man proceeded, however, they were loud murmurs of disapproval from these men. They surrounded the preacher with angry gestures, threatening to seize him and drag him through a horse-pond close by. Others, on the contrary, stood up in his defence, and a quarrel seemed imminent. Arthur, whose generous disposition always led him to take the weaker side, was the more disposed to do so now, because he had been impressed and touched by the old man's words. There was something grand and brave too, he thought, in this feeble and venerable clergyman standing up to rebuke these wild, rude folk for their evil ways. His calm fearlessness pleased him, and when one of the miners advanced to seize the preacher and carry their cowardly threat into execution, Arthur rushed forward with the intention of placing himself between the old man and his assailant; but at that moment he felt a heavy hand on his shoulder, and turning round he perceived Roger Barlow, who, with an old servant's freedom, explained, "Come away, Master Arthur, this is no place for you; the squire would storm for an hour if he heard that you had been listening to the Methodists."

"I'll not leave this spot, Roger, till I have seen fair play," said the boy boldly. "Stop these fellows from ill-treating that old man, and then I'll go with you at once."

Roger, whose sympathies went with the Methodists, stepped forward. The crowd was quieted by threats that, if a disturbance was made, the justices would interfere, and Mr. Wesley was allowed to depart quietly.

But the story, a few days after, reached the squire's ears; at once he fell into a violent passion. He sent for his son, and with a volley of oaths and curses (too common, alas! in those days among the upper classes of society), told him that if he ever went near the Methodists again, he would disinherit him, and turn him out of doors to beg his bread. His hatred of religion seemed then even stronger than his love for his son.

Arthur did not make any reply to his father's angry words. When he found that his silence only irritated the old man, he told him that pure accident had brought him to the spot, and that a sense of honour and fairness had made him stand up to protect the weak against the strong.

Neither threats nor entreaties could extract from the lad a promise that he would never listen to the preacher again. The idea that his son might become a Methodist haunted the squire by day and night, caused him great trouble and vexation, and made him more violent and passionate than ever. All that he could hope was, that when the boy returned to school, he would forget the matter. Such, however, was not the case. Arthur's heart had been too deeply impressed by what he had heard, the arrow of conviction had shot home. He now studied his Bible diligently, was attentive to the services of the Church, and joined fervently in the prayers. He was as diligent in his studies and as fond of games as before; but he was often laughed and jeered at by his schoolfellows for refusing to use or tolerate bad language, for being religious, and, in fact, he was actually called by the then opprobrious name of "Methodist."

The next vacation his father observed that his son's manner was changed, and that his worst fears were realised. To him the most alarming symptom in Arthur was his regular attendance at the church service which was celebrated on alternate Sundays at the three churches of St. Buryan, St. Sennen, and St. Levan, these three benefices being held in those days b y one clergyman. Great as was the distance, and however wet and stormy the weather, Arthur might always be seen at his place in church, while his example drew others with him. In the week, too, his father discovered that he now and then attended meetings held in the village for reading the Bible and prayer. This made the squire furious, and he threatened to send his son away to London, or abroad, unless he returned to his senses, as he expressed it. In the midst of his rage Arthur went back to school for the last time. During the term a Confirmation, then a very rare event, was to take place at Truro. He was one of the candidates. Though the preparation he received was very different from that given in these days, and defective in many ways, yet Arthur derived the greatest benefit from the sacred rite; fresh grace and renewed strength for the battle which in Holy Baptism he had been pledged to fight being then vouchsafed to the faithful young soldier and servant of Christ.

He now made up his mind to seek Holy Orders, and do his best in that dark age to make the knowledge of God and of the Saviour known to the rude miner and fisher folk of his native county.

Arthur was between sixteen and seventeen when he left school. He told his father boldly that he wished to go to Oxford, and that he intended to become a clergyman. The grief and indignation with which the squire heard this announcement may well be imagined. At first he refused his consent. He swore at his son, and used every term of contempt he could think of, to express his wrath at the decision. He accused him of being lazy, cowardly, a weak milksop. Why did he not go into the army or navy! Had he no desire, like most young men of his age, to enjoy the gay life of London for a time? He would do anything for him if he liked; - but that he should be a parson, the idea was repugnant to him in every way, he could not consent to it.

But menaces, sarcasm, and ridicule were alike ineffectual. Arthur was firm in his decision. He was respectful and affectionate to his father, but he had the courage of his convictions – he would not give up his religion, nor his intention of serving God.

He must now remain quietly at home, doing all the good that came in his way, till his father gave his content for him to depart to University. The boy had a hard time before him; his faith and courage were severely put to the proof. The squire had constantly parties of his neighbours to dinner, and, as was then the custom, they rarely left the table sober; but Arthur always retired from the room, amid the jeers and mockery of his father and his guests, before the drinking commenced. He bore all this meekly and bravely, regarding it as a stern discipline to fit him for the future combats he saw he must engage in with the ungodliness everywhere around. He though, too, of all his Blessed Master had endured for him, and amid these many trials he was peaceful and happy. He would often leave his father's table to repair, through storm and rain, to one of the villages, or to a solitary cottage, to read the Bible to some lonely sufferer on a sick-bed, or join with a few of the awakened miners or fishermen in the reading of God's Word and prayer. He prayed constantly that his father's heart might be touched, that he might relent at last and grant his wish. God heard his prayer, but in a way he little expected. The squire was taken seriously ill, his life was despaired of. Arthur never left his father's bedside, he waited on him with tender and affectionate care. At first the old man was surly and morose towards his son, swearing at him as usual, and constantly reminding him that he had blighted his dearest hopes, and caused him bitter disappointment by his obstinacy and folly. Gradually, however, Arthur's love, self-sacrifice, and unremitting attention began to make an impression on the squire's hard heart. As he grew weaker and more dependent on his son, the old affection for him, - the one soft point in his character, - returned; he felt that he had acted harshly and unjustly, and that he was not worthy of all this love and devotion now lavished upon him. He spoke more kindly to Arthur now, and when, through his tender nursing, he began to grow stronger, he confessed to him, with tears in his eyes, that he felt he had been wrong, that he might have his way now, and go to Oxford if he wished. He never should like his being a parson, but if nothing else would satisfy him, he must give his consent.

For Arthur that was a doubly happy day, for not only with returning health was his father's former affection to him restored, but the one earnest wish of his heart was at last about to be satisfied, his prayer was heard and answered. Fervently did he thank God that night for His mercy and goodness towards him.

A few months after he bade farewell to his father, who had now completely recovered, and started for Oxford. Here he studied with diligence and industry, - not that there was any necessity for exertion to obtain a degree, for examinations were in those days made so easy that any could pass them. Arthur led a quiet, studious life, associating with the very few young men who were like-minded with himself. Occasionally they were exposed to jeers, mockery, and even persecution; for anything savouring of Methodism, as all earnest religion was styled in those days, was most unpopular, not only with the under-graduates but with the authorities of the University. Only a few years before six students had been expelled by the Vice-Chancellor, because "they held Methodistic tenets, and took on them to pray, read, and expound the Scriptures in private houses" – such was the toleration of that age.

After a residence of between two and three years at Oxford, Arthur took his degree and returned to Cornwall. His father had given his promise, and he was not a man who would go back from his word, - still he did all in his power to dissuade his son from taking Holy Orders. He pictured to him the life of ease and independence before him when, after his death, he should succeed to the estate; he offered him money to travel, - in short, promised to gratify any wish he might express, if he would only abandon his long-cherished idea. He spoke to him of the folly of sacrificing himself to a life which was regarded in those days almost as one of degradation by most people, and in which he would acquire neither fame nor profit. However, when he perceived that neither argument nor persuasion could shake his son's firm determination to become a parson, he once more reluctantly gave way, and submitted to the inevitable.

There was very little difficulty in obtaining ordination in those days. The old clergyman who held the three livings of St. Buryan, St. Sinnen, and St. Levan, led an easy life, and did not trouble himself more than he was obliged to do in the fulfilment of his clerical duties. He baptized, married, and buried his flock; he said the prayers once a Sunday at one of the churches in his charge, and preached one sermon, a dry, moral essay, not always of his own composition; he celebrated the Holy Communion once in three months, as well as on Easter-day and Christmas-day. It never entered his head to visit the poor among his parishioners, though he was a frequent guest at the squire's table, and shared his dislike of Methodists. Master Arthur, with his zeal for religion, was quite a marvel to the old gentleman. He was a thorn in his side, too, for he asked him questions difficult to answer, and urged him to set on foot works of piety and benevolence in the parish of a troublesome nature, and subversive of that indolent ease in which he passed his days.

Arthur's ambition was to succeed Mr. Somers as rector of these united parishes, and during his lifetime to act as his curate. The latter proposal was not very palatable to the rector, but as the squire wished it, because he desired to keep his son near to him, he had to give way, and Arthur was ordained at Exeter as his curate.

The village of St. Sennen with the adjoining Cove became the special sphere of his labour, which had begun there about a year before the commencement of our story. There was not a cottage here that was not visited, not a man, woman, or child that Master Arthur – for he still went by that name – had not a kind word for; all in distress found in him a friend and helper. The only men who hated him were the wreckers, for he had, from the first, firmly set his face against their cruel and iniquitous way of life. He was determined, whatever it might cost him, to put a stop to it, and his pluck and daring were so well known, that the men were always more or less alarmed when at their wicked work of luring a vessel on the rocks, lest Master Arthur, well armed, and with a few trusty followers, whom he had warmly attached to him, should be down upon them, and suddenly bring to naught their projects.

During the autumn, which had been a very stormy one, there had been more wrecks than usual. The absence in those days, not only of life-boats, rocket apparatus, and all those many skilful and benevolent means by which, now, lives are rescued from perishing at sea, but also of lighthouses and lightships, round the coast, greatly increased the number of disasters, so that it did not need the evil arts of the wreckers, to cause vessels to lose their reckoning, and to be dashed upon the rocks which skirt the Cornish coast. Sometimes driven by storms, sometimes bewildered and helpless through fogs, the hapless sailors returning from long voyages, when in sight of the beloved shores of England, perished in the waters without a hand being stretched out to save them.

Within the last few years the minds of many charitable persons in England had been directed to this question. Arthur had long felt that something ought to be done to guide the mariner to safety, instead of luring him to destruction, and that a lighthouse must be erected on some prominent point of that iron-bound and dangerous coast.

3

Arthur's Plan

"Then he and the sea began their strife
And worked with power and might;
Whatever the man reared up by day,
The sea broke down by night.
He caught at ebb with bar and beam,
He sailed to shore at flow,
And at his side by that same tide
Come bar and beam also.

For ah! His looks that are so stout,
And his speeches brave and fair,
He may wait on the wind, wait on the wave,
But he'll build no lighthouse there."

- J. Ingelow

When Arthur Pendrean was once fully convinced of the necessity of any project upon which he had set his heart, he never rested till all the means in his power to carry it into execution, had been employed. He succeeded in persuading his father, who since his illness had become far more susceptible to kindly and benevolent impulses, that a lighthouse ought to be erected at some point on the coast. He had corresponded with shipowners in London, and in the large seaport towns of the kingdom, and the result at last was, that a wealthy merchant, who had lost several valuable ships and cargoes on the Cornish coast, determined to build a lighthouse near the Land's End, on the condition that the Government allowed him to levy a toll upon the shipping which passed it, for a certain number of years.

It is a wild but grand scene which surrounds the traveller who stands on the extreme point of the Land's End, the most westerly spot in England. Behind him the rugged plain, strewn with great boulders, with here and there bright patches of golden gorse; on either side rise large granite cliffs of fantastic shape, advancing into the sea; before him dashing in clouds of snowy spray against the fringe of rocks which skirts the coast, and roaring with terrific sounds in the dark and mysterious caverns beneath. Rather more than a mile from the Land's End, a lighthouse may now be seen, built on the largest of a cluster of rocks, the Carn Bras, and called the Longships. This building was in course of construction when our story commences; it owed its origin to Arthur's endeavours, as well as to the enterprise of the merchant above alluded to.

On a stormy winter afternoon, two men were standing on the Land's End gazing out to sea, and watching the vessels as they sailed by, buffeted by the billows. One was a man between fifty and sixty, short, thick set, with dark features and forbidding aspect; the other was much younger, probably about thirty, he was tall and stalwart, fair-complexioned, but with a weather-beaten face. Both looked as if they had lived hard lives, exposed to storms, tempests, and dangers of every kind. They were dressed like fishermen, with high boots and sou'westers. The eyes of both rested on the rising walls of the lighthouse.

"Ben," said the elder, "that lighthouse, if it is ever finished, will be our ruin. A curse on him who ever thought of building it!"

"That was Master Arthur Pendrean," said his companion; "we heard nothing about it till he came among us."

"That's what they call charity, taking the bread out of our mouths," rejoined the other with an oath.

"It'll never be finished, John," was the reply; "look, every now and then, the waves cover it over altogether, so that nothing can be seen of it, and lately we have had such high winds, they have not been able to get on with the works at all."

"Don't go and comfort yourself with any fancies of that kind, Ben.

That lighthouse will be finished before next winter, I know; look how steadily they worked all the summer, and though we have had worse weather than usual this autumn and winter, that there work has stood as firm as the rock on which it's built. I had a good look at it last time I was round that way in my boat."

"I wish a lot of our fellows would go and pull it down, some fine night, John," said the other, "I'll be the first to join them."

"Pull it down, man, why you're a fool to talk of such a thing. If you'd only see'd it as I have! Why, them there stones are all fitted and nailed and cemented one into another, as I say, it's as strong as the rock itself."

"And when it is finished, John, who's a going to live there, I should like to know? There must be some one to keep the lamps lighted," said Ben Pollard.

"Of course, there must; and a nice life he'll have of it. Why, there's such a roaring and a raging of the sea, even in calm weather, in the caves underneath them rocks, that you can scarcely hear yourself speak, however loud you shout; and I should like to know how that there lighthouse keeper'll get his food. Sometimes it's a week at a time before any boat can get near the rock, and there's not many of our Sennen folk that'll take any great trouble to go out and help him. He'll starve perhaps, and a good job too," he said with a malicious laugh.

"Not so sure of that, John, there are three or four of our men's heads already getting turned by that young rascally Methodist, Pendrean. Look at Owen Tresilian, for instance."

"I tell you what it is, Ben," said the other, and an expression of bitter hatred passed over his repulsive features; "if there's any one on earth I owe a grudge to, it is to that Tresilian. He was bad enough before his wife died, but since her death he's become a regular out-and-out Methodist; he used to wink at smuggling, and I have known him have a hand in it, too, on the sly; but now I believe if he had the chance he'd peach about it, and get us into trouble."

"Twice, I know, John, he profited by a wreck."

"Yes; and I'll not forget that against him, should it be convenient."

"He's become lately Master Arthur's right hand man, John; and as to that boy of his, why, he's always with that young fool of a parson."

"We'll pay them both off some day. I have got another plan in my head, Ben," said the elder man, with a chuckle. "The lighthouse is not built yet, and we may still have some fine wrecks before the winter's over."

"Hope we shall, John, for business has become very slack of late."

These two men, John Nichols and Ben Pollard, were probably the worst characters and the most daring wreckers in the neighbourhood. They, associated with others, had carried on their wicked traffic for many years with great success, but it did not follow that they were at all comfortably off in consequence. All the gains of these men were no sooner made, than they were spent in drinking and gambling. John, as the older, was the more hardened of the two; he had led a wild, desperate life, both in England and abroad – a life stained with many crimes of the blackest dye. Ben, on the contrary, had never left his native village, he had a cottage at Sennen Cove, and was a married man with a young family, who, owing to his recklessness and selfishness, lived in extreme misery and want.

It may well be imagined how obnoxious to such men was the prospect of the erection of a lighthouse on the Longships. That would decrease their gains there could be no doubt; that it would be the means of saving life, they were too selfish, too unfeeling, to take into consideration; they cared for no one but themselves. They, and in fact the majority of the men in the village, were bitterly incensed against Arthur Pendrean, not only because he was the originator of the lighthouse scheme, but because he never hesitated boldly to remonstrate with them upon their evil manner of life, and frequently urged them to amend their ways. Then they had another grudge against him, for his genuine sympathy, had already won over a few of the men, who had begun to lead honester and steadier lives. Arthur's position, not only as the parson, but also as the squire's son, prevented them from treating him openly, as they would have done, had they dared. They knew, too, that this young parson was not a man to be trifled with; many of them, when they were boys together, had felt the weight of his arm, and there was not a man in the village who did not wince before the calm, stern glance of his eye. He could manage a boat as well as any of them in a squall, he knew how to haul in the lines, and could handle an oar perhaps with greater skill and power than any man along the coast. From a boy he had grown up with the fisher folk, and now, as a man, he was still not ashamed to join them on their cruises, and took as deep an interest in these expeditions as if his own livelihood depended on their success, as much as theirs did. Not a cottage in the place, the inside of which he had not seen; not a man, woman, or child whose name he did not know, as well as the whole history of their lives.

With the Tresilian family Arthur had long been on intimate terms. He was absent when Ellen Tresilian died, having gone to Plymouth to further his lighthouse scheme, but on his return he did all he could to help and comfort Owen and his motherless children. To Philip he showed special kindness, he took deep interest in the boy, employed him, when he was not out at sea with his father, in various ways, and took care of that, during the whole winter which followed his mother's death, the family should not suffer from want. He would often go and spend an hour with them in the evening, reading the Bible aloud while father and son mended their nets, and Mary busily plied her needle; then he would tell them stories, too, that he had read in other books, or that had been told him – tales of heroism and adventure, of brave deeds done by bold men in bygone ages and other lands.

Arthur often discussed with Owen his lighthouse project. From the first, the latter had favoured the scheme, for his experience proved to him how many gallant vessels might by its means avoid a shipwreck, and thus valuable property and precious lives be preserved. He, too, had helped with his advice, when the survey was made, to determine which was the fittest spot for the erection of the building; with Arthur and others in his boat, they had thoroughly explored the Longships, and came to the conclusion that, though the undertaking would be an arduous and tedious one, yet that by perseverance it might be accomplished, and that for the benefit of the shipping interest, the Carn Bras rock was the most suitable site for the lighthouse.

Owen's advocacy of a plan which was so unpopular with the inhabitants of the whole district, naturally, as we have seen, made him more hated than ever by the majority of his fellow-villagers. All possible means were devised to vex and annoy him. He had a hard life of it now. The light of his home had gone out, and he had far more to bear than formerly from the jeers and scoffs of those with whom he must daily associate out of doors. Now, too, he had no good wife, ever ready with comforting words to welcome and cheer him when he came back at night sad and cast down. Still, little Mary did all in her power to make up to her father for his loss; Philip, too, was a good and dutiful son, and had, poor boy, quite as much persecution and ridicule to put up with from the lads of the village, as his father had from the men.

More than a year had passed away since Ellen Tresilian had been laid in her grave. As we have gathered from the conversation of the two men at the Land's End, business had been slack during the winter, which meant that the wreckers had not been so successful as usual, and that the smuggling trade had, owing to sharper look-out on the part of the coast-guard authorities, not been very brisk.

Philip was growing up a strong, smart lad, and a great help to his father in his fishing. They were often out from early morn till long after sunset in their boat, occasionally, indeed, they had been absent all night, but it was only through unavoidable circumstances that this occurred, as Owen never liked to leave Mary quite alone in the cottage by herself. She, however, did not mind it in the least. She was never afraid; she would get her father's and brother's supper ready for them, put dry clothes for them to change (if they came in wet) before the fire; then she would read out of the big bible, and if they did not come by nine o'clock, she would say her prayers, and asking God to watch over and protect them from the dangers of the sea, she would go quietly to bed, and soon fall asleep. If the wind howled much, and the rain beat against the window panes, she would feel somewhat anxious about them, and pray more earnestly to God to guard them. Once, indeed, when they were out for two nights running, when she knew that the wind had changed and a gale had come on, the poor child was alarmed, her courage quite gave way, and she sobbed and wept, as if her heart would break. All the second night she lay awake, and when, early in the morning, her father and brother appeared, they found her looking very pale, and her eyes red and swollen with weeping. Owen assured her that never, if he could help it, should this occur again.

4

Philip And His Foes

"When He hath blessed and called His own,
He tries them early, look and tone,
Bent brow and throbbing heart;
Tried them with pain, dread seal of love,
Oft when their ready patience strove
With keen o'er mastering smart."

- Keble

The day following the conversation between John Nichols and Ben Pollard related in our last chapter, Philip Tresilian went down early in the morning to the beach to clean out his father's boat, and get it ready for fishing, as Owen intended to start on a cruise in an hour's time.

The boy was accustomed to meet with annoyance from lads of his own age, so he was not surprised to be greeted on his arrival at the beach by jeers from some half dozen lazy young fellows, who were amusing themselves by throwing stones into the water, and occasionally pelting each other with sand and shingle. Philip's appearance was the signal for them all to turn upon him. "Here comes the young Methodist!" shouted one, and the whole set immediately surrounded him as he walked quietly on to his boat, taking no notice of them, and making no reply to their insolent speeches.

He commenced busily mopping the inside of the boat, and preparing the tackle for fishing. But he was not allowed to do this in peace, for the boys had discovered an amusement which was most congenial to their feelings and tastes, and which consisted in flinging sand and dirt into the boat, so that it was utterly impossible for Philip to go on with his work of cleaning. The more he begged them to desist, the more active did they become in throwing sand. While this was going on John Nichols sauntered down to the beach. He perceived what the boys were doing, and by a malicious burst of laughter, encouraged them in their ill-natured proceedings.

A lad who was a great deal bigger and stronger than Philip, a nephew of Nichols', was the ringleader in the mischief. "Come on, boys," he cried, "let's pelt the parson's pet well, the fellow who sets himself up to be so much better than any of us." A fresh volley of mud and sand was the answer to this appeal.

"We'll teach him that we've had enough of his fine airs," he continued; "he'll grow up a regular coward, like his fool of a father!"

"Who dares to call my father a coward?" exclaimed Philip, starting up from the boat, and gazing at the mocking faces before him.

"Oh! he's found his tongue at last, has he, the young rascal!" cried Bill Nichols; "why, I call your father a coward, he's afraid to go wrecking now, because of the parson!"

"You dare to say that again," said Philip, springing out of the boat, and standing in front of his insolent adversary in an attitude of defiance.

"Dare say it again, indeed. Your father's a coward, and a fool, and so are you."

Philip's blood was up now. He was quite accustomed to bear any amount of insult and mockery which only concerned himself. The parson had often taught him that those who are trying to live a good, honest, true life in the midst of evil men, must endure such trials, and hard as they are for flesh and blood to bear (and especially for young blood), still our Blessed Master has by His life set us up the example, and by His words enjoined us, "Bless those that curse you, do good to them that hate you, and pray for them which despitefully use you and persecute you." But to hear his father insulted – whom he had ever considered the bravest of the brave, a man who had done honour to the British navy, and was reckoned one of the boldest seamen on the coast – that he should be called a coward and a fool to his son's face. No – that was too much for any son to bear – he could not, he would not, stand it.

He rushed upon Bill, who was quite unprepared for the assault, as he imagined the young Methodist, as he called him, would take any insult. His clenched fist fell heavily upon Bill's eye, and then the fight began with fury. Bill was, of course, the stronger of the two, but Philip had gained some advantage by beginning the attack, and he made good use of it. All the other lads gathered round, cheering and encouraging Bill, his uncle too approached the combatants, and, of course, warmly espoused his nephew's cause.

Most of the lads, badly disposed as they were, had in them enough of an Englishman's sense of fair play not to interfere in the struggle, though they bitterly regretted to see that Bill was plainly getting the worst of it. Not so, however, John Nichols. His hatred towards Owen Tresilian and all his family was so inveterate, that it blinded him to every other feeling, and extinguished any sentiment of honour, which might still be lingering in his heart. When he perceived that his nephew would soon be prostrate on the beach, and Philip completely victorious, he was cowardly enough to interfere by dealing Philip a blow from behind, which sent him reeling on the ground, where he lay bleeding and unconscious. The cheer which rose from the bystanders at this new turn of events was a very faint one, for now the majority sympathised with Philip, who was, in fact, regarded as the victor. A cowardly act, even if successful, is never applauded, except by the most degraded. "That ain't fair," shouted four or five of the boys, "that's a shame, John Nichols!"

But another spectator, who had only arrived in time to witness the final act in this drama, at this moment interfered. He was no other than the young parson himself, whose tall and manly figure now advanced into the thick of the fray.

"What mischief are you up to here?" he demanded sternly. "How many – five, six, seven, against one – eight, and the last, a full-grown man, too. What, you, John Nichols! and it was you I saw deal the boy the blow which has laid him there unconscious, a cowardly act," he continued in a tone of withering contempt. "I should say you ought to be ashamed of yourself, if I thought you had any shame left in you."

The boys hung their heads and skulked away without saying a word. Arthur then turned towards Nichols, who winced beneath his gaze. He went close up to the man, his vigorous frame so quivering with indignation, and such fire in his eye, that the miscreant really trembled; he did not know what was coming next. "John," said Arthur, as he laid his hand heavily on his shoulder, "this kind of thing shall not go on here; I'll not have the lives of steady men and lads made miserable by you and a lot of lazy drinking fellows, who only gain their livelihood by robbing and murdering others. I have marked lately how Tresilian and his son have been set upon by you and your set. But this sha'n't go on, I c an tell you, for I'm determined to see justice done, and if all other means fail, I must call in the law to help me. Are you really lost to all sense of shame, John? don't you feel that you acted like a coward in striking yonder boy?"

"I wish parsons would mind their own business, and leave poor folks alone to get their bread as best they can," grumbled John Nichols, as with a scowl of bitter hatred, he turned away from Arthur, and hastened up the village.

The young clergyman with a heavy sigh then went up to Philip, who still lay senseless on the ground; he raised him up, placed his head upon his knees, wiping the blood off his face and whispering kind words into his ear. The boy soon opened his eyes, and smiled, when he saw the loved and well-known face which was bending over him.

"Oh, sir!" he said in a faint voice, "is it you? You will forgive me, won't you? It was wrong to fight perhaps, but then Bill called father a fool and a coward, and I could not stand that, indeed. He called me bad names enough before, but I didn't say a word till he called father a coward."

"Well, my boy, I mustn't blame you, for I can't say what I shouldn't have done myself had I been provoked as you were. May God forgive you; but you are terribly bruised and knocked about, poor lad – ah! here comes your father, this will be another sore trial to him, who has already so many to bear."

Owen, who knew nothing of what had taken place, was quietly coming down the beach, prepared to set out with his son on his fishing cruise. He started back with terror when he saw the parson sitting on the beach, with Philip's bleeding head resting on his shoulder.

"Don't be frightened, Owen," Arthur called out to him, "matters might be much worse. A lot of young rascals set upon poor Philip, some seven or eight against one, and of course he got rather the worst of it."

"No, sir," interrupted Philip, starting up and forgetting his pain, "no, sir, I got the best of it. I had thrashed Bill well, and should have got him down in another minute if his uncle hadn't given me that blow from behind, on my head, which knocked me down senseless."

"Come, let's hear all about it, Philip," said his father, sadly and anxiously.

Philip related in a few unvarnished words all that had occurred.

"You're a brave boy," said Owen, "and I'm proud of you. I thank you, sir, too," he continued, turning to Arthur, "for if you hadn't have come just at the right time, and interfered, they might have killed the lad – set of cowards that they are."

"That they are indeed, Owen," said Arthur, "but you had better take Philip home now to his sister. I don't expect he'll be fit for any work, or to go out fishing with you, for a day or two."

"Oh! I'll soon be all right again, father," said Philip, cheerfully; "black eyes soon get well."

"I want to say a few words to you, Owen," said Arthur; "if you will go back with Philip to your cottage, I will wait here till you return."

"Very well, sir," replied Owen, who now turned homewards with his son, leaving the young clergyman sitting alone on the beach.

The scene of what he had just been a witness had filled Arthur's breast with sad and gloomy feelings. Even the most sanguine are at times discouraged, and Arthur, in all the pride and vigour of youth, with his naturally cheerful disposition, was in the habit almost always of looking on the bright side of things. But now he felt utterly cast down and disappointed. For more than a year he had been labouring among these people, he had tried in every way to influence them for good, he had lived among them, shared their joys and sorrows, affectionately, but solemnly, endeavoured to impress upon them how sinful and evil was their manner of life, which must, if unrepented of, bring a curse upon them in the next world, if not in this. He had drawn upon himself insults, mockery, even hatred. Notwithstanding this unworthy requital, he earnestly loved their souls, he longed that these poor ignorant misguided men, cruel and brutal as many of them were, should be led to see their sin and turn to that Saviour Whose arms are ever open to welcome the vilest and most degraded. But how few as yet had been impressed, while the majority appeared more hardened and defiant than ever. He was brooding over these melancholy thoughts, when Owen came back, and stood beside him. The first words the sailor uttered, spoke with some degree of consolation to the young clergyman's troubled heart.

"Ah, sir," he said, "I have had trouble enough since my poor wife's death in one way and another, and particularly from the ill-will these fellows round here bear to me and my boy. But you, sir, help us all to bear the burden God lays upon us. I always feel thankful that He sent you to us just at the right time."

"I am glad to hear that I have been of use to any one, Owen," said Arthur sadly. "I was just thinking, when you came up, how little good I have been able to do here; it seems as if nothing could touch the hard hearts of the folk around us."

"Don't say so, you haven't been here overlong yet. Besides, don't forget all the good you've done to me and Philip and to my little one up yonder; you've taught us all very much, sir, and we shall always be grateful to you for it."

"Have I, Owen? Then I'll thank God and take courage; yes, I have been wrong to despond; it is sinful to mistrust Him Who hitherto has helped me on, and answered so many of my prayers; only I do long to see more fruit of my labours."

"That you will, sir, in time, I am sure," said Owen. "Only last night little Mary was reading to me out of the Psalms, a verse which often comes into my mind when I feel low-spirited, 'O taste and see that the Lord is gracious: blessed is the man that trusted in Him'."

"A good lesson, indeed, Owen; God seems to have sent you to cheer me up just at the right moment. Yes, we will trust Him, and then we shall never be confounded."

They were silent for a few minutes, then Arthur continued –

"But now, Owen, what I wanted to speak to you about was my scheme of the lighthouse. That you know has a great deal to do with my being so unpopular with the Sennen folk, and all the men round the coast; still I feel I am right about it, and no power on earth should make me desist from carrying out the plan, and if God permit, the lighthouse will be finished this summer. The work, I am thankful to say, has bravely stood all this winter's gales, and before the long dark nights of autumn, I hope to have the satisfaction of seeing a bright light burning on the Longships, to warn all mariners how near they are to a dangerous coast. But you know some one must live in that lighthouse, the lamps can't be kept burning without hands, and the man who takes up his abode there must be honest, steady, and thoroughly trustworthy, above taking a bribe, able to bear the scorn, mockery, and annoyance which he is sure to meet from the Sennen people, who of course will regard him as an enemy. The salary will be good, but the life will be – I can't conceal it – a very hard and trying one. For days, perhaps for weeks, there may be no means of communicating with the shore, so the lighthouse must be well stored with provisions. Then, too, it will be a lonely life and one not unattended with danger, for the strongest building might yield before some tempest of unexampled fury, as the Eddystone did in the great storm at the beginning of this century. It will be a life of peril as well as of discomfort to the man who consents to accept the office, at the same time it will be a noble life of self-sacrifice for the welfare of others."

"Yes, sir; a man who undertook to live on the Longships' Rock would be doing a great service to his countrymen, and especially to the shipping interest. I believe if there had been a lighthouse there, hundreds of vessels would never have gone to the bottom; but a dismal life that'll be for any man, and especially if he's to live there all alone."

"I don't think a man ought to live there all alone, Owen; but it seems to me there's no chance just now of finding two men who would go there, I doubt if we shall get one; moreover, I don't know whether Mr. Smith would provide a salary for two."

"The lighthouse-keeper, whoever, he is, won't get much help from the Cove men, sir. They'll lead him a pretty life," said Owen.

"They can't do him much harm out there, Owen; they can only annoy him when he comes on shore for his provisions; and means must be taken to ensure that he is protected from anything like violence. Well, now, Owen, to come to the point, I want to know if you will be the lighthouse-keeper?"

"Ah, sir, I thought that was what you were driving at; but that's a matter which requires consideration. It will, as you say, be a very hard and very lonely life, and then I should have to give up my cottage which I am fond of, and what would become of Philip, and little Mary? They couldn't go and live in the lighthouse."

"I don't want to hurry you to decide, Owen; it will be months before the lighthouse is finished, and you shall have plenty of time to think over the matter. I've considered the objections I knew you would raise about your children, and all the difficulties in the way; but who else can I find here? there's no one I can thoroughly rely upon except you. There are indeed one or two fellows who are honest enough, and seem to be trying to mend their ways; but they all have large families, and I could not depend upon them. Think, Owen, of the good you will be doing, try not to shrink from making a sacrifice, which will confer such great benefits on mankind. Remember Him Who loved you with so deep a love that He came from heaven to die for you on the cross – there is the noblest, most glorious example of self-sacrifice for you to follow. Dreary and lonely as your life on the rock may be, what can it be in comparison with His,, when He left His Father's throne to dwell on earth to suffer and to die for us sinners!"

"Yes, sir, I quite feel all you say; but you see there's Mary – she never would be separated from me, she'd fret so, poor child, brave and good as she is. Why, once when I was out two nights running, she was so frightened, poor thing, fearing Phil and I were drowned, that it made her quite ill."

"I could get her a comfortable berth where she would be well taken care of up at my father's place, Owen. I thought of all that, I knew Mary would be the difficulty in your way. As to Philip, my idea was that he could go and live in the lighthouse with you for the first winter, till you get accustomed to being there alone. But there's no need to come to any decision now; only don't say a word about it to anybody, for if the fellows here thought you were going to be the lighthouse-keeper, they wouldn't give you much peace, I'm sure."

"I believe my life wouldn't be worth much if they did," said Owen. "to hear the way they talk about the lighthouse you'd think it had been built on purpose to prevent them getting their living, and to drive them to starvation. They threaten often that they will never allow the lamp to be lighted, and breathe vengeance against the man who is appointed to live there."

"All the more reason they should know nothing about our plan, then, Owen," said Arthur, "and now farewell; I shall come and see how Philip is getting on to-morrow."

5

A Plot

"Not one can say he's safe –
Not one of you so humble, but that still
The malice of some secret enemy
May whisper him to death – and hark, look to it!
Have some of you seemed braver than their fellows,
Their courage is their surest condemnation."

- Taylor, *Philip Van Artevelde*

Philip soon got over the effects of the affray with his tormentors, and as usual accompanied his father on his fishing cruises. His pluck and courage had gained him the respect of the lads of the village, who had moreover been disgusted with Nichols for his interference, and Philip was now not nearly so much molested as hitherto.

It was a fine spring, there was a plentiful harvest of pilchards, and the walls of the lighthouse continued to make steady progress. There was no doubt that by September the building would be completed.

The violent opposition which its erection had created was not in the least abated, but rather increased as the work progressed; and Arthur, as the originator of the scheme, was more and more hated by the lazy and evil-disposed of the Sennen people.

In these days of peace, liberty, and prosperity, we can hardly realise how different the condition of this same England was some ninety years ago. The nation then was constantly at war, rebellions and mutinies were frequent; there was not that security of life and property which exists at present, yet the penal laws were so harsh and severe that they might almost be said to have been written in blood; it was death then to steal to the value of five shillings, and in 1785, ninety-seven persons were executed in London for theft alone. There was great difficulty at that time in obtaining a sufficient number of men to serve in the Army and Navy, and the Government was obliged to resort to means which, interfering as it did with the liberty of the subject, was hard and grievous enough then, but would never be endured now. Men were impressed for both services, and pressgangs, as they were called, would, with the sanction of the authorities and on board government cruisers, sail round the coast, land at various seaport towns and villages, and carry off by force young men and lads of sixteen or seventeen to serve on board His Majesty's fleet. Money or influence could often obtain protection or release for the unfortunate victims, but when neither the one nor the other were forthcoming, the poor fellows were dragged from their homes, and often from a calling in which they were earning an honest livelihood, and forced for years into unwilling service.

The men who composed these pressgangs were often a drunken ruffianly set; in many places they were used by bad and malicious persons as a means of paying off old scores, against their enemies, and not a few instances could be given, in which young men had been pointed out to the pressgang as eligible for their purpose, by those whose interest it was to get rid of them. Men who made themselves obnoxious to their ungodly neighbours, by living pure and honest lives, and doing the best in their power to urge others to abandon their wicked ways, were frequently denounced to pressgangs, and carried off to be soldiers and sailors. The poor Methodists, as they were called, were very often pressed; and at this time, in Cornwall, not only along the coast, but in the interior, several pressgangs were going their rounds.

One evening in May several of the worst characters in Sennen were sitting together drinking in the public-house, among them our previous acquaintances Ben Pollard and John Nichols. The conversation soon turned on the favourite topic of the lighthouse on the Longships' Rock, which every day was exciting fresh opposition and ill-will.

"I tell you what it is, mates," said John, "our trade is pretty nigh done for, unless we can put a stop to the building of that lighthouse. I'm told the whole affair's as good as settled now, and Mr. Smith has got permission from the Government to levy a toll on shipping as passes this way, to pay for the expenses of the lamps and lighthouse-keeper."

"I see no help for us, " said another man. "Ever since Master Arthur took it into his head to become our parson, there's been little chance of us poor fellows gaining a living."

"I don't see that we should submit to this tamely," protested Ben; "we should show them that there's some spirit left in us, and that we're not a-going to be ruined by all their arts and devices."

"I should like to know what we can do, Ben," replied John. "Haven't we tried every way to stop the work – worried the workmen, stolen their tools, capsized their boats, and landed on the Rock to see if we could destroy or injure the building, didn't we find it so strong that there was no good making the attempt?"

"True enough, John," remarked another of the party, "I say we can do nothing till the lighthouse is finished; then we must drown the keeper and put out the lights."

"Yes, if we can," said Ben; "but I doubt it."

"We'll do our best," exclaimed John with a loud laugh; "we'll show Master Arthur that we're not such fools as to submit to all his whims and fancies without resistance. I've got an idea in my head, comrades, I want to talk to you about. You know I've long had a grudge against that sneaking fellow, Owen Tresilian."

"Ha! Ha!" roared all the men, "so have we."

"I believe that he and his rascally son," said Ben, "are set by the parson to spy upon us and report to him all we say and do."

"I'm sure of it," said John, "and I've never forgiven that young rogue for the drubbing he gave my nephew Bill last winter."

"A nice mistake you made, interfering as you did," remarked one of the party; "lots of young fellows took Philip's part after that, because he showed so much pluck, and you acted like a coward, they say."

"May be so, Jenkins, but it won't last," replied John, "and I wasn't going to see my own flesh and blood mauled about by that young scoundrel;

but now, for what I was going to say when you interrupted me. – Look ye here, comrades, the pressgangs a-coming our way!"

"The pressgang?" they all exclaimed.

"Yes, sure enough. They're hard up for men for the Navy, and there's no chance of peace with the Frenchmen for many a long day, and the pressgang is cruising in a cutter round the coast. Only yesterday a friend of mine, just come from Pendeen, told me they had been there a day or two ago, and had carried off four young fellows. He said, too, they always took the Methodists by choice, if they could find them out."

"Well, if they come here, it's to be hoped they'll carry off both the Tresilians, father and son," said Ben; "that would be a good riddance."

"Not the father," said John, "he's too old. They never take men much over thirty; besides, he has served in the Navy already, and would get off on that score, but that drivelling young fool – his rascally son – I think we might get rid of him in that way."

"A very good thought of yours, John," said one of the company. "And when are we to expect the pressgang?"

"Why, any fine day their cutter may anchor off our bay. They're at Pendeen now, and that ain't far off. I mean to keep a sharp look-out for them, and have my eye on that Philip Tresilian too; he sha'n't escape, I promise you."

"And we must be on the look-out to get out of the way ourselves when that cruiser comes," said the youngest man of the party; "I don't want to be pressed for the Navy."

"You will, if you don't make yourself scarce, Ned," said Ben, "and I don't feel at all safe myself. I believe, John, they'll come after us all of a sudden in the night, and drag us out of our homes."

"There's no telling; they may. But forewarned is forearmed, and I have told you what to expect, so be on your guard!"

We do not sully our pages with any allusion to the oaths and vile language which were thickly mingled in this conversation. In those days swearing was fashionable among even the highest classes of society, and never absent from the everyday talk of the lower orders. Only those whose lives had been changed by the religious revival of the time, and had been taught to see its wickedness and profanity, abstained from blasphemous and impure language.

The men, delighted that an opportunity seemed likely to occur by which they could avenge themselves on Tresilian, now separated, after agreeing that a keen watch should be kept on Philip's movements, that he might be denounced to the pressgang as soon as they made their appearance.

6

A Cornish Parson And His Work

"Think not of rest; though dreams be sweet,
Start up and ply your heavenward feet,
Is not God's oath upon your head
Ne'er to sink back on slothful bed,
Never again your loins untie,
Nor let your torches wastes and die,
Till, when the shadows thickest fall,
Ye hear your Master's midnight call?"

- Keble, *Christian Year*

The same evening, on which the conversation related in the previous chapter occurred, Arthur Pendrean had gone to pay Owen Tresilian and his family a visit. His main object was to have a talk with Philip on the subject of Confirmation. This sacred rite of the Church was thought very little of in those days. Bishops did not then visit all the towns and villages in their dioceses annually, as they do now, for the purpose of holding confirmations. They occurred then but rarely, and were held only in some large and central place in the country. In the coming autumn it was announced that the bishop would hold a confirmation at Truro. None could think of taking so long and expensive a journey who were not impressed with the importance of the ordinance, and very few in Sennen or its neighbourhood thought anything about it. But Arthur was anxious that several young men and women, who had been influenced by his teaching, should be confirmed at this time. He meant to go with them himself, and send them at his own expense; and having already spoken to Philip on the subject, he wished that evening to converse with him more fully about it.

Though, as we have related, Arthur Pendrean's heart had been first touched by hearing the preaching of John Wesley, yet he was in no sense what would now be called a Methodist. That was a term of reproach, applied in those days, to all people who were striving to live a religious life. John Wesley himself was a thorough Churchman, and the schism which arose after his death, and which unhappily will ever be connected with his name, was far more owing to the apathy and worldliness of the Church dignitaries, who refused to recognise the movement, and to direct it into the right channel, than to its reputed founder, who would have shrunk back in horror from raising any opposition to a Church, of which he had ever been a faithful and devoted son. Arthur, who deeply venerated the holy and truly apostolic man, from whose lips he had first heard the words of life, could not altogether agree with the exaggerated opinions taught by many of his followers, and was wholly opposed to those who had separated themselves from the Church of their baptism. But in his parishes there were none of these. Arthur's energetic and pious labours among the people, his zealous and constant preaching of the true and whole gospel, his visiting from hamlet to hamlet and from house to house, the meetings he held for instruction, prayer, and the reading of God's Word, supplied all the spiritual wants of the few who had been roused to care for higher things; the so-called Methodists were in consequence thoroughly at one with him, attended all this services, and assisted him by all the means in their power.

He had during his residence at Oxford devoted much time to the study of theology, and especially to the doctrines and teaching of that branch of the Catholic Church to which he belonged, as expressed in the services and offices of the Prayer Book, the Articles, and the works of her greatest divines. He perceived how many good men of his day stopped short of the whole truth, and by constantly inculcating the doctrines of justification by faith alone, neglected to enforce the necessity of good works, without which faith is dead, and also seemed entirely to overlook not only the importance, but almost the very existence, of those two Sacraments ordained by Christ Himself, as generally necessary to salvation, and which He appointed as channels of grace. Both from Holy Scripture and the Prayer Book, Arthur perceived how the divine life begins in Baptism, in which holy ordinance all are made children of one great Father in heaven, but he saw as plainly how few there are, who can preserve their baptismal innocence, and how necessary and all-important is the need of conversion. He recognised, too – which few at that period did, - the solemnity and force of our Lord's injunction, "Do this in remembrance of Me," and was shocked and pained to observe how in those days that command was utterly neglected, and how rarely the Blessed Sacrament of the Holy Communion was celebrated in the churches of England.

Mr. Somers, the old rector of the three united parishes which Arthur served, did not at all concur in his views. All zeal he called Methodism, while his young and energetic curate looked upon John Wesley as his model, only differing with him so far, that he disapproved of those measures which he had taken late in life, and which had caused his followers to separate from the Church of England. But for the sake of peace Mr. Somers left Arthur to do much as he liked, especially at St. Sennen; he was glad to be spared a journey there every third Sunday, and he now confined himself mostly to the larger and nearer church of St. Buryan. There, however, and at St. Levan too, Arthur's influence was felt, for he generally managed to preach at both these churches once a month, besides diligently visiting the poor.

St. Sennen Church stands on a bleak and elevated plain; scattered round it are the few cottages which form the village. Externally the church presented no striking features, the roof being rather dilapidated, and the churchyard ill kept and overgrown with weeds; the interior was dismal in the extreme, but not worse, nor perhaps so bad, as many of the churches in England at that day. The walls were thickly covered with whitewash, here and there stained with dark green patches and streaks from the damp, the paved floor was rough and broken, the windows were filled with panes of very dirty glass which had once been white, the stained glass having been broken and removed in Puritan times. The only ornaments were a rude mutilated figure of alabaster, possibly intended to represent the patron saint Senanus, of Irish celebrity, and a very large and gaily painted representation of the royal arms, the lion and unicorn, over the chancel arch; the altar was a very shabby table with a faded red baize cloth, the pulpit a huge unsightly wooden structure, painted a bluish-green, the high pews were allowed to remain in their original worm-eaten deal, though one or two of these were furnished with cushions and rounded with curtains. At the west end of the church was a gallery for the singers, the balustrades of which were painted a very bright blue. There was no organ, but occasionally a bass viol, a violin and a couple of flutes were played by village musicians. Here and there in this dreary and depressing interior, in the arches and tracery of the windows some remnant might be seen of its original design, and of those graceful proportions to which it has, at the present day, been once restored.

This, then, was the building in which Sunday after Sunday Arthur Pendrean ministered to his little flock. Dismal as it was, with the winds often howling round it, and the rain and hail beating against the windows, yet he did his best to warm the hearts of his hearers, and to make the prayers and psalms a reality to them. The liturgy in which that little congregation of poor fisher folk united was the same, word for word, that we use now in our beautiful churches and cathedrals, where we have so much to help our souls to devotion and to add to the dignity of our worship. They joined in the same solemn litany, its petitions coming with special force to men whose calling led them to expose themselves for days and nights to the perils of the treacherous deep. Arthur, after he was ordained priest, had instituted a monthly celebration of the Holy Communion at St. Sennen, an unheard-of innovation even in a town, in those days, but very few gathered round the holy Table to partake of the Bread of life. Two or three women who were not ashamed to confess their Lord, and perhaps now and then an old and decrepit man, were generally the only communicants, but they gradually increased, for several in hamlets and solitary farmhouses around, who had been awakened by the preaching of the Methodist missionaries, and who were glad to welcome in Arthur a godly and pious minister, would walk to St. Sennen and join in its heart-stirring services.

The singing at St. Sennen's Church if not melodious was warm and hearty. Arthur had a fine voice and always set the tune. John and Charles Wesley and others had written many hymns which are now still universal favourites, but hymn-singing, except Bishop Ken's morning and evening hymns, was unheard of in churches at the period of which we are writing; and the metrical psalm to be found at the end of our old Prayer Books were used instead.

Philip Tresilian, since his encounter with Bill Nichols, had become more popular with the lads of the village; he had consequently been led to associate more with them than formerly, and to take part occasionally in their games and pastimes. This was but natural, and Arthur, who liked to encourage manly sports among the youths of his flock, had nothing to say against it, but he could not help observing with sorrow that Philip's manner towards him was altered, especially when he accosted him in the company of his companions. He was beginning to get ashamed of his religion, and did not so boldly show his displeasure at the scoffs and jeers which were levelled at the parson and at the Methodists, as he had been wont to do. Arthur had several times spoken to

Philip about Confirmation, but he apparently did not relish the subject, for he always gave very short answers, or made an excuse to get out of his presence as quickly as possible. This evening, however, Arthur Pendrean found Philip alone, for his father and sister had gone to Sennen village, and left him to mind the cottage and repair some nets which were wanted for to-morrow's fishing. He had no means of escape, therefore, and must listen to all that the parson had to say.

"Philip," he began in a kindly voice, "I've come to have a talk with you on the subject I spoke to you about last week, when you said you were so busy you could not listen to me then, but would hear what I had to say another time."

"Oh yes, sir, I remember; about my going to the bishop at Truro," replied Philip; "but I think, sir, I would rather not go at present."

"Why not, Philip, you are quite old enough I am sure to be confirmed, between sixteen and seventeen now; why put off what ought to be done to a time that may never come?"

"I don't see the good of it, sir; none of the lads about here are going to be confirmed, I fancy; and it's enough I have to bear now, being laughed at for going to church, and being with the parson so much; and when it once gets to their ears that I am going to Truro to be confirmed, why I shall never hear the end of it; I shall be called a saint, and a Methodist, and all kinds of names."

"I am sorry to find, Philip," said Arthur solemnly, "that you are becoming ashamed of your religion. You would not have spoken like this a year ago. It is not what your good mother would have expected of her son."

"I am not ashamed of my religion, sir, but I don't want to put myself forward to be better than others, and thus make myself a laughing-stock. Why should I be confirmed when others are not?"

"Because they neglect their duty, should you do so, Philip? Are you 'to follow a multitude to do evil'? The very reason why I urge you to this sacred ordinance is,, that you may therein receive fresh strength and renewed grace to resist those temptations which beset you, and to enable you boldly and manfully to confess your Lord and Saviour Jesus Christ."

Philip sighed, but did not reply. Arthur continued,

"I know, my lad, you have a great deal to bear, but I have seen, too, that you are beginning to waver in your allegiance to our great Master. You are not so bold as you used to be in standing up for what is right and good. You can listen to bad words without a shudder. It does not give you so much pain to hear religious people – Methodists, as they are called – laughed at and spoken against. Is it not so, Philip?"

Philip reddened and kept his eyes fixed on his work.

"Come, answer me, my good fellow, is it not so?" said Arthur earnestly.

"Well, sir, I can't say what isn't true, so I must confess it is."

"If we confess our sins, He is faithful and just to forgive us our sins', as you hear every Sunday in church Philip. I thank God that He has given you a conviction that all is not right in your heart. Think now how dangerous it is to begin to tread the downward path. Before it is too late, before you are led to commit some sin which may destroy your soul, stand up boldly and confess Christ; and seek every means of grace which He has appointed to help you and strengthen you to walk in the right way."

"I'm sure I try to do my best, sir; I have not missed once to go to church on Sundays, and I can't see the harm of having a game with the other lads of the village now and then."

"I know, Philip, your place in the church has never yet been empty; but take care; 'let him that thinketh he standeth take heed lest he fall.' I should be the last to wish you to lead a morose and selfish life apart from your fellows, or to forbid you to join in their pastimes, only remember when you take part in their games, not to take part in their evil ways too, and not to let them think that you countenance their profane language or dishonest deeds, but let them see plainly that you are a Christian and are not ashamed of being one. Be as bold to confess your Saviour as you were to resent the insult on your father's name and character that day when I found you lying stunned upon the beach."

Tears started into the lad's eyes as he turned them affectionately upon the young clergyman. "Oh, sir," he said with deep emption, "I never can forget how kind you were in coming to my rescue; that brutal fellow Nichols might have killed or maimed me for life, if you hadn't appeared at the right moment. Yes, sir, I have been wrong. I am ashamed of myself, I am indeed; sometimes when the lads have said things against you, and called you names, I have let it pass and said nothing, and once I laughed; and then I haven't liked to speak to you when I have been in their company, and have felt vexed when you have talked to me. I have been very, very ungrateful, but I won't be so again, sir; I won't indeed."

"Philip, my dear boy," said Arthur kindly, "don't think about me, it isn't much I have done for you, and for that little, I see by your looks, and hear by your words, that you are grateful. No, is not man, but God, that you offend when you are ashamed to stand up for the right, and to confess that you are His. If you feel gratitude towards me who have done so little for you, what ought you not to feel towards Him Who died to save you. Ah, Philip, in your baptism you were made His child, you were enlisted into His army, it was then promised for you that as His faithful soldier and servant you would fight manfully under His banner till your life's end. Are you striving to keep that promise? Will you be a good and brave soldier in that great army of the living God, or will you be a coward and deserter?"

"I often feel, sir, that I have not enough strength to resist all the temptations I have to endure from companions I cannot always avoid. I pray to God to help me indeed, but now and then I have given way, and said and done what I have afterwards been ashamed of."

"That is the very reason, Philip, why you should come to be confirmed, that you may obtain more strength, for this daily conflict against sin and the great enemy of souls; and still more help will be supplied to you, if afterwards you receive prayerfully and worthily the Blessed Sacraments of our Lord's Body and Blood."

"I'll think over what you have said, sir; you have put these matters in a new light to me this evening; but if, after being confirmed and taking the Sacrament I should do something wrong, be led away by the bad fellows I must be with every now and then" –

"If you pray to Him, God will give you His Spirit so that you will be able to resist temptation, however strong it may be. Remember you are enlisted in an army the final victory of which is absolutely certain, the great Captain of our salvation can never be defeated. Trust in Him only, look not to yourself but to Him; 'Commit thy way unto the Lord, and put thy trust in Him, and He shall bring it to pass,' says the Psalmist, and further on in the same psalm is the comforting assurance 'The Lord ordereth a good man's goings, and maketh his way acceptable to Himself; though he fall, he shall not be cast away, for the Lord upholdeth him with His hand.'"

At that moment Owen and his daughter entered the cottage. After exchanging friendly greetings with them, and chatting for a few minutes with Owen about the fishing season and other matters, Arthur took leave of the family, telling Philip he would take an early opportunity of seeing him again and continuing their conversation.

7

The Capture

"Thou who in darkness walking did'st appear
Upon the waves and Thy disciples cheer,
Come, Lord, in lonesome days, when storms assail
And earthly hopes and human succours fail:
When all is dark may we behold Thee nigh,
And hear Thy voice, - 'Fear not, for it is I.'"

The next day was Sunday. It was a glorious morning, not a cloud on the bright blue sky, the sea was smooth as a mirror, and fell in the gentlest ripples on the shingly beach where all the fishing boats were drawn up; as more from the force of habit, than from any sense of religion, the Sennen folk did not as a rule go out fishing on Sundays. Out in the offing lay a cutter at anchor. She had arrived in the night, and was recognised by those who were earliest astir in the morning as a revenue boat. On board her was the dreaded pressgang.

Just as Arthur was about to ride to St. Sennen for morning service, his faithful servant, old Roger, came up to him and said,

"I hear, Mr Arthur, that a cutter with the pressgang on board is at anchor off Sennen Cove. Sunday is a favourite day for those chaps to land; they always find the men at home then, and so they are easier to catch. I thought I would warn you about it, sir, because their game now is to carry off all the men and lads who are called Methodists; so you had better tell some friends of ours to make themselves scarce for the day."

"This is bad news, indeed, Roger," said Arthur; "I knew a pressgang was in the neighbourhood, but never thought of their coming our way. I will gallop down to Sennen Cove at once; I shall have time to ride there and see what's going on before service begins."

When Arthur arrived at the Cove he found everything as usual; there lay the cutter indeed quietly at anchor; a few men and boys sitting or lying lazily on the beach were watching her, and speculating as to the intentions of those on board. To Arthur's inquiries, they replied that no one had landed yet, and some asserted that there was no pressgang with the cutter, but that she was probably sent to look out for smugglers. Arthur left the beach and proceeded to church.

Being so fine a day there was a larger congregation than usual. Philip, with his father and sister, was in his accustomed place. Arthur's manner to-day was unusually grave and earnest. His long talk with Philip on the previous evening had left a melancholy impression on his mind. He felt that the few who were striving to do right, who had some faith in God and some love towards their Saviour, were exposed to trials, temptations, and persecutions, which he feared lest they might not have strength to withstand. For Philip he was specially anxious, and fervently had he that morning prayed to his Father in heaven to guide and protect the lad, and not suffer him to be tempted above what he was able to bear. Then this new cause of trouble, the idea of the pressgang coming down upon his flock, had filled him with alarm and apprehension. It was with difficulty that during the service he could keep his mind calmly fixed on Him without whose permission not a sparrow falleth to the ground. Before the sermon he gave out a psalm which was a favourite both with himself and the villagers – the 121st –

"To Zion's hill I lift my eyes,
From thence expecting aid,
From Zion's hill and Zion's God,
Who heaven and earth hath made.

"Sheltered beneath th' Almighty's wings
Thou shalt securely rest,
Where neither sun nor moon shall thee
By day or night molest.

"From common accidents of life,
His care shall guard thee still,
From the blind strokes of chance and foes
That lie in wait to kill.

"At home, abroad, in peace, in war,
Thy God shall thee defend,
Conduct thee through life's pilgrimage
Safe to thy journey's end."

These, indeed, were words of cheer and solace which had often breathed comfort into sad and desponding hearts. To those whose lives were spend for the most part on the treacherous deep they came with peculiar force; but never had Arthur himself felt their power as he did that day. The little congregation sung the psalm very heartily, as if fully convinced by their own experience of its truth. When Arthur ascended the pulpit his confidence had returned, and he felt that he could trust his own future and that of his flock in the hands of the Almighty, Who had hitherto helped and sustained him. He spoke on a theme of which he was never weary, he told them of a Father's loving care over His children, how He yearned over them all, though they had wandered far away from Him; how it was His will "that all men should be saved and come to the knowledge of the truth." The terrors of the law, he said, might indeed sometimes startle men in the midst of a career of sin, and rouse them to a sense of their danger, but it was the story of God's great love to the world, in sending His Son to die for poor fallen men and women, which moved and melted hardened hearts far more than fear, - that must not be the element of our religion, but love, for God is love, and, "His tender mercies are over all His works." And then, if they loved Him, and trusted Him, help would come to them from above, when they most needed it. "I will lift up mine eyes unto the hills from whence cometh my help." Now all might be peaceful and secure with them, the sky bright and cloudless, health, happiness, and quiet days secured to them. But who could tell how long such pleasing prospects might last? How often had they seen, after some calm brilliant day in summer, the little cloud rise out of the sea, which as it rose became larger and blacker, till it burst in a furious storm, and the lightning flashed, the thunder roared, and the winds raged. So it might be with many among them. The cloud might come, but no cloud was too dense for God's love to penetrate, no storm so fierce that He could not keep those who loved Him and trusted Him safe beneath His sheltering wing. "The Lord shall keep thee from all evil, it is even He that shall keep thy soul."

The sermon over, the little congregation began to disperse. Arthur, who was still apprehensive of danger from the pressgang, had marked two or three members of his congregation whom he thought would be likely victims. Among these was Philip Tresilian; a strong healthy fisher lad of seventeen was just the sort of fellow the rough gang would be likely to seize. Moreover, he knew that Philip; and his father had enemies ready enough to denounce him to the men who were collecting forced recruits for His Majesty's Navy. But there was another man in church, the father of a family, who had served some years in a merchant vessel, a good and able seaman, who had latterly begun to lead a steady life, and came regularly to church, this man Arthur thought was very likely to be pressed, so he was anxious to put him on his guard. He meant to catch both him and Philip before they had time to get far from the building, and hurried out of the vestry after them. He succeeded in overtaking David Abbott, who was walking quietly homeward to Sennen Cove with his wife and family; but while he was talking to him Philip escaped him, having gone on quickly with his father and sister. Abbott was very grateful to Arthur for his caution; as there seemed no means by which he could get a legal protection against impressments, he said he would walk off into the interior, some way from the coast, and spend the night at the house of a married sister who lived at a lonely farm, which the pressgang were not at all likely to discover.

Arthur now determined to go to the Cove and to Tresilian's cottage. His intention was to take Philip home with him. At his father's house he knew he would be quite safe, and there he would keep him till all danger was passed. However, "man proposes, God disposes." Just as Arthur had taken leave of David Abbott, a girl ran up to him, and implored him to come at once to see her mother, who was at the point of death. Arthur dared not delay so sacred a duty, and he had now to turn back to Sennen village. Here we must leave him for the present, while we follow the fortunes of Philip Tresilian.

The three had walked quietly home from church to their cottage by the sea-shore. Owen perceived the cutter, but took no particular notice of it. He sat down with his family to their frugal meal. That finished, he handed down the big Bible to Mary, and she, as was her usual custom on Sunday afternoon when there was no service at church, read out of it to her father and brother.

This lasted for about an hour. All the time Philip was restless and ill at ease. The fact was, that good and evil were struggling within him; he was hesitating between duty and inclination.

As he was going to church in the morning, two lads of his acquaintance had said to him, "It's a pity, Philip, after being at church all the morning, that you should shut yourself up for the whole afternoon; come out for a stroll with us along the shore, then we'll have a bathe and a swimming race round the point, the sea's so smooth, it's just the day for it!"

The proposal was a tempting one; but those who made it were lads who did not bear the best of characters. Philip hesitated. It was hard to say no. It always is to refuse what is pleasant, and harder still when mockery and ridicule are likely to follow the refusal. "Come, Philip," said the elder of the two, "we'll be quits, - Bob and I'll go to church this morning for a change, if you'll come along with us in the afternoon. What d'ye say to that?"

"Well, I'm sure the parson will be glad to see you in church, Dick; but as to this afternoon" –

"Come, come, don't be a fool, Philip, what's the harm of taking a walk along the shore, and having a bathe? I don't believe your friend the parson would even object; besides, it's a bargain; if we go to church this morning, the least you can do is to go with us this afternoon."

"Very well, Dick, I will if I can, but mind you, I can't quite promise."

"Stuff and nonsense, Phil; you'll come, I know; the matter's settled, we'll say no more about it. Come along to church, Bob."

The two young fellows kept their promise and went to church. Arthur had perceived them there with surprise and pleasure. Dick tried to go to sleep, but Bob was very attentive and well-behaved during the whole service.

Now Philip's mind was occupied during the afternoon, while his sister was reading, thinking about his half promise to go with these lads. He knew they were not just the sort of fellows the parson would like to see him with, and especially on a Sunday afternoon; and he thought too of all he had said to him yesterday about the effects of bad company; on the other hand, just for once, it surely could not matter, and it was such a fine bright warm afternoon, and the sea so smooth, perhaps he mightn't have another chance so good for a long time. Yes, he would go. He looked out of the window, and saw Bob and Dick waiting for him on the beach; that settled him at once. He took his cap off the peg and was going to the door, when Mary said to him, "What! are you going out Phil? Can't you stay a little longer, and then I should like to go with you, after I have read father one more story."

"No, Mary, I can't wait any longer; it's such a fine day, I'm going for a walk, and shall go much farther and faster than you are able."

"I'm sorry you won't wait for me, Phil," said his sister reproachfully;

"I was thinking this morning what a nice ramble we might have together this afternoon, and I could gather a nosegay of wild flowers, which I have not done once this spring."

"I'll go with you next Sunday, Mary, I can't do-day, I'm in a hurry now, so good-bye." And he rushed out of the door, and down to the beach.

"You shall come with me, Mary," said her father kindly. "I'll go out with you whichever way you like."

"Thank you, father," said Mary. "I wonder what Phil is up to. He seemed so determined to go out; he isn't often like that." She went to look out of the window and then continued, "Oh! there he is, yonder, walking along between two lads of about his size; one of them is Dick Evans, I know, but I can't make out who the other is."

"Dick Evans!" exclaimed her father, "a very bad companion for Philip; I don't like that at all, Mary, the boy's not as he used to be; he'll be led astray at last I'm afraid, and get into bad ways, and become like the rest of the young fellows here."

"Oh, don't say so, father. Think how mother used to pray for him when she was alive."

"And we pray for him too, I hope, Mary," said Owen.

Philip didn't feel comfortable as he left the cottage, and walked quickly down to the beach. But he had no presentiment of what was in store for him; he little thought of the fatal consequences of that Sunday afternoon walk, and of the important influence it was to have on his future life.

The plot had been schemed the night before in the alehouse by Nichols, Pollard, and a few other men, who were sworn enemies to Tresilian and his family. The lads had been bribed to decoy Philip away from the village to a lonely part of the sea-shore. One of the conspirators had rowed out to the pressgang cutter while service was going on in church, and had told them the exact spot, where they might that afternoon secure a prize. Nichols and Pollard were lurking about on the beach waiting for Philip and his companions. They hoped to see and take part in the capture, and were gloating in anticipation on the dismay and sorrow which Philip would suffer at being thus dragged away from his home, and the grief which is father would experience at the loss of his only son.

The three lads walked slowly onwards. Dick proposed that they should stroll round to the next point, on the other side of which was a sandy bay, the usual bathing-place of the lads of the village. To this Philip consented. When they had got round the point, they observed a small boat drawn up on the shore. There was no one in it. "Whose boat is that?" said Philip, "we don't often see boats drawn up here in this bay, and on a Sunday too!"

"Oh," said Dick, "I know all about it. The punt belongs to yonder cutter which has come to look out for smugglers. They've got an idea that there are some smuggled goods hid in one of the caves in the cliff here, or buried under the sand, and they've sent some of their men to look for them."

Oh, that's all, is it!" said Philip. "Come on then, Bob, here's a capital place for a swim, let's go and undress by that rock, it's in the shade there."

Near to the spot the lads chose was a cavern, the entrance to which was low and narrow; but it extended some way under the cliff, becoming at last large and spacious. They rapidly undressed, and then one after another ran off into the bright sparkling sea, which looked so inviting and refreshing on that sultry afternoon. They swam about for some time, Philip in the race always surpassing his companions, for he was a first-rate swimmer.

They were all in high spirits when they returned to dress, making the cliff re-echo with their merry peals of laughter. Philip was nearly ready, when he was suddenly startled by hearing loud voices proceeding from the interior of the cavern near the boat, and before he had time to get on all his clothes he felt himself seized by strong rude hands and thrown upon the ground. His assailants, he at once perceived, were sailors of His Majesty's Navy, but where they came from, and why they attacked him, was a riddle he could not solve. At the same time Dick and Bob were likewise captured by the gang. All three were then dragged into the interior of the cavern. Here Philip perceived Nichols and Ben Pollard. The former with a burst of malicious laughter exclaimed,

"Come, Philip, you're paid off at last, you're pressed now for His Majesty's Navy, and you may say good-bye for a long time to Sennen, to your friend the Methodist parson and to your father, to whom we owe so many grudges. Well, Ben, we're revenged now, ain't we?"

"Yes, that we are, John," said Ben cheerfully. "But what do you mean, my good men, by seizing hold of those other two fellows; it's only this one" – pointing to Philip – "we want you to carry off."

It's not who you want us to carry off," said the leader of the gang gruffly, "we're not here to pick and choose; we shall press all the young fellows we can for the Navy, - that's what we've orders to do."

"That's not fair play," said Nichols, "we only promised you this fellow here we're longing to get rid of – not the other two lads."

"Stuff and nonsense!" said the sailor, "we've got them, and we'll keep them now."

"Where are you going to take me to? What does it all mean?" exclaimed Philip, trying to release himself from the strong grasp of the sailor.

"No struggling, young chap, or you'll get more than you bargain for," said the man who was holding him. "It means that you're pressed for the Navy, and you'll have to come with us on board yonder cutter till you're sent to join the fleet."

"Let me go, let me go!" exclaimed Philip. "I must tell my father about this, he'll get me off, I'm sure; and he's expecting me home by this time."

"Well, he'll have to wait long enough, then, if that's the case, we mean to carry you off this minute – there's our boat; you won't see Sennen Cove again for many a long day."

Philip now burst into tears, he begged and implored the men to let him go home only to say good-bye to his father and sister; he promised to go with them then, and so all they required of him. But his prayers and entreaties were of no avail, they only laughed and mocked at him, while Nichols and Pollard continued to express their satisfaction at the success of their plot, so far as Philip was concerned, though they were evidently vexed that Dick and Bob should have also fallen into the trap.

These two lads naturally enough were much incensed at the turn affairs had taken. They bitterly reproached the elder men, for they did not believe their assertion that they had not desired their capture. However, they well deserved their fate: they had themselves fallen into the trap they had been bribed to lay for their companion. Resistance was useless. At first, indeed, they howled and struggled to get free; but the sailors were too strong for them, they were six in number and well armed; they threatened to bind and gag them if they did not at once submit.

Nichols and Pollard were so overjoyed at the success of their scheme as regarded Philip, that they soon forgot their vexation at the capture of the other two lads. After all, the fewer hands there were in the place the more money would be earned by those who were left behind. Dick and Bob might well be spared. Dick's uncle would grumble at first, perhaps, but he would soon find that it was a good riddance to lose his lazy nephew. Bob's mother would doubtless fret a good deal, and if she found out they had a hand in the business, it would be a long time before they heard the end of it. Still that wouldn't do them any great harm, so they must make the best of a bad job.

The sailors of the pressgang whose hearts were as hard as stone, and who were accustomed nearly every day of their lives to take part in similar scenes, now proceeded to seize their victims, and drag them to the boat which lay on the shore awaiting them. The hoarse laugh of the sailors, and the jeers and scoffs of Nichols and Pollard, were mingled with the sobs of poor Philip, and the yells and angry protestations of Dick and Bob.

Let us now turn away from this scene of violence to see what has become of Arthur Pendrean during this eventful afternoon.

We left the young clergyman just as he was summoned to the sick-bed of a poor woman. She was one of those who had been converted years ago by the preaching of John Wesley, and who had welcomed with joy and gratitude the advent of the zealous young clergyman to St. Sennen. She had ever been a regular attendant at the services of the church, she was a faithful communicant, and now in her last hours she thanked God that He had sent His minister to be at her side to cheer her as she passed through the dark valley of the shadow of death. Arthur administered to her the Communion of the sick, and in those sacred offices to the weary pilgrim, whose earthly race was so near its close, he forgot for the time his anxiety about the other members of his flock, and the danger with which they were threatened. He could not leave that bedside till all was over, and the faithful servant had peacefully passed away into the joy of her Lord.

When he had said a few words of comfort to the sorrowing relatives, he left the cottage, and looking at his watch, perceived that he had only just time to ride over to St. Levan where he had to perform evening service that afternoon. His thoughts naturally reverted to Philip and the pressgang, but he could do nothing now, he could only hope that he was exaggerating the danger, and utter a fervent prayer that God would protect that lad and others from being dragged from their homes, against their will, into a life which in those days was full of the gravest peril to the soul, and in which it seemed to Arthur almost impossible that any one, and especially a young lad, could lead a godly and moral life.

The service at St. Levan was not a long one, and immediately it was over, Arthur galloped off to Sennen cove, which he reached about half-past five in the afternoon. He went at once to Tresilian's cottage. He knocked at the door several times, but there was no reply. The fine afternoon had doubtless tempted the family out for a stroll on the beach or the cliffs. If Philip was in his father's company, probably all would be well. The cutter still lay at anchor in the bay. All was calm and quiet. He saw none of the inhabitants about, of whom he could inquire in which direction the Tresilians had gone. He felt uncertain as to what he should do next. The danger he saw was still there, but how could he warn those who were likely to be its victims?

He rode down slowly to the beach. As he found no one about, he went into one of the cottages, and inquired of an old woman who lived there, if she had chanced to see anything of Owen Tresilian and his son and daughter, during the afternoon. She replied that more than half an hour ago, she had seen Philip walking along the beach with Dick and Bob, and that they had disappeared round the point to the eastward. They seemed in high spirits, and were laughing and talking gaily enough. To Arthur this was by no means cheering intelligence; he was sorry to think that Philip should have chosen such companions on Sunday afternoon, especially after the talk he had had with him on the previous evening. The appearance of the two lads in church that morning had greatly surprised him; he began to fear that no good motive had brought them there, and, still more, to suspect foul play. At all events, he would follow them in the direction indicated by the old woman; so, tying up his horse close to her cottage, he hastened along the beach, and towards the point which hid the adjoining bay.

Before he turned the point, shrieks and yells, mingled with loud laughter and horrid curses, met his ear. He shuddered at the profane language, though in those days, alas! every one was accustomed daily to hear it; but this was more blasphemous than usual. Arthur felt certain now that the pressgang men had landed, and that a struggle was going on between them and some of their victims. God grant that Philip might not be among them! But he prepared himself for the worst; he knew that a hard conflict was before him, and he lifted up his heart in prayer to his Heavenly Father, asking Him to give him strength and courage to say and do what was right, and to guard him in every danger with His all-powerful hand.

To fear, Arthur was a complete stranger. His natural disposition was bold; physically strong, and with the heart of a lion, he had never cared since his boyhood what odds he faced, if the weak were to be defended against the strong, or injustice, meanness, or cruelty to be resisted. When, therefore, on turning the point he found himself in the presence of the scene we have previously described, - the six pressgang men, dragging the three lads struggling against them to their boat, while the two cowardly betrayers looked on, standing with their hands in their pockets, chuckling and mocking at poor Philip's despair, - he drew himself up with the air of one accustomed to command and be obeyed, and in a stern bold voice, in which there was no hesitation, nor the smallest sign of fear, exclaimed,

"What are you doing here, men? take your hands off those lads at once; what right have you to drag them away?"

The six men were so startled at this most unexpected apparition, and by this loud authoritative voice, that they did in fact let go their grasp of the boys for a moment, which Philip at once took advantage of. He ran up to Arthur, threw himself at his feet, clung to his knees, and cried –

"Oh, save me, sir! save me. They are going to take me away from you and my father for ever, and force me to be a sailor in the fleet."

But the rough tars, so suddenly startled, soon recovered their self-possession. They now perceived that this new-comer was a parson, - a very different sort of parson, indeed, from those to whom they were accustomed – nevertheless he was one; and of all the men, parsons were treated with the least deference and respect by ruffians, who mostly came from the scum of the population. Sailors, in those days, who had been forced into the service by impressments, were glad enough to employ themselves in pressing others, and many of them, too, were criminals who had been released from gaol, on condition that they joined the fleet.

"Who are you, I should like to know," exclaimed the leader of the gang with a volley of oaths, "who dares to interfere with us and our duty?"

Arthur had felt from the very first that he had no authority whatever to resist these men, in seizing any who were not provided with legal protection and who were between the ages of seventeen and forty-five. Happily he remembered that Philip was not seventeen, and it was only on this ground that he could claim his release.

"Your warrant does not allow you, my men, to press any lad under seventeen, and Philip Tresilian here is not seventeen yet. Therefore you will not take him with you," said Arthur firmly.

"We shall take whoever we please without the permission of a canting parson like you," said the sailor with more oaths and curses, "if you dare to resist His Majesty's warrant, we'll carry you off too," he continued with a loud and jeering laugh.

"A precious good thing too for us, mates," chimed in John Nichols, with an impudent leer at Arthur.

"You'll touch me at your peril," said the parson. "Neither shall you carry off this lad, so long as I stand here to protect him. He's not seventeen, and till he is you dare not press him for the service."

"Well, this beats all I've ever seen in my born days," cried another of the gang. "To have a parson come and defy six strong tars like us, doing our duty in His Majesty's service. What next, I should like to know?"

"The fellow is seventeen, I'll swear," said Nichols, approaching the leader of the gang.

"So'll I," said Ben.

"And I, too," yelled Dick, "but I swear I'm not sixteen; so, come, let me off, good sirs, won't ye?"

"Hold your tongue, rascal," said the man. "If ye were only twelve I'd press the whole lot of you."

"I assure you, sir, it's true, and I'm not seventeen," groaned Philip, still clinging to Arthur.

"Who cares what you say, any of you; and nobody can prove it. The fellow is big enough for seventeen at any rate, and what's certain is, that we are going to take him off to His Majesty's fleet, so you'll do best all of you to come away quiet, and don't force us to use violence; as if you resist us, we shall have to do," said another of the men.

"If you care to do what is right, you will come back with me to Sennen Cove and see his father," said Arthur.

"Go back to Sennen, indeed; catch us doing that," said the head of the gang. "No, now; no more parleying or halting. Come, lads, we must be off, we can't waste any more time here. Seize hold of that fellow, never mind the parson."

Philip still clung convulsively to Arthur. The men now advanced to drag him away – the other two lads were already in the boat with one of the men.

"You'll not take him if I can help it," exclaimed Arthur, who grasped Philip's shoulder with his left hand, while with his right he hurled back the man who had attempted to seize him.

The man was furious at this repulse. "We'll soon settle that game," said the leader, and he at once gave a signal to the other men, who fell upon Arthur from behind and dragged him to the ground; while he himself seized Philip with an iron grasp, forced him to release his hold of the parson, and dragged him to the boat.

"Cowards, that you are!" cried Arthur, as he sprang to his feet, but only to be dragged down again by his assailants. "Six against one, but I'll be equal with you yet. I'll have the lad released when he gets to Plymouth, and have you punished for this act of violence, and for acting beyond what your warrant allows."

"We're not afraid of that, Parson" said the leader of the gang, "and I hope you'll learn not to interfere with His Majesty's officers again."

"Oh, sir," cried Philip from the boat into which he had been dragged, "say good-bye to father for me, tell him not to fret about me; I know you will get me released," and the poor lad sobbed as if his heart would break, "ah! perhaps I shall never see them again."

"Come, stop all this noise," said the sailor. "None of this here," as he pushed the boat off the sand; "come along, you chaps," he called out to his companions who were still holding Arthur down, "you can leave that fool of a parson, he can't get after us in the water."

The men leaped into the boat. No sooner was he free than Arthur, who saw now that, in the face of such superior numbers, all resistance was in vain, put his hand into his breast pocket and drew out a small Testament. "One moment," he said to the men, "I know I can't resist you now; one word with the lad," and advancing up to his knees in the water he handed Philip the Testament. "Take that," he said to him, "read it whenever you can, and think of me and of those you leave behind at Sennen. Be a brave lad, Philip, and a credit to your family and your country. Trust in God. Remember what I told you yesterday. I will get you off, if I can, my boy; if not, I commend you to God, and I know He will guard and guide you, till one day we meet again – if not here, - above."

"Why, here's the parson preaching a sermon out of the water!" said one of the men in a tone of mockery. "Shove off, shove off, lads, pull away, my lads!"

Philip's sobs prevented him from saying a word in reply to his faithful friend and pastor. He gazed at him through his tears till he was out of sight.

8

A Fruitless Search

"He groans in spirit for his wife and son,-
Sore troubled like his Lord: he weeps and cries,
I have lost her: yet, O Lord, Thy will be done
And he – oh now, within Thine arms he lies,
O Father; and I thank Thee; yet, I pray,
Oh, spare him!" ...

- Rev. S.J. Stone

Arthur Pendrean stood alone on the sea-shore. The two Sennen men, to gratify whose malice and spite this wicked plot had been conceived and carried out, had slunk away, not wishing to expose themselves to the clergyman's indignant reproaches, which they knew they so well deserved. There he stood, solitary, cast down, overwhelmed with bitter grief and anguish. All seemed to have gone against him that day. Had he but arrived earlier at the Cove he could have saved Philip, and now he only owed his defeat to the superior numbers arrayed against him. This was the severest blow which had fallen upon him during the short course of ministerial labours. There was no lad in the parish he took so deep an interest in as Philip: perfection in a world so exposed to manifold temptations he could not expect, but Philip had promised well, his heart was still tender and open to receive God's truth, as the conversation he had had with him the previous evening had proved. And now this gentle-spirited but brave-hearted boy, who hitherto by a mother's love and a father's care had, in a measure, been sheltered and protected from the evil and vicious influences of his native village, was suddenly to be plunged into a world, where vice in its most hideous forms reigned paramount, where his companions would be ruffians gathered from gaols, or men hardened by a career of sin and infamy; and where there was little hope that the good seed planted in the lad's soul could ever grow up to perfection, but be choked or crushed out by constant contact with the vile and reprobate, by whom he would henceforth be surrounded.

But Arthur's disposition was not one to give way to despair. As he gazed at the little boat, whose oars fell rapidly into the glassy surface of the tranquil sea, while it grew smaller and smaller as it receded from the shore, and in the bright sunlight he could still distinguish the figures within it, he lifted up his heart in fervent prayer to God, to give strength and courage to that poor sorrowing lad, that he might be faithful and purer as Joseph in the house of Potiphar, and bold and steadfast as Daniel at the court of Babylon. He who had begun the good work in the boy's heart, surely would not allow it to come to nought. He never would suffer him to be tempted above what he was able to bear, but would with the temptation make a way for him to escape. He who had chosen the weak things of the world to confound the things which are mighty, had perhaps chosen the lad as a special instrument whereby His name should be glorified in the midst of an ungodly generation.

The young clergyman now bethought him of a sad duty he had to perform, and this was to break the evil tidings to Philip's father. He hurried back to Sennen Cove, but he was too late to be the first to inform Owen of his son's hard fate. With villainous glee Nichols and Pollard had hastened up to Tresilian's cottage, and met him and his little daughter just as they were returning from their quiet stroll.

"I've a piece of news for you, Owen," exclaimed Nichols with a malicious grin. "Your young chap's been carried off by the pressgang to yonder cutter: I saw the sailors drag him off myself."

Owen stood rooted to the spot with horror and amazement.

"What does he mean, father?" said Mary; "has anything happened to Philip?"

"Yes," said Ben, "you'll not see your brother again, little one, for many a long day, perhaps never at all; he has been pressed for a sailor on board His Majesty's fleet, and that's the long and short of it."

"Scoundrels that you are!" cried Owen in a burst of passion, "I don't believe a word of it, it's a lying tale you've invented to vex and worry me; only one of your old wicked tricks."

"It's true enough, as you'll find out to your cost," said Nichols with an insolent laugh. "You'll hear all about it from your friend the parson, and we're very glad it has happened, pleased enough to get rid of the young cub, only wish his father'd gone to keep him company, and the parson too."

Mary burst into tears. She began to understand now that Philip had in some mysterious way been carried off. Owen's rage, indignation, and anguish knew no bounds. "If this story is true," he exclaimed, "I believe you two villains have been at the bottom of it; you must have laid some vile plot to entrap the boy. Ah! I'll have justice done, I'll be a match for you!"

"Talk as big as you like, Owen, but there's no question of justice in these days, when the government has given order to press all the men they can lay hands on to man the fleet. You'll get no redress, I warrant," said Nichols, "and if we've had a finger in the pie, we shall only get His Majesty's thanks for presenting a promising seaman to his Navy, and the gratitude of many folks hereabouts, too, for getting rid of that prating young rogue, who was always running after that fool of a parson."

With these words the men turned quickly away, for they were eager to go to the village ale-house, to tell their companions there how well the plot had succeeded.

Scarcely were their backs turned, than Arthur, flushed and excited, came up to Owen's cottage. He found him standing outside, dismay and anguish depicted on his countenance, while Mary, her face hidden in her hands, was sobbing aloud. He perceived at once that the bad news had already reached Owen's ears, and the retreating figures of the two villains in the distance, told him by what means. He grasped the poor father's hand and said in a low tone of deep sympathy,

"I see you know the worst, Owen, but cheer up; it's not so bad, after all. I'll never rest till I get the lad released. He's not seventeen, I know, and below that age he is not eligible for impressments."

"Ah, sir, you've always been a friend in need to me and mine. There is a little comfort in what you say, for it's true the lad's not seventeen; but I fear when they've once got him into their clutches, they won't so easily give him up," replied Owen.

"Yes, I hope they will, if proper representations are made," said Arthur.

"Ah, sir, can't you save my brother?" sobbed Mary.

""Is it true what those bad men said, I shall never see Philip again?"

"No, Mary, we'll hope for the best, and that I shall be able to bring him back in a few days. So cheer up. Remember, too, our dear Philip is in his loving Almighty Father's hands; think of the psalm we sung in church this morning, the words still seem to ring in my ears, and God grant that Philip too may be feeling comfort in these words –

"'At home, abroad, in peace, in war,
Thy god shall thee defend,
Conduct thee through life's pilgrimage
Safe to thy journey's end.'"

Owen's eyes filled with tears, he could not utter a word; but he grasped the young clergyman's hand warmly.

"Come," said Arthur, "let us go into the cottage and talk the matter over calmly. Let us ask God to bless us in all that we mean to do, and to aid us in obtaining Philip's release, and to give us grace too, that we may in everything submit ourselves to His holy will, and feel that He doeth all things well."

When seated in the house Arthur told them the whole story of Philip's capture; how he had suddenly come upon the scene, and done his utmost to save the lad, but that in face of violence employed against him and of superior numbers, his efforts had been unavailing. Then they all knelt down and prayed to God that He would give them strength to bear this trial; that it might turn out to His glory; and asked that if it were His will Philip might be restored to his family; but if not, that He would graciously preserve him both in body and soul.

Arthur decided to start with Owen the next day to Plymouth, where they would seek an interview with the naval authorities, to protest against Philip's capture as illegal.

At night-fall the cutter was still at anchor in the same place. It was expected that the gang would land and make a raid upon the village. This, however, did not come to pass. They had secured as their prize three strong healthy lads, and they knew that all the village would now be on the alert, and the most eligible men conceal themselves. They might, too, get involved in some trouble about Philip – if he were really, as asserted, under seventeen. The young parson who had confronted them so boldly was evidently not a man to be trifled with, and they felt certain he would use every possible means to rescue their victim. But they would foil him, nevertheless. The next morning at dawn, not a trace of the cutter was to be seen. Owen, who had been on the look-out all night, thought she had sailed to the westward, but he could not be certain – if such were the case she would round Land's End and probably make for Falmouth or Plymouth.

The capture of the three lads caused great excitement both at Sennen Cove and the village. The part played in the affair by Nichols and Pollard was by no means regarded with unanimous satisfaction by the inhabitants. The majority, indeed, joined them in their grudge against Tresilian, who was regarded as friendly to the parson and those who promoted the obnoxious lighthouse scheme, so they rather rejoiced that Philip had been pressed; but the relations of the other two lads were loud in their expressions of indignation, they asserted that Nichols and Pollard had taken a large bribe from the pressgang men, to entrap the three young fellows and deliver them over into their hands, and as this was believed by most of the villagers, the two men were henceforth regarded with distruct and aversion by all except the most degraded and vicious.

Arthur consulted his father that evening on the unhappy event of the day. The squire, as lord of the manor, and as a county magistrate, naturally possessed a good deal of influence, and this his son persuaded him to employ energetically, to obtain the release of Philip Tresilian. Letters were dispatched in all directions, the naval authorities in Plymouth were communicated with, the Admiralty in London was petitioned. Everything was done to obtain the release of the youth who had so illegally been pressed for the service.

Next morning the young clergyman, accompanied by Owen, started for Falmouth. They thought it not unlikely that the cutter would put into that port before proceeding to Plymouth. There were several men-of-war, too, in Falmouth harbour, and the victims of the recent impressments might possibly be immediately put on board one or other of them. But nothing had been heard or seen of the cutter in Falmouth. The clergyman and the anxious father then proceeded to Plymouth, but here no greater success awaited them; they were assured by the authorities that the cutter had not put in there. Arthur made every possible inquiry, he sought an interview with the Admiral who commanded the fleet, and with the governor of the citadel; they promised that if the yacht with the young men on board put into Plymouth, the matter should be fully investigated, and the lad who had been illegally impressed, immediately released and sent back to his home. But those were days of war and great political excitement, when the country's honour was at stake and mighty issues were hanging in the balance. The fate of one poor fisher boy was of little consequence to the men who had fleets and armies at their command, nor were the zealous efforts and petitions of a village parson likely to be remembered by boards and councils who were wielding the destiny of the nation, during so critical a period.

Arthur was obliged to return at the end of the week to Cornwall for his

Sunday duties. Owen, more anxious and more desponding than ever about his son's fate, determined to take a passage in a fishing smack to Portsmouth, where he hoped to learn some tidings of the missing cutter. As he was furnished with an order for Philip's release, he trusted that if the lad could only be found, he might be liberated at once. But their ill success both at Falmouth and Plymouth did not encourage the afflicted father. When men were so scarce, and the pressgang men were rewarded for every recruit they captured, it was unlikely they would land at ports where inquiries would be instituted, and their victims released. Most probably Philip was already on board a man-of-war which was sailing to some scene of action, far away from the shores of England. But Owen would leave no stone unturned to find his son. Therefore commending his little daughter, who had been sent to the squire's house during her father's absence, to Arthur's care, he sailed for Portsmouth, with but faint hopes of success.

A fortnight passed away, and no news of Owen Tresilian reached Sennen Cove. Poor little Mary, who was most kindly treated at the squire's, and whom Arthur did all in his power to cheer and comfort, pined and fretted sadly at the absence of her father and brother. Letters in those days were very rare occurrences; indeed, if any inhabitant of so remote a village as St. Sennen received one, it was an event – in fact, a nine days' wonder. Neither the parson nor Mary therefore expected to get any news of Owen by post, but they daily hoped to see him. The men at the Cove were overjoyed at his departure.

"We did a good stroke of business last Sunday week, Ben," said Nichols one day as the two friends met on the beach. "We thought we had only rid ourselves of the young 'un, but the old 'un seems to be gone too. He's fallen into some trap, we'll hope."

"He sailed in a smack from Plymouth to Portsmouth; perhaps he's been pounced upon by a French cruiser," said Ben.

"That would be too great a piece of luck, Ben," said Nichols, "no; I expect he'll turn up one of these days; but as to the young chap, he's not likely to trouble us again."

"They be hard at work at the lighthouse now, again, John," said Ben.

"Yes," he said with an oath, "and a poor look-out for us next winter if it's finished by that time."

It was nearly a week after this conversation, late one Saturday night, when a man weary, foot sore, with haggard face, and clothes torn and ragged, knocked at the door of the manor house. When it was opened, Mary at once recognised her father's voice and rushed into his arms.

"O father!" she said, "you've come at last. How long you've stayed away. I thought you'd never come, and I've cried myself to sleep at night, though everybody has been so kind to me. How ill you look, father, and how tired, and where is Philip? I thought you had gone to bring him back, but he is not with you. Isn't he coming then?"

Owen sank down exhausted in a chair. He clasped his daughter, now his only remaining treasure, to his heart; his voice was so choked with grief and emotion he could hardly speak. At last he said, "Yes, Mary, thank God I have come back to you; but a hard and weary time I've had of it, and I've not been able to get any news of Philip; I fear I shall never see my dear boy again."

"Oh, don't say so, father," sobbed Mary. "Surely, some day he'll come back to us."

At that moment Arthur entered the room; he warmly grasped Owen's hand.

"My good friend," he said, "I'm glad, indeed, to see you back again. I have been quite anxious about you, and as to poor Mary here, it was all that I could do to keep up her spirits at all. Ah! I read in your sad face that you have had no success; but come, tell me, have you heard anything about him?"

"No, sir, nothing whatever," said Owen sadly. "I sailed, as you know, to Portsmouth in the smack, working my passage. My shipmates were good-hearted fellows, and said when we got to Portsmouth they'd do all they could to help me to trace the cutter. Well, we had a very long, rough passage, contrary winds all the way. We reached Portsmouth at last, and there I set to work to get some tidings of my poor boy. Furnished with the letters and papers you and your father gave me, sir, I went before every one who possessed any influence – magistrates, naval boards, dockyard authorities; some refused to hear me, and sent me rudely about my business, others assured me that the cutter had not put in there, and that all the men who had been pressed along the Cornish coast had been taken at once to the fleet, which was somewhere cruising in the channel. One gentleman who seemed to have a kinder heart than the rest, and who said he had a son himself, a midshipman, on board the fleet, and so could feel for me, told me that there was no use my troubling myself any more about the matter. It was too late now. There was such a scarcity of seamen, that every one was being pressed they could lay hold of, and that even the gaols had been emptied to man the fleet. My boy, he was certain, was far off at sea by this time, and I must take the best of a bad job, and submit to my fate. He hoped some day he would return to me safe and well, and be a credit to his country. And that's all the comfort I got, sir. But I didn't give us yet. I persevered in my inquiries, but all was no use. Then I thought of my little one here, and felt that it was time for me to return home. I looked out for a passage back to Plymouth or Falmouth, and finding a brig bound for Falmouth just about to sail, I arranged with the master to work out my passage to the port. But I had fallen upon a very rough lot, they drank, they swore, they blasphemed in a way it was horrible to listen to; and because I would not join them in their wickedness, they ill-treated me, giving me all the hard work to do, and very little to eat. We had had stormy weather too, as is not usual at this time of year, but very thankful was I when we got to Falmouth at last, and I was once more at liberty. I walked home at once, and never stopped till I reached your father's door, and faint and tired I am now, sir, I can assure you."

"You shall have a good meal and a good night's rest, Owen," said Arthur with kindly sympathy, "but this is bad news you bring us, though it is what I have expected; and now we can only submit to God's will. To his heavenly Father's care and protection we must commit the dear lad. Daily have I prayed for your Philip, Owen, and I have such faith in God's love to His children that I often feel comforted about him. Think of the words of the hymn in Mr. Wesley's little book, which Mary sometimes reads to you, Owen –

'Thine everlasting truth,
Father, Thy ceaseless love,
Sees all Thy children's wants, and knows
What best for each will prove;
And whatsoe'er Thou will'st
Thou dost, O King of kings:
What Thine unerring wisdom chose,
Thy power to being brings.'
and this verse too –
'Leave to His sovereign sway
To choose and to command,
So shalt thou wondering own His way,
How wise, how strong His hand:
Far, far above thy thought
His counsel shall appear,
When fully He the work hath wrought
That caused thy needless fear.'

Tears flowed down the weather-beaten cheeks of the rough sailor as he listened to these words which Arthur repeated in an earnest tone, as if he thoroughly realised their power and their truth.

"Ah, sir, it is hard, very hard," he said, "to lose both my wife and my son in so short a time."

"Don't say that they are either of them lost, Owen," said Arthur cheeringly. "She is not lost but gone before! and as to Philip, by God's mercy, I trust we shall all see him one day again among us. Then there is Mary left to you; she will do all she can to comfort and help her father, won't you, Mary?"

"Yes, that I will, sir, and father knows it," said the child through her tears.

The next morning, Owen Tresilian and his daughter returned to their lonely cottage at the Cove. Few were there who showed him any sympathy, or gave him a friendly welcome. Most of the men, by their manner and looks, gave him to understand that they were sorry to see him among them again, and wished he had never come back. Mary, deeply as she felt the loss of her brother, set bravely to work to cheer her father, and to render his home as comfortable as possible, but nothing seemed to make up to the poor man for the absence of his son. His manner was quite changed, he was gloomy and almost morose. Without saying a word to any one he would shove off his boat, jump into her, and go out fishing alone for the whole day, and whether he caught much or little seemed to have no effect upon his spirits. In the evening, when he sat mending his nets, Mary would, as she was wont, take down the big Bible and read to him out of it, or sometimes she would repeat one of Mr. Wesley's hymns; but he seemed to give little heed, and to take hardly any interest in the sacred words. The absence of Philip, the waves of sorrow which one after another had rolled over him, and deeply affected poor Owen's mind. Still Mary did not despair. She was indeed the sunlight of that desolate home; she had always a smile ready to welcome her father when he returned from his day's toil. Her affectionate greetings and loving embrace almost seemed as if they must in time dissipate the gloomy clouds which encircled his brow, and pour a cheering ray of sunshine into his afflicted soul.

Arthur was a frequent visitor to the cottage. Though all his efforts had as yet failed to discover what had become of Philip, he always spoke to Owen of his son as of one who was only absent for a time, fighting the battles of his country, and who would one day be restored to his father and his home. The more he thought of the matter, the more confident he felt that his prayers would be answered with respect to Philip, and deeply as he regretted his capture, and the barbarous circumstances with which it had been attended, he felt convinced that the Almighty had some wise end in view in permitting it. Repeatedly he did by every means in his power, try to make Owen look at the sad event in this light, but the poor father was a man of little faith, and that little faith was now as it were flickering in the socket, and it was all Arthur could do to keep it alive at all. Sorely, indeed, did the good clergyman feel that this poor man had been tried, and he often endeavoured to impress upon him that "whom the Lord loveth He chasteneth;" and that "no chastening for the present seemeth to be joyous but grievous: nevertheless afterward it yielded the peaceable fruit of righteousness unto them which are exercised thereby." But Owen regarded his trials in another way, he chafed and repined under God's chastening. Why, he said, should others be spared and allowed to go on prospering, who, instead of trying to lead a good and honest life, were getting gains by smuggling, wrecking, and all sorts of evil means? He had prayed to God, but he had received no answer. He had prayed that his wife might be spared, but she now lay in the cold grave. He had prayed that his son might be restored to him, but his prayer had not been heard, he knew not whether he were alive or dead. Like the Psalmist, he envied the prosperity of the wicked, but he had not yet learned the truth which the Psalmist experienced, he had not patience to wait to see what the end of these men would be, how "they are brought into desolation in a moment, and are utterly consumed with terrors," he could not yet say, "I waited patiently for the Lord, and He inclined unto me, and heard my calling." But Arthur did not despair, he was full of true, earnest sympathy for the poor fisherman, and he knew that the day would dawn at last, when God would make all things plain to him, when he would see "the bright light which is in the clouds," which he saw not now, and acknowledged that "His tender mercies are over all His works."

And thus spring changed into summer, and then the long, warm summer days shortened, and autumn came with its equinoctial gales and cheerless skies, heralding the storms of the approaching winter. But during this time the lighthouse had made great progress, and by the month of October, Arthur, and all those interested in this work of true humanity, hoped to see the bright, cheering light shine over the waste of stormy waters, to warn the mariner of the dangerous rocks, and by its cheering beams to tell him of his nearness to his home, to the shores of Old England.

9

On Board The Fleet -
The Battle Of The First Of June

"O Lord, be with us when we sail
Upon the lonely deep,
Our guard when on the silent deck
The midnight watch we keep.

"We need not fear though all around,
Mid rising winds, we hear
The multitude of waters surge,
For Thou, O God, art near.

"If duty calls from threatened strife
To guard our native shore,
And shot and shell are answering
The booming cannon's roar;

"Be Thou the mainguard of our host
Till war and dangers cease;
Defend the right, put up the sword,
And through the world make peace."

We must now take leave of our friends at the Land's End for a time, and follow the fortunes of Philip Tresilian.

The three lads, who soon ceased to offer resistance to their captors, were at once taken on board the cutter, and put down into the hold. When Dick and Bob protested against this, and began to yell, howl, and swear, the captain threatened to put them in handcuffs, if they showed the slightest violence. Philip was perfectly silent and passive; he was so completely overwhelmed by the suddenness of the blow which had fallen upon him, and which he had yet scarcely realised, that he could not utter a word.

"Well, my lads," said the captain to the men, "you've done a good day's work. It's a long time since we've caught three finer, stronger looking lads than these. First-rate sailors we'll make out of them, though they all look rather down in the mouth just now."

"And a nice piece of work we've had to get 'em, I assure you," said the sailor who had been the head of the landing party. "One of these here chaps is a regular Methodist, and a pet of the parson of the place, who is said to be a Methodist too. Whatever he may be, he's the strangest parson I've seen in all my born days. He's a young fine-looking fellow of about five-and-twenty, fitter, I should say, to be a life-guardsman than a parson, and what does he do but come down on the shore, just as we were a-going to carry off these young chaps, and he shows fight too, and says we shan't take off this pet of his. But strong as he was, and determined too, we were too many for him; so we dragged the chap off, and the parson preached us a sermon while we were getting into the boat. Didn't he just, Tom?"

"Yes, that he did," said the comrade appealed to, "and gave the lad a book to read to keep up his spirits."

"It's not often we catch chaps as can read," said the captain.

"No, and not much good it'll do him," said the sailor. "But, look ye here, captain, this parson says this young chap, that he took on so about, isn't seventeen, and so we've no right to press him. He'll move heaven and earth, he said, to get him released, so the best thing we can do is to make sure of our prize."

"We mustn't put into port, then," said the captain.

"No. Sure enough, he'll be off to Falmouth and Plymouth to-morrow, to be on the look-out for us, and if he gets, as he says, the chap's father to come and swear as he isn't seventeen, it'll be all up with us, and we shall lose our prize."

"I know what I'll do, Jack," said the captain; "the fleet's somewhere in the channel, bearing down for the French coast. We must just cruise about, too, till we fall in with a man-of-war, then we'll put these fellows aboard. In these days one or other of His Majesty's ships is sure to be short of hands, and the admiral will be glad enough to take the chaps, and pay us well for our prizes."

"Just what I was going to propose, captain," said the other.

"Very well, then, we'll lay here till nightfall, and then round the Land's End, and straight up mid channel, till we hail His Majesty's fleet."

The lads in the hold heard all this conversation, and poor Philip's heart sank within him. He felt that he must now bid farewell to all hope of release. Oh! had he only been allowed to take leave of his father and sister, just to see them once more, it would have made his hard fate more endurable! But, no; he had parted from his dear sister somewhat sulkily he felt, then he had yielded to a temptation he ought to have withstood in accompanying the other two lads, he had been vacillating and weak, he had known what was right and done what was wrong, and alas! now there was no means of repairing his fault. He buried his face in his hands and sobbed aloud. Should he ever see his father, his sister, the good parson, his home again? and what a hard lot was in prospect for him, how different from that of a quiet fisherman in the remote little Cornish village.

His two companions took no notice of his grief; they remained sullen and morose. They, too, saw that there was no escape for them. Their anger and vexation arose from a different motive. Instead of leading a lazy easy life at Sennen, they would now be submitted to the severest discipline, and to all sorts of hardships. Dick, the idlest and most mischievous lad in the village, who thought himself his own master, and never was accustomed to obey any one, would now be forced to submit to authority. Bob was not such a bad fellow, lazy enough he certainly was, but he was kind-hearted and had some affection left for his mother, though at times he caused her a great deal of trouble. He began to feel now that she would miss him, and to regret much of his unkindness and undutifulness towards her.

In the hold of the cutter were seven other men and lads, who had been pressed at various places on the coast, where the pressgang had landed. Some of these, being respectable men, were silent and depressed; others, who were bad and desperate fellows, swore and scoffed, and delighted in mocking at the grief of the new-comers.

At night the cutter weighed anchor, and favoured by a fair wind sailed round the Land's End and made for the English Channel. Philip, overcome by his sorrow, sank into a heavy slumber and did not awake till dawn next morning.

A fresh breeze sprang up as the sun rose, which increased during the day. Towards evening, in the rays of the setting sun, they perceived the fleet in full sail bearing down upon them. To lie to and run up a signal was the next step. A boat was put out from one of the men-of-war ships, and rowed up to the cutter. As the captain had expected, they were only too glad of fresh hands, so long as the men were strong and healthy, and not unfitting for a seafaring life.

Their ship, the "Royal Sovereign," they said, had been obliged to sail from Portsmouth without her full compliment, though every possible effort had been made by impressments and other means to obtain men. It was arranged that the cutter should sail up as close as possible to the "Royal Sovereign," on board which the men should be sent to undergo the usual inspection; those who were considered capable would be enrolled among her crew, but if any were not so, the cutter was to land them at the nearest English port. This was done. Two out of the ten, one a lad, the other a man of about five-and-thirty, were rejected as too weakly for service. The other eight, Philip among them, had to remain on board the "Royal Sovereign." Some, however, as the whole fleet was short-handed, were subsequently drafted on board other vessels, among those was Philip's companion, Dick.

And now quite a new life began for Philip, a rough one it was certainly, but the lad had learned to feel that he must submit without murmuring to a fate which was inevitable. He regretted, indeed, his happy home, his kind father and loving sister, and he grieved when he thought how hard it would be for them never to get any news of him. But like a brave English lad, he determined, God helping him, to do his duty in that state of life to which, by no wish or act of his own, he had been called; he would try to become a gallant seaman, and be an honour to his father and his country.

When he first went between decks on board the man-of-war, had his hammock pointed out to him, and mingled with his messmates, he perceived at once with what a rough set he had been cast; still, with the hopefulness of youth, he trusted that there might be some honest fellows among them, who, like himself, had been pressed into service against their will. The oaths, the vile language which greeted his ear, surpassed anything he had heard from the very worst characters at Sennen. This was indeed to be expected, for there was a proverb in those days, "that a king's ship and the gallows refused nobody," and really honest tars were obliged to number among their messmates jail-birds and felons. Philip set about his work quietly and unobtrusively, hoping that he would be let alone and lost in the crowd. His companion, Bob, kept as close to him as possible; the unexpected trouble which had come upon him had softened this lad considerably; he was by no means of a bad disposition, and already, as he told Philip, deeply regretted the cowardly and deceitful part he had played in the plot which had led to Philip's capture, and with it to his own. As soon, too, as he was removed from Dick's evil influence, he became more friendly with Philip, so that the lads were much together.

Those were stirring and anxious days, not in England only, but all over Europe. The horrors and crimes of the French Revolution had startled and disgusted the civilised world. When at last the wretched mob who ruled in Paris had performed the crowning act of infamy, and sent their king, Louis

XVI, to the scaffold, shortly to be followed by his heroic wife, Marie Antoinette, and his saintly sister, Madame Elizabeth, all the powers of Europe, Great Britain included, declared war against the French Republic, and in the year 1793 a fearful struggle commenced, which, with little interruption, lasted for two-and-twenty years.

Twenty-one line of battle ships and several frigates had been put into commission early in the year. This fleet, which was subsequently increased, was placed under the command of Lord Howe, one of the ablest admirals of the day. For more than a month it had been cruising in the channel, and was escorting a number of merchant vessels clear of the Lizard, when it had been met by the pressgang cutter. Lord Howe was keeping a sharp look-out for a large French fleet, which he expected either had, or shortly would, put out from Brest. The Republican government had, after much exertion, fitted out this fleet, consisting of twenty-six ships of the line, and as a famine was raging in the country, they were eagerly on the watch for the arrival of a convoy of 350 sail from American ports, laden with provisions. Earl Howe's object was first to capture or destroy this convoy, and secondly to fight the Brest fleet. From the crews of several vessels he had captured, he obtained accurate information of the enemy's movements; and finding that the French fleet had actually put to sea, he determined to engage it as soon as possible.

The "Royal Sovereign," on board which were Philip and Bob, was one of the finest line of battle ships in Earl Howe's fleet. As both the lads were strong and active, and from earliest childhood accustomed to a seafaring life, they soon fell into the duties allotted them, and in a few days could climb the rigging and reef the sails as handily as if they had been a year in the service. But it was not long before Philip's quiet, sober manner attracted the attention, and drew upon him the ridicule, of his messmates. Not to swear or use bad language was alone enough in those days to render a lad peculiar on board ship, and as an oath or a filthy word had never been heard to escape Philip's lips, he soon became the butt of profane and ill-natured among the crew. It was not often that he got a chance of reading a few verses out of the Testament which had been the last gift of the clergyman; he could only do so when no one was near to observe him, as, if discovered, he would have to encounter, besides ridicule, the danger of losing his precious book. One evening in the twilight, retiring to a remote corner of the deck, when he perceived that most of the crew appeared to be occupied in their own affairs, he drew out the little book, and soon became deeply immersed in the sacred story. Suddenly he was interrupted by a gruff voice behind him; he looked up with a start of terror, and saw a rough tar who was distinguished above the rest for his brutality and profanity.

"What have you got there, lad?" he said with an oath. "Reading indeed, and setting yourself above your fellows like us who never learned a letter in our lives!"

Philip immediately put the book safely away into the pocket of his jacket, and replied quietly,

"It's a book that was given to me before I left home; surely it can't do any harm to any one, my reading it; and I don't want to set myself up above anyone else, I'm sure."

"And what's the book about, and what' the name of it, you young vagabond?" said the man.

"It's a New Testament," said Philip.

"A Testament!" cried the sailor with a volley of oaths; "a Testament, why, then, you must be a Methodist, you rascal; who ever heard of any one on board ship reading a Testament? That kind of thing's not allowed here, you'll soon find out, my fine chap;" then he hollooed out to the group of men nearest to them, "I say, messmates, come here, we've got a young rascal here who can read, and is a regular Methodist into the bargain. Here's fine fun for you!"

The men were all attention at once; they gathered round poor Philip, who felt both abashed and troubled. Hitherto he had managed to avoid notice, now he felt the time had come when his faith would be put on trial. He prayed to God to give him strength and courage not to deny his Saviour, but to act as bravely in defence of His cause as he would in that of his earthly sovereign.

"A Methodist, indeed!" exclaimed the men with a loud shout of derisive laughter.

"We'll soon drive these notions out of your head, my lad," said one of the boatswain's mates, who, as one of his chief duties was to inflict the punishment of the cat – only too frequent an occurrence on board that ship – was utterly hardened to all feelings of humanity or kindness.

"Young chaps like that shouldn't be allowed to waste their time over books on board a man-of-war," remarked another sailor.

"Nor to fill their heads with such rubbish," said a third.

"No fellows are such cowards as Methodists, sure to flinch before the enemy, and hide themselves in the hold if they can get away during a battle," observed another of the group.

"Come on, give us up that book," said Edwards, the man who had been the origin of all the disturbance, addressing Philip in an authoritative tone.

"No, I shall not," said Philip firmly. "The book belongs to me, and you've no right to take it from me."

"Well, you are a cheeky young vagabond. I'll teach you how to speak to your superiors. Right, indeed! we'll soon see who's right here. Come, give us up the book, or the worse for you," declared the man angrily.

But Philip showed no signs of giving way.

"Give it up, I say," roared Edwards again, with a fearful oath; and the other men who stood round all shouted in chorus, "Yes, give it up, or we'll make you!"

"Well, then," said Philip, "you may take it if you can, but I will not give it up to you, for you've no right to it."

Edwards, now furious with passion, seized Philip by the arm and dragged him along the deck. Meanwhile the boatswain's mate, and several of the worst disposed among the men, kicked and cuffed the poor lad unmercifully.

"Now, will you give it up?" cried Edwards.

"Never!" said Philip as decidedly as ever.

Edwards and another man proceeded to force the book out of Philip's possession; they held him down on the deck, but he kept his arms tightly clasped over his breast, in which his Testament was concealed.

"You won't hold out long now, I'll warrant," said Edwards, accompanying the words with a series of cuffs and blows which rendered his victim nearly unconscious.

Just at this moment Bob, who had been employed at the further end of the ship and whose work was now done, came upon deck, and perceiving the crowd and hearing the noise, hurried to the scene of action. There, to his horror and indignation, he saw Philip, bleeding and prostrate, while several strong sailors were belabouring him on every side, and evidently trying to get something out of his grasp, which he was determined not to give up. Naturally impetuous, and fearless of consequence, when he saw the only friend he had on board in trouble, he pushed his way through the crowd in spite of every obstacle, bent over Philip, wiped away the blood which was flowing form his face, and exclaimed in an angry voice,

"I say, messmates, fair play; what has the fellow done that you should treat him like this?"

"Why, there are two of them then," said Edwards with a wild burst of laughter; "another Methodist, are you? Yes, I remember you both came aboard the same day. I suppose you've got a Testament too; well, you have to give it up as well as your mate here."

"I'm not a Methodist, and I've got no Testament," said Bob, "but he's my friend, and there ought to be fair play."

"The impudent young beggar," said Edwards in a fury, as leaving Philip he sprang upon poor Bob, and dealt him such a number of blows, that he soon rolled down utterly senseless on the deck. It was small use Philip springing to his feet, to try and defend his comrade, he was soon seized and the Testament was at last, notwithstanding all his efforts, wretched from him.

The poor lads were now completely overpowered, and as they lay on the deck, their cowardly foes amused themselves by kicking them. At that moment, however, a quartermaster appeared, who was noted equally for his justice and severity. Edwards, who had got possession of the Testament, was debating with his companions as to what should be done with it, and was on the point of throwing it overboard, when the quartermaster demanded an explanation of this disturbance. He glanced angrily, now at Edwards, now at the prostrate forms of the two lads, whom he perceived at once had been severely handled.

"Now then, my lad," said he to Bob, who was with difficulty attempting to rise, "tell me the truth, what's all this row been about?"

Bob explained as well as he could, and as Philip was beginning to revive, the quartermaster soon made out the story. The ruffianly character of Edwards was well known to him, the breach of discipline and order he and his mates had committed well deserved a flogging, but just then, as an important action was daily expected, they escaped with a severe reprimand, and a command to give up the book, which the officer restored to Philip, remarking that he must keep it to himself, and not be seen reading it on deck, for no Methodism was allowed aboard ship.

Edwards sauntered off with a growl of suppressed rage, vowing vengeance against Philip and Bob. The two lads were henceforth greater friends than ever.

The hostile fleets frequently sighted one another, and a battle evidently was imminent, only indeed delayed by the thick fog which every now and then came down upon the sea and hid them from each other. At last, on the first of June, a day noted as glorious in the annals of the British navy, the sun shone forth with unwonted splendour, and disclosed the French fleet steering in order of battle and ready for the combat.

There was great enthusiasm on board every vessel in the English fleet, the "Royal Sovereign" among the number, and Philip and Bob looked eagerly forward to the struggle. At seven in the morning, Lord Howe signalled that he should attack the enemy's centre and break though their line. The crews were now piped for breakfast, the drums beat, and all hands got ready for action. Each ship was ordered to steer for and engage the ship opposite to her in the enemy's line, keeping to leeward of her antagonist, so that if worsted she could not get away. Six of the ships succeeded in breaking through the compact line of the French fleet; the first of these was the "Defence," and the next the "Queen Charlotte," the flag ship, with the Admiral Lord Howe, on board. He gave orders to his pilot to lay him alongside the "Montagne," of 120 guns, the largest vessel in the French line, and directed that till then not a shot should be fired, though in passing she received the fire of the "Vengeur" and the "Achille." With awful force did the Admiral, at last, pour his whole broadside into the stern of the "Montagne" as he passed between that huge three-decker, and the "Jacobin," of 80 guns. So close were the ships on this occasion that the great tricolor which waved on the "Montagne's" flagstaff touched the rattlins of the "Queen

Charlotte," and so terrible was the effect of the Admiral's broadside that the decks of the French vessel were drenched in blood, and strewed with the bodies of 300 killed and wounded.

The other vessels of the British fleet were, meanwhile, engaged in as desperate encounters with the remaining French ships. But we will confine ourselves to the "Royal Sovereign," on board which were our two friends.

After having been struck by several shots, she bore down upon the "Terrible," and commenced firing at her. Her batteries promptly answered in return. An awful struggle now ensued, the vessels came to close quarters and opened their broadsides on each other, pouring shot upon their decks, which were soon strewn with the dying and the dead. But on board the English ship every man did his duty bravely, all stood to their guns. Some of the young lads, indeed, and a few of the men too, who had been so recently impressed, could hardly repress a shudder at the sight of the carnage around them. It was the first time they had been face to face with death. Philip, when he saw the first man who was struck down carried off bleeding to the cockpit, thought involuntarily of his home, of his father, and his sister, whom, perhaps he would never see again; but he breathed one short earnest prayer to his Father above, to shield him in the danger, and to give him a brave heart in the terrible combat, and then he stood unflinchingly at his post till the end. His conduct was not unobserved by some of his superiors. In the very midst of the engagement Admiral Graves, his commander, was badly wounded, and carried off the deck; and the charge of the "Royal Sovereign" devolved on Captain Nichols. But still the battle raged, the main and mizen masts of the enemy were shot away, but she did not give up, bravely continuing the struggle, till perceiving that further resistance was useless, and that she might still effect an escape, she bore away, the "Royal Sovereign" in pursuit of her. Other ships which came to her aid were beaten off, and the "Royal Sovereign" hauled up as well as the disabled state of her sails and rigging would permit.

It was a grand victory! Ten of the French line had struck, though only six had been secured, and five of their ships were dismasted and slowly going off under their sprit-sails. They had 690 men killed and 580 wounded, whereas the English had only 68 killed and 129 wounded.

During the battle Philip and Bob had been posted at a long distance from each other. Philip often longed for a word with Bob, and would now and then strain his eyes in the direction where he knew he was, hoping to get a glimpse of him.

But smoke and fire constantly obscured his view, and he could see nothing of his friend. Desperate as the battle had been, it did not last long; and the first thing Philip thought of, when he had a moment's liberty, was to seek for Bob. He traversed the deck, sad marks of the recent carnage everywhere meeting his view. It was a sickening sight. Bob was nowhere to be seen. Philip's heart began to sink within him, he scarcely dared asked information about his friend. At last he summoned up courage to consult a marine who was stationed on guard very near the spot where he knew that Bob had been posted.

"Oh yes," was the reply. "I remember a young fellow about your age and size. He stood there by yonder gun; he fought well, but towards the close of the battle he was badly wounded, shot in the breast, I believe, and carried below. It isn't likely you'll find him alive now, but you'd better go down into the cockpit and look around."

Terrible groans and sighs met his ear as he descended the ladder into the cockpit. The pale, flickering light of a lantern which hung from the roof increased the ghastliness of the scene. Surgeons were everywhere at work. The agony which was depicted on many faces was enough to touch the hardest heart. Not a few sufferers were already stiffening in death, while many, alas! even in their last hour, were breathing oaths and curses against the enemy, or blaspheming the hard fate which had cut them down in the full vigour of life and in the hour of victory.

Philip shuddered at the sight he beheld, and the sounds he heard, but with a keen and eager glance to the right and left he quickly made his way among the dying and the dead, expecting in every face to recognise the well-known features of his friend. He began to think he had been misinformed, for nowhere could he discern Bob among the wounded, till reaching the very furthest end of the cockpit, he perceived, in a corner, by the faint light of the lamp, a form which was just about Bob's size. Could this be he? He bent over him, his face was turned away; it was very pale and his eyes were closed. Yes, there was no doubt of it now. It was Bob, but whether alive or dead Philip could not tell.

"Bob," he said to him in a low voice, "Bob, is it you?"

The boy opened his eyes, and tried with difficulty to turn his head round towards Philip, then the reply came in a faint voice,

"O Philip, thank God that you have come. How did you find me out here?"

"I searched the ship for you, Bob, as soon as the battle was over, and when I could not find you, I asked the sentry near where you were posted, and he told me that you had been wounded, so I hurried down here as fast as I could to look for you. But, tell me, are you very bad, Bob?"

"Yes, I am done for, Philip, shot in the side. The surgeon has just been to me. The ball can't be extracted, and he says it's only a question of an hour or so."

"O Bob!" replied Philip with a burst of anguish. "It can't be true, the surgeon has made a mistake, - they do sometimes, it mayn't be so bad as you think."

"No hope, Phil," he replied in an utterly despairing and very faint tone. "No hope. Oh, my poor mother! I shall never see her again; how she will fret, for I am her only child, torn away from her, too, without even saying farewell, or asking her pardon for all my undutiful conduct. We've won the victory, Phil, haven't we? ah! I'm glad of that; and you'll tell mother about me, and ask her to forgive me the trouble I've given her. And, Philip, you'll forgive me too, won't you?"

"Forgive you, Bob? I've nothing to forgive," said Philip.

"Nothing, Phil? Not for joining in that wicked plot with Dick and Nichols and the rest, to get you pressed, just to spite your father and the parson?"

"Don't talk of that, Bob. I've forgotten your share in it long ago. You were over persuaded by the others; don't think of it again."

"Ah, Phil," he sighed, "it can't be much longer now, I feel weaker every minute. I'm going to die, and what'll become of my soul? I've been a bad lad, Philip, not good and steady like you."

"Don't call me good, Bob, I've been anything but that. But think of Jesus Who died for you, He's waiting for you above, and if you believe in Him, and trust Him, you will go to a happier and a better place."

"He won't have me, Phil. I've not served Him as you have. I've told lies, and sworn, and done many bad things beside. I used to laugh at the parson down at Sennen, and never went to church except that once."

"That may be, Bob, but if you're only sorry for your sins, as our parson's often told me, and as it says here in this Testament, God will forgive you for Jesus Christ's sake. Did you never hear the story of the thief on the cross?"

"I don't recollect as ever I did."

"I'll just read it to you, then," said Philip; and he took out his Testament and read slowly and earnestly that beautiful touching story. The tears rolled down bob's pale cheeks. "Now, Bob," he said, when he had finished, "think that the Lord Jesus is saying those words to you, 'To-day shalt thou be with Me in paradise.'"

"Raise me up a little, Phil; I feel that I'm choking," said the poor boy, a cold perspiration coming over his forehead. "Thank you," he added, in broken accents; "that is more comfortable. Now, I shall die in your arms. Yes, it is quite true what you say. Jesus loved sinners and gave Himself for them. So, perhaps He'll save me like that poor thief. Read some more, please."

Philip found the 15th chapter of St. Luke, and read the parable of the prodigal son, that wonderful story of Our Father's love, which has cheered so many sin-burdened and desponding souls.

Eagerly did the dying sailor-lad drink in every word as it fell from his friend's lips; he felt that even for him there was hope of another life in the world to come.

When he had finished, he said – "Were not those the words the parson began the service with that day, Phil? 'I will arise and go to my father.'"

"Yes, Bob, that's right."

"That's what I want to do now, Phil, to arise and go to the Father in Heaven as you've told me of. Good-bye, Phil," he murmured after a pause. "You'll see my mother, and tell her – Lord, remember me" –

He did not finish the sentence. His spirit – may we not hope – had already passed into Paradise.

For some time Philip sat by the side of the earthly remains of his departed friend, his face buried in his hands, and quite absorbed by his grief. The death of poor Bob was a terrible blow. He had been the only link which bound Philip to is home, the sole friend he possessed on board that crowded ship. Henceforth he must bear his burdens, his sorrow, his home-sickness, alone; he would not again be cheered by Bob's kindly face and hearty good-natured sympathy. His lot was a harder one than ever now; now could he bear it?

He was roused from the stupor of his grief by the rough voice of one of the petty officers.

"What are you after down here, my lad?" he exclaimed, as he observed Philip sitting in the corner of the cockpit; "go aloft and join your watch at once. What's all this snivelling and drivelling about? Oh, I see!" he continued, as he observed Bob's lifeless body, "been attending to a friend who won't give you any more trouble, plain enough, so don't loiter here any longer, d'ye hear?"

Philip knew he must obey. He took one last parting look at Bob's beloved features, calm and placid in death, and making a desperate effort to stifle his grief, returned to the deck and to his ordinary duty.

A still, starlight night succeeded that eventful day – a sad and memorable one it had been to Philip; for the first time he had witnessed and taken part in an engagement, and beheld the pomp and glory, as well as the horrors of war.

And now that the din of battle was over, and the traces of carnage banished from the deck, Philip stood at his post on the forecastle, and gazed up at the bright stars, and listened to the sea gently rippling round the keel, and reviewed in the stillness the events of the day. All did not appear so dark to him now; he seemed to see God's purpose in allowing him and his comrades to be torn away from friends and home. Had Bob remained at Sennen among his bad associates, he would probably have become more and more like them, and been hardened in sin and wickedness; but the sudden trial had softened his heart, causing him, while on board the man-of-war, to show not only a brave spirit, but an inclination to listen to better things. It seemed to draw upon him now, that Bob and he had been thrown together on board that ship, that he might be the means of leading his friend back to the Father from Whom he had wandered, and pointing him at his last hour to Him who saith, "Come unto Me, all ye that labour and are heavy-laden, and I will give you rest." And in all the dangers of the day God had protected him; His Fatherly hand had been outstretched to guard and shelter him from the enemy's fire. The words of the psalm, the last he had heard sung in the little village church at home, came back now forcibly to his mind, and he felt how truly they had hitherto been fulfilled in his case.

"At home, abroad, in peace, in war,
Thy God shall thee defend;
Conduct thee through life's pilgrimage
Safe to thy journey's end."

At dawn of day the bodies of those who had fallen, gloriously fighting for their country in the famous battle of the first of June, were with full honours committed to the deep. Among these departed heroes was Bob. When the solemn words were spoken, and the sea received those mortal remains, "to keep till the day when she shall give up her dead," Philip could not restrain his tears. To him the separation and the loss were bitter indeed; but he cheered himself with the thought of the happiness and rest his friend was now enjoying, in that Paradise into which he felt assured that he had entered.

10

The First Watcher On The Longships

"The startled waves leap over it; the storm
Smites it with all the scourges of the rain;
And steadily against its solid form
Press the great shoulders of the hurricane."

- Longfellow

The long, bright summer was drawing to an end, the days were gradually closing in. Autumn, with its gloomy skies, its dense fogs, and furious equinoctial gales, was nigh at hand. The lighthouse on the Longships Rock was all but completed, a fine summer having favoured the workmen. Mr. Smith, who supplied the means, had, at the urgent entreaty of Arthur Pendrean, vigorously pressed on the work, in the hope that ere winter and dark nights set in, a warning light might send forth its friendly beams to the mariner, pointing out the maze of treacherous rocks which girded that rugged coast.

One beautiful September afternoon, just before the sun sank in all his glory of gold and crimson into the sparkling sea, Arthur Pendrean stood alone at the extreme point of the Land's End, and gazed with mingled feelings of pride and gratitude at the slender column of strong granite masonry which, about two miles distant, rose a solitary object in the midst of the green waters.

Proud, indeed, the young parson might be of this structure, for it was mainly owing to his own perseverance and indomitable energy that it had been raised. The scheme had been in his mind for years; he had been baffled and opposed in every way; but now, at last, he had gained his object. But in his pride and pleasure he did not forget to thank Him, without Whose aid and gracious permission not a stone could have been laid, Who had prospered the work by granting fair weather, Who had protected the workmen from accidents, and Who, above all, had put it into the hearts of men to provide the money for an enterprise at once so costly and so benevolent.

That was a happy day in the young clergyman's life, for the work was now, so far as the masonry was concerned, completed; the gear and the lanterns had indeed yet to be supplied; while the important question of who was to perform the office of lighthouse-keeper was still undecided. Arthur trusted that all in good time this would be settled also. He was standing on a spot where he often loved to meditate, to look back on the past and forward to the future; before him was the vast expanse of ocean, now calm and smooth as a mirror; behind him was the grey barren moorland, all so still and quiet, not a sound to be heard but the thud of the waves against the rocks below, and the shrill cries of the sea birds whose nests were in the cliffs around. It was here on this very spot that Charles Wesley had composed a hymn, a favourite of Arthur's, and very popular with the Cornish folk.

> "Lo! On a narrow neck of land,
> 'Twixt two unbounded seas, I stand
> Secure, insensible!
> A point of time, a moment's space,
> Removes me to that heavenly place
> Or shuts me up in hell.
> O God, my inmost soul convert,

And deeply on my thoughtful heart
Eternal things impress;
Give me to feel their solemn weight,
And tremble on the brink of fate,
And wake to righteousness."

Much as Arthur had to be thankful for, and many as were his causes of rejoicing, there was yet enough to make him feel sad. A glorious thing, indeed, he felt it was to be allowed to work for God; but he grieved at the very little he had been able to accomplish for his Master, during the time he had been allowed to labour in His vineyard. How few, comparatively, were the souls won to God; here and there, indeed, he could point to one or two who showed signs of repentance and conversion, who were striving to lead a better life; but on the other hand, the notorious evildoers seemed to be growing worse, more hardened and desperate, more bitter in their opposition to all his efforts to benefit their souls or bodies. It was a hard struggle he knew that he had to look forward to, but he must thank God and take courage.

Full of these thoughts, Arthur now turned homewards. In a month's time he hoped that the lighthouse would be provided with all that was requisite, but unless an honest and trustworthy keeper could be found, the whole undertaking would prove a failure. Intimidation from the stronger party – those who had from the first been opposed to the scheme, because it must interfere with their godless gains – was sufficient to prevent any of the more well-disposed men at the Cove from accepting the office.

Since the loss of his son, Owen Tresilian had sunk into a deep melancholy, from which nothing seemed able to rouse him. His brave little daughter did her utmost to cheer her father, and to brighten by her smiles and living attention his solitary hearts. But rarely indeed was she rewarded. As usual, she would read to him out of the great family Bible, choosing the most consoling passages, those especially which spoke of the love and tender care of our Father in Heaven.

Arthur constantly visited the cottage, he always spoke hopefully of Philip, he reminded the desponding father that Philip's name had never appeared among any lists of killed and wounded, so they might reasonably trust that he was safe, and likely to become an honour to his family and his country. The day might come ere long when he would once more be restored to his home, and they would then be shown clearly that God's way was the best way, and that He had had some wise purpose in permitting the son and brother to be dragged away so ruthlessly from them. But Owen could not be brought to acknowledge this, he repined at his hard lot, he could not humbly resign himself to the Divine will.

When Arthur spoke again to him on the subject of the lighthouse, Owen told him plainly that he could not and would not leave Mary; she was his only treasure and comfort now. In his present melancholy state, too, the young clergyman felt that Owen might be almost driven to insanity if shut up alone in the lighthouse; for in stormy weather he would be days without communication with the shore. He had, therefore, given up for the present all idea of Tresilian being the keeper, and latterly, had not alluded to the subject in conversation with him.

All over the country Arthur had ordered inquiries to be made for a suitable man to fill the important office. Several, attracted by the large pay, had volunteered their services; but all were found on examination to be in some way unfit. But the day following that on which Arthur had regarded with so much satisfaction from the Land's End the completed work, he received a letter from Penzance, which informed him that a man had offered himself for the vacant post who seemed in every way fitting. He had been a preventive man on the coast, was about fifty years of age, a widower, of robust constitution and very steady character. Mr. Smith, Arthur was informed, was thoroughly convinced that this man, Stephen Jordan, was competent and suitable to act as lighthouse-keeper on the Longships, his testimonials being excellent. Arthur, as may well be imagined, rejoiced when he received these welcome tidings; he rode over to Penzance next day, where he saw Jordan, and was quite satisfied with him. In a fortnight's time it was settled that he was to come to Sennen and enter on his duties; the lanterns and other gear he hoped would then be fixed in their places.

It soon got wind among the Sennen folk, that a man had at last been found who would consent to live at the Longships; this was very bad news to the most of them, for, latterly, they had consoled themselves with the idea that though the lighthouse was now built, no one would ever dare to take up his abode there. They vowed vengeance against the coming keeper, against the parson, and against Mr. Smith, all three of whom, they said, had contrived together to enrich themselves at the expense of the poor fishermen of Sennen Cove. Was not Mr. Smith to levy a toll on every vessel that passed? And doubtless the parson would get his share of the profits? The lighthouse, too, would also probably avert wrecks during the winter, and leave them to depend only upon fishing and smuggling. All Arthur's endeavours to conciliate these men were futile, they would not listen to argument or reason, they received him with scowling looks and suppressed curses. Some half-dozen of the worst men, with Nichols as their ringleader, had leagued together to foil him in every possible manner, to place every obstacle in the way of carrying stores to, and communicating with, the lighthouse, and to persecute and vex, by every means in their power, any one in the neighbourhood who was at all friendly with the parson or who favoured his schemes.

The lanterns and reflectors had arrived, as well as all the necessary furniture for the lighthouse. The government, who warmly took up the project, had, at the request of Arthur and Mr. Smith, send down several preventive men to aid in the conveyance of these articles to the lighthouse, as so few of the Sennen people could be relied upon. Jordan, too, came shortly after; but Arthur, fearing that he might be exposed to severe personal violence from the Cove men, kept him at the manor house.

Stormy weather for several days prevented all communication with the Longships; but at last the winds moderated, and the sea once more became calm as it ever can be along that coast, so strewn with rocks and agitated by conflicting currents.

It was necessary, immediately, to profit by such an opportunity, which at that time of year might not occur again for along time. Early in the morning, therefore, on the 29th September, the lanterns were shipped in Owen's fishing-boat, another boat belonging to the preventive service following with stores and furniture.

Arthur himself determined to visit the lighthouse on this occasion, and accompanied Owen in his boat, Jordan being in the other, which was manned by the coastguard. Two men only had been found, who, on the promise of a large reward, consented to help Owen in his boat, and one of these did not belong to Sennen.

A crowd of men and boys had gathered on the beach to witness their departure. They greeted the party with wells of execration, curses, and insults, but they were powerless either to injure them or to hinder their departure.

At low water the Carn-Brâs rock, on which the lighthouse stands, emerges forty-five feet above the sea level.

Landing here is always difficult, owing to the surf which dashes round the rock, and the swirl of the sea caused by the fierce currents which rage round the multitude of granite islets on every side. Caution and skilful navigation were therefore necessary to approach the rock, and when at last they reached it, their difficulties seemed but to have commenced, for to land and remove the boat's cargo to the lighthouse was not easy work.

Favoured, however, by the smoothness of the sea, they succeeded, after many hours' labour, in conveying everything they had brought to the rock. The lanterns, nineteen in number, with their reflectors, were carried into the cupola of the lighthouse, and the stores into the room below. The lamps were Argand burners, the latest invention, then considered very brilliant, but vastly inferior to the splendid lights which now on all sides flash out around our coasts. A bed, a table and chair, with a few other necessary articles of furniture, had been brought for the use of the lighthouse-keeper, as well as a goodly stock of provisions, in case continued bad weather should interrupt communication with the shore.

It was late in the afternoon before the work was completed, and Arthur Pendrean and the men who accompanied him prepared to quit the rock, and leave Jordan in his solitary home. Before they sailed away Arthur solemnly thanked God for having permitted them to accomplish their work, and prayed that His blessing might rest on the lighthouse, and enable it to be as the means of saving many lives. He asked that the Holy Angels, whose Festival they that day celebrated, might be sent to guard the building from destruction, and to watch over those whose lot it might be to dwell therein; the men, with bent knees and uncovered heads, listened reverently to the prayer and joined heartily in the "Our Father" which concluded it. Then they all took leave of Jordan.

"God bless and protect you, Jordan," said Arthur, as he warmly grasped the sailor's rough hand. "You may do a great service to your fellows by remaining here. Some calm day ere long we'll come out again, and see how you're getting on. Meanwhile, keep you your spirits, and remember that you are not really alone, for God is always with you."

"All right, sir; I'm not a bit afraid," said Jordan. "I've passed through greater dangers in my life than I'm ever likely to meet with this here lighthouse, which seems to me to be built strong enough to stand the fiercest storms that ever blew. You need not give yourself any trouble about me, sir. I never knew what fear was, and this isn't the place where I'm likely to make its acquaintance."

Jordan, though a good, honest fellow, was by no means a religious man, and though he couldn't help admiring and respecting the energetic young parson, who seemed as if nothing could daunt him, yet rather despised him for being what was called a Methodist.

The men gave a hearty cheer as they sailed away from the rock, to which the lighthouse-keeper, as he stood at the door of his new abode, responded, waving his sou'-wester.

That night, for the first time, on the Feast of St. Michael and All Angels, the friendly warning light shone forth clear and distinct from the Longships Rock.

Arthur beheld it with feelings of joy and gratitude. The Sennen men, who felt that they were utterly baffled and defeated, could only shake their fists with rage, and utter the old string of senseless curses.

Those were the early days of lighthouses. Experience had hardly yet proved the risk and danger of leaving one man alone on a solitary rock to attend to the lights; often cut off for days, or even weeks, from communication with the shore. Men, too, were very scarce at that period, as all the able-bodied were seized for sailors and soldiers. Very great, indeed, had been the difficulty to secure the services of one man, and long indeed would it probably have been before a second was forthcoming. In these days it is very different. Three men, and sometimes four, are appointed to take charge of lighthouses, such as the Longships, the Eddystone, and others. Tales terrible, but true, of suicide and murder have long ago proved the inexpediency and danger of smaller numbers.

The fine weather lasted till the next evening, when a stormy sunset was succeeded by a dark and cloudy night, through which the lanterns on the Longships shone out brighter and more cheerily than ever. During the whole of the following day the wind rose and freshened, till towards the evening it amounted to a gale. As Arthur and Owen stood at the Land's End watching the lighthouse, they beheld the fierce billows raging round the rock, the waves leaping upon the tall column, and at time dashing over it with such fury as completely to hide it from their view, yet still permitting occasional glimpses of the beacon light.

"Thank God, Jordan is all right," said Arthur; "but what a gale he's caught in? It's long since we've had one as violent."

"Yes, sir," replied Owen gloomily; "but we have not seen the worst of it yet, we shall have a very dirty night: and, in spite of the lighthouse, there's many men down at the Cove who are hoping for a 'good wreck,' as they call it."

"I hope they may be disappointed," said Arthur; "why cannot these men lead honest lives? If they were sober and industrious, they could gain their living by fishing alone; but they seem to me to do nothing except look out for chances of wrecking and smuggling."

"And when they make any money by those means," replied Owen, "they spend it very quickly in drink, I can assure you, sir."

"Yes; it is the gold of the wreck which pays for the accursed abomination of drink, as I have heard it said," remarked Arthur.

"I almost wish, sir," said Owen, after a pause, "that I had stayed out in that lighthouse with Jordan. I've blamed myself ever since for not doing so."

"Why, Owen?" asked Arthur surprised; "you long ago refused to be lighthouse-keeper. Have you changed your mind now?"

"No, not exactly sir; you know I never wished to be lighthouse-keeper for many reasons. I felt I could never stay there alone, and since I lost my poor Philip, I haven't the heart for anything, and can't stand what I could before. Then I wouldn't on any account be separated from my little Mary, that would break my heart and hers too. But it's not about myself I've been thinking, it's because of Jordan; he is a stranger to these parts, and no one who hasn't been there before can have any idea of what an awful noise there is on the Longships Rock when a gale is blowing."

"I have no doubt it is very bad," said Arthur; "but Jordan, who has passed all his life at sea, must be well inured to such sounds, Owen."

"Ah! but this is quite a different kind of noise, sir, to what one ever hears at sea; it is the roaring and raging of the waves in a cavern underneath the rock. There is nothing you ever heard like it, sir; I can assure you, it's enough to frighten the bravest man, and if Jordan has not been warned about it, it will give him a fright."

"You should have mentioned this before, Owen, and prepared him for it."

"I wish I had, sir, but the day we took him out was so calm that it never occurred to me; I wish now I had kept him company, at all events for the first few nights."

"Well, I wish you had, Owen, for many reasons; but at the same time I don't think Jordan's one to be easily frightened," replied Arthur.

That night a furious gale from the south-west raged along the coast: many were the watchers at Sennen, and at other villages along the shore, keeping a sharp look-out for wrecks; but whether owning to the lighthouse, or to the fact that there were not many vessels about just then, the evil hopes of those who were longing to profit by the misfortune of others were frustrated. There were watchers of another kind too that night. Owen Tresilian never closed his eyes; he was uneasy and restless, he could not help thinking of the lonely lighthouse-keeper trimming his lamps on the solitary rock, with the roar of the ocean around and below him. Arthur too, though at first he had given little heed to Owen's words about Jordan, felt anxious, when he came to reflect more seriously on the subject; he perceived what a mistake it might prove leaving one man by himself in such an isolated spot, surrounded by so many elements of terror and danger.

He passed a sleepless night, and early next morning rode to the Land's End again, eagerly gazing over the seething waters, till, through the mist and surf, he discovered the lighthouse safe on its rock. Fervently did he implore his Father in heaven to protect its brave keeper. All that day did the tempest rage. At nightfall Owen and Arthur again repaired to the shore, anxiously watching for the lamps to be lighted. Long ere this had they shone forth yesterday, but as yet not a ray of light proceeded from the buffeted and storm-stricken column. What could be the reason, what had happened to the keeper? The clergyman was full of alarm, and Owen more than ever rebuked himself for not having proposed to keep Jordan company in his lonely watch. This new anxiety seemed to have roused him from that melancholy lethargy into which he had sunk ever since he had lost his son. The surf was flying around the two men, the drifting rain and spray soaked them to the skin, they could scarcely stand against he violence of the wind, but still they lingered on, hoping against hope that each moment the lamp might flash out is friendly rays over the dark abyss, and prove to them that the lonely guardian of the lighthouse was alive and at his post. But all in vain. Night threw her gloomy pall over the vast Atlantic; there was neither star in the sky nor light from the sea to cheer them, and they were as helpless to give aid as to discover the cause of this misfortune. Silently at last, and with heavy hearts, they turned towards their homes.

"Ah! parson, what's become of your light now?" cried a jeering voice out of the darkness. It was that of Nichols; he had also been on the look-out not far from them on the cliff, and with equal surprise and pleasure had perceived that no lamp was burning on the Longships Rock.

There could be no reply to those insolent words. Arthur and Owen hastened back to the village.

There was revelry that night at the public-house; wild shouts of laughter, mingled with cries of exultation, might be heard, too, from groups of men who stood on the shore, or round the cliffs. The lighthouse which was to do them so much mischief had very soon proved a failure; the second stormy night had sufficed – though none knew how – to extinguish the lanterns. The parson was baffled now, thoroughly defeated in his scheme to take the bread out of their mouths.

At dead of night, too the evil men of Sennen had another cause for rejoicing; a small vessel, driven by the fury of the gale, ran upon the rocks at some little distance to the north of the cove, and as no helping hand was stretched out to rescue the poor mariners, they all found a watery grave within sight of their native land; while the ship's cargo, which happened to be a valuable one, fell to the share of the heartless and rapacious wreckers.

But why had not the lamp been kindled on the Longships lighthouse? Let us now turn thither to discover the cause.

As soon as the clergyman, Owen, and the other men had sailed away from the lighthouse, Jordan had set to work to arrange his furniture and make himself as comfortable in his new abode as circumstances permitted. He then went up into the cupola of the tower, and as it was getting dusk, proceeded to light the lamps. On descending to his living room below, he heard peculiar rumbling noises underneath the lighthouse, such as he had never experienced before, but he did not take any particular heed of them, and as he was tired with his long hard day's work, he soon fell into a sound sleep.

Day was dawning when he awoke. His first care was to go and extinguish the lamps; this done, he lighted his fire and got his breakfast ready. He had seen, on looking out from the tower, that the weather was going to change, but he was quite prepared for that, since storms and squalls were likely to prevail at that season, and the equinoctial gales couldn't be far off. While Jordan was hard at work trimming the lamps and polishing the reflectors, the wind was rising; already did the waves beat with violence against the strong masonry of the lighthouse, and shake it to its very foundation, and the mysterious sound below became louder and louder. He went up aloft once more, gazed out first to the west, where the Atlantic loomed before him a wild mass of angry billows, then to the east, where the dark jagged coast line was fringed with a broad belt of foaming surge, above was a leaden sky; there was nothing to relieve the monotony of the stormy prospect, but here and there the white speck of the sail of some vessel which was battling with the elements, and striving to double the Land's End.

The lonely man now went back to his quarters below, and looked over his stores. This was soon done. He could neither read nor write; so, with nothing whatever to do, shut up in that isolated tower, it was natural enough that time should begin to hang heavily on his hands. He sat down in his gloomy chamber, his head drooping on his breast, brooding over his fate, and already repenting that he had been tempted by a high salary to undertake the office. He had done so without much consideration, he had never reflected on, nor tried to realise the horrors of complete solitude. Here he was, imprisoned in the midst of the sea, more than a mile from land, with no chance of seeing a human face or hearing a human voice for days, or it might be, weeks. Perhaps he would get accustomed to it, he thought, to cheer himself; at any rate the evil must now be endured, and he had better make the best of the lot which he had himself chosen. He had made his bed, and he must lie upon it; happily he bethought himself of some twine and a netting needle he had brought with him; he would begin a net and sell it to the Sennen fishermen, or use it himself if he got the chance to catch fish in calm weather, this seemed a bright idea. He worked diligently for an hour or so, and then it was time to cook his dinner, which gave him some occupation. Meanwhile, the wind was still rising, from all appearance there would be a heavy gale at night.

After dinner Jordan continued his netting, though every now and then the building shook and quivered as a giant wave dashed against it, leaping up its sides and enveloping cupola and all in its rough embrace.

As soon as it grew dusk, even before sunset, he went up to light the lamps, the thick glass all round was dimmed by the spray, and when a wave rolled over the hop, he was left for a moment in almost complete darkness; tightly as the glass was fixed, and substantially as the whole frame-work of the cupola was constructed, the fierce wind seemed to penetrate into the interior, and made the lamps flicker considerably.

Nevertheless they burned brightly, so that Jordan felt sure that the tempest-tossed mariner would that night be warned in time of the proximity of the destructive rocks which lined that dangerous sea-board.

On such a night as was coming on, Jordan felt that sleep would be impossible. Moreover, he was a man animated by a stern sense of duty, brought up in that strict school of discipline and integrity, the British navy. He had undertaken to keep the lamps constantly burning bright and clear from sunset to sunrise, and should the fury of the tempest break the glass and extinguish the lights, he must be on the watch to avert what evil he could, so he descended into his chamber, lighted his own little dim lamp, and paced up and down the room smoking his pipe, starting occasionally as some fiercer wave shook the structure to its very foundation.

As the gale increased in violence the weird sounds below the lighthouse grew louder and louder. Had Jordan had a companion with him they would scarcely have been able to hear each other's voices, so deafening was the sound, added as it was to the perpetual roar of the sea and the noise of the winds. It was the mystery about them which shook the man's usual courage more than any other of the horrors by which he was surrounded. Sailors are generally more or less superstitious, and though Jordan was not naturally so, yet now all sorts of ghastly stories that he had heard years ago, told by his mates in the forecastle about the ghosts of the dead holding revels during storms in caverns beneath the ocean's depths, came back into his mind. What could this strange noise be? – now it sounded like the angry roar of hundreds of imprisoned wild beasts, now like the shrieks of myriads of souls in torment. He grew every minute more restless and excited. At first he was ashamed of himself for feeling afraid; had he not boasted to the parson that he did not know what fear was, and now, before three days had elapsed, he had already experienced it. Oh! that he had never been tempted to come to this accursed haunted rock – for haunted he felt certain it was. He thought of his past life, of the happy home he had once had with his wife and daughter. He wondered if he should ever see his daughter again, and recollect how opposed she had been to his applying for this post.

Thus the hours passed away till midnight, the gale still increasing in fury; several times did Jordan go up to the lantern to trim the flickering lamps and polish the reflectors, dimmed by the particles of spray which even penetrated into the cupola. The waves now leaped up far above the lighthouse, sometimes completely covering it. Intense was the darkness out at sea, not the faintest glimmer to be seen except the reflection on the water of the lamps from the lighthouse, which displayed the violence of the storm and the immense size of the foaming billows which seethed and boiled around.

As Jordan descended the spiral staircase into his cheerless chamber, the strong man fairly gave way to the mysterious terrors which assailed him. He fancied that demons were holding their fierce revels below, that every moment they might appear and drag him down to their awful abode; or that they were working to undermine the foundation of the lighthouse, which, with its solitary watcher, would fall an easy prey to the fury of the winds and waves, and at last be swallowed up in the wild abyss of waters.

Again he went aloft, the building rocked and reeled beneath him, several panes in the lantern were already cracked and the water was pouring in. He went down once more, fierce yells and shrieks from below fell upon his ear, his brain became confused; now he paced hurriedly and feverishly up and down his narrow chamber, now in despair he flung himself on the bed; when the noise had grown more deafening, more appalling than ever, he was left in utter darkness, he had forgotten to trim his own lamp, it had for some time been flickering in the socket, and now had suddenly gone out. He groped about for his tinder-box, but could not remember where he had put it, so taking up his lamp he felt his way to the staircase, and reached the cupola, where the lights were all burning, though they flared and flickered in the wind which, through the broken glass, forced its way to the lantern. He rekindled his lamp, but it was with a trembling hand; he had just turned to descent the stairs to the room below, when suddenly there came such a shock that it seemed as if the strong tower must yield to its force, a louder roar than ever from below seemed to respond to it, followed by a fearful crash, a rattle of broken glass and lead, and Jordan felt himself drenched to the skin and plunged into total darkness. A huger, stronger wave than any which the angry Atlantic had yet rolled in towards the shore, had shattered the cupola, carried away the cap of the lantern, smashed the glass, and extinguished the lamp, as well as the light Jordan carried in his hand. Utterly overcome with terror, the poor fellow groped his way to his room, where in an agony he threw himself on his bed and sank into a state of unconsciousness. When daylight dawned, it found him in the same condition, while still the raging hurricane drove billow after billow against the lighthouse; the water through the broken lantern now penetrated the interior, and in drenching showers poured down into the chamber where the unfortunate man was lying.

11

A Hazardous Voyage

"Guide our barque among the waves,
Through the rocks our passage smooth,
Where the whirlpool frets and raves,
Let Thy love its anger soothe;
All our hope is placed in Thee":

- Miserere Domine
A.A. Proctor

During that terrible night the hurricane had reached its height, and with the next day it gradually abated. Arthur and Owen again stood on the extreme point of the Land's End eagerly gazing at the lighthouse. Wreathed as it was by the snowy surf, and ever and anon hidden from view by some gigantic wave, yet there it stood, unharmed, firm, and immovable, amid the mighty billows. But what had happened to its brave guardian? Why had no light shone from it yesternight? These were the questions which pressed anxiously on their minds.

"The wind has fallen very much, Owen," said Arthur, "the storm has evidently spent its fury. When do you think we shall be able to get out to the Longships and see what has happened to Jordan?"

"Certainly not to-day nor tomorrow either, I fear, sir. After such a gale has been blowing for the last forty-eight hours it will be very long before the swell goes down enough to allow a boat to approach the Longships without danger of being dashed in pieces."

"Danger or no danger, we must risk it at the very earliest opportunity," said Arthur decidedly; "I shall not have a moment's rest till I know why the lamp was not lighted last night. I bitterly blame myself for allowing Jordan to be there alone. I wish heartily I had remained with him the first night or two."

"It was my place to do that, sir, not yours," said Owen.

"I begin to see now that it is my duty to take the post of lighthouse-keeper; I was wrong to refuse it, but since I lost my poor boy, sir, I don't know what's come over me, I don't seem as if I had heart to do anything."

"Don't talk of Philip as lost, Owen," said Arthur, in a more cheerful tone, "I expect he is somewhere fighting bravely the battles of his country, and the day will certainly come when we shall see him back at Sennen. I am glad you have changed your mind about the lighthouse; a man who lives there is doing a grand and noble work, helping to save the lives of many fellow-creatures. But I shall never consent to you being there alone, Owen. I have learned a lesson to-day in that respect."

"I should not be afraid, sir, it's only I shouldn't know what to do about my Mary; but after all there mayn't be much amiss with Jordan, perhaps the sea got in to the lantern and put out the light, we can't tell till this evening."

"I wish it were only that, I'm sure, Owen," said Arthur; "if we don't see the light to-night, to-morrow we must get to the Longships, I cannot stand the suspense, I shudder when I think of that poor fellow alone on that solitary rock, with the waves roaring round him."

"So do I, sir, and with God's help I trust we'll get there to-morrow, but it'll be a hard job, however much the wind goes down meanwhile."

It seemed as if a calm were about to follow the storm, the wind fell till there was scarcely a breath to move the leaves or stir the air, the sky maintained its dull leaden hue, the sea, a turbid mass of tossing, tumbling waves, kept up its incessant and almost deafening roar, still dashing up with violence upon the coast, which it lined with a broad fringe of creamy surge, and raging with impotent fury against the Longships Rocks.

As soon as it was dark, many eyes were strained in the direction of the lighthouse, but with very different hopes and wishes. The party who, for their own wicked and selfish reasons, had always been opposed to the erection of the friendly beacon, had been triumphant all day, but they looked forward with some anxiety to the evening, feeling a little doubtful whether their victory would be maintained, some thinking that the lamp had only been put out by a wave breaking the lantern, and that it would probably burn again that evening. Others, however, boldly asserted that the whole affair was a failure. Anxiety for the safety of poor Jordan, which could only be proved by his showing a light, was the absorbing feeling in the minds of the clergyman, of Owen, and a very few others. At dusk some twenty or thirty of the Sennen men and lads had assembled on the Land's End to watch the lighthouse. Dense clouds covered the sky, not a star was to be seen. It was quite time now for the lamp to be lighted, but in the direction of the Longships not a ray was to be seen, no friendly beacon glistened over the gloomy waters.

"It's all right," said Nichols, "if he'd been going to light up at all, he'd have done it before this."

"Don't make too sure, Bill," said Ben, "it's early yet, though it's a very dark afternoon."

"Well, we'll give him another half hour, and if he doesn't show himself alive by that time, I shall feel certain that the parson's lighthouse-keeper has regularly come to grief."

"And a good thing for us poor folk if he has," said another.

"Yonder's the parson with that set-up fool Tresilian," said Ben, "and very long faces they've both of them put on."

"The longer their faces, the better chance for us," said Nichols.

As time wore away, the sea became shrouded in darkness, and still no light beamed from the lighthouse. Arthur and Owen were confirmed in their fears that something must be wrong. Both were determined that at all risk the lighthouse must be reached on the morrow.

Shouts of triumph and roars of mocking laughter from the men who had been as eagerly watching the lighthouse, but with such different hopes, now rent the air. They cut Arthur to the heart. Seldom had he felt so thoroughly despondent and downcast – slowly he returned home. The Sennen men betook themselves to the public-house, where they celebrated their triumph by drinking harder than usual, so that not one of them left the place that night sober.

The weather still continued calm, but next morning there was the same dull leaden sky, not a ray of sunlight over the waters. Both Arthur and Owen were astir early, eager to see whether it was possible for them to reach the Longships on a boat. There was still quite enough surf and swell to make the undertaking a very dangerous one, however much care and caution they might employ. Both, however, were bent on making the attempt. The great difficulty was to obtain two other men to join them, for four was the smallest number with which they dared to venture to put to sea when their object was to effect a landing on the Longships Rock.

One of the preventive men, a daring fellow from the nearest station on the coast, was at last prevailed to join them, another volunteer was found in David Abbot, already alluded to in these pages, over whom Arthur exercised great beneficial influence. They at once began to get Tresilian's boat ready to sail, while the Cove men hardly recovered from their drunken bout of the previous evening, came one by one lazily out of their cottages to sneer at what they called this mad game, not one of them could ever get back again alive, they said, since the boat would certainly be dashed to pieces against the rocks. They tried hard to frighten the two men whom Arthur had persuaded to join them, hoping they would go back, and thus the expedition might come to nought, but they were both too brave to change their minds, after having given their word to the parson. Arthur's example, his courage in going himself to the rock, his contempt for danger when the life of a brother-man was at stake, filled them with admiration; none except the most degraded of characters could fail to respect such heroism, and at the last moment, when the boat was on the point of being launched, two other men offered their services, which, of course, were only too gladly accepted.

At first all went smoothly enough. There were scarcely a breath of wind, and though the swell was heavy, it only somewhat impeded their progress. The men pulled heartily, and rounded with no little difficulty the last point, which brought them to that maze of rocks which surrounds the Longships. Here the sea swirled and boiled round the granite islands, driven hither and thither by fierce contending currents, and still violently agitated by the effects of the recent gale. Strength, skill, and coolness were now requisite, and Arthur was very thankful for the aid of the two men, who had been the last to volunteer.

The boat was tossed and swirled in every direction. To steer her so as to meet the waves and to avoid the rocks was no easy task; this was Owen's work, while Arthur took his turn at the oars, like the other men. All were soon drenched to the skin, and it was more than one man could do, to bale out the water which constantly filled and threatened to swamp the boat. The nearer they approached the rock, the greater was the danger; the rougher and more agitated the sea. The waves still leaped upon the lighthouse, burying it in clouds of surf. The enterprise seemed more and more hopeless, and all expect Arthur felt inclined to abandon it in despair. But he cheered on the men, telling them it would never do for them to show their faces at Sennen Cove, returning crestfallen from a fruitless expedition. Somehow or other a landing must be effected on the rock. And then he lifted up his heart to Him who holdeth the waters in the hollow of His hand, and Who alone can assuage the fury of the waves, imploring Him to great success to their endeavours.

The tide favoured them, as it was nearly high water, when it was always easier to effect a landing on the rock. Weary and exhausted, buffeted by the waves, cold and wet, beaten back at every effort, they still persevered with dogged energy, but seemed no nearer achieving their purpose. If they came too close up to the rock, they exposed themselves to the risk of having their boat dashed to atoms against it by the next breaker. Their hope was that, by dodging the waves, they might land a couple of men between the intervals. But the waves were so irregular there was no calculating on them; it was not a heavy sea rolling in regularly, but a boiling, foaming mass of tumbling water.

Arthur proposed that two men should be ready to spring on the rock if the boat could be brought sufficiently near, and that ropes should be tied round their waists, so that in case they missed the land, they might be dragged back again into the boat. None of the men, however, seemed willing to incur this risk with the exception of Owen, who could not be spared, as he was indispensable as coxswain. Arthur, therefore, insisted on making the attempt himself. All tried to dissuade him from it, but he was resolute. He was, he said, the youngest man there, he had no wife nor family to lament his loss, if he perished. His example so wrought upon another man, Harry Ellis, one of the last volunteers, that he offered to make the attempt with him. All was made ready, and they again approached the rock, but just as they seemed near enough and Arthur was about to spring on shore, a huge wave threw them back a greater distance than ever from the lighthouse. Still they persevered, over and over again did the same thing happen, till at last, when even Arthur was beginning to despair, there seemed to be a sudden lull, the men pulled hard, the boat approached nearer to the rock than it had ever done before. This time Arthur was determined to make the attempt; if he failed, he new that with the rope round his waist his mates would be able to drag him back; he was a first-rate swimmer, too, and even in a heavy sea could keep himself up for a long time, so without a moment's hesitation he took a bold leap, springing safely upon a projecting ledge of the Longships; Ellis, eager to follow, was almost immediately behind him, but he was less successful; at that moment a huge wave driving the boat far away from the rock, he fell into the raging surf, and his companions with no little difficulty dragged him back into the boat, exhausted and almost senseless.

Arthur stood upon the rock alone. He has loosened the rope from his waist, and now held it with both hands round a ledge of rock, hoping by this means to keep the boat near enough to enable Ellis or one of the rest to make another attempt to leap on the rock beside him.

But this was found to be impossible. With the turn of the tide the swell seemed to have increased, and though repeated efforts were made to approach the Longships by the brave men in the boat, they were every time driven further from their object. Owen would not hear of Arthur being left alone on the rock; he urged the men on with far more energy and vigour than he had done when the parson was in the boat, but he soon became convinced, as all the other had been long before, that there was not the slightest chance of success, and that the clergyman must be left on the Longships with Jordan – whether dead or alive they knew not – till the next day, when the attempt must at all hazards be renewed.

Arthur himself, who had watched their heroic efforts to reach him, made signs to them now to abandon him and return to Sennen, for he clearly perceived that they were only vainly wasting their strength and their time.

Sadly and reluctantly Owen had to yield. With a heavy heart he steered his boat away from the lighthouse in the direction of the Cove. Borne on by the tide and surf she bounded rapidly over the waters, leaving behind her another watcher on the Longships, one who would ill be spared from other and higher duties, to occupy such a post, but who had a heart bold and brave enough to feel no fear to remaining there, or having to occupy the singular position to which the force of circumstances, or rather the Providence of God, had so unexpectedly called him.

The sensation caused on shore by the strange tidings which the boatmen brought back, can well be imagined. The partial failure of their enterprise, and the forced imprisonment of the parson in the lighthouse for a period, the length of which must entirely depend upon the pleasure of the winds and waves, caused no little joy to Nichols, Pollard, and the more badly disposed of the Sennen folk. Fortune seemed now decidedly to favour them, and to have set thoroughly against the parson and his lighthouse scheme. Still there were very few who could withhold their admiration for Arthur's heroic conduct. There was no doubt that on the morrow many would volunteer to aid in setting the parson at liberty, if the weather permitted the attempt, and that Tresilian's boat would not be the only one launched from Sennen beach, to sail to his rescue. It is very seldom that true courage does not gain adherents to the cause it represents; only the most degraded can fail to be inspired with admiration and regard for the bold, self-sacrificing deeds of a really brave man.

But we must return to the lighthouse, where we left Arthur standing alone upon the rock. He watched the boat as it was driven along by the waves, now and then almost completely hidden by the surf. It seemed to be the last link which bound him to the shore, to his home, to the flock he had learned to love so well. How long would he have to stay here? what would be his fate? and what had been the fate of the luckless man who had been left in this awful solitude alone? Whatever it was (and he would soon know), he knew that he ought to share it, for it was his want of thought which had occasioned it. But he felt no fear. God, his Father, was with him in that lonely rock, quite as near as He was in his home on shore; no harm could happen to him unless He willed it.

So he turned towards the lighthouse, and finding the door was closed, but not locked, he opened it and entered. He stopped at the threshold to listen, but not a sound could he hear except the beating of the surge against the granite rocks, and the singular rumbling and roaring of the waves beneath. He lost no time in ascending the spiral staircase which led into the living-room of the lighthouse-keeper. The apartment was in great confusion, the floor was covered with pools of water, broken glass, and pieces of lead, here lay a lamp out of which all the oil had poured, there and overturned saucepan, no fire was burning in the grate, but some coals were strewn about the room; while partly on the bed, partly resting on the floor, Arthur perceived the motionless body of Jordan, his face hidden in the clothes.

Was he alive or dead? For a moment the young clergyman stood horror-struck, then recovering himself, "Jordan," he asked in a low voice, "what is the matter? Are you ill?"

Not a word came in reply, there was not the slightest movement in the recumbent form before him. He now approached nearer and bent over the apparently lifeless body, and put his hand on the man's shoulder. "Jordan," he said, "it is I, Arthur Pendrean, come to see you, don't you know me?" A shudder passed through the man's whole frame, and Arthur, to his inexpressible relief, felt now that he was alive. But Jordan did not move nor look up, he only heaved a deep sigh.

"Jordan, my good fellow, what is the matter?" continued the clergyman. "Are you ill? I am come here to keep you company; don't be afraid."

Slowly now, and very cautiously did the poor man turn round to see who was addressing him in such kindly tones. Arthur, when he saw his face, could not help the involuntarily starting back with horror, the features were so altered that he could scarcely recognise them – while the vacant stare and rolling eyes betokened idiocy or madness. A still more striking change in his appearance had taken place since Arthur had left him on the rock three days ago. Jordan's hair, which had been jet black then, had now turned snowy white, like that of an old man, - the effect of extreme terror.

So horror-struck was Arthur that he could not recover himself for several minutes, nor utter a word. Meanwhile Jordan kept his eyes fixed upon him.

"Jordan, my poor fellow," he said at last, taking his hand and sitting down beside him, "you have suffered terribly from your lonely watch, I know, but I have come to take you away, and to-morrow you shall leave the lighthouse for ever."

There was not a word in reply, only the same fixed and vacant stare. There was no doubt, Arthur felt, that the poor man's mind was affected, he trusted, however, only temporarily. He seemed to have lost the power of speech, and it appeared doubtful, too, whether he understood the kindly, soothing words addressed to him. But he was perfectly quiet and docile. He would sigh and groan occasionally, cover his face with his hands, or throw himself upon the bed, but there was no violence in his madness. He looked so weak and exhausted that Arthur felt certain he had not tasted any food for a couple of days, and he at once set to work to prepare some for him, and lighted a fire, which soon made the room look more cheerful.

Jordan closely watched all his movements. He ate eagerly of the food which Arthur offered him, even seemingly to enjoy it, but still he did not utter a word.

Arthur having done his best to put the room in order, and to repair the damage which the storm had made there, now went up to the cupola to examine the lanterns. Here he at once perceived what destruction the gale had wrought, and noted for future guidance and precautions that must be taken to protect the lights against the fury of the winds and waves. Every pane of glass was broken, a part of the cupola, too, had been injured, the lamps and reflectors were so drenched with salt water that he doubted very much whether he would be able to get any of them to burn that night, an object he was not desirous to effect, only to relieve the anxiety of his friends on shore.

When, after taking these observations, he returned to the room below, he found that Jordan had sunk down asleep on the bed. He rejoiced at this, for he had hoped that rest and sleep might have a beneficial effect upon the poor fellow's mind. Moreover, as he did not require his attention, it gave him more time to clean the lamps, and repair, as far as possible, the mischief done in the cupola. If the night were only calm, and the wind did not rise again, he hoped that the lighthouse would once more send out a cheering ray, and proclaim to those on shore that one watcher, at all events, was there to guard it. But should a storm arise, with the broken glass and cupola, there would be no hope of keeping the lamps alight. It was no easy task to clean the lamps and reflectors; he had to seek for fresh wicks and for a new supply of oil. However, when it began to grow dusk, Arthur's arrangements were quite complete, and to his great delight he succeeded in getting most of the lamps to burn. There was still but little wind, and he hoped that if this calm weather continued, to-morrow, or at all events the next day, he would be released from a confinement, which he had so little anticipated.

He remained for some in the cupola, trimming the lamps and gazing over the vast waste of waters which stretched around him. How strange was his position! alone – almost worse than alone – shut up in that narrow space, with nothing but sea around him, no means of communicating with his friends, the length of his captivity entirely dependent on the mercy of the winds and waves.

Now for the first time he understood how isolated, how terribly monotonous, is the life of a lighthouse-keeper, and how wrong and dangerous it was to leave one man alone in such a position. His long-cherished scheme, which he thought had been so happily accomplished, was still far from successful. He glanced at the broken glass and wood-work, which would take some time to repair; it would be no little expense, too, and there would be great difficulty in persuading workmen to come out at that time of year, not to speak of the difficulty of embarking them on the rock in mid-winter. Then who was to take Jordan's place? Tresilian undoubtedly was willing to do so, but never would Arthur consent to his remaining there alone, and he could not think of any one who was in the least likely to volunteer to join him. On the other hand, Arthur felt the importance of keeping the lamps lighted as far as possible during the winter. Now that they had once sent forth their cheering ray, it would never do for them to be extinguished, the shipping interest would suffer, lives would be sacrificed, and wreckers would triumph; but greater difficulties than those which now faced him had been overcome, and, with God's help, he hoped to conquer these too.

Finding Jordan still asleep, he put the lamp he carried in his hand on the table, and to calm himself took out of his pocket the Bible and Prayer Book he always carried with him. He read the Psalms, lessons, and daily office, and grew gradually composed as he realised the presence of Him Who alone could still the ranging of the storm, Who Himself had walked calm and unmoved over the fierce billows of the Galilean lake.

After sitting thus for about an hour, he again went up to look at the lantern. The wind had slightly risen, and two of the lamps had been blown out, these he lighted again with difficulty. Clouds were gathering in the west. Was another gale coming on, and was he to be condemned to a week's sojourn in the lighthouse?

On returning below, he heard for the first time that extraordinary roaring and rumbling of the waters about which Owen had told him, and which, from its remarkable and mysterious sound, had so terrified poor Jordan. It did not alarm Arthur, but he could well understand that on the ignorant and superstitious mind, in so lonely and isolated a spot, its effect might be very appalling.

Jordan was now becoming restless. Arthur, who had kept the fire alight, had food ready for him. The poor fellow now awoke with a start, resting on his elbow he gazed at Arthur wildly, as if he had never seen him before.

"Where am I?" he exclaimed, springing out of bed, "who are you?"

"I am the parson of Sennen, Mr. Pendrean," said Arthur quietly. "I have come out to keep you company in the lighthouse, till we can both go back to shore together."

"In the lighthouse!" he exclaimed, as he sprang up in terror. "Am I still in that accursed place, with all those demons, yelling around me, and the sea threatening every moment to swallow me up? Good God! I thought I was out of it. Ha! ha! it was only a dream then, and I have been asleep, and am still in this awful prison. Ah! I hear them again – there is that horrid sound, that hissing and roaring as of imprisoned devils, and they may break loose any moment, and come and drag me down to their den below," and he threw himself down upon the bed again, in an agony of terror.

Arthur was shocked, when he saw the state of the abject fear into which the poor fellow was plunged, though thankful he had recovered the use of his speech. He went up to him as he lay, taking his hand and doing his best to sooth and comfort him. It was long before he could make him realise that he was no longer alone, but when at last he was convinced that he had now a companion in his solitude, who would never leave him, he became quieter and more reasonable.

Still, when the rumbling sound in the cavern below increased, as it did with the rising of the wind, the strong frame of the poor sailor trembled as a leaf in a breeze, making him shudder and cling to Arthur like a child. The clergyman soon discovered that argument was of no avail, he had to treat the poor fellow as he would a child. Jordan eagerly ate the food prepared for him, but he did not fall asleep again as Arthur had hoped. A long and weary night was it for the poor young parson, he could not leave his charge for a moment, he dared not even go up to the cupola, to see if the lamps were still burning. He feared the effects of the least interval of solitude on his companion's disordered mind. That the wind was still rising he heard plainly enough, what a prospect was this in store for him if another gale were coming on! For a week or more he might be imprisoned on this lonely rock, his only associate a man who had been driven to the verge of insanity. He had need indeed to exercise all his faith and trust in the ever-watchful care of Him who never forsakes His children.

12

The Second Watcher On The Longships

"Yet, were I fain still to remain
Watch in my tower to keep,
And tend my light in the stormiest night
That ever did move the deep.

"And if it stood, why the 'twere good,
Amid their tremulous stirs,
To count each stroke when the mad waves broke
For cheers of mariners."

- Jean Ingelow

There was no little excitement at Sennen Cove that evening. That a parson should be shut up in a lighthouse was such a strange and unprecedented circumstance that nothing else could be talked about, and the news of it spread like wildfire all through the neighbourhood.

When the old squire heard the tidings he was seriously alarmed, giving orders that no pains nor expense should be spared in trying to reach the rock, and in liberating the prisoners.

Towards evening crowds, not only from Sennen, but from the other villages and hamlets around where the parson was well known and beloved, gathered on the cliffs eager to catch the first glimpse of light from the Longships. They had not long to wait. A hearty cheer broke from the throng, when, fainter than usual certainly, but still bright and clear, the lantern once more sent forth its friendly ray. The parson at all events was safe, it was his hand that had kindled the lamps, and to-morrow, if all were well, the mystery would be solved; they would know what had happened to Jordan, and why the lamps had not been lighted for two evenings.

Nichols, who was standing in the centre of a group of men like-minded with himself, uttered an oath when he saw the beacon, and exclaimed, "There's that parson again in our way; when he can't get any one to do it for him, he goes and lights up that cursed lantern himself; I wish he'd only stay there. I'd almost stand the lighthouse, if we could get rid of him for good."

"It strikes me he'll be there for a day or two longer," said Ben. "I'm very much mistaken if the wind doesn't rise again to-night, and there'll be no getting at the rock to-morrow."

"I'd be glad if a gale came on, and blew hard for a month," said Nichols. "Starve the parson out, I say."

"Hardly likely to last so long as that, Bill, but at this time of year one can't expect calm weather to hold out for long."

Owen also had been anxiously watching the sky; he was too weatherwise not to perceive signs of rising wind, and perhaps of a coming storm. He had so set his mind upon rescuing Arthur on the morrow, that he could not endure the idea of anything thwarting his intentions; but he knew well enough that if the sea were in the least degree heavier than it had been to-day, all attempts at reaching the lighthouse would be futile. He turned away from the cliff with a sad heart, and walked slowly back to his cottage, where the bright face of his little daughter greeted him as usual with a friendly smile, and with the eager question –

"Did the light burn in the Longships this evening, father?"

"Yes, Mary, it did, I am thankful to say."

"Oh, that is good news! then Mr. Pendrean is quite safe, for he must have lighted the lamps, and to-morrow you'll go and fetch him home. Won't you, father?"

"Yes, my child, if the weather only allows us."

"Oh, it certainly will, father; I hear no wind to-night; it's sure to be fine and smooth to-morrow."

"Not at all so sure, Mary, there's every sign of the wind rising. I am very uneasy about it. It might happen at this time of year that we couldn't get to the rock for a week or more, and think of poor Master Arthur being shut up in the lighthouse all that time. We don't know what's happened to Jordan, he may be dead, or very ill, or gone mad, and in any case Mr. Arthur will have a terrible time of it. Only to think of a gentleman like him having to light the lamps, make a fire, see to the stores, and all that kind of thing. I wish I had prevented him landing on the rock; for all the mischief that's been done, I'm more to blame than any one else."

"O father! don't say that; and I'm sure, too, you've been a great help to Mr. Arthur in many ways. He's always come to you for advice, and you have often taken him out in your boat when he wanted to go and see how the works were going on."

"Ah, but I mean, Mary, that I ought to have taken the post of lighthouse-keeper, as Master Arthur wanted me to do. This wouldn't hve happened then."

"You might have been ill – or whatever has happened to Jordan might surely have happened to you, father."

"Not likely, my child. I believe that poor fellow has been frightened to death by the horrible noise that the sea makes under the rock. I forgot to warn him about it, as I ought to have done."

Owen sat down before the fire, and left his supper, which his daughter had ready for him, untested, burying his head in his hands and heaving a long deep sigh.

"Come, father," said Mary, "don't take on so. Eat your supper and you'll be better afterwards. Perhaps it will be fine after all to-morrow, and then you'll fetch Mr. Arthur back again, and how glad everybody will be to see him."

It was some time before Mary could induce her father to come to the table, and even then he ate his supper gloomily and in silence. When he had finished he again sat brooding over the fire.

"I tell you what it is, Molly," he said at last, "I shall have to go and be the lighthouse-keeper at last – there's no one else fit to take the post, and I see it's my duty to do it, so we'll have to be separated, my dear," he continued in a choking voice; "and I must find a home for you, and some one who'll look after you while I'm away."

"No, father, I shall go with you," said Mary firmly. "I'd as soon live in the lighthouse as here; we can't have any garden, of course; and we'll have to give up the fowls and the pig, but then you'll be with me all day; you won't ever go fishing and stay out all night as you've had to do some times. Why, I daresay I shall like living in the lighthouse very much."

"Nonsense, child, I should not think of such a thing; I'd never expose you to the dangers of such a place; there would be all the risk of getting there; and then that dreadful notice from underneath, you'd never stand it a day. Think of the building trembling and quivering with every wave – no, no, Mary, that would never do, you must find a home somewhere on shore."

"O father! let me go with you; if you're in danger I'd like to share it. I'm sure I sha'n't be afraid of the noise, besides you'll always be with me. Of course I shouldn't like to be quite alone there, though I don't see what there is to be frightened at; think how much pleasanter it will be for you if I'm there to get your meals ready and light the fire. I'd rather live with you in the lighthouse than in the squire's fine house without you, - do let me go, father."

"You're a dear good girl, Mary," said her father, embracing her tenderly, "the only comfort I have got in this world now, all the more reason I should be careful of you, and not think of running such a risk as allowing you to live in a lighthouse. No, no, my child; it can never be."

Mary burst into tears. All her father's efforts to soothe her were in vain. He wish he had said nothing about the lighthouse. He felt how hard separation would be to both of them. But the idea of taking such a young child to spend months, or perhaps years, on a lonely rock, gazing upon nothing but a wild expanse of sea, and hearing no sounds but the roaring of the waves and the cries of the sea-birds, was so repugnant to him that he could not admit it for a moment. He could only quiet her for the time by saying that perhaps, after all, he should not have to live at the Longships, and that Mr. Arthur might find another and more suitable guardian for the lighthouse.

But poor Mary went to bed sad at heart, and passed a restless a night as her father, who was listening to the rising wind and to the waves beating against the sore. She wouldn't mind at all going to live at the lighthouse; but that he beloved father should be there quite alone, that she should hear nothing of him for weeks or months, was an intolerable thought to her. When Mr. Arthur came back, she made up her mind she would speak to him about it, and get him to persuade her father to let her go with him to the lighthouse if he indeed became the keeper. Next morning Nichols' hopes and Tresilian's fears were only too fully confirmed. It was blowing hard. It would be utterly impossible for any boat to approach the Carn-Brâs rock. The lighthouse was every now and then completely hidden by the waves which dashed over it. The old squire was in a great state of excitement. He rode down to the Land's End, and was vexed and irritated when he heard that no boats had put out that morning to the Longships, but when he saw the state of the sea, even he was convinced that all attempts must be utterly fruitless, and turned away homeward anxious and downcast.

Owen, feeling how powerless he was to afford any aid to the imprisoned, parson, paced the cliffs agitated and restless, vainly scanning the sea and sky in hopes of observing signs of more favourable weather. Nichols and his companion passed the greater part of the day in the alehouse, celebrating the defeat and imprisonment of their enemy by a drunken bout.

In the evening the light was again visible, but it was much fainter than it had been yesterday; several times it vanished altogether, but reappeared after a short interval. The men on shore understood from this that the lantern was damaged, so that the sea at times put out the lamp, which was as soon as possible relighted. Next morning happily brought a very favourable change in the weather, the wind had veered round to the east and fallen altogether, the sky was bright and clear, and there was little doubt that on the morrow a landing could be effected on the rock, though not unattended with difficulty and danger.

In the evening the light burned steadily, though it was somewhat faint; this was a cheering and encouraging sign to Arthur's many friends on shore. Meanwhile calm weather continued, and the sea was already smoother. Owen was in better spirits than he had been for a long time. He made every arrangement for an early start next morning. The four men who had accompanied him before were again to form his crew; to them were added two others. A second boat manned by five of the Sennen men, who could not help admiring the young parson's bravery and unselfishness, was to put off for the Longships at the same time, and to render all assistance in its power.

We will now return to the lighthouse. Arthur had passed an anxious and sleepless night. He could not leave Jordan for a minute, the wind continued to rise, while the waves dashed more and more violently against the building. The weird noises below, too, had greatly increased; he could scarcely feel surprise at their effects on his unhappy companion. At early dawn he went up to the lantern, to find the lamps drenched and put out by the sea and spray, which penetrated unhindered through the broken glass. It was blowing hard, the sea was rough and there was every indication of squally weather. It was Thursday now; if he did not get released by Saturday, there would be no one to minister to his flock on Sunday, and the church would have to be shut up. This grieved him far more than the prospect of the trials and inconveniences he would personally have to endure, if he remained here much longer. Provisions would soon run short, and the strain and anxiety on his mind entailed by Jordan's still helpless and agitated condition, and by the necessity of performing himself the duties of a lighthouse-keeper, was as much as he could bear. Still he would not despond, but seek for comfort in his Bible and Prayer-book, and then set to work to prepare his sermon for Sunday, though he felt there was not much chance of his getting ashore to preach it. He selected for his text the 24th verse of the cvii Psalm, "These men see the works of the Lord, and His wonders in the deep," for he felt now that he could speak more than ever from his own experience of the dangers and terrors of the deep, and could also prove how a firm trust and confidence in Him, who ruleth the raging of the storm, is able to keep a man calm and fearless amid them all, because he knows that a Father's hand is stretched out to guard and protect him.

He was thus occupied when Jordan awoke with a start from the heavy stupor in which he usually lay. At first, when his ears were greeted by the same howling of the wind and the rumbling of the sea beneath, he looked terror-stricken and began to tremble violently, but when he saw Arthur standing at his side and looking kindly down upon him, he was reassured. "Ah, you are still here, sir," he said; "I was afraid it was all a dream that you had come to share my dreadful prison, but I began to think it's real now."

"Yes, quite real, Jordan," said Arthur, taking his hand; "and I hope we shall both get out of our prison before many days are over; but we must make the best of it now, and try to keep up each other's spirits."

"But how did you come here, sir? and why are you all alone with me in this dreary place?" said Jordan like one awaking from a dream.

Arthur was delighted to see these signs of returning intelligence. He told him of their alarm and anxiety about him on shore when no light was seen, of the perilous voyage of the Sennen boat, and of the accident which had left him as his companion and on the rock.

"It was very kind of you to come, sir," said Jordan at last; "and to give yourself so much trouble about a poor fellow like me. There are not many gentlemen who would have risked their lives as you have done, to see what ailed a poor lighthouse-keeper."

"It was only my duty, Jordan," said Arthur, "and any one with a sense of humanity would have acted in the same way. Besides that, I was partly responsible. I was to blame for allowing you to be here all alone. One solitary man should never be left to guard a lighthouse, as I have now learned from experience."

"You are quite right there, sir," said Jordan with a shudder. "I've had a terrible time of it. I believe, too, sir," he added after a pause, "that I've been quite out of my senses with the fright."

"But you're getting right again now, I hope," said Arthur.

"I still feel very queer and weak in the head, sir; but I am not like what I have been, for sometimes I did not know whether I was dead or alive, asleep or awake. These horrid noises that come up from below, it's that what's frightened me so, sir; never in my life have I heard anything like it. I take it – it's demons dancing and howling in some cave below. Ah, sir, don't your hear them now? If you were not here I'd go mad, sir, at once with terror." He spoke excitedly, and began to tremble afresh, till Arthur put his hand on his should, saying kindly –

"My good fellow, do put such foolish notions out of your head. God does not permit demons to come near us in this world. You are as safe from them here, as you would be on shore. The noise proceeds from natural causes. There is a great cavern underneath this rock; when the sea is rough, this strange noise is produced by the air confined within it; to this is added the roar of the ocean and the beating of the waves against the rock. You ought to have had all this explained to you, before you came out here.

"Well, sir, I suppose you're right; but it's hard to believe that such a noise as this can be caused by anything else than by the power of the evil one. I never could spend another night alone here, sir; it would be the death of me!"

"You never shall, Jordan," said Arthur. "I remain with you here till we are both released, then you go on shore never to come back hither. You shall never want for anything as long as I live."

"Thank you, sir," said Jordan with a more cheerful expression than he had ever yet assumed. "Ah, how glad I shall be to feel myself on shore again!"

In the course of the afternoon Jordan related all he had experience in the lighthouse during the three days he had passed in it before Arthur's arrival. He told him also a great deal about his past career. He had seen a great deal of wild, rough life beyond the seas, had endured a good share of hardships and trials, and he was as superstitious as most sailors, that have little or no religion. Arthur was surprised at his ignorance of sacred subjects. On these he spoke to him for a long time, and read to him also from the Bible. Jordan was much interested in what he heard; his heart was so touched by Arthur's kindness that it was open to receive God's truth, and in his present condition it made a deep impression on his mind.

In the evening Arthur went up to light the lamps, Jordan, who was quite quiet and composed, remaining below. With joy did the young clergyman perceive that the wind had fallen, and that the sky was evidently brightening. One by one the stars came out. Tomorrow perhaps they would be rescued. He went down and told his companion the good news.

Both passed a much quieter night. Jordan slept well, and Arthur, wearied out with all the fatigues and exertions of his new life, did not awake till daylight. When he mounted the cupola he found to his joy that the storm had abated, and that though swell and surf were still too heavy to allow a boat to approach the rock, yet in a day or two there would be every hope of deliverance.

On returning below he told Jordan, who was just awaking, the happy tidings; and a smile of pleasure passed over the poor fellow's face.

"Oh! what it will be, sir, to feel myself on shore again. I shall be thankful indeed. But never shall I forge the terrible time I have passed here."

"I am glad you are a little more cheerful this morning, Jordan," said Arthur; "it does me good, too, to see you so. I feel I have nothing to regret in the accident which left me here with you alone. God's hand was in it! I now know from experience what a lighthouse-keeper's life is, and shall be able better to sympathise with whoever is brave enough to take this post after us. I fear, however, I sha'n't discover the right man in a hurry, and that some time must elapse before the lamps are lighted again."

"Yes, sir, I am afraid there'll be trouble to find any one to take the post. You say you will have two men now, and you are quite right there. Yet you won't find two in this neighbourhood, I am sure."

"I fear not," said Arthur; "I have one who has volunteered – Owen Tresilian – I only wish he had done so before, and came out with you a week ago; but I have made up my mind not to allow him to be here alone, willing as he is to come."

The day passed away quietly. When in the evening Arthur and Jordan went up to light the lamps, there was scarcely a breath of wind, the air was clear and frosty, and the sky was bright with countless stars. There was every reason to hope that the morrow would bring them release from their prison. With ligher hearts than either of them had for several nights experienced, Arthur and his companion retired to rest.

13

Deliverance

"O God! Who wert my childhood's love.
My boyhood's pure delight,
A presence felt the livelong day,
A welcome fear at night, -
Oh, let me speak to Thee, dear God!
Of those old mercies past,
O'er which new mercies day by day
Such lengthening shadows cast."

- Faber

Morning dawned, still clear and frosty, scarcely a breath of wind ruffled the surface of the bay, and there was no doubt that although there would still be surf and swell round the Carn-Brâs Rock, yet perseverance and caution would enable the brave Sennen fishermen to overcome all difficulties and effect a landing. Owen naturally was the leader of the party; all who had formerly taken part in the enterprise joined him again; and when the two boats put off from the shore, a hearty cheer greeted them from the crowd assembled on the beach. Nichols and Pollard did not show themselves that morning. Feeling they were in a minority, they thought it best to keep out of the way.

The two smacks safely reached the rock, and greatly were their crews cheered to behold two figures standing at the door of the lighthouse, who waved their hands to them in token of encouragement. Jordan then was alive at all events, and there stood their good friend the parson safe and well. Every effort must be made to rescue them and bring them once more to shore. But this, owning to the heaviness of the swell, was no easy matter. Towards noon when the tide began to ebb, the sea become somewhat smoother, and after repeated attempts Owen at last succeeded in getting his boat sufficiently near to the rock to throw out a rope, which Arthur caught and made fast to the capstan there. The clergyman, who had been keenly watching the hitherto unsuccessful efforts of his brave friends to rescue him and his companion, was convinced that Jordan ought to be the first to leave the rock, for with his present disordered mind and unstrung nerves, to be left for however short a time there alone, might have the most serious effects upon him.

"Now, Jordan," he said, when they had made fast the rope, "spring into the boat when it comes close enough; don't wait for me, for I sha'n't leave the rock till I see you safely away from it."

"All right, sir!" he replied, "I'll take care not to be left here alone again, if it were even for a few moments; I could hardly help throwing myself into the sea, I fear, sir."

"Make yourself easy, my good fellow, I won't leave you alone; look, here they come nearer than ever this time, now a good pull at the rope – no, they're off again – better luck next time, I hope."

At last, after three vain attempts, Owen succeeded in getting his boat near enough for both the men to spring into it almost simultaneously. A hearty cheer rose from the crews of both smacks, Owen grasped the parson's hand – "Thank God, sir," he said, "that we have you among us once more, and that you are safe and well; we have been very anxious about you, sir, on shore, and the squire has done nothing but gallop up and down along the coast all day, and far into the night too; we'd have put out before this, sir, I can assure you, but it was quite impossible."

"I know that, Owen; I never expected you before; I was certain you would come the first moment there was any chance of landing here, and I've nothing to complain of. I've experienced what a lighthouse-keeper's life is, and I've been some little help to my friend here, I hope, haven't I, Jordan?"

"That you have, sir," replied Jordan, and now that he spoke for the first time, the attention of Owen and the other sailors was directed towards him. So startled and horrified were they by his changed appearance, his white hair, his sunken cheeks, the scared look in his eyes, that some of the men almost dropped their oars from their hands; they scarcely recognised the sturdy, hale, determined-looking man whom but a few days before they had landed on the rock. They all gazed at the poor fellow askance, as if he were some inhabitant of another world, but none ventured to ask a question or make a remark.

Arthur of course noticed their amazement.

"Poor Jordan has had a hard time of it," he said; "I am very thankful I reached him just at the right moment."

None of the men liked to ask for further explanations, but Owen said, "We have only done half our work, sir, we have got you into the boat and off the rock, but now I must land on the rock till you get some one else, I feel it's my duty to be the lighthouse-keeper."

"No, Owen," Arthur said firmly, "nothing of the kind. It is indeed a grief to me that the lamps won't be lighted to-night, and that we can't tell how long it will be ere they burn again; but on this point I'm determined, no one must pass a night on that rock alone if I can hinder it."

"But, sir, I'm not in the least afraid; I'm not a stranger to these parts like Jordan; and think of what a bad effect it will have that, after the lights have once begun to burn, they should cease even for a time. How all the bad fellows down at the Cove will rejoice; they'll say that the parson is foiled after all, and that his scheme has turned out a regular failure. You'd better let me land, sir; in a day or two perhaps you'll find me a companion, then you'll feel more easy about me."

"No, Owen, I have made up my mind; so, say no more about it, it is settled for the present."

Much as Arthur admired Owen's bravery and spirit of self-sacrifice, nothing would induce him to alter this decision. That his scheme had failed, he must now confess, but he trusted it was only a temporary failure, and that erelong the lamps would shine brighter than ever.

Anxiously had the progress of the boats been watched from the shore. The squire stood at the extreme point of the Land's End and gazed through his telescope at the lighthouse. Every attempt and failure to effect a landing was observed by him, as well as by the groups of men and women who gathered together at spots where they could obtain a good view of the smacks and their proceedings. When the brave young parson was observed on board, and the boats were seen to turn homewards, shouts rent the air, and when he landed, many of the men who had formerly looked upon him as an enemy, grasped his hand as warmly as if welcoming a friend. Arthur was deeply gratified. He felt that the two days spent in the lighthouse had by no means been lost ones; he had gained experience, he had won friends. But he dared not be too sanguine, he knew how easily the ignorant are moved by what appeal to their feelings – how transient are the opinions of an excited multitude.

The squire was overjoyed when he once more held his son's hand in his. He had passed a terribly anxious time, but now that he had him safe home again, he was proud of his valour and daring; though his son was a parson (which he never ceased to regret), he had proved by his pluck that he had spirit and courage enough to have made a first-rate solider or sailor. He was never tired of talking and hearing about Arthur's expedition to the Longships, and of the days and nights he had spent there.

On the evening of that day it was the turn of Arthur's enemies to rejoice. No friendly light beamed from the Longships that night. There was a noisy carouse at the village alehouse.

"The parson's fine scheme for taking the bread out of our mouths has come to nothing," said Nichols; "what's the good of a lighthouse without a light in it, I should like to know? They'll never get any one to live there after what's happened."

"No, indeed," answered Pollard. "Did you ever see such a poor wretched object as that fellow Jordan? why, I could scarcely believe my own eyes when I saw him pass up the road, his hair is a white as old Harvey's, and when he walks he totters and trembles."

"I could not have believed it either," said another of the party, "couldn't have thought that a few days could have made such a change in a fellow. He was strong and hearty enough when he started the beginning of last week."

"Ah! I always told you how it would be," said Nichols. "It's what the Methodists would call a judgment upon him, I suppose!"

"I'm told," said another, "it was all owing to that horrible howling and roaring in the cavern under the rock. It frightened the fellow so, that he lost his wits and nearly went mad."

"And would have gone so quite if the parson hadn't got to him," said Pollard.

"He seems none the worse for it, though," remarked Nichols. "I only wish he'd stopped there."

"Well, his fine plans are all baulked, there's no doubt," said Pollard, "and that's a good job."

"He'll be up to some fresh pranks erelong," replied Nichols, "we must make the best use of the time while we can, dark nights and stormy weather coming on, let's keep a good look-out for wrecks, and hope for a better season than we had last winter."

As may well be imagined, Arthur lost no time in trying to find a successor to the unfortunate Jordan. On the following Monday he started for Falmouth and Plymouth, making inquiries of the naval authorities, of well-known ship-owners, and shipping-agents, but all his efforts were fruitless. There was a great scarcity of men in those days; all who were strong and able-bodied were draughted into the army and navy, and it was above all things necessary for Arthur to secure a man of good and trustworthy character. Such an one he could nowhere hear of. Mr. Smith, the shipowner, who had furnished the money to build the lighthouse, was equally unsuccessful in his endeavours, and much vexed that his benevolent scheme had so early proved a failure. Baffled and bitterly disappointed, Arthur at the end of the week returned home.

It was hard to bear the ill-concealed mockery and exultation of his enemies. Sneers often greeted him as he passed through the village. The ground he had gained by his courageous adventure on the Longships seemed to be already lost.

The story of Jordan's adventure on the Longships soon spread throughout the country and along the coast. It is needless to say that it was marvellously exaggerated; but that the man's hair had turned white from fear in a single night was a fact terrible enough without any exaggeration. His fate was quoted as a warning to others. He had gone back to live at Truro with his daughter, and many had seen him and spoken to him. Any man who undertook the post of lighthouse-keeper after what had occurred to Jordan, must either be of unexampled coolness and bravery, or come from some remote part of the country to which the tale of that wretched man's troubles had not penetrated. Though Arthur really required two men, he would for the present have been content with one, as Owen was quite willing and ready to do his share of the work, in fact he constantly urged the parson to consent to his going to the Longships alone. But on this point, anxious as he was that the lighthouse should be manned, Arthur was still quite decided.

14

A Cruise And A Long Fight

"In our sails all soft and sweetly,
Yet with bold, resistless force,
Breathe the winds of heaven, and fleetly
Wing us on our watery course;
Swift and swifter furrowing deep,
Through the mighty waves that keep
Not a trace where we have been:
On we speed to lands unseen.
Be our voyage, brethren, such
That if direst peril come,
Wreck and ruin could not touch
Aught but this our weary frame;
That may gladly sleep the while,
Still and blest the soul shall smile
In the eternal peace of heaven
That our God hath surely given."

- Fouque

It was not very long after Lord Howe's glorious victory on the 1st June, when Philip, who had been commended by the officers for his bravery in the action, was transferred from the "Royal Sovereign" to another vessel. Since Bob's death he had more than ever been a victim to persecution and annoyance of every kind from the rough and ungodly fellows among the crew. Edwards had never forgotten his struggle with Philip, in which, partly by Bob's timely interference, he had been foiled. He never lost an opportunity of injuring or tormenting Philip, and setting on the other lads to do what he dared not attempt himself. He was nicknamed the Saint and the Methodist; he had not now a single friend from whom he could get any sympathy; he therefore had no reason to regret the order which moved him to another ship. The "Redoubtable" was a fifty-gun frigate; she formed part of a squadron which was despatched to look after British interests in the West Indies. Philip found but little difference between his new and his old messmates. When the former observed, as they soon did, that he did not swear or use bad language, that he was quiet and retiring, they soon singled him out to be a laughing-stock. His kindly disposition, indeed, as well as his fearlessness of danger, which had already on several occasions been displayed, won him a few friends among the steadier of the crew, but the worst characters soon found out that he was religiously inclined – an offence on board the "Redoubtable" as everywhere else in those times.

There was, too, at that period far greater hatred and opposition to religion among the officers than is now the case. Not only was it singular and unpopular to be religious, but it was also held to be cowardly; none could believe that a Methodist solider or sailor would be as fearless in the presence of an enemy, or fight with the same bravery, as a man who never spoke without an oath, and who was utterly indifferent to every principle both of religion and morality. The officers, too, had far more power than at present over the persons of the men, the horrible system of flogging for the most trivial offences, as well as for acts of insubordination, was in full force, and often Philip had shuddered when he had seen this punishment mercilessly inflicted on some of his messmates, but hitherto he had escaped it himself.

The captain of the "Redoubtable" was a hard and severe man; he maintained the strictest discipline, coolly standing by while the lash was inflicted, and utterly unmoved through the victim fainted beneath this brutal treatment. The officers and midshipmen, while they were as cruel and heartless towards their subordinates as the captain, were in other respects even worse, and more to be feared than he was, for though the captain was stern and cruel, yet he was just; and though he was destitute of sympathy and kindly feeling, he was never vindictive. But many of the officers did not hesitate to punish men to satisfy their own spite; they were selfish and dissolute in character, petty tyrants who loved to feel their power, and delighted in nothing so much as being able to inflict degrading punishments on those who ventured to oppose their will.

Philip had not been long on board the "Redoubtable" before several of the officers discovered that he was in many respects above the ordinary run of seamen – better educated, able to read and write, neat in appearance, and respectful in manner. These, however, were not regarded as recommendations, and when they remarked that his language was free from the oaths and impurities in which they indulged themselves quite as much as the men, they began to suspect that Philip was a "Methodist," and therefore a fit object for mockery and persecution.

One young lieutenant, Bayley by name, had conceived a particular spite against Philip. He would always put him to the most degrading work, speak to him as if he were a dog rather than a human being, and garnish his language with a great number of vile oaths and horrible expressions, than he was in the habit of using when he addressed the other men.

One evening this lieutenant came on deck, and in his usual brutal manner, seeing Philip unoccupied, ordered him to perform some degrading office. He was about to comply with alacrity when the officer, who was rather the worse for drink, turned round upon him, give him a severe cuff on the head without the slightest provocation, and said with a volley of oaths, "Take that, you wretched young milksop. I'll teach you to be like other men, and not set yourself up for a saint here on board ship."

Philip, accustomed to Lieutenant Bayley's brutality, made no reply, but this only further irritated the officer. "I say, why don't you ever swear, you young fool? Don't stand there staring at me; answer my question," he shouted.

"I don't think it right, sir," said Philip quietly, "and I don't see the use of it."

"Hang the use of it!" said the lieutenant. "I'll soon have such ideas thrashed out of your head, and teach you how to set up yourself above every one here."

"I don't wish to set myself up as better than others, sir," said Philip respectfully.

"Then why don't you act like others and talk like others?" said the officer.

"Because I can't do and say what I know to be wrong, sir."

"You know to be wrong! and how do you know it, I should like to know? If that isn't setting up yourself above others, I should like to know what is?"

Philip did not reply. The officer continued, "I tell you what it is, young rascal, and I've made up my mind to it; I'll not put up with any of your Methodistical doings here, I'll have them flogged out of you before long, so take warning in time, and let me hear you swear and talk like the other lads, -

for if you don't, you'll repent it."

With these words the officer turned away to join a companion who had just come on the deck, leaving Philip at his work, and to no very pleasant reflections. What could he do? Swear he never would, rather would he endure the dreaded lash, than utter a foul word or blasphemous oath. He knew how Lieutenant Bayley hated him, but he hoped these words were only threats which is obedience to orders and general good conduct would make it impossible for his enemy to carry into execution. But the poor lad felt very downcast; he had not a single human soul to whom he could tell his grief or ask advice; he could only lift up his heart in silent prayer to his Father in heaven, beseeching Him now to give him strength and courage boldly to stand up for Him, and to submit to pain and suffering rather than deny or dishonour Him.

Philip often, as he stood on duty, gazed into the star-lit sky so glorious in that tropical zone through which they were cruising, and thought of his beloved home far away in old England; wondered how his father fared, and his little sister, whether they often spoke of him, and if they were beginning to recover his loss. Would the day ever come on which he should again look upon that beloved cottage on the wind-blown height by the stormy sea in dear, far-off Cornwall? When he thought of the many dangers to which his life was exposed from war and tempest, and the thousand accidents which beset a seaman's career, the chances seemed against it. On the other hand, God could bring him back "to his father's house in peace," and fervently did he pray that such might be His will.

Cruising about among the West Indian Islands the "Redoubtable" constantly captured valuable prizes; now and then, too, her crew had sharp engagements with the enemy, which hitherto had ended in victory to the English cause, and resulted in no loss of life to the victors.

Lieutenant Bayley meanwhile grew more incensed against poor Philip since the interview we have described. He kept the sharpest look-out that he might catch him at some neglect of duty, and tried to irritate him so as to make him commit an act of insubordination – but all was to no avail. Yet Philip's life, it can well be imagined, was a very wretched one. Latterly, however, he had noticed that one of the petty officers, an elderly man with kindly features, as well as one of the ordinary seamen, who seemed steadier than the rest, were inclined to treat him differently from the others, and often, when no one else was near, would say a cheering word to the poor lad.

Beneath a cloudless sky on a glassy sea they were sailing among the spicy islands of the West Indies. It was winter now in England, but here the climate was warm and delightful; how different Philip often thought from the cold stormy weather to which at that time of the year he was accustomed on the bleak shores of Cornwall.

One morning Philip and another lad of about his own age, a lazy dissolute young fellow, who never lost an opportunity of worrying and tormenting his companion, were ordered to wash the decks. Philip as usual set to work with a will, and his portion was soon done. Sam Wilks, on the contrary, dawdled over his task, amusing himself by throwing dirty water at Philip, feeling sure he would stand any amount of bullying and insult, as if a Methodist must be a coward and dared not fight.

However, there are things which it is hard for human nature to bear, and young blood, even when under the best and holiest influences, is apt occasionally to rebel and assert its rights. So it was at last with Philip Tresilian. To be called cowardly and lazy by one of the laziest and most cowardly fellows on board, to hear his religion and all that he held dearest on earth scoffed at and abused with oaths and filthy language, to be hindered in his work, while every remonstrance he made was responded to by fresh annoyances – all this was at last too much for his temper.

"Sam," he exclaimed at last, "stop this foolery, or you'll repent it, I can tell you."

Repent it! I should like to see that! I'm not afraid of a Methodist like you.' You daren't touch me, I know," said Sam in an insolent voice, coming close up to Philip and shaking his fist in his face.

"You'll pretty soon see that I do dare to make you pay for it, and pretty smartly too, so you'd better shut up and leave me alone."

Sam, coward as he was, did not feel at all alarmed by Philip's words or by his fierce look. He did not believe he would fight him. He imagined that he would stand any amount of ridicule. He knew, too, how unpopular Philip was, and that in a quarrel none would be found to espouse his cause; so he went back a few steps, and taking up the dirty mop with which he had been washing the deck, dashed it full into Philip's face with a loud laugh, exclaiming –

"Ha! ha! I'd like to see you touch me indeed. Why your parson at home would find it out if you did, and preach you a nice sermon for it. I'm not afraid of a fool of a Methodist like you – there, take that."

Philip without a moment's hesitation sprang like a tiger upon his assailant, blow after blow fell heavily on the head and shoulders of the luckless Sam, whose roars and yells soon called up spectators to the affray.

Among the first of these was Lieutenant Bayley – certainly not a little surprised when he perceived Philip Tresilian fighting. Sam Wilks lay bleeding and howling on the deck. There was no doubt as to who was the victor, and the battle had been of very few moments' duration. The officer was delighted that he had at last an opportunity to punish Philip for a breach of discipline, as well as of heaping insults upon him and ridiculing his religion.

"What's all this?" he said, in a loud voice; "I'll have no fighting here!

Neglect of duty, too. Why is not the deck washed down?" he continued, glancing at Sam's unfinished portion.

"My part is done, sir," replied Philip, turning round and facing the lieutenant with flashing eyes; "that is Sam's."

"Then it is you who have prevented him from doing it by fighting," said the officer. "I thought Methodists never fought – if they do they must be punished like others," he continued with a sneer.

"I was provoked, sir; it is more than any lad can bear to stand the insults I have to meet with every hour – and from Sam Wilks more than any one. My blood was up, sir, when he stuck the dirty mop in my face."

"It's all a lie, sir," yelled Sam; "he began it. He came upon me all unawares, when I was hard at work, nasty coward that he is – to pay off an old score. If I'd only had fair play, I could have thrashed him easily, sir."

"Oh, that's the truth of the case, is it?" said the lieutenant, "just like a Methodist and a coward – you shall pay for this, Tresilian; you won't escape this time without a flogging – twenty-five lashes at the very least."

"I have told the truth, sir," said Philip; "why should you believe Sam more than me. Have I ever told you a lie, sir, and isn't Sam known to be the biggest liar on board? I know I was wrong to strike him, but to be called a coward is more than"-

"Hold your tongue, you impudent young beggar," said the lieutenant with an oath, "I'll have none of your arguing with me. I'd sooner believe Sam than a Methodist like you, any day. This evening you'll make the acquaintance with the lash for the first time, and I shan't be sorry."

Lieutenant Bayley would gladly have had the punishment inflicted at once, but the captain was on shore, as they were then at anchor off one of the smaller islands, and it required his consent before the flogging could be administered. Meanwhile he ordered his victim to be incarcerated in the dark cell set apart for men guilty of insubordination and misconduct.

Here Philip had plenty of time for sad reflection. Again had his temper got the mastery over him. He had broken through his good resolutions, he had not yet learned to bear insult and persecution as his Divine Master had done for his sake. Tears of deep penitence flowed down his cheeks, as he prayed his Father above to pardon his son and to receive him again into His favour.

The captain did not come on board till late in the evening when orders were immediately given to weigh anchor and sail in a northerly direction to join some other vessels of the squadron, information having been received that the enemy were in considerable force in those waters, and that there was some risk to his frigate being surprised and overcome by superior numbers.

There was so much bustle and excitement on board that evening, that poor Philip was forgotten even by Lieutenant Bayley, and he remained alone and unnoticed in his cell, which was so small that he had not room either to stand upright or to lie down in it.

He was faint and hungry, for he had had nothing to eat all day, but his physical sufferings were small in comparison to his mental pain, and to the disappointment and shame which he felt at having given way to passion, and thereby brought disgrace upon the religion he professed.

Time passed away slowly enough in that dark hole, where there was nothing to distinguish day from night; but the rattling of cables, and the heaving of anchors in the evening informed the prisoner that the frigate was about to leave her moorings and again set sail. The captain had come on board then. The terrible moment poor Philip thought could not be far off when he would endure the dreaded punishment. It was not so much for the pain that he cared, intense and fearful as that must be – for often he had seen strong men borne away fainting and bleeding after the infliction of the lash – but it was the disgrace that he minded most of all. He felt, too, that he was innocent, - he had not neglected his duty. No officer who had any sense of justice would have ordered him to be punished on the accusation of a lad like Sam, notorious for lying. He knew he was about to be flogged merely to gratify Lieutenant Bayley's spite against him. However, he made up his mind he would bear it bravely. His Lord, to Whom he had confessed his sin, would, he hoped, pardon the weakness of his erring nature, and he felt sure would also give him strength to endure the cruel punishment.

With such thoughts in his mind, wearied and exhausted, he sunk into a restless slumber, starting at every sound, and expecting every moment to be summoned on deck and to hear the captain's loud voice order the boatswain's mate to carry out the sentence.

In this state he remained for some two or three hours, when he was aroused by the sound of voices near him. As it was part of the vessel not much frequented, he was sure now that his time was come, and he almost wished it might be so, - anything would be better than suspense. But no, he was wrong. The voices seemed close to the door of the cell, and they were very low, but he soon was able to distinguish what they said, and to his utter amazement and pleasure, he heard the blessed words of Holy Scripture, the 42nd Psalm, read almost in a whisper, in a tone he had certainly heard before, but could not recognise.

"Like as the hart desireth the water-brooks, so longeth my soul after thee, O God … My tears have been my meat day and night, while they daily say unto me, Where is thy God?"

Every verse as it fell upon Philip's ear seemed more and more appropriate to his case. He felt indeed as if an angel from heaven had been sent to him to pour the balm of consolation into his wounded heart.

There was silence now, for a few moments, then a short fervent prayer was offered up in plain familiar words, like those of a child asking a favour of its father. There was a petition for more faith and love in Him Who loved and died for us, for protection from danger in storm and battle, for courage not to deny or be ashamed of Him, and for all on board the ship that they might be converted and brought to the knowledge of the truth. Then the "Our Father" was repeated by two voices slowly, and with great fervour. This was followed by another interval of silence. Then he heard the following conversation –

"We can't sing to-night, Tom, we might be overheard, there are so many moving about, but I'll say one of Mr. Wesley's hymns to you if you like."

"Yes, do, Bill, it always does me good to hear one of them, and I'm not in the best of spirits to-night."

"Well, listen, I don't know all of it, but only some verses; it'll cheer you up a bit, I hope, Tom; it always does me, it's something like the psalm I've just been reading to you:-

> "'Commit thou all thy griefs
> And ways into His hands,
> To His sure truth and tender care
> Who earth and heaven commands:
> Who points the clouds their course,
> Whom winds and seas obey,
> He shall direct thy wandering feet,
> He shall prepare thy way.
> Thou on the Lord rely,
> So safe shalt thou go on,
> Fix on His work thy steadfast eye,
> So shall thy work be done.
> No profit canst thou gain
> By self-consuming care;
> To Him commend thy cause, His ear
> Attends the softest prayer.
> Give to the winds thy fears,
> Hope and be undismayed,
> God hears thy sighs and counts thy tears,
> God shalt lift up thy head;
> Through waves and clouds and storms,
> He gently clears the way;
> Wait thou His time, so shall this night
> Soon end in joyous day.'"

"Well, I never heard a finer hymn than that, Bill. How well you've got it off, too."

"Oh, there's ever so much more of it; but that's all I can remember now."

"It's done me good. I've been feeling downcast all day. This little meeting of ours down here, Bill, though we don't often manage to get it, is a mercy we have to be thankful for."

"It is indeed, Tom. To get a word together now and then to cheer one another up, and to feel that we are fighting the same battle, and serving the same Master, is a comfort indeed among our trials."

"You remember that lad, Tresilian I think is his name, who came aboard some months ago from the 'Royal Sovereign.' Well, have you heard what happened to him this morning?"

"No, Tom; but I'm sure he's a God-fearing lad. I never hear him swear, I've never seen him drunk, and I don't know any one else on board I can say that of. I'm always trying to get an opportunity of saying a word to cheer him up, for he has a deal to bear, not that I haven't gone through it all myself before; but what were you going to tell me about him?"

"Why, this morning, it appears that he and Sam Wilks were set to wash the decks, they got up a quarrel between them, and Tresilian gave Sam a drubbing that he won't forget for many a long day."

"I shouldn't have thought the lad would have fought. But I suppose he was provoked. I'm not sorry that lazy rascal Wilks got a thrashing."

"But that's not all the story, Bill. Up comes Lieutenant Bayley, and finds Wilks bleeding and blubbering on the deck. He tells, as you might expect, a lie about the whole affair, which, as you would also expect, the lieutenant believes; he won't listen to a word Tresilian has to say, sends him down to the blackhole, and says he will have him flogged when the captain comes on board."

"Poor lad! and it'll be done too, sure enough, to-morrow. I suppose he's forgotten all about it to-night. I am heartily sorry for him."

"I suppose he's in the prison yonder? Can we go and say a kind word to him through the door, Bill?"

"He may be in the other cell; but if he's in this one he must have heard all we said, unless he's asleep, poor fellow. Well, I'll go and speak to him at once."

Not a word of this conversation had been lost on Philip; but his hopes of kindly sympathy were dispelled by sudden shouts from above, and the shuffling of feet as of many men running up and down the ladders. Then there was a whisper of "Come, Tom, all hands are wanted aloft. We mustn't be found down here. We'll get a chance of speaking to the poor fellow another time perhaps." And then he was left once more in trouble.

Though Philip was disappointed, he felt far more cheerful than he had done since the sad events of the morning. Here were two men who felt for him, and who, like him, were endeavouring to serve God in the midst of this ungodly crew. Who could they be? At last he remember the petty officer and the sailor whom he so often saw together, and who occasionally had given him a kindly look, though they had never yet spoken to him. Surely these must be the two men whose conversation he had overheard.

Soon after the frigate had set sail, Lieutenant Bayley informed the captain of the occurrence of the morning. He naturally exaggerated Philip's misdemeanour, and it was settled that Philip should be flogged early the next morning.

The glassy surface of the sea was scarcely stirred, so gentle was the breeze, and very slowly did the "Redoubtable" advance through the calm waters. A sharp watch was kept up at the maintop. The squadron lay some distance off, and the captain felt a little uneasy at the accounts he had received of the nearness and superior strength of the enemy. The frigate was not a fast sailer, so there was great need of watchfulness, and some cause for anxiety.

It was one of those brilliant moonlight nights such as are only to be seen in tropical regions. Near midnight the men on watch at the maintop announced that they perceived in the far away distance three sail, but whether they belonged to friend or foe they could not as yet distinguish. As English ships were not expected in that quarter, the captain and officers had but little doubt that they belonged to the enemy's fleet, if so, strenuous efforts must be made to escape from them. Every inch of canvas was ordered to be spread to catch the feeble breeze; the hope that, as was usually the case, it would freshen in the morning, was damped by the reflection that it would serve the enemy as well, if not better, and it did their own ship.

It was the excitement caused by this discovery, and by the stringent orders of the captain for all hands to set to work, which Philip had heard in his cell, and which had hastily sent his two friends aloft, when they were about to speak to him.

At daybreak the crew were mustered. Philip alone was missing. Lieutenant Bayley reminded the captain of Philip's misconduct, and of the punishment he had promised should be inflicted on him that morning.

The captain was irritated at the mention of flogging.

"I can't spare any hands to-day, Bayley. Absurd to maim a strong lad when, in all probability, we shall want every able-bodied fellow we can get to fight the French. If he fights well he'll be let off the flogging, if not, he shall have it with interest another day. Quartermaster, release the prisoner at once, and set him to work."

Lieutenant Bayley did not reply, he turned away on his heel, vexed and disappointed. Common sense and right were on the captain's side, so he dared not dispute with him. However, he would remember Philip, and take precious good care that though the flogging was deferred, it should be administered in the end.

Philip, pale and exhausted, was now brought on deck, the captain swore at him, and informed him that he had been let off the flogging he so richly deserved for the present, but that he was very much mistaken if he fancied he was going to get off it altogether. But when he saw how ill the lad looked from want of food and confinement, he gave orders that he should have his breakfast before going to work.

The greatest excitement now prevailed on board the "Redoubtable." With dawn of day the breeze freshened, and every sail was spread to catch the favouring gales, but notwithstanding all the exertions of both officers and crew, the three vessels, which none doubted now belonged to the enemy, were slowly and surely gaining upon them. Their only hope was, that they might come up with the English squadron before they were overtaken and outnumbered by the foe. Every eye was strained to northwards, but not a speck was to be seen on that horizon.

Towards noon there was a dead calm, during which no advance was made by either side, and though with evening rose a gentle breeze, and the exertions of the crew were again renewed, they could not but feel very anxious as night fell, and concealed the pursuers from their gaze. Morning, they all felt, must decide their fate, either revealing the friendly squadron near enough to come to their aid, or disclosing the enemy's ships in such close proximity that escape would be hopeless. When the day dawned all eyes were strained first to the north, then to the south, striving to discern through the faint mist which covers the horizon the outline of friend or foe. The keenest eye could not discover the trace of a sail to the north, while the three French vessels had gained so rapidly on the "Redoubtable" that their gay tricolour flags were distinctly visible.

A council was now held by the captain and officers of the "Redoubtable" to consider the line of action it was best to take under the circumstances, whether they should continue their flight, or to lay to at once and await the enemy's attack. Some were for immediate action; the battle, they said, could not be avoided, terrible as were the odds against them, and the sooner, therefore, it was over, the better. Others were for continuing to press on with vigour to the north, since help might not be far distant, while experience taught them that on the appearance of any English ships in all probability the French would at once take to flight. The latter council prevailed. At noon they perceived to their no little delight that one of the French ships was lagging behind the others, some accident had probably disabled her, but the other two slowly continued to gain on the "Redoubtable".

"Well, what do you think'll come of it, Bill?" said Tom Marriott to Bill Forster, the two praying men to whom we have previously alluded.

"I can't say, I'm sure, Tom. We shall have to fight for it, there's little doubt – two, if not three to one, against us, so there doesn't seem much chance."

"No, indeed; still there's no telling. Such things have been known before as one English ship beating three French men."

"Oh yes, Tom, and there's no doubt it will be a desperate business, for our captain will fight to the last; but what makes it worse for us is, that those three French line-of-battle ships are all of them bigger than our frigate."

"True enough, Bill; and whatever comes of it, there's no doubt there'll be precious slaughter among us."

"There will indeed, Tom, and it's just what I've been thinking all the morning. How few there are among us prepared to die, to appear with all their sins before the presence of God!"

"May the Lord have mercy upon them, and on us too, Bill. For my part, I feel that I am a great sinner, and not fit to die."

"None of us are, Tom, but it is from our sins that Jesus has died to save us. We must look to Him and trust Him, and He will be our refuge and strength in this great danger. If it's His will that either of us fall doing our duty, fighting for our king and country, He will be with us at our last hour and receive us into His eternal kingdom."

"Your good words always cheer me up, Bill. I wish I had as much faith as you. But did you hear that the poor lad who was in prison last night, and sentenced to be flogged, has been let off by the captain? and there he is at work as usual, just coming down from the maintop."

"Yes, it's an ill wind that blows nobody good, as they say; our French pursuers have done that poor fellow a good turn certainly. I'll go and say a kind word to him, Tom; I've never yet had the chance to do it."

Forster went up to Philip and told him how glad he was to see him released. "I'm sorry your temper got the better of you, my lad, yesterday, but I know how greatly you were provoked. There's a hard time in prospect for all of us now. Ah! which of us can tell where he will be this time to-morrow, for ere then we must fight those Frenchmen."

"There seems no doubt of that," replied Philip. "I know what a battle is too, for I fought under Lord Howe on the 1st June, when we won that splendid victory."

"Did you, indeed? I've been in many battles myself too, but they've been pretty even ones; this is likely to be a desperate affair, we're so outnumbered."

"Yes, no doubt of it," said Philip. "Was it you and your mate I heard talking and reading down near the cockpit last night?"

"Yes, - you heard Tom and me then?"

"I scarcely lost a word. I was locked up in the black-hole, more miserable and down-hearted than ever in my life before, but the psalm and the hymn you read cheered me up wonderfully. I felt that in answer to my prayers God had sent me comfort in my trouble, and that whatever happened to me – even flogging and disgrace – I'd be able to stand it."

"The Lord be praised for His mercy," said Forster. "I little thought that any one but Tom was within hearing. But now, my lad, farewell, we mustn't stand talking here. May God guard and keep you both in body and soul!"

When evening came the third French ship was some distance behind her companions, which were still gaining on the "Redoubtable." Not a speck of any kind was to be seen to the north. There was no doubt now that at early dawn the battle would take place.

It was a busy night. But few hours of rest were snatched by either officers or crew. Decks were cleared, guns got ready, every preparation made for a desperate action. There was to be no surrender, they were all determined to fight to the last man, and to stick to their ship till she sunk beneath the waves.

With every inch of canvas spread, and speeding on with a favouring breeze, the officers and crew of the "Redoubtable" hailed the dawn of another day. One of the French ships was now almost within gunshot of them, evidently ready for battle.

Drums were now beat to quarters on board the "Redoubtable," the signal was given to prepare for action, and the frigate's course was altered that she might be in a better position to pour a broadside into the first enemy's vessel which approached her.

Though the captain was a man of few words, he endeavoured by a short address to inspire his crew. Such is the indomitable pluck of the British tar that all hearts beat with confidence, for, notwithstanding the unequal nature of the approaching conflict, they still hoped to snatch a victory.

It was a magnificent morning, the sun had risen in unclouded splendour, pouring his brilliant rays on the sparkling sea, and shining on the spreading sails of the hostile vessels, giving them an appearance of snowy whiteness. All the crew on board the English frigate now stood to their guns, while every officer repaired to his appointed station.

The foremost French vessel ran up a signal demanding immediate surrender, instantly replied to by a shout of defiance from the "Redoubtable," which now lay-to awaiting the enemy's nearer approach. On she came – a monster, an eighty gun ship, nearly twice the size of the frigate. The first shot was fired by the "Redoubtable," striking away the enemy's jib-boom. She at once opened a heavy cannonade on the English ship, which, however, being avoided by a skilful manoeuvre, fell harmlessly into the sea. It was now the turn of the British crew. They poured a furious and well-directed broadside on the deck of the Frenchman. Every shot seemed to take effect. The groans of the wounded now mingled with the exulting shouts of the English sailors. The French vessel's next cannonade did some amount of damage to the "Redoubtable". One man was killed and a few wounded, some spars, too, were shivered, but the well-aimed broadside given them in return was bestowed with such murderous effect that not only was the deck covered with the dead and wounded, but the French vessel was so crippled and damaged that her commander began to have serious fears as to her safety. But as the "Redoubtable" – her captain and crew eager for closer action, as well as desirous of disabling one antagonist before another came up – approached nearer, the French ship was able to pour a volley of shell and shot which raked the "Redoubtable's" decks, and brought down not a few of her brave defenders.

The second French man-of-war was now within cannon shot. She was smaller than her companion, about the same size as her English foe. The third ship, anxiously watched form the "Redoubtable's" maintop, was described to be also making rapid progress, and in less than an hour she too would be able to take part in the battle.

Every man on board the "Redoubtable," from the captain downward, felt that a desperate effort must now be made, and a tremendous broadside was poured into the flanks of the French ship, while at the same time a sharp musketry fire was showered upon her deck from the yards of the English frigate.

But a fresh and more formidable foe was now ready to engage the "Redoubtable," already in some degree weakened and damaged by her first encounter. The second French vessel, her crew fully prepared for action, and confident of victory, had borne up in such a way as to place the English ship between two fires. She, however, was more skilfully and rapidly handled than the French vessels, and by a clever manoeuvre her captain avoided this danger as well as the first cannonade from the second French ship. There was little now to be feared from the first of the enemy's vessels, her crew had enough to do to prevent her from sinking. But there was no escape from a conflict with the second; yet the heroic Englishmen were anything but disheartened by the issue of the battle so far, and as confident of victory as they had been at its commencement. A desperate struggle now ensured. Broadside after broadside was poured from either ship, shot and shell raked the decks, now strewn with the maimed and mangled bodies of their brave defenders. Smoke and fire obscured the brilliant sunlight, riddled sails hung drooping down, shouts of triumph were mingled with the groans of the wounded. Victory seemed to incline to the English, though they had lost many men, but the issue of the battle must ultimately depend on the arrival of the third French vessel. If the "Redoubtable" could even overcome her present antagonist, it was hardly likely she could withstand a third foe, coming fresh into the fray, and with her damaged masts and torn sails escape would be impossible. The captain, officers, and some of the more thoughtful men among the crew, began to feel this, - still they did not relax their efforts, determined as they were to fight to the end.

And how had it fared with Philip during this desperate conflict? He had stood as bravely at his post as he had done on the 1st of June on board the "Royal Sovereign." To him a battle was not a new experience, but this was a far more terrible combat than the first in which he had been engaged. There are two things at which it is said a man cannot look steadily, the sun and death, but Philip had now to look death very steadily in the face, for it came near to him, as well as to every one else on board, that eventful morning.

But his trust was in God, were it His will that he should share the fate of those he saw lying dead around him, he was ready to submit, hard as it was to part with life, and give up all hope of seeing again in this world those he loved the most. Still he was not afraid to die; with sorrow he remembered how often he had offended his Saviour, and the disgrace he had recently brought on his religion by allowing his temper to get the better of him; but he knew how merciful his dear Lord was to all His children, and that "if we confess our sins He is faithful and just to forgive us our sins, and to cleanse us from all unrighteousness."

Thoughts such as these filled his mind, when the clouds of smoke by which he was surrounded cleared away for a moment, he perceived standing close by the petty officer Forster who had spoken so kindly to him the previous day. In the discharge of his duty he had come close up to Philip; both recognised each other at the same moment. "Ah! my lad," said Forster, "so you too are still alive and unwounded, thank God; but it is hot work, isn't it?"

"Yes, it is indeed," replied Philip, "and what a terrible slaughter is going on everywhere. However bravely we fight, we must be outnumbered."

"I fear so; we shall pretty well fight to our last man, I expect. But it is sad to think how many of us are unprepared to enter into God's presence," said Forster solemnly.

A fresh roar of cannon drowned his voiced, and a cloud of smoke hid him from Philip's view. As it slowly vanished, it disclosed the French ship so close that a hand-to-hand fight must soon ensue; Forster was at Philip's side, while at a very short distance off they perceived Lieutenant Bayley.

"A last word, my lad," said Forster. "I shall be called off from the forecastle ere long, if another grimmer messenger does not come for me before; stand up bravely as you have already done for what is right and true and honest; be as fearless of the mockery of your fellows as you are now of the enemy's balls, continue in the right way, and it will bring you peace at the last – a peace which, perhaps, is not far off for you and me. Remember Him who said, 'Behold thou faithful unto death, and I will give thee' –"

He did not finish the sentence. At that moment a hail of musketry poured down upon the "Redoubtable's" decks from the enemy's yards. Forster, struck by several shots, fell apparently senseless by Philip's side. "Where is your God, Forster, now?" said Lieutenant Bayley with a sneer, as he turned and looked at the prostrate form which lay bleeding on the deck. The wounded man opened his eyes, and turn them full in the face of the lieutenant. "He is here, sir, with me, yes, in the valley of the shadow of death. Oh that He were with you too, sir; it is not too late if you seek Him now."

The lieutenant winced before the earnest gaze of the dying man, and turned away. Philip bent over Forster and tried to staunch the blood which flowed from his wound. "Leave me, lad," he said, "it is all over with me, God bless you; if you see Tom, tell him I'm gone to my home above, and give him my Bible and Hymn-book, which you'll find in my pocket, and if you can read, lad, read them to the poor fellow, for he's no scholar himself."

He could say no more, but with a kindly look at Philip, he heaved a deep sigh, and all was over.

Philip had scarcely been absent three minutes from his post, but the keen eye of Lieutenant Bayley had observed him. Just as the poor man has breathed his last, and Philip was about to fulfil his last request, and take possession of his Bible and Hymn-book, the lieutenant came up angrily to him, exclaiming, with an oath, "Back to your post instantly, you young vagabond; what are you up to, rifling a dead man's pockets? Thieves and liars as you Methodists are!"

While the lieutenant was speaking, the French vessel poured her last broadside upon the "Redoubtable's" deck, which it strewed with fresh victims, and the return volley from the English following almost instantaneously, the cloud of smoke was so dense that Philip could not see the officer. After securing Forester's Bible and Hymn-book, he was groping his way back to his post, not more than four paces off, when the first object he beheld, so close to him that he must have stumbled over it at the next step, was the lifeless form of Lieutenant Bayley, whose head had been shattered by a cannon ball. At this terrible sight Philip shuddered and started back. "May God have mercy on his soul!" he murmured. How different, he thought, had been the last moments of these two men! But this was no time for reflection, no attention could be paid to the dying or the dead; the contending ships, now close alongside, had grappled with each other, and an obstinate battle, in which Philip had to take part, was proceeding. The English, diminished as were their numbers, were getting the better of their antagonists; many of them had already pressed over the sides into the French ship, when the near approach of the third frigate at last finally decided the issue of the conflict. The "Redoubtable's" drums sounded retreat, and those who had boarded the Frenchman returned to their own decks, a desperate effort being now made to disentangle the vessel from her adversary. Before this could be effected, the third ship had approached sufficiently near to pour a terrible broadside into the already disabled "Redoubtable," while the French sailors from the second vessel, cheered by the timely arrival of their consort, now succeeded in boarding their antagonist, and transferring the battle from their own deck to hers. The captain fell at his post, the majority of the officers had shared his fate. Still the remnant fought on like heroes, still they refused to give up the ship.

Exposed to a double fire, to which she was unable to reply, riddled with ball, masts and yards shattered, canvas and cordage rent and torn, and every effort to plug the shot-holes, through which the water was now pouring, being useless, further resistance must be in vain. The "Redoubtable" was not only sinking, but, as her crew soon discovered, on fire also. In such a condition it was useless for the bravest to prolong the fight, even had they not been contending against six times their number. The captain of the third French ship, who was a humane man, and filled with admiration at the intrepidity of the foe, at last induced the little band to surrender and quit their ship.

The first French vessel had sunk soon after the second had come up. Her crew had taken to the boats, and finally been received on board the third vessel, to which the prisoners and wounded from the "Redoubtable" were now transferred. The second Frenchman was utterly disabled, and it was feared that she would share the fate of her first consort, so well and bravely had the heroic gunners of the "Redoubtable" done their duty.

Philip had stood valiant to the last, but he had not escaped unhurt. He was severely wounded in the arm, and, worn out by exhaustion and loss of blood, was borne fainting to the cock-pit of the French ship.

15

Tom's Story

"Our ship lay tumbling in an angry sea,
Her rudder gone, her mainmast o'er the side;
Her scuppers from the waves' clutch staggering free
Trailed threads of priceless crimson through the tide;
Sail, spars, and shrouds with hostile cannon torn,
We lay awaiting morn."

- J.R. Lowell

Half-an-hour after the conflict had ceased, the gallant "Redoubtable," a mass of flames and smoke, sank beneath the clear blue waters of that tranquil sea, taking with her the remains of many heroes who had fallen in the service of their king and country.

Every effort, meanwhile, was made to save the injured French ship, but though all hands were sent to the pumps, it was at last found necessary to abandon her, and the captain, officer, and crew, together with a large number of wounded men, had to take refuge on board her companion.

The English might well claim the victory, for out of three antagonists they had sunk two, and only yielded at the last moment, when weakened and disabled, to superior numbers.

The French vessel was fearfully overcrowded, and as English cruisers might anywhere be met with in those seas, it was necessary that she should without delay make for a friendly port, or join a large French squadron known to be about in those waters.

When Philip revived, he found himself in almost complete darkness. On raising himself upon his elbow, his eye fell upon a sad scene. The wounded men, French and English, lay huddled close together beside him in the cockpit of the French vessel. Groans and sighs, too, fell upon his ear. As his eye got more accustomed to the light of the one dim lantern, he recognised two or three comrades, but most of the men near him seemed to be French. Tortured with thirst, and suffering acute pain from his wound, he soon sank back again exhausted. But the events of the day passed vividly before his mind. How terrible were the scenes of carnage which he had witnessed, how many brave comrades had he seen hewn down in all the strength of their manhood! He thought, too, of the good Forster, now nobly he had met his death, and how ready he seemed to answer his Master's call, and – of his enemy, of him who had persecuted and unjustly condemned him to a harsh and cruel punishment – he too had died a brave man's death. Oh! that Forester's solemn words might at the last moment have moved him to make his peace with God. And then he thought of himself – again had God preserved his life and guarded his head in the day of battle, again has He been his "refuge and strength – a very present help in trouble;" he was a prisoner, indeed; he was wounded, suffering, and among strangers and foes; but with life there was hope that he might once more, by God's gracious providence, be restored to his country and his home. He closed his eyes, but he was in too much pain to be able to sleep. Hearing steps soon after, and looking up, he saw two men moving about among the wounded. One of them he recognised as the surgeon of the "Redoubtable." In the darkness he could not quite make out the other, till the doctor approaching to examine his wound he perceived that his attendant was no other than Tom Mariott, poor Forster's great friend. A thrill of joy passed through Philip's heart; here was, indeed, a new instance of God's mercy towards him. His arm was dressed and bound up, and on the surgeon leaving him to attend to another patient, Philip pulled Mariott by the sleeve. "Tom," he said, "don't you know me?" The man bent down and looked into Philip's face. "What, is it you, my lad? thank God, you are alive; I didn't think I'd ever see you again. But can you tell me anything of my friend Bill. I fear he's gone. I've seen nothing of him."

"He is gone, Tom," said Philip; "I was by his side when he fell, and I heard his last words, and received a message from him for you, Tom, as well as these books which I have got in my pocket, but I am too helpless to get them out now."

"Ah! he's gone is he, then; the best friend I ever had in the world. I feared it was so – " Tom could say no more, and the tears rolled down his cheeks.

"Come on," called the surgeon in a harsh tone; "what are you dawdling about there for? I've seen to that chap, and I want you here."

"I mustn't stay, Philip, you see," said Tom, as he tried to stop his tears; "I'll hear more of poor Bill's last hours another time – there's no one but me fit to help the surgeon."

The vessel was much overcrowded, and the little wind there was generally contrary. She made, therefore, but slow progress. Martinique was their destination; here the captain hoped to get rid of his prisoners, as well as the officers and crew belonging to the other French ships.

The English prisoners were few in number compared with their captors, and as most of them were wounded, there was no danger of their showing insubordination or making any attempt to escape. The captain, therefore, who was a generous man and honoured bravery, even in an enemy, allowed them a great deal of liberty, permitting those who were able to leave the cockpit, and enjoy the fresh air on deck. Philip was one of the first to profit by this privilege. He had not been long on deck when he was joined by Mariott, who, sitting down beside him, remarked, "Now, Philip, my duties with the surgeon are over for the next few hours, and I can have a long chat with you, and hear all about poor Bill's death; but you are looking pale, my lad, are you still suffering much?"

"I shall be better now I'm able to get some fresh air, I hope," returned the lad; "that stifling cockpit alone's enough to kill a man, I'm not nearly in so much pain as I was. It will do me a great deal of good to have a talk with you, Tom."

"It's what I've been looking forward to ever since I saw you that morning when I was going round with the surgeon – ah! that was a shock when you told me about poor Bill – though I'd feared the worst ever since the battle, because I couldn't find him anywhere."

Philip now related to Tom Mariott very minutely all the particulars of

Forster's death; he told him, too, how Lieutenant Bayley had been cut down at the same time; then he delivered to Tom the well-worn Bible and Hymn-book, which at his friend's request he had taken from his pocket after his death.

"Well, he's happy now," said Tom, "God grant that we may both meet him some day above – and Lieutenant Bayley gone too, poor man, I'm sorry for him indeed, though I know he bore me no good will, nor you either, Philip."

"Had you known Forster long?" asked Philip.

"We've been a couple of years in the 'Redoubtable' together, and a blessed time it's been for me, Philip."

"Did you know him before you went on board her, Tom?"

"Well, if you like, I'll tell you my story, and how we became acquainted."

"Yes, do, Tom, then I'll tell you mine if you care to hear it."

"I'm sure I shall, Philip, but now for mine. I belong to Devonshire" –

"And I to Cornwall," interrupted Philip.

"You're Cornish, are you? then we both come from the West – well, I was born at Brixham. I daresay you've heard of that town, Philip, for our trawlers are to be found in every port of England, and abroad too – when there's peace. Every man there is a fisherman, we're a hardy lot, there's no doubt of it, too much used to danger, too often out in storms to know what fear means, but we're a rough set too. There's hardly any religion amongst us. When the Methodists first came to preach in the town they were soon driven out of it by having stones and rubbish thrown at them, - they couldn't make much of us, however they persevered, and there was one or two who joined them, and stuck to them too, through thick and thin, and one of them was my friend Bill Forster; but we weren't friends at that time I'm now speaking of. Bill, poor fellow, was much older than I am, twelve or fifteen years I should think, and when he joined the Methodists I was only a boy, and one of the worst and wildest lads in Brixham, and that's saying a good deal. I was up to all sorts of mischief and wickedness. The smugglers, of whom there are a great many in those parts, always used to get me to help them either to watch the coastguard and give them a signal if they were coming, or to look after their goods while they went to fetch more. But I couldn't always be in Brixham; I had to go out trawling like the rest, sometimes in my father's boat, sometimes in that of another man who was looked upon as about the worst character in the place. One Saturday afternoon when we returned to the harbour, after having been out for a week's cruise, we heard a piece of news which only amused me, but made some of my comrades sad and others angry. The pressgang had been at Brixham the day before, and carried off eight of our fellows. Among them was the son of our captain, and wasn't he in a fury about it? Two or three of the men were married, and their wives were left unprovided for; I couldn't help giving a chuckle of delight when I heard that Bill Forster was among the young men who had been pressed. He used to rebuke me, kindly enough always, for my wild ways. Only the Sunday before, as he was going to church with this very Bible in his hand, he had stopped me in the street and asked me to go with him; 'Tom,' he said, 'there's another world after this, I wish you'd think a little more about it.' I turned away from him with an oath, but all the week I couldn't get the words out of my head, and now that I heard he was gone, I thought, well I sha'n't be bothered with him any more. He left an old mother at Brixham, who was quite dependent upon him, and when she heard he had been pressed for a sailor, carried off without being allowed even to say farewell to her, she took on so, poor soul, and fretted so about her William, that though kind neighbours, especially the so-called Methodists, took care that she should want for nothing, she pined away, and in a little more than a year she was carried to the churchyard.

"I still went on in my bad ways, and the older I grew the more wicked I became. Three years after Bill had been carried off, when I was rather over twenty, as seamen were very scarce, we had many visits from pressgangs. I so far had managed to escape, for I wasn't much at home. But one Sunday I was caught. Late in the evening I was with a lot of other fellows as desperate as myself in the public-house; we were the most of us the worse for liquor, when we heard a great noise outside, the door was burst open, and in rushed the fiercest set of ruffians I had ever seen; they were armed with cutlasses and pistols, and far outnumbered us. It was vain to resist, we were all of us gagged and bound, and carried off to their boats, lying between the town and Berry Head; they soon took us on board their corvette at anchor in Torbay. I didn't much care about parting from my relations, for I had very little feeling for anyone except myself, but I regretted my free, wild life, how I should no more be my own master, and must submit to discipline; and I knew well enough how severe that was on board His Majesty's fleet. I trued to escape and swim ashore, but I was only captured again, flogged and put into irons, and I saw that I must give in, but I did with desperate ill-will. We were all taken to Plymouth, where we were distributed among different ships of the navy. I was sent on board the 'Impregnable.' We sailed at once to the Mediterranean. At first I was surly with my messmates, and not over civil to the officers. I often narrowly escaped flogging, but being strong and active, and never having the slightest fear, I won a certain amount of popularity, which, after I became more accustomed to life on board a man-of-war, increased. I was the first in every hazardous enterprise, in every wild prank, whether at sea or on shore. In swearing, drinking, and other vices, none surpassed me. But I seldom got into trouble, my impudence and daring helped me out of many a scrape. I saw a good deal of active service, was in several battles, and once was slightly wounded. For more than two years I served in the 'Impregnable.' We then returned to Plymouth to refit, and shortly after I was transferred to the 'Redoubtable;' here I fell in with my old acquaintance Forster. To me it was anything but a pleasant meeting, for the words which he last said to me at Brixham at once came back to my mind; he, however, was hearty and cordial; he said nothing to offend me, but I learned from the crew that he was what is called a regular Methodist, and that though mocked at and persecuted in every way on account of his religion, he still continued the same – never swore nor drank, and was not afraid of saying a word of warning to those who persisted in leading an evil life. But with all this, he was so much respected by his superiors for his bravery and consistent conduct, that in time he was promoted to be a petty officer. I took precious good care to avoid him as much as possible, and we weren't thrown very much together; when we did meet I defied him by using viler language and worse oaths than ever, loud enough for him to hear. He looked sad, but said nothing. Once or twice indeed my conscience smote me, and I bethought me, why should I annoy a man who had never done me any harm? Well, we cruised about, now to the Baltic, now to the Mediterranean; once or twice we had smart encounters with French ships, and took several prizes. Then we sailed along the coast of Africa, and here an adventure occurred which had a very important influence on my future life. We were short of water; a party was sent on shore in the cutter to explore, and if possible obtain some. Forster was the head of the expedition, and I was told off among the number. We landed all right, seeing no trace of human beings anywhere. Through tangled bush-wood we penetrated some way into the interior, where we at last discovered a stream of excellent water, with which we filled our barrels; our object being now accomplished; we retraced our steps to the shore. When from a height we had to climb we came in sight of the coast, we perceived that our boat was waiting for us at some distance from the shore, and was no longer in the creek, where we had left her. We did not understand the meaning of this, till we looked again and saw the shore black with savages, who evidently had come down during our absence and tried to capture our boat. Thus our retreat was intercepted, and to regain our boat we must cut our way through this crowd of natives. We halted to take counsel. Some thought that if we waited the natives would disperse; others that more would probably arrive, and that the sooner we fought our way to the coast the better. We signalled to the two men we had left in the boat that we were coming. Meanwhile our danger had been observed by our mates on board the frigate, and we perceived two boats making towards the shore. Forster put himself at our head. 'Come on, my men,' he said; 'we shall have sharp work enough. May God protect us, and bring us safe through!' Fortunately we had our muskets with us, so when near enough we fired a volley at the enemy, which threw them into confusion for the moment, and enabled us by the use of our cutlasses to pass right through the crowd. Showers of arrows fell upon us, happily they were not poisoned; but many of our men were wounded by them, and when we reached the shore, a desperate hand-to-hand fight with these savage niggers took place. Of course we were better armed, but they so terribly outnumbered us that we couldn't fail to suffer. Many of our party had succeeded in getting through the shallow water to the boats, still we had some way to wade up to them, and not all the men could swim. I was the last. I never had to fight so desperate in all my life. Strong and active as I was, I felt that the savages were too many for me. I was bleeding in a hundred places from their arrows. The blows from their clubs fell like rain upon me. I saw my companions plunging into the water, and getting into the boats which I could not reach. I felt sick and dizzy. At last I stumbled, and fell to the ground at the very feet of a savage bigger and stronger than the rest, who with uplifted club was about to dash my brains out, when suddenly Forster, who was just making for the boat, observed my danger, rushed back, and with a desperate blow from his strong arm felled my assailant to the earth. 'Back, my lads,' he cried; 'here's Tom half slaughtered by the niggers. You won't leave a brave comrade to perish, I'm sure.' Immediately five or six of our fellows darted back, hewing down the natives on either side, and I, more dead than alive, was dragged by Forster and another man into the nearest boat. When we got on board the 'Redoubtable' again, and our wounds were examined by the surgeon, he thought my case was more serious than any; but next day three of my mates, whose wounds at first hadn't bee thought so bad as mine, died, but still I lived on. Forster, whenever he could get away from his duty, was at my side; no woman could have nursed me more tenderly than he did. He put up with all my fretfulness and ill-temper, and did all he could to cheer me. At first I didn't like him near me. He had saved my life I knew, I couldn't help feeling grateful to him for that; but, on the other hand, I was under an obligation to him now, and that vexed me very much. My constitution was naturally so strong that I gradually got better, and had time to reflect seriously on Forster's conduct to me, and on mine to him. I began to feel really ashamed of myself. What motive but a good one could he have had in trying to induce me to forsake a manner of life which he held would lead me to ruin? For this I hated him, mocked him, and turned on others to do the same. And now he had not only saved my life, but he came down day after day into the stifling cockpit to nurse me, and try to cheer me, surly as I was, scarcely ever greeting him with a grateful word. Such thoughts as these were in my mind when one day Forster came up to me.

'"Tom,' he said, 'you're looking much better to-day. You'll soon get over the mischief the niggers did you. I'm sure I never thought I should see you able to move about again.'

'"Well, Bill,' I said in a much pleasanter tone than I had ever used to him before, 'there were no bones broken in my case, only cuts and bruises; but it's all thanks to you that I'm here now – indeed, that I'm alive at all. You not only saved my life when those black brutes were just about to put an end to me, but you've helped to keep me alive since by all your kindness, sitting with me, and giving me drink when I was thirsty, and trying to keep up my spirits. I've been an ungrateful dog, I know, Bill, but I'll try to make up to you for it now.'

"I shall never forget the happy expression of surprise and pleasure which passed over Forester's face, and shone forth from his eyes as I spoke these words.

"'I'm sure I've been glad enough to help you, Tom, as much as I could in my poor way,' he replied; 'it's what we ought all to do for each other in trouble, especially if we're fellow-townsmen, as you and I are. You'd have done the same for me, I know.'

"I was silent, for I didn't feel at all certain that I should. Hitherto I had hated Forster, and now that my feelings with regard to him were beginning to change, I was ashamed for my former conduct. I was never so thoroughly base that I hadn't generous impulses now and then, and I had done kind acts to my shipmates occasionally; but I don't think I would have gone out of my way to give Forster a helping hand.

"'You've had a bad time of it, Tom,' Forster continued; 'but now you're able to get about a little, you won't find it so dull as it's been for you down below.'

"'No,' I said, 'and I hope I'll not forget what you've done for me, Bill. I know I've behaved very badly to you ever since I came aboard this ship. You have meant me well, I am sure. I can't understand why you should have given yourself so much trouble about me, trying to bring me to your way of thinking, and warning me of the consequences of my own bad ways. You never have got anything in return from me and the other chaps but scoffs and oaths and hard names. Why do you persevere so, Bill? Why don't you leave us alone, and keep your religion to yourself?'

"'Just for the same reason, Tom,' he replied, 'that I wouldn't leave you to be beaten to death by the savages. I can't see you or others of my shipmates wounded by sin and enslaved by the devil, without putting out a helping hand to rescue them. I know your evil courses and bad ways will lead you to ruin at last, and because I know this I feel I should be a coward if I didn't do my best to try and save you. The scoffs and sneers and surly answers I get in reply may make me sad, but they do me no harm. God has had mercy on me, He has given His Son to die for me, and should not I, in return for His love, have pity on my brethren, and do all I can to persuade them to accept that great salvation so freely offered to all?'

"I was much struck by Forster's words. I had not looked at the matter in that light before. 'Now I see that you did it all for a good motive, Bill,' I replied; 'and you acted so bravely in that terrible skirmish with the niggers, that I shall never say again, as most of us do, that Methodists are cowards, and never make good sailors or soldiers.'

"'I know that's what folks say,' said Forster with a smile, 'but if you come to think of it, Tom, you will see what a mistake it is. A man who strives with all his might to lead a godly life, who loves God and trust in Him, who repents of his sins and knows that they are pardoned through the blood of his Saviour, must go into the battle with far more courage and confidence than one who has never thought of entering things at all, and to whom, should he fall, the future life – which comes after death – is all dark and uncertain.'

"'Yes, Bill,' I said after a pause, 'I felt that when I was struggling there among the savages. Death stared me in the face; I thought what will come after? I knew I was not ready to die.'

"'God was very merciful to you, you see, Tom' for He spared your life, and has given you time for repentance and amendment. Profit by this warning, then, you may not have another. O Tom! I have by His mercy been the means of saving your life, let me help you to save your soul!'

"'The tears ran down his cheeks, and I could not restrain mine. I was still very weak form the effects of my wounds, and was therefore more susceptible than I should have been under ordinary circumstances to Forster's warnings and entreaties. Just at that moment he was called away, and it was some days before we had any talk alone again. I rapidly recovered, but, thank God, as I grew stronger I became more and more convinced that I had been leading a wicked life, and more determined to change it. Of course when my messmates perceived what an alteration there was in me, I had to endure mockery and persecution of every kind; now and then, too, I was led into sin, passion overcame me, and I would break out into oaths and curses, to the no little delight of my ungodly comrades. I didn't all of a sudden become as good as Forster – alas! No, I shall never be like him – but he was always ready to comfort and encourage me. Sometimes after I had fallen into grievous sin, I would despair altogether, then Forster would talk with me, and read to me out of his Bible and Hymn-book, and pray with me too, if we could get a chance, down below somewhere, when no one was near, and so by the help of God's Spirit I gradually began to love my Saviour and to lead a more Christian life. This happened more than two years ago; ever since, Forster and I have been firm friends; we've stuck to each other through thick and thin, and now he's gone, and our ship's gone too, and my future is dark enough. Ah, my heart sinks within me when I think how sad and lonely I shall be without my friend!'"

Tom's voice had often been very husky as he told his story, but at the close the tears started to his eyes. Philip, too, was deeply moved as he listened to Tom's simple tale. When he could speak he said –

"Well, Tom, I thank you very much for telling me your history; we have indeed both suffered a great loss in Forster, but how thankful I am that I was with him when he fell, and able to receive his last message to you. Ah, Tom, we mustn't grieve for him, he's happy now, he is with the Master he so well and nobly served. God grant that our last end may be like his."

"Amen," said, Tom earnestly; "and here are his books he valued so, and out of which he used to read to me, and I, alas! can't read a word."

"Can't you, indeed Tom?" said Philip; "but I can, so I'll read to you whenever we get a chance, as Forster asked me to do."

"Just now you could often manage it; we sha'n't be molested much here; the Frenchmen can't understand us, and our few messmates are not likely to interfere with us. But now, Philip, I want to hear your story."

"So you shall, Tom," said Philip, and he began to relate his whole history, which greatly interested his companion.

"And so you were pressed too!" he said at the end. "What a wonderfully good parson that must be, down your way!"

Ah, that he is," said Philip; "this is the Testament he gave me that Sunday when I was dragged away from my home. God grant that I may see him one day again. It's he that taught me the right way, he and my good mother that's gone. He's such a brave gentleman too, he does not care for any man, and he's enough to put up with from our chaps at Sennen."

"Pity those who mock him ain't like him, I'm sure!" said Tom.

Their conversation was now interrupted by the "Redoubtable's" surgeon, who called Tom to help him to attend to the wounded below. But he and Philip were often together afterwards. The latter was able to read to Tom out of his friend's Bible and Hymn-book. They had plenty of leisure time, and were rarely interfered with. Philip's arm rapidly healed. His heart was full of gratitude to God, who had not only saved his life in the terrible battle, but who had also granted him a companion of like mind with himself, so that they were able mutually to cheer and encourage each other in leading a godly life.

Contrary winds and calms continued to impede the French ship, so that it was not till ten days after the battle that she anchored in the roads of Martinique. Here the prisoners were landed, and here we must leave Philip and his friend for the present, and return to Cornwall.

16

The Light Burns Again

"Said one – she was the elder child,
And older yet in all her ways,
She was so motherly and mild,
So meekly wise beyond her days –
'O'er sea or land I'll never roam
While father wants his maid at home.'"

- Rev. S.J. Stone

Arthur Pendrean was still indefatigable in his exertions to find a lighthouse-keeper. But hitherto no success had crowned his efforts, for a month all had been darkness; the lighthouse indeed stood firm and immovable as the rock on which it was built, but so long as no friendly light shed its warning rays over the sea around, it was practically useless. There had been much stormy weather and several wrecks. The Sennen men had profited by them; one vessel, it was said, had been lured by them on to the rocks, by the false lights they had displayed along the shore. All hands had perished, but much plunder had been washed on shore. For the next few days drunkenness and riot reigned at the cove, and in the village, for it was always the gold from the wreck which paid for the cursed abuse of drink.

Owen frequently had implored the parson to allow him to go and live in the lighthouse alone. But in this Arthur remained inflexible. Jordan's example was always before his eyes. A few days after the storm which had caused so much mischief, Arthur called at Tresilian's cottage; he had gone out fishing, but Mary was there to welcome the parson. He sat down by the fireside and talked kindly to her, asking about her father, if he was in better spirits now, and if he had made much by fishing lately.

"Oh, sir," she said, "father does take on so about the lighthouse, he scarcely talks of anything else. He wants to go and live there all alone, and keep the lamps burning to prevent there being wrecks. After that shipwreck last week, when so many poor fellows were drowned, father did mope terribly; he said he must go; if he had only been there then, they might all have been saved."

"Yes, I know, Mary, he is willing and anxious to sacrifice himself, and go and live in that desolate rock, but I will never consent to him or anyone else going there alone. I've been there myself, and I know what it is," said Arthur.

"But, sir, why should he go alone?" said Mary decidedly. "Why can't I go with him? I'm not afraid to live in a lighthouse, or anywhere else, if my father's with me. I hope you won't let him go alone, sir, for it would break my heart to be separated from him; but why we shouldn't live together in the lighthouse, and be quite happy there, I can't see."

"I fear it could never be, Mary," said the parson. "A lighthouse is not a place for a child like you; days, weeks would pass away without you being able to go on shore and get fresh provisions. You'd have to live on poor fare there, Mary; and suppose you or your father should be unwell, what help could you get? to say nothing of the fearful noise there always is there, enough to frighten you out of your wits. You know the story of poor Jordan, Mary."

"Oh, sir, I should never be frightened, if my father was with me; and as to the noise, it's only the sea roaring underneath the rock. Jordan was afraid because he didn't know what it was; he thought it was ghosts, but you have taught me not to be afraid of such things, so it wouldn't matter to me."

"Ah, Mary, you little know what life in a lighthouse is like – now if your brother Philip were at home it would be a different thing, he might well go and live out there with your father."

"Poor, dear Phil," said Mary with a sigh, "I wonder if we shall ever see or hear anything of him again. What a long time it seems since he was so cruelly dragged away from us."

"I don't despair, Mary. I never forget him in my prayers – neither do you, I am sure. I have not seen his name in any list of the killed. God, I know, is watching over him wherever he is, and I hope some day to welcome him home safe and well."

"I wish father thought so, sir; he looks upon him as quite lost to us for ever."

Just at that moment Tresilian entered the cottage. He looked worn and sad, but he warmly greeted the clergyman, his face brightening when he recognised him.

"I am very glad to see you, sir," he said; "I want to talk to you about the lighthouse again. With all the mischief that has been going on the last few weeks, surely you'll consent now and let me go, so, won't you?"

"It's a difficult question, Owen, and very hard to decide upon. I have indeed felt keenly the loss of life which has occurred latterly, which might have been avoided had we only had a light on the Longships; but I can't send you there alone, I feel it would not be right."

"But, sir," said Owen eagerly, "isn't it better that one man should expose himself to a slight risk to save hundreds from perishing? I'm not a bit afraid to go to the lighthouse alone, as I've often told you, and in time I've no doubt you'll find someone to keep me company."

"If you go I shall go with you, father," said Mary. "Won't that be better, sir, than that he should go there all alone?"

"Nonsense, child," said Owen, "that can never be. If I go the parson'll find some comfortable berth for you."

"Though it's not the place for a child like her, Owen, I'd rather she went with you than you went alone," said Arthur thoughtfully.

"There, father, I knew the parson would say so; we'll both go and live in the lighthouse then. I'll help you to light the lamps, and there'll be no wrecks after that, I'm sure."

"It's all very well for you to talk, child, but you know nothing about life in a lighthouse; you'd soon have enough of it, I'm sure," said Owen.

"Only let me try, father," implored Mary, "just for a month, and then if all doesn't go well, and you don't like to have me, I promise you I'll come back and go wherever the parson likes to send me, though it will break my heart, I know."

"You're a dear, good child, Mary," said Owen as he kissed her affectionately, "and I'm sure I can't bear the thought of being separated from you; but if it's my duty to go to the lighthouse, go I must, and I don't like the idea of taking you there for ever so short a time."

"Well, Owen," said Arthur, "I would not myself propose that Mary should go and live at the lighthouse. I see much to object to in her plan; but, on the other hand, it is far better that she should go with you than that you should go alone, and if nothing else can be done, and you consent, I would not forbid her trying it for a month."

"Thank you, sir, thank you," said Mary, jumping up from her seat. "Now, father, you'll let me go with you," and she put her arms coaxingly round his neck.

"I don't like it at all, Mary; no good'll come of it, I fear. I must think the matter over till to-morrow, before I make up my mind altogether."

"Very well, Owen," said the clergyman, "I'll look in again to-morrow and hear the results of your consideration. I fear there's no chance of my finding any one else to join you, I have been trying long enough now without any success."

"Ah, I wish you could, sir," said Owen, "because that would settle the matter."

The clergyman now took leave of Tresilian and his daughter. As he rode home he meditated on Mary's plan. That she should be willing to go proved what a brave and affectionate heart the little maiden possessed. But what a hard, dreary life it would be for a child of such tender age. He feared lest her health might suffer from the extreme cold, as well as from the constant storms which shook the lighthouse. However, as nothing else could be done, and it was important that the light should again shine forth from the Longships, he was willing to consent that that the trial should be made, if Owen saw his way to agree to it.

That evening, as they sat by the fireside, Owen mending his nets, and Mary reading to him out of the big family Bible, or from the "Pilgrim's Progress" which the parson had lately given her, both father and daughter were thinking about the lighthouse. A hard struggle was going on in the mind of the former, a struggle between love and duty. Mary was his greatest, his only treasure on earth. His wife had been born to the silent grave; his son, of whom he had been so proud, had been ruthlessly torn from him, and he could not endure the thought of exposing his beloved daughter to any peril. To shield her from danger, to do all to make her happy, was the greatest object of his life, and to take her to live in that dreadful lighthouse, on that lonely storm-beaten rock, out of the reach of help, in case of need, from any human being, was exposing her to terrible risks, from which he instinctively shrank. On the other hand, he was not allowed to go there alone, no one else could be found to accompany him; so long, too, as the lamps were unlighted, gallant ships would continue to be dashed on the merciless rocks and brave lives to be sacrificed, whilst the wicked and unprincipled wreckers who dwelt round the coast would successfully ply their evil trade. Was it not, then, his duty to go? Would not God watch over and protect his little daughter on the lonely rock out yonder as He had done in their snug little cottage on shore? Plainly there was no other way out of the difficulty. It was the stormiest and darkest period of the year – the middle of December – each day's delay might involve a sacrifice of life and property.

Mary had finished reading, and had taken up her needlework, when Owen, silently gazing into the fire, remarked, "Are you still bent on going to the lighthouse, Mary?"

"Yes, father," she replied cheerfully; "you'll let me, won't you?"

"Well, child, I've been thinking the matter over ever since the parson was here, and though I don't like the thought of it, yet as nothing else can be done just now, it seems as if it must be; just for a time, Mary – remember only for a time – till we find some one else, some man to keep me company."

"Oh, there's a good father!" cried Mary delighted; "I knew you'd let me go at last, and we'll be so happy together, and save every so many vessels from being shipwrecked," and she threw her arms round her father's neck.

"Ah, Mary, it won't be the pleasant life you think," said her father sadly "you'll repent it ere long, I know."

"Never fear that, father; if you're with me I sha'n't be afraid, and we'll take the Bible out there and the 'Pilgrim's Progress.' But what shall we do on Sunday? I never thought of that – we shall never be able to go to church all the time we're out there."

"There, Mary, you see you've already found out one happiness you must give up, if you go; it'll not be long before you find a great many more," said Owen.

"Well, it's very sad, certainly, that we can't go to church," replied Mary; "but God will be with us, all the same, out on the rock. We must read the prayers together every Sunday, I suppose, and the lessons and psalms, and make the best of it we can."

And thus Owen and his daughter talked the project over. Now that the father had reluctantly given his consent, he was anxious that no time should be lost in taking up their abode in the lighthouse. Next morning, Arthur called at the cottage. Owen told him his resolve, but he could not conceal from the parson how much he dreaded the risk to which he feared he was exposing his child.

"I can well enter into your anxieties, my good Owen," said Arthur; "in fact, I share them all, but I trust in our gracious Father above; it is clearly His will that you both should go; I know He will protect you, and that He will be to you both a Refuge from the storm and a Covert from the tempest. You and Mary will sadly miss the church privileges you have had on shore, our Sunday services in church, our meetings now and then for reading God's Word, and prayer, but you'll have your Bible and Prayer-book with you, and you can keep Sunday in the lighthouse, and think of us in church, remembering you in our prayers, and perhaps some day when it is quite calm I may be able to come out and pay you a visit."

"Ah! that would be nice, sir," said Mary; "how glad we shall be to see you."

"I'm thinking, sir, the sooner we go the better," said Owen; "the weather is unusually calm for the time of year, and we can well be ready to leave the day after to-morrow. It'll be hard parting from the old home. And what's to be done with our cottage, sir?"

"It shall be well taken care of till you come back again, Owen, for I hope ere long you'll be relieved from your post, and that I may get some one else to fill it. I am looking out now for a berth for a poor widow; so I'll put her into your cottage to take care of it while you're at the lighthouse."

"Thank you, sir," said Owen; "that'll be one trouble off my mind; but we shall have to take a good many things with us; I want my Mary to be as comfortable as possible out there."

"All right, Owen," replied Arthur; "we'll see to that, and you must be well stocked with provisions, too, of all kinds, plenty of coals and wood to keep yourselves warm; of course, whenever we can, we'll send you out fresh meat, and if you take flour with you, I suppose Mary can make bread if necessary."

"Oh yes, sir," said Mary; "ever since poor mother died I've done that. I can cook too, in the lighthouse, I hope as well as in our cottage."

"Hadn't we better go out to-morrow and take some of the stores, sir," said Owen, "and overhaul the lighthouse to see that all's right there?"

"Yes," said Arthur; "and I'll go with you. I want to see how the new work done to repair the damage caused by the gale, in which poor Jordan was caught, has stood; you mustn't go to live there till all is made as tight and comfortable as possible."

"Shall we start at eight o'clock to-morrow, sir? the tide'll suit very well then."

"Yes! I'll be ready, Owen; you ask Abbott to go with us, and I'll ride round by the preventive station, and get a couple of men to join us."

"There'll be a precious row among the men at the Cove when they hear the light is to burn again on the Longships, sir; they've always boasted that you were dead beat, and that you'd never get any one to go out there again."

"Never mind, Owen, they can't do us any harm; they'll be much put out, doubtless, for since the light has ceased shining they have made a lot of money by their deeds of darkness."

The calm weather continued during the night, and early next morning two boats were launched ready to sail for the Longships.

"What are they up to now?" said Nichols to his nephew as they strolled together down the beach and perceived Owen, Abbott, and the two preventive men getting the boats ready.

"Some mischief," replied Bill, "for here comes the parson riding down to the shore."

"They've never found anybody, surely, to go and live in that cursed lighthouse," said Nichols.

"It looks like it," replied his nephew; "where else could the parson be going to?"

"That's it, you may be sure," said Ben Pollard, who came up at that moment; "the parson's regularly got hold of that fool of a fellow, Abbott, and can twist him round his finger almost as easily as he does Tresilian. They've got stores of provisions in one of them boats, so you may be certain where they're agoing to."

"Yes, Ben; but who's going to live there? it would surely have got wind among us, somehow or other, if the parson had found any one to take Jordan's place. It can't be that Tresilian, surely."

"Not alone, John, certainly, for the parson vowed after that Jordan was so nearly made crazy, that no one should ever liver there alone, but it's possible he's found some stupid chap to join Tresilian. Well, I wouldn't be in his shoes."

"At any rate, it's a bad lookout for us, Ben," said Nichols; "the only comfort is, it can't last long, the lamp's get put out as they were before."

Meanwhile, both the boats had pushed off from the shore; they reached the rock and landed on it without any difficulty. Everything was found to be in repair – the cupola had not been in the least damaged by the recent gales, and no water seemed to have come in. The provisions and coals they had brought with them were safely deposited in the storeroom below the building. Owen could not help sighing as he glanced round the gloomy chamber in which his dear little daughter was to sojourn.

"It does look dreary, Owen," said Arthur; "I half repent that I gave way to the child's fancy, but it sha'n't be for long, I promise you; I won't rest till I find another lighthouse-keeper – at last I'm sure I must succeed."

"I hope you will, sir," said Owen, "for I feel it ain't at all the place for my Mary; but you'll send some one to us in a day or two, I daresay, to see how we're getting on, so that I may have a chance of sending the child ashore, if need be."

"Never fear that, Owen, I shall be too anxious to hear of you both to lose any chance of communicating with you."

The two boats reached Sennen Cove on their return early in the afternoon. Next morning it was settled that they should start for the lighthouse at the same hour, taking with them the remainder of the stores required, as well as some furniture from Owen's cottage, to make the living room of the lighthouse look a little more comfortable and cheerful. The parson and the other men were then to return leaving Tresilian and his daughter in their new abode.

All the afternoon Mary and her father were busy making their preparations for an early departure the next morning. Their cooking utensils, as well as a good supply of blankets and warm clothes, were put up, the large family Bible, the Prayer-book, Hymn-book, and "Pilgrim's Progress" not being forgotten by Mary, and a long discussion took place between her and her father as to whether the large tabby cat who constantly sat purring before the fire, and added not a little to the comfortable look of the cottage, should be left behind, for Mrs. Beavis, the new tenant, to take care of, or should accompany them to the lighthouse. Mary, who was more anxious for the cat's comfort than her own, suggested that she would prefer to remain, for it would be impossible to provider her with milk, while it was most unlikely that any mice were to be had in the lighthouse. Owen, on the other hand, though the animal would be an amusement to his daughter, so it was at last decided that puss, too, was to be of the party.

The next morning was bright and frosty. Owen was early down on the beach, when the same party soon assembled as on the previous day; and very eagerly were they watched by a group of Sennen men, among whom Nichols and Pollard were conspicuous. The riddle they knew would now be solved, and they would see how the new lighthouse-keeper was. When they saw Mary lifted into one of the boats, while furniture and household good were put into the other, they guessed at once that she was to be Owen's sole companion on the lonely rock.

"Well," said Pollard, "I never should have thought it; - the idea of sending that child to live out in a lighthouse; - the parson must be hard up indeed!"

"Well, this is a joke!" said Nichols with an oath; "I was right about Tresilian going there, you see; oh, that'll soon come to an end, - the girl'll never stand it; they'll soon be back again, and all the better for us."

A burst of derisive laughter rose from the men when, after Arthur had jumped on board, the boats put off from the shore.

"It doesn't please them, you see, sir," said Owen; "I told you what a rage they'd be in; from their way they evidently think that this experiment will be another failure, and that the lamps won't b urn for long in the lighthouse."

"There's no doubt that's what they wish, Owen," said Arthur; "let us hope their wishes will not be realised."

Mary greatly enjoyed the voyage. They safely reached the rock, when she, the cat, and all her little property, were successfully landed. She followed the parson and her father up the narrow staircase which led to the apartment designed, for the present, to be her home.

"Well, it is a queer place, father," she said; "the walls look so bare and rough, and the room quite round, too! How dark it is; such a very small window; we shall have to burn plenty of oil – sha'n't we?"

"Yes, it is a dark room, Mary, there's no mistake," said Arthur; "I've spent three or four days in it, so I know what it is; you must try and make the best of it, however. Come now, we'll go up and look at the lantern."

They mounted into the cupola, where the parson showed Owen how the lamps were lighted and regulated.

"I like this place best," said Mary; "I shall often come and sit up here – such a fine lookout over the sea, and there's the Land's End looking so close and the cottages along the cliff."

"In a storm you won't find it such a pleasant place, child," said her father.

They returned to the room below, were the fire which they had lighted was now burning brightly, and making the place look more cheerful.

"I suppose you must be going soon, sir," said Owen to the parson. "You won't forget us, I'm sure."

"No, that I won't, Owen," returned Arthur; "and whatever betide, I am sure our gracious Father above, into Whose holy and all-powerful keeping I have committed you both, will never forget or forsake you. Tempests may rage and seas swell around, still He will ever be near to guard and watch over you. In the path of duty and self-denial which He made so plain before you, in the noble work of helping to save the lives of your fellow-men, which you have so bravely chosen to perform, He will, in His own good time and way, give you a blessing. Has He not said, 'Inasmuch as ye have done unto one of the least of these, My brethren, ye have done it unto Me'?"

"Well, I trust we shall do some good, sir," said Owen, "and so long as God gives us health and strength we mustn't mind putting up with little discomforts, and feeling rather lonely. We'll make the best of it; won't we, Mary?"

"Yes, father, that we will," Mary replied hopefully.

Arthur now took his Bible out of his pocket, and they all sat round the fire while he read the 107th Psalm. Then they knelt down, and the clergyman offered up a short prayer, in which he commended Owen and his daughter to the ever-watchful care of the Almighty.

When they rose from their knees it was time for Arthur to go. Owen and his daughter accompanied him to the landing-place, where the other men were waiting in the boats. "Good-bye, Mary," he said to her cheerfully. "I'll try to come over to see you again before long; and mind you don't let your father get into low spirits. Keep the lights burning, Owen," he added, grasping his hand; "when we look at them we shall think of you and Mary. God bless you both!"

He jumped into the boat. The men pulled immediately off from the rock. Owen and his daughter went up to the cupola and watched them till they turned the point, and were hid from their eyes. For the first time they seemed to realise how completely they were isolated from the world.

They set busily to work, however, arranging their furniture and making the place as comfortable as possible. Puss was very restless and unhappy; she did not easily adapt herself to her novel situation – even Mary's caresses failing to make her feel at home. Then Owen had his lamps to trim and polish, while Mary prepared her father's dinner, as she had been used to do at home. This she managed very cleverly, and at its conclusion Owen smoked his pipe by the fireside.

When it grew dusk, Owen went up to light the lamps, accompanied by Mary. One by one they shone cheerfully forth, till all were kindled, and sent their bright rays across the gloomy waters.

"There, you see, Mary, they're burning once more, thank God!" said Owen. "I hope that nothing'll occur to put them out again."

The sea was still calm, and father and daughter passed a happy evening in their new abode.

"Ah! there burns that cursed light again," said Nichols to Pollard and several others who had accompanied him to the Land's End to see if the parson's new lighthouse-keeper had really succeeded in performing his duties.

"Yes! no mistake about it, John," returned Pollard. "Well, for the present, I suppose, business'll be slack enough with us."

"It's a bad job, indeed," said another man – "a poor lookout for us this winter."

"Trust me. I'll be a match for 'em somehow or other," said Nichols with an oath; "I've got an old grudge against that Tresilian, and I mean to pay him out. As to that parson, you all know what I think of him."

"Well, John, there's many a chap here'll be glad enough to help you," said Pollard.

17

Christmas

"It came upon the midnight air,
That glorious song of old,
From angels bending near the earth
To touch their harps of gold.
'Peace to the earth, good will to men,
From Heaven's all gracious King,'
The world in solemn stillness lay
To hear the angels sing."

- E.H. Sears

"The bells – the bells – the Christmas bells,
How merrily they ring!
As if they felt the joy they tell
To every human thing.
The silvery tones o'er vale and hill
Are swelling soft and clear,
As wave on wave the tide of sound
Fills the bright atmosphere."

- J.W. Brown

Regularly every evening did the lantern on the Longships send forth its friendly rays over the dark ocean.

Arthur gazed at it with pleasure and thankfulness; the evil men of Sennen, whose dishonest and cruel schemes it arrested, beheld it with increasing hatred and disgust.

Mary and her father, who both felt it dull and lonely at first, in about a week's time began to get accustomed to their new life. The confinement, indeed, was irksome to both of them; the only exercise they could get was running up and down the spiral staircase of the building, walking round the lantern, or pacing the very small platform at the base of the lighthouse, which latter exercise could only be done on a calm day, and at low tide.

Hitherto the weather had favoured them. There had been no storms, though a fresh breeze now and then considerably ruffled the sea. But the surf was not too heavy to prevent communication with the shore.

The Christmas festival was close at hand, and Arthur had not forgotten his two friends condemned to spend it on the solitary storm-beaten rock, far away from church and home. On the fourth day after their exile they were visited by a boat rowed by David Abbott and another man who was friendly with the parson. In this Arthur sent them fresh provisions, not forgetting a good Christmas dinner, with plenty of apples and oranges for Mary, as well as friendly messages and hearty good wishes to her and her father.

Christmas Day dawned, the dreariest, coldest day they had as yet experienced in the lighthouse; but Mary kept up a good blazing fire, which made even the bare walls of their chamber look cheerful, and the thoughtful parson had not forgotten to send some branches of holly and laurel, which Owen had hung over the fireplace and round the narrow window and door, so that the little room had quite a Christmas appearance. As the wind was blowing from the eastward, they heard the bells of St. Sennen Church ringing out merrily in honour of the birthday of Him Who came to the earth to save us from sin, and to reconcile us for ever to His Father, and to summon the villagers to join in praising Him for this His inestimable gift.

Mary felt rather sorry that she could not be there when the sounds of the chimes first fell upon her ear. She remembered last Christmas Day when she and her father and Philip had all sat together in church on the bench just under the pulpit, how beautifully the building was decorated with evergreen and holly, how heartily and sweetly the Christmas hymn, "Hark! the herald angels sing," had been sung, and what an interesting sermon the parson had preached on the story of the Babe of Bethlehem, told so simply, and yet in such thrilling language, that it was all quite fresh in her mind now, thought it was a year ago since she had listened to it. But she tried to conquer her regretful longings; her father was with her, so she felt she ought to be happy. She would read the service to him presently, the psalms and hymns that would be sung in church, both morning and afternoon, and the story of our Lord's birth in St. Luke's Gospel.

Though it grew gloomier and gloomier without, a snow-storm coming on so thickly that they could not see the land from the gallery round the cupola, yet the room within looked bright and cheerful, and the blessed words they had read from the holy Book filled their hearts with joyful thoughts and blessed hopes.

"I hope the parson will come and see us before long, father," said Mary; "he said he would."

"I am sure he will, child, if the weather permits," he replied, "but it looks very dirty indeed just now. Though Mr. Arthur wasn't able to come himself, he hasn't forgotten us. What a good dinner he sent us yesterday; you cooked it, too, very well, Mary."

"Yes, indeed, the dear, kind gentleman," said Mary; "whatever should we do without him? Look at all the presents he sent me – books and pictures and oranges and warm clothes for both of us; - everything he can think of to make us comfortable out here."

"Yes, Mary; I never met a man with such a kind heart as Mr. Arthur; and yet how brave and fearless he is! I shall never forget his leaping on the rock that day when we put out to rescue Jordan, and then only to think of his being left alone here with him for three days."

"Yes," said Mary; "and how he tried to drag poor Phil out of the hands of the pressgang!"

"Ah yes! Philip, poor dear boy! shall I ever see him again?" and Owen sank into that melancholy mood which always came over him when his son was mentioned.

"Yes, father, I hope we shall some day," said Mary cheerfully. "Mr. Arthur thinks so; - bad news, he says, travels fast; and if Philip had been drowned or killed in battle, he is sure we should have heard it."

"It may be so, Mary," said her father sadly, "but I'm apt to look at the dark side. Ah! how the wind is getting up. I must go and light the lamps."

The wind was howling, and the waves were beating against the walls of the lighthouse with greater violence than they had done since it had received its present tenants. When her father went up to light the lamps, and Mary was left alone, she could hardly help shuddering as the building rocked and vibrated as each fresh wave dashed against it. How dreadful, she thought, it must be to be quite alone in the lighthouse, as poor Jordan was. With her father, however, she need fear nothing: when he came back, she remarked, "There will be a great gale to-night – won't there father?"

"Yes, my child, there's every appearance of it; there is a good deal of shipping about too, which makes me glad that the lamps burn so clearly."

"What a dreadful noise I hear every now and then from underneath the lighthouse, father!"

"Yes, Mary, that's beginning now; it was these unearthly sounds which frightened poor Jordan so, and turned his hair white in one night."

"But there's nothing really to be afraid of – is there, father?"

"Nothing whatever, child; it's only the air compressed in the caves under the rock; but to any one who doesn't know what it is, it sounds awful indeed."

"And it's getting louder and louder, father."

"It'll be worse, I expect, when the gate gets to its height."

Owen was right, for soon the noise was so loud that they could scarcely hear each other speak. Mary was obliged to give up reading aloud to her father, and study the "Pilgrim's Progress" to herself. When she went to bed, it was long before she could get to sleep.

Owen, anxious about the lamps, and fearing lest the glass of the cupola might be broken by the violence of the waves, sat up all night on the watch. The gale increased in fury till morning, when it seemed somewhat to die away.

On shore, Christmas had been kept with more solemnity and cheerfulness than usual. Arthur, during the previous week, had diligently visited his parishioners from house to house, urging them to come to church on Christmas Day. He had done his best to encourage those who were striving to turn over a new leaf, and had fearlessly rebuked those who still persisted in leading an ungodly life. He had found an opportunity, which he had long been seeking, for saying a few earnest words to Nichols and Pollard separately. Whatever might be the results, he felt that such was his duty; some good, he knew, there must be in every man – some soft spot in the hardest heart. In none could the image of God, in which he was created, be entirely effaced. His interview with Nichols filled him, however, with despondency; the kindest words he repaid with brutal insolence and mockery. It seemed impossible to make the least impression on him. After this rebuff, he had not much heart to encounter Ben Pollard; nevertheless, he must pass his cottage, and he wanted to give some Christmas gifts to his poor, struggling wife and her young family; so if Ben were at home he must speak to him. He opened the door, and there he was, alone, his wife having gone into the village to buy provisions. Ben received the parson in a surly manner, but he was never quite so insolent as Nichols, especially when he was not in his company. When he found, too, that Arthur had come with presents for his wife and children, and that he was going to provide them with a dinner for Christmas Day, of which they sadly stood in need, he softened very much towards the parson. Arthur even ventured to remonstrate with him on his way of life, and tried to point out to him how much happier he and his family would be, if he would only work honestly and steadily, give up smuggling and wrecking, and cease from preferring the village alehouse to his own home.

"It's all very well for you to talk, sir," said Ben, "but it isn't so easy for a man to change his way of life all of a sudden like, even were I disposed to, which I can't say I am. I think you may mean well enough towards me, but there's many who'll never forgive you, sir, for taking the bread out of our mouths by building that ere lighthouse."

"Your bread you could earn honestly, Ben," said the parson, "if you choose to go out fishing regularly, instead of idling about from morning to night. What the lighthouse deprives you of, is ill-gotten gains, wrung from the sufferings, often the deaths, of innocent men, which you no sooner get than you spend in drink."

Ben was about to reply when his wife came in, to whom the parson addressed a few friendly words before leaving the cottage.

Though Christmas Day dawned dull and gloomy, and the sky was overcast with dark clouds, never had the little church of St. Sennen looked so gay and cheerful, for, under the parson's directions, it had been decorated with laurels, evergreen, and bright red hollyberries; the congregation, too, was much larger than was usual on Sundays, and the service was warm and hearty. The Psalms and the Christmas hymns had been well practised during the week, and were therefore sung with more spirit and correctness than generally was the case. The sermon, earnest and simple, as usual, was attentively listened to by the congregation. Arthur, on looking round from the pulpit, observed many faces that he had never seen in church before, and among them, to his astonishment, was that of Ben Pollard, sitting behind a pillar, and accompanied by his wife. He was greatly encouraged at this sight. As the wind howled round the little church, he did not forget his friends in the lighthouse, and offered up a silent prayer that they might be preserved from danger and cheered in their solitude.

When service was over, many of the parishioners lingered in the churchyard to shake hands with the parson, and wish him a happy Christmas. Ben Pollard was not of this number; he felt half ashamed of having been persuaded by his wife to go to church, and was thinking how he should get laughed at by his friend Nichols and several others if it ever reached their ears.

There was no afternoon service, for the parson had to go to St. Levan to say Evensong, and there to preach a short sermon to the few poor folk who assembled in that damp, quaint little church. It had been a happy day for him, and he rode home filled with brighter hopes and more encouraged in his work than he had ever felt before. Many of the men, whose utter insensibility to kindness he had so often deplored, seemed at all events softened towards him; he might have to lament indifference, but rarely had to complain now of mockery and ridicule. He hoped that the good seed which he had so diligently striven to sow was at last about to spring up and bear fruit.

He passed a happy evening with his father; but when he heard the wind howling round the old house, while the snow beat against the window panes, he thought of poor Owen and his little daughter out at the Longships. How gloomy must this Christmas evening appear to them! Such weather, too, he feared, would for some time make it difficult to communicate with them.

About nine o'clock he was informed that a young man dressed like a sailor, was anxiously waiting to see him in the kitchen; he had walked all the way from Plymouth, he said, and seemed exhausted.

Who could it be? Arthur hastened down at once. A lad in sailor dress, drenched with snow and rain, his countenance worn and haggard, stood before him.

"Well, my friend," he said, "you look cold and tired; draw a chair to the fire; you are probably hungry too, you shall have something to eat. I don't seem to know your face. Have I ever seen you before?"

"Yes, sir," said the young man dejectedly; "my name is Evans, Dick Evans. I was pressed for a sailor last spring along with Bob Harris and Philip Tresilian."

"Philip Tresilian! and do you know where he is?" asked the parson eagerly.

"No, sir. I've heard nothing of him since we parted. A few days after we were pressed, we were put on board different ships, he and bob in the 'Royal Sovereign,' and I in the 'Duke of Marborough.'"

"And what has brought you back here now, Dick?"

"Well, sir, I've had a hard time of it; I've been passed from one ship to the other, and in the last one I was in, a corvett, we were shipwrecked on the coast of South America."

"How, then, have you come here, Dick?"

"After spending several weeks on a barren island, I and three of my messmates were picked up by an English merchant vessel, in which we worked our passage home, and were landed last Tuesday at Plymouth, sir."

"Well, Dick, I'm glad to see you safe back after so many dangers and adventures; but what made you come to see me first before going to your old home at Sennen?"

"Why, sir, I wanted, the first thing I did when I came back to these parts, to thank you for words you've said to me, which I never heeded at the time, but only laughed at, but which made me feel afterwards what a bad life I had been leading, so that I hope now, sir, I'm different from what I used to be when you knew me before."

"Thank God for it," said Arthur. "I remember, Dick, that you were a wild fellow enough; you often made my heart ache when I heard one so young swear as you did, and keep company with the wreckers and the worst fellows in the village. How long is it since you were brought to a better mind?"

"Well, it's rather a long story, sir."

"I'll hear it after you've refreshed yourself with a good meal, and dried your wet clothes by the fire. Then you shall come to my study, and tell me all about it. You shall sleep here to-night, Dick; I'll have a bed prepared for you."

"Thank you kindly, sir; I am hungry, there's no mistake, for I've had nothing to eat to-day, as I had no money to pay for food, and I've been walking since seven o'clock this morning."

Arthur having seen that Dick was served with a substantial meal, retired to his study, where he pondered over this singular and unexpected incident. Dick Evans was the very last of all the lads he had known in Sennen parish whom he would have expected to turn to a better mind. It was he who had joined the plot so heartily for getting Philip seized by the pressgang, falling himself into the trap which he had laid for that poor lad, he remembered, now that he had seen him together with Bob in church on the morning of that eventful Sunday, but he had never heard of the motive which brought them there. Truly wonderful and mysterious are the dealings of the Lord; "how unsearchable are His judgments, and His ways past finding out!"

Half-an-hour after, there was a knock at the door, and Dick, looking brighter and refreshed, entered the room.

"Sit down by the fire, my lad," said the parson, "and now let me hear your story."

"Yes, sir, willingly," said Dick; and then he told the parson plainly the part he had taken in the plot to lure Philip into the hands of the pressgang. "But, sir, you see me and Bob fell into the trap ourselves. You must have wondered that morning at seeing us in church; but we bargained with Philip to go if he's consent to come bathing with us in the afternoon. I did my best, I confess, not to listen to what you said; but I couldn't help hearing some things which stuck, as it were, in my heart, so that I couldn't get them out – always coming back again when I least expected them. I was mad with rage at being dragged away from home where I was leading an idle life, and was pretty much my own master. That I knew well enough, I shouldn't be in the Royal Navy. I cursed Nichols and all the fellows who had led me into the plot, and I hated Philip more than ever as the cause of all my trouble. But I wasn't long in his company. As I said, he and Bob were put aboard the 'Royal Sovereign,' and I was sent on the 'Duke of Marlborough,' both vessels belonging to the same squadron. I was very obstinate and sulky at first, and was flogged several times for insubordination. I kept company with the worst and roughest fellows on board. In actions in which I was several times engaged, I was daring and fearless; and though on these occasions I was once or twice commended by my superiors, I longed for my old free life at home, and always meant, had I the chance, to desert; however, we cruised about, and never put into any port. When, after a couple of months, we anchored in Plymouth Sound, a very sharp lookout was kept over the crew. I was then transferred to a small corvette, the 'Tiger,' which was bound for South American waters. Only two of my former messmates went on board the vessel with me. The crew were as rough a lot as those on the 'Duke of Marlborough,' but they just suited me, for, young as I was, I was as bad as any of them, and up to any amount of sin and wickedness. We had a long voyage across the Atlantic, but fair weather, on the whole; when we reached the coast of South America, however, we encountered terrible gales. We were beaten about hither and thither, our ship became disabled, and we could not make for any port in which to refit. One fearful night I shall never forget; the wind, which had been blowing hard all day from the east, rose to a hurricane; we were driven fiercely on the rocky coast, for our disabled corvette was powerless to resist the violence of the gale. Now and then, indeed, by desperate efforts, we got her head to the wind, but we couldn't keep her in that position for long, so that we continued to drift towards the shore; and all on board came to the conclusion that the loss of the vessel, and probably of our lives, was certain. There were the boats, indeed, as a last resource; but when we looked at the raging sea and the size of the huge waves which dashed over our ship, there didn't seem much hope of any boat weathering such a storm. Nevertheless, as we were being driven faster and faster on to the rocks, the captain ordered the boats to be lowered. The first was smashed against our vessel's side before any one could get into it; the second, filled with some of our officers and crew, was swamped within a hundred yards of us; - all hands were drowned – we couldn't save one, though we tried hard. In a few minutes our ship must be dashed upon the rocks. All discipline was at an end. The men, uttering oaths and curses, rushed to the spirit-room to drown their terror in drink, and for the first time in my life I was face to face with death. Somehow or other, I couldn't defy it as the other fellows did. My conscience so long asleep now awoke, and began loudly to accuse me. I thought of the ships I had helped to lure into destruction in my old Cornish home, and now it was my turn to perish. Then I tried to stifle these thoughts by joining in the wild oaths of my messmates, but it was no use. With a violent crash we at last ran upon the rocks, and immediately the ship went to pieces. We were all cast into the cold sea. I managed to seize hold of a plank, and being a good swimmer, succeeded in keeping myself afloat. I had, however, to dodge the waves, and try to hinder myself from being dashed by their fury against the rocks. Before me I could see a line of coast rising in bare and rocky ledges; I hoped to be able to reach this. The cries of my drowning companions rung in my ears; a few only were able to keep their heads above water as I was doing. I felt my strength failing me – should I ever get to the longed-for shore? The words I had heard in my childhood came into my mind now. I remember, too, several things you, sir, said in your sermon that Sunday, when I went to church with Bob and Philip. You said that God was like a loving Father Who never forgot that we were His children, and loved us still, though we were rebellious and disobedient, and never thought of Him; that when we turned to Him and prayed to Him, He would certainly hear us, and come and help us if we were in trouble and distress – but would He listen to one so vile as me, who had always despised and insulted Him, and laughed and mocked at religion? Just when these thoughts were in my mind, and when I was feeling so exhausted, I knew I could bear up no longer, and must allow myself to sink in that raging surf, I felt a footing for the first time. Above me, like a stair of huge steps, rose the black rocks; another stroke and I was able to stand up to my middle in the water. The deep gratitude I felt to God as I gazed up to the dark cliffs towering above me, I cannot describe. Standing in the water as I was, with the waves still dashing against me, in a few words I prayed – really prayed – for the first time in my life. I thanked God for His mercy in saving me from the raging sea; confessed how sinful my life had been, and vowed to amend my ways. Then I clambered up the rocks, and sank utterly exhausted upon the ground. When I came to my senses I saw three or four of my messmates at a sort distance from me; they seemed as weak and faint as I was. When we had a little recovered from our fatigue, we began to explore the country. We could find nothing to eat but the eggs of sea-birds. Some few miles further up we discovered a spring of rather brackish water, and glad we were to slake our burning thirst even with this. We soon came to the conclusion that we were in a desert island, not far, however, from the mainland, the coast of which we saw in the distance. This was a bad lookout for us, for we must starve here unless we were picked up soon. We found shelter in a cave, from the cold wind which blew from the sea. Some provisions, too, were washed on shore from the wreck. We were six in number, all the rest had perished; some of their bodies were washed on shore, and we buried them in the sand. After a week had passed away, and not a sail had been seen, we grew very melancholy and downcast; and when one of our party died of exhaustion from want of proper food, we felt still more low spirited. We had stuck an old flag we had rescued on the highest point of the island, so that passing vessels might know we were here. The weather now was much more favourable, being calm and bright; but another of our men sunk beneath the hardships and privations we had to endure. Our party was now reduced to four – hope was dying out of our hearts. We felt that in our turn we must share the sad fate of our two mates. I did not fear death now, as I had done that day when I struggled for my life amid the waves. It wasn't much I knew about religion; I often wished I knew more; but things came to my remembrance now which had long ago been forgotten – words I heard at the dame school and in church, when I used to go as a little boy, and especially that Sunday when I went with Bob and Philip, and heard you preach there, sir. I felt that I was a great sinner; but I remembered hearing you say that it was for the greatest of sinners that Jesus Christ came to die, and the words which the service began and which I recollected having heard before – 'When the wicked man turneth away from his wickedness, and doeth that which is lawful and right, he shall save his soul alive.' Yes, sir; I was sure that for me, sinner as I was, there was a Saviour, and to Him I turned, asking Him, if it were not His will to save my life, at least to save my soul. I tried now and then to speak to my poor messmates of these things. Two of them mocked and laughed at me, but one listened quietly, and seemed to be comforted by what I said. But I am making my story too long, sir; I must cut in short. After we had lost another of our men, and had well-nigh given up all hope of being saved, one morning we saw a sail; it came nearer and nearer - our flag had been seen. The weather was calm, so they put out a boat and rowed to the shore. How thankful we were to greet our deliverers! The three weeks we had passed on that desolate spot had reduced us three survivors, to skeletons. The vessel that rescued us was a merchant, homeward bound. The captain was a humane man, and treated us very kindly. When we were well enough, as he was short of hands, we worked with a will, for we were all grateful to him for saving our lives. We had a fair wind and a prosperous voyage, and three days ago we anchored in Plymouth Sound. Then I took leave of my mind friend the captain, and came on here at once, determined to seek you out, sir, first, and ask your advice as to my future course. I hope to lead a very different life from what I did when I was in these parts before. Will you help me, sir? I know I shall be laughed and jeered at but I trust God, Who has hitherto helped me will grant me courage to stand it here, as I did on the desert island and on the voyage home."

Arthur had been deeply touched by Dick's story. What a lesson it was to him, never to despair; what a confirmation of the truth of the text, "Cast thy bread upon the waters, and thou shalt find it after many days." How often had he grieved and repined at seeing no fruit of his labours, and said in his heart, like the desponding disciple, "Lord, we have toiled all night, and taken nothing." Here was an encouragement to him to work on more vigorously than ever in that portion of his Lord's vineyard to which he had been called. He warmly grasped the lad's hand, and said –

"Yes, Dick; I will indeed to my best to help you. God, who has begun the good work in you, will, I am sure, not forsake you, but strengthen you by His Holy Spirit manfully to stand up for His cause, and show yourself to be His faithful soldier and servant. To-morrow we will talk further over your affairs; meanwhile, I will reflect as to what is best to be done for you. Now go and get a good night's rest, which I am sure you need."

Dick, who was an orphan, had lived with a drunken uncle at Sennen, but this man had lately left the village; there was therefore no home for Dick to go to. Arthur pondered over the question as to what could be done with the lad, and it suddenly struck him that he might share Owen's duties as lighthouse-keeper. It was, indeed, a gloomy post for a young fellow of his age, but here, at all events, he would be out of temptation, and he need only stay there for a while, till something else was found for him to do. The parson determined to propose this to him next morning.

18

A New Conspiracy

"O conspiracy!
Shams't thou to show thy dangerous brow by night,
When evils are most free? Oh, then by day,
Where wilt thou find a cavern dark enough
To make thy monstrous visage?"

- Shakespeare

That was a rough, stormy Christmas-tide. Though the wind fell somewhat on the morning of St. Stephen's Day, it increased in the afternoon, and rose to a terrible gale in the evening. None felt it more severely than the two lonely dwellers in the lighthouse. All night long the wind howled, while the sea roared and raged, dashing with fury against the granite walls of the building. For the first time since they had removed thither, Mary experienced what a real gale was like on the exposed rock. The noise in the cavern below was awful. The child could only sleep by first and starts, while her father sat up all night to watch, lest any accident should extinguish the lamps. Next day, when the fury of the gale seemed to have spent itself, Mary looked so pale and exhausted that her father was quite anxious about her. "Ah! Mary," he said to her, "I see you'll never be able to stand such a life as this for the whole winter. You don't look at all yourself to-day; and no wonder, after the night we've had."

"Never mind, father," she said, trying to speak more cheerfully; "I'm only a bit tired after such a bad night. What a howling and roaring there was, and how the lighthouse shook when a great wave beat against it! I'm not at all surprised now that Jordan's hair turned white, and that he almost went mad."

"Neither am I," said her father; "but I'm sure this ain't the place for you, child. Next time the boat comes I shall have to send you back in it, and stay here alone for a time."

"No, no, father, you won't; there's not so much wind now, and after a good night's rest I shall be all right again."

There had been no wrecks along the coast during this gale – thanks probably, to the new lighthouse. On Innocent's Day the wind sank, the sun shone out brightly, and there seemed every prospect of a spell of fine weather.

In a couple of days, Mary was as bright and cheerful as ever, and her father said no more about sending her back to Sennen. Before the Christmas week was over, they were gladdened by a visit from the parson. He had a great deal to tell Owen and his daughter. He related his interview with Pollard on Christmas Eve, and described the Christmas services, and how surprised and pleased he had been by Dick Evans' appearance on the evening of that day. Owen listened eagerly to Arthur's account of Dick, but now without many a sigh, for he thought of his own lost son who had been carried off at the same time, and whose fate was still veiled in mystery. "And so he's come back, - Dick Evans! Who'd have thought of such an idle vagabond as he was, becoming so changed?" he said. "And my poor Philip! I often think about him, and pray for him; and what you've been telling me, sir, about this Dick has brought the whole story up to my mind afresh. I wonder if we shall ever see him again in this world?"

"I don't despair of it, Owen. I am all the more hopeful now, since Dick has returned to us," said the parson.

Arthur mentioned to Owen his idea that Dick might share his duties as lighthouse-keeper for a time, and thus relieve Mary. Her father was at first greatly pleased at the proposal, but, on further consideration, he feared lest her health might suffer, even more owing to the grief at separation from him and from the solitude and confinement of her present rough life. Arthur told him there was no need to decide yet, as Dick was laid up ill at the manor-house, and it might be weeks before he was himself again.

As it was a calm bright morning, Arthur suggested that Owen and Mary should take a trip to Sennen Cove in the boat, while he and Abbott remained on the rock till their return. It would be a nice treat for Mary. Owen, too, would be able to have a look at his house and garden, and they need not be absent more than two or three hours.

Mary was overjoyed at this kind proposal. She had been longing for several days to go on shore and see some of her old friends in the village.

Owen at first hesitated; he was afraid lest the weather should change, and the parson be again imprisoned on the rock. He at once raised this as an objection.

"Don't be afraid of that, Owen," said Arthur. "There's every prospect of the weather holding up. It's bright and frosty, the wind north-east, not a cloud in the sky. Come, look sharp, and be off, if the worst comes to the worst, too. I shall have Abbott with me this time, you know."

"Well, sir, it's very kind of you, - and we'll go, then; but I'll take care to be back as soon as possible. It's true I want to go on shore very much for several things; and Mary'll be pleased, I know."

Ten minutes after, Owen and the two other men were pulling heavily at the oars, while Mary, who looked the picture of happiness and contentment, sat at the helm. When they landed at the Cove, some fishing-boats had just come in, and a large quantity of fish was being landed. Several of the men stopped in their work when they perceived Owen and his daughter. Very few gave them a friendly greeting; the majority received them in sullen silence.

"What's brought that fellow Tresilian on shore, I wonder?" said Nichols. "I wish he'd stay here; he did us mischief enough when he was on shore, certainly, but he does more still by keeping that cursed light burning on the rock. Can't we manage to lock him up somewhere, Ben, and keep him here, so that the lamp sha'n't be lighted for a night or two?"

"What a fool you are, John," said Pollard, "to think of such a thing. Don't you see he's left the parson and Abbott out there? They're a precious deal too sharp to leave their lighthouse untenanted for a moment; and if we did kidnap Owen, the parson would stay there till he turned up again, and keep the lights burning as he did before."

"You're right, Ben, I see," replied Nichols. "Still I hope I'll be revenged on the fellow yet."

Owen took no heed of the savage way in which his friendly greetings were met by most of his fellow-villagers. He and Mary proceeded to the cottage, where they found all in good order; the garden, too, was as neat and trim as when they left it. Mary then went up to the village to make a few purchases and see some old friends, while Owen set to work to repair a small punt of his, which he wanted to take out to the rock with him. On fine days he thought he might vary the monotony of his life by going out fishing in this boat close to the rock. It was so small and light hat he would easily be able to drag it up and stow it away in the lower storeroom of the lighthouse; and he would nave no difficulty in launching it himself. To secure this boat, indeed, was one great object he has in coming on shore that day.

Mary had soon executed her commissions and seen her friends. Owen's punt was fastened behind the boat. With a fair wind, they started on their return to the lighthouse; the sail was hoisted, and in a short time they safely reached the rock, when Arthur and Abbott at once prepared to depart. Owen and Mary heartily thanked the parson for giving them the chance of making this pleasant little visit on shore. When he perceived the boat which Owen had brought with him, and when he dragged it up into the storeroom, Arthur remarked, "Don't be rash in going out in that boat, Owen; and never venture far. Think, if a sudden squall came on, and you were capsized, what would poor little Mary do alone here in the lighthouse? I'm rather sorry you've brought it."

"Oh, never fear, sir; it isn't often I shall go out at all, and only in very smooth weather, and certainly never out of sight of the rock. It'll be a great thing for us to get fresh fish now and then; we can't do much in that way with our lines from the rock."

"Well, Owen, remember how frail the punt is, and how suddenly the weather changes; but now I must say goodbye. I shall try and come out again before long."

"Good-bye, sir; God bless you; thank you for your kind visit," said Owen.

"And come again soon, sir," cried Mary, as the parson waved his had to her from the boat.

The stormy weather which had been so prevalent during the winter appeared now to have come to an end, and was succeeded by a calm sea and a hard and long-continued frost. Every morning the sun shone like a red ball of fire through the thick mist in which he rose, and after shining brilliantly through the day would set in the afternoon in gorgeous colours of crimson and gold. Undisturbed by squalls and tempests, the fishermen round the coast plied their trade with success, and the sea all around was studded with the white sails of their smacks. Owen was one of those who profited by this long spell of fine weather. Every day he went out fishing in his little boat, while Mary watched him from the gallery round the lantern. Not only did he catch sufficient to supply food for himself and his daughter, but he was able to sell a good deal to the fishermen he fell in with. One very calm day indeed he had ventured to run his boat on shore just below the Land's End, and sold a good haul of cod he had taken that morning to a group of fishermen there. The lighthouse was not far off, and it was such a clear day that Mary could see him all the time. When he came back half an hour after, he asked her if she had been frightened at his absence.

"Oh no, father," she replied, "I am getting quite accustomed to it now; such fine weather as this there is nothing to fear; and I'm so glad you are able to make a little money by selling the fish. Of course I like to keep you in sight, father, but if it did happen that for an hour or so on a fine day like this I couldn't see you, I don't think I should be very much afraid."

"Never fear, my child," said Owen; "I won't go out of sight if I can help it. I wonder when Mr. Arthur'll come to see us. It's more than ten days since he was last here."

"Yes, I can't think why he doesn't come' he's very busy, I expect," said Mary.

"To-morrow the men will come to bring us fresh provisions, most likely then we shall hear something of him," rejoined Owen.

He was right, for next day Abbott and another man came out to the rock with stores for the lighthouse-keeper, and they brought a message from the parson. He hoped, he said, to be able to pay them a visit next week, must now his time was fully occupied; there were a great many sick in the parish he had to visit. Moreover, Dick Evans had been very ill ever since the night he had arrived at the manor-house, and now he was in such a violent fever that his life was in very great danger.

"The parson is very anxious about the lad," said Abbott; "he doesn't think he'll ever get over it, and he takes it to heart very much. He sits up all night with the poor fellow, trying to soothe him when he's delirious, and it's wonderful how quiet Dick is when he's got the parson by his side."

"Oh, how kind and good Mr. Arthur is," said Mary; "he'll wear himself out, he works so hard. I wish people were more grateful to him than they are."

"Would that they were!" said her father.

They sent word back to the parson how sorry they were not to see him; they hoped Dick would soon be better; as for themselves, they were well and happy, and enjoying this fine weather, which, so long as it lasted, made their residence in the lighthouse quite pleasant.

The more industrious of the population in the villages round the Cornish coast had profited by this favourable weather, and made a good sum by selling the fish which it had enabled them to catch, but to the lazy and evil-disposed, who lived from hand to mouth, and whose real trade was smuggling and wrecking, it was by no means so welcome. The storms indeed which had heralded the approach of winter, when no light shone out from the Longships to guide and warn the homeward-bound mariner, had brought the Sennen wreckers a rich harvest; but all these ill-gotten gains had long since been spent in drink; women and children were famishing; men, gaunt and morose, hung round the alehouse, or lounged upon the beach, uttering curses upon the weather, the lighthouse, or the parson, whichever at the moment seemed to them the cause of their present misery and poverty – never once reflecting that their own evil an idle conduct was alone to blame for it.

March had come with its cold east winds, clear skies, and lengthening days. It was more than a month since a drop of rain had fallen. Such fine weather, all agreed, could not last much longer. Nichols and his nephew were standing on the shore gazing out to sea, on which there was scarcely a ripple; the sun had just set, and the western horizon was a mass of glorious colour. The features of both men bore a sullen and discontented look. At last Nichols turned sharply round, and, followed by his nephew, walked towards the village. A thought seemed to have struck him, and a malicious grin passed over his face as he said to his nephew, "This won't do, Bill; we can't go on much longer like this, but it's a long lane that has no turning. I expect the equinoctial gales will come early this year."

"They won't do us much good, uncle, so long as the lamps burn in that lighthouse," replied Bill.

"But they sha'n't burn any longer, Bill," the elder man exclaimed with an oath, as he stamped his foot on the ground. "As sure as my name's John Nichols I'll devise some plan for ousting that fellow Tresilian from his present nest in spite of all the parsons in the world."

"You'll be clever if you do, uncle. Hasn't the parson always foiled us, always got the better of us at the last?"

"He can't get any one to live in his lighthouse except Owen, you know well enough, Bill. Didn't he scour all the neighbourhood round to find somebody? Why, I know he sent to Plymouth, and even to London, but all to no purpose. I tell you, if it hadn't been for Tresilian, there'd have been no light in the Longships now."

"You're about right there, uncle."

"Yes; and once get rid of Owen, and you put out the lights, for no one knows how long, perhaps for good," said Nichols.

"But how to get rid of him, is the question, uncle."

"Ha! Bill, I've got my plan; but here we are; let's see which of our chaps are to hand."

A few of the worst and most desperate characters of the village were sitting smoking and drinking in the alehouse; among them was our old acquaintance, Ben Pollard.

The two new comers were heartily welcomed, and room was made for them at the table.

"What's the news, John?" said Pollard.

"News! why, that erelong we shall have a change of weather, and equinoctial gales too, if I'm not very much mistaken," said Nichols.

"Your news is too good to be true, John; no such luck for us just yet," returned one of the men.

"And if we did get foul weather," remarked another, "what good would it bring us now? for there's not much chance of wrecks with that light burning night after night in the Longships!"

"Yes, yes, I know," said Nichols, "but with your help, mates, I've made up my mind to put out those lamps."

"You'll never succeed in that, John, and if you did they'd be lighted again the next evening. We should have a nice piece of work to do it, get ourselves into a scrape, and gain nothing in the end," remarked another of the party.

"Wait till you've heard my plan, then perhaps you'll change your minds," said Nichols.

"Come, out with it, then," said they all.

"Well, you know last time Tresilian was ashore here, he fetched away his punt, and I'm told since he's had it out on the rock; he goes out fishing in it every day if the weather's at all fine. He's been known at times, too, to land just close below the Land's End, and sell his fish there to some of our fellows, or to chaps from Penberth. Now, my plan is, that we keep a sharp lookout, and next time he comes ashore we just carry him off by main force, and keep him imprisoned for as long as it pleases us in the smuggler's cave between this and the Land's End. We can make that prison secure enough; the gate has heavy bars and bolts, and no one is likely to pass near it to whom he can call out. Meanwhile, there'll only be the child left on the rock, and most likely she'll die of terror, or go mad like Jordan; anyhow, she won't be able to light the lamps, that's certain—

"But," interrupted one of the men, "if we do this on a fine day like today, it won't do us any good; the parson'll hear directly that the light does not burn; he'll send off at once to the rock, find Owen not there, and move heaven and earth till he discovers him, and when he does, a nice mess we shall be in."

"We must watch our opportunity," said Nichols; "a fine day is often followed by a stormy night. I don't say my plan'll succeed, but it's worth trying. We can't go on like this; we shall starve soon. Nothing ventured, nothing have, I say. Even if we fail, we'd better make the attempt."

"My opinion, John, is, that you'd better leave the matter alone," said Ben Pollard; "no good'll come of it, I warrant; the parson'll get the better of you somehow or other. I'm no friend to Tresilian, you all know well enough, and glad I should be to see the lamps put out on the Longships. But we've already robbed Owen of his son; we've made the poor fellow's life wretched ever since, and as to kidnapping him and shutting him up in a cave for nobody knows how long, and leaving that poor child alone to die of fright in the lighthouse, it seems to me a cowardly plan, and it'll be a long time before I can make up my mind to consent to it."

"That's just what I feel about it," said another man.

"Why, Ben, you're the last chap I should have thought would have taken that view on the matter." Said Nichols angrily; "you and I have hitherto always stood together, what's changed you now?"

"I'm not changed, John, but I don't like your plan; you've got no children of your own, so you can't feel as Charley and I do, and it's what may happen to the girl all alone in the lighthouse sets me against your designs."

Nichols was bitterly disappointed and vexed at meeting with opposition in so unexpected a quarter. Nevertheless, most of the men were in favour of his plan, though they considered it too rash to ensure success. Still they were so desperate, and times were so bad, that they felt inclined to risk anything to better their condition; Nichols hoped, too, that when he got Ben alone, he would be able to talk him over to his way of thinking. It was his wife, he felt sure, who had made him so soft-hearted, and she, he knew, was influenced by their common enemy, the parson.

The conspirators sat on, drinking and talking, till very late. With the exception of Ben and another man, who also had a large family, all agreed to aid Nichols, and it was arranged that they should meet again next evening to consult further upon this cowardly enterprise.

Ben went home that night not in the best of humours. He did not wish to offend his old friend, but still he could not like the idea of the poor child being left alone, to perish perhaps on that lonely rock. When he found, however, that his children had gone hungry to bed, and was met by the reproaches of his weeping wife for his idleness in not trying to make something by fishing, as other men did, his temper was by no means improved. Matters seemed to him so bad that he began to think he had better join Nichols after all.

In this frame of mind he sauntered down to the beach next morning, meeting Nichols immediately, who was indeed on the watch for him. "Well, Ben," he said, "you look very down in the mouth this morning; what's the matter now?"

"The old story, John," said Ben; "no bread in the house, the children are crying, and my wife abusing me; but it's not my fault, I tell her, that times are bad."

"It will be your fault, Ben, if you let slip a good opportunity for bettering yourself. What made you stand out against my plan last night?"

"Well, it struck me as cowardly and cruel, and I think the same now," he replied; "but when one's brought to such sore straits as I am now, one's ready to catch anything. I've pretty well made up my mind to join you, John."

"That's right, Ben; I knew you'd come round to my way of thinking at last. It's the first time we've ever differed, and I hope it'll be the last."

"But it's a desperate plan, John, and I doubt whether it will succeed," said Ben hesitatingly.

"It's our only chance, Ben – once get rid of Tresilian, and we're certain that during the coming gales no light'll burn in that cursed lighthouse; then we're sure to get one or two good wrecks, as we always do at this time of year."

"Well, as you say, John, there seems nothing else to be done, and I shan't stand in your way, I'll do my best to help you."

"You're a good fellow, Ben," declared Nichols, clapping him on the shoulder. "I knew you'd come all right at last. We'll meet again, and have a glass, to-night, and talk the matter over."

The two men then separated, Ben turning homewards, looking still downcast and gloomy; Nichols, with beaming face and a chuckle of delight, making for the beach, to meet his hopeful nephew, whom he perceived in the distance.

That same evening Mary and her father were sitting beside a cheerful fire in their little room in the lighthouse, Owen was busy mending his nets, Mary had the big Bible open before her.

"What a long spell of calm weather we've had, Mary," said the former; "I'm very thankful for it; since I've taken to fishing my life here has been much pleasanter, and besides the good wages I get for being lighthouse-keeper, I've made a nice little sum by selling fish. I'll be able to provide you with more comforts now, Mary."

"O father! I'm sure I'm comfortable enough. I never thought I should take to living out on this rock, so far away from home, as I have done. I'm quite used to it now; why, even Puss has got to like her new home in the lighthouse. Look how happy she is before the fire!"

"Yes, my child; fine weather has made a great difference to our life here," said Owen; "but we must remember it can't always be fine. In a few days, I feel sure, we shall have storms again."

"Well, I hope they won't be very bad, father. If the sea gets all rough, you won't go out fishing, will you?" she asked anxiously.

"No, no, my child; never fear that; I'll run no risk for your sake," said Owen. "To-morrow, I think, we're pretty sure of a fine day, but I shan't be surprised if that the last for a long time."

"What makes you think so, father?" asked Mary.

"I've lived at sea, or by the sea, all my life, child," said Owen, "and I am pretty well acquainted with the sings of coming weather."

"Well, we must try to make the best of it, father. I hope it won't be worse than it was six weeks ago."

"I hope not, Mary; but you'll be more used to it now, and won't mind the noise of the roaring down below as much as you did then."

"Oh no, father; there's nothing to be afraid of when one knows what it is causes the noise; and besides, with you close to me, I shall never be afraid."

Next morning dawned bright and fine again; the wind, however, had changed, and the air was milder. Owen felt more certain than ever that the fine weather would soon come to an end. The sea was everywhere studded with the white sails of homeward-bound vessels. If foul weather came on suddenly that night, how many of these, Owen thought, would be saved from shipwreck by the warning light which it was his duty to keep burning! But he must profit by the fine morning, and get a few hours' fishing, he might not have another chance for a long time; so after breakfast he kissed his daughter, gathered up his nets, launched his little boat, and rowed out towards the westward. Mary, telescope in hand, watched him from the gallery; every now and then he made signs to her when he had been particularly lucky in securing a large fish; and that morning he was more than usually successful. After he had been out about a couple of hours the sky grew overcast, and as his boat was nearly full of fish, he determined to row to the shore at once, sell all his fish, except what he wanted for his own consumption, and then return to the lighthouse by their usual dinner-time.

As he rowed past he called out to Mary, who was still in the gallery, that he would soon be back, and that she had better begin to cook the dinner.

"Make haste, father," she replied; "the weather's going to change. Look at those black clouds!" and she pointed to the west.

"Never fear, Mary," he cried cheerfully, "they are a long way off yet. I shall have plenty of time to get back before that squall comes."

The little girl watched her father through the telescope till she saw him run his boat on shore, and she perceived men coming down to meet him as they always did. "He'll soon be back now," thought Mary; "I won't watch him any longer, but go and see about getting his dinner ready."

She ran merrily down the stairs, stirred up the fire, and began her preparations. "In half an hour he'll be back," she said to herself cheerfully.

More than half an hour had passed. Mary ran up to the gallery to look out. She saw nothing of her father; and on pointing the telescope towards the shore, she perceived his boat lying in the same position as when he landed, but not a trace of any human being could she discern near it.

The child was alarmed. Her father had never been away so long before – never, indeed, had he gone out of sight of the lighthouse. He would not willingly remain long ashore, there must be some very strong reason for it. Perhaps the parson had sent for him, but that was not likely. Mr. Arthur was the last person who would do anything to frighten her, and he would know she must be frightened if her father was detained on shore and kept out of her sight. But he couldn't be long, she thought, he would come soon. Already the sky was darker, and the black clouds were rising higher and higher in the western horizon. Some drops of rain were beginning to fall, and here and there the waves were tipped with white foam, and no longer broke noiselessly and gently against the rock below. All these signs of bad weather would surely hasten her father's return. Again she went downstairs, and busied herself with the dinner; yet she could not stay there long, but soon returned to the lantern, and now with trembling hands grasped the telescope, to be disappointed once more at sight of her father's boat still in the same place, but no trace of its owner, and the wind was rising more and more, and the rain descending in torrents.

What could have happened to her father? It was two o'clock now, and still there were no signs of him. The poor child did not know what to do; slowly she went down the staircase into the room, and throwing herself into her little chair, she burst into tears. For some time she sat sobbing as if her heart would break. The dinner was well ready, but her father was not there to eat it, and she had no appetite to touch a morsel. She listened to the rising wind and to the sound of the waves, which now began to beat with violence against the rock. She perceived how dark it had become – the sky overcast by black clouds, and the rain, too, coming down more heavily than ever. She went up to the gallery again. Alas! it was only too plain to her that it would be impossible for her father to land on the rock in such a surf as was now foaming around the lighthouse. The only hope was that he might have gone to Sennen, and would come out in a large fishing boat, from which he might possibly effect a landing. But why should he have gone there? The more she thought of it, the more mysterious and inexplicable seemed his extraordinary disappearance. Could he have been suddenly taken ill? had an accident happened to him on the beach? Surely, had this been the case, he would have sent some one off in the boat to tell her. The real truth the poor child never guessed; she was too young, too innocent, to fathom the depths of human malice and wickedness, or to imagine anything so base and cowardly as the vile conspiracy of which her poor father and herself were the victims.

She stood in the driving rain and mist, the wind rapidly rising to a gale, howled around her, while she strained her eyes in the direction whence she hoped to discover the sail of the Sennen boat. But thought the sea all around was dotted with sails, from the large three-master to the humble fishing boat, the familiar and so eagerly desired smack nowhere showed itself, and now the wind had risen greatly, and so violent were the waves, that, if the boat were to come, it was plain enough no one would be able to land on the rock. All the horror of her situation seemed to burst upon the unfortunate little girl; she ran down into the room below, covered her face with her hands, and burst into a paroxysm of tears.

But now let us turn to her unhappy father, and follow his fortunes. After he had rowed past the lighthouse, he made for the shore as rapidly as possible. He saw the bad weather coming, and knew that Mary would not be easy till she had him safe back with her again; but he also saw people waiting on the sand; he knew they were looking out for him, and that the bargain, there-fore, would soon be concluded. When he ran his boat on shore, two men came forward at once and helped him to pull her up. He recognised them both, as he was constantly in the habit of selling fish to them. They did not belong to Sennen, but to a village some five miles along the coast to the east-ward. The contents of the boat wee son emptied on the sand. Then there was more bargaining than usual. Owen asked a very moderate sum for his fish, but the men disputed his charge, a circumstance which had not occurred before. Owen did not choose to give in, as he knew his price was a fair one. At last a compromise was effected; then the men said they had no money to pay him, but their mate, who was a few yards off sitting under the cliff cooking their dinner, would settle with him. Owen, perfectly unsuspicious of treachery, followed as desired. He had not gone ten yards from his boat, and had just turned round the corner of a huge rock which lay on the sand, when he heard a yell of mocking laughter, and saw before him Nichols, his nephew Pollard, and three or four more of the Cove men, notorious smugglers and wreckers, who feared neither God nor man. Im-mediately he perceived that he had fallen into a trap. It was clear enough now why the fishermen, bribed by these villains, had detained him on the sand. What the men meant to do with him he could not guess – perhaps kill him outright, for he felt they were bad enough for that, and when he saw that Nichols was their ringleader he could not hope for much mercy. And, indeed, Nichols – as he dared – would gladly have made an end of his enemy altogether, but, like most thorough villains, he was a coward too. Moreover, he was not sure that all his companions would have consented to so desperate a measure as this. Ben certainly would not; and in that case they might have informed against him. He kept, therefore, to his original plan of confining Owen in the cave, so that the lighthouse might be left without a guardian. All had been planned the night before in the alehouse. The fine weather seemed the great obstacle to their schemes, for should that continue, the extinction of the lamps would bring them no great advantage; but, as Nichols had foretold, a change was at hand, heavy gales were coming on, and thus all chances seemed to combine to favour their iniquitous designs.

Owen, when he found himself surrounded by these men, drew himself up, and standing with his back to the rock awaiting the attack which he knew to be imminent. Yield without a struggle, he certainly would not. If he were to lose his life, he would sell it dearly. "Ha! ha!" cried Nichols, "the bird's caught in a trap. You're our prisoner now, Tresilian, and we mean to keep you as long as it suits our purpose."

"Your prisoner, indeed!" said Owen contemptuously. "You don't think I'm going to yield to such as you. Give me the money you owe me, Sam, at once," he said, turning to the fisherman, "and I'll be off this instant."

The man thus spoken to made no reply, but slunk away with his companion. Their part in the plot was already played out, and they had received their reward in advance.

"We'll pretty soon let you know that you are our prisoner and in our power," said Nichols with a malicious grin.

Owen looked so resolute and determined, that no one of the men ventured to lay hands on him, Of course he was not a match for all of them together, but singly there was not one who was his equal in strength.

"Whoever touches me does so at his peril," he exclaimed, and he fixed his eyes with contempt on Nichols, who winced beneath his glance.

Nichols, the ringleader, making no reply, the men all looked rather sheepish, and a few moments' silence ensued.

As long as he maintained his defiant attitude with his back to the rock, Owen felt certain that no one of the men would attack him, but he could not stand thus inactive all the afternoon. He must make a desperate effort to regain his boat, and push off to the lighthouse. Now or never, he thought, with his opportunity. His assailants looked cowed; a resolute move on his part might be successful – at all events, he would make the attempt.

He left his position of security, and rapidly, with a bold air, turned back towards the beach. But the villains who had so skilfully laid a trap for him were not going to let their victim slip out of their hands so easily. Moreover, he was now assailable in the rear. At a sign from Nichols they fell upon him simultaneously, endeavouring to seize his arms, throw him on the ground, and bind him.

Now a desperate struggle ensued. Owen struck out right and left. There was not a man who did not feel the weight of his arm. Young Nichols soon lay howling on the ground, his uncle's face streamed with blood, while another of his assailants fell prostrate and stunned. Twice did Owen succeed in ridding himself of his foes, and making further advance towards his boat.

"Cowardly ruffians!" he cried, "let me go. Don't you see I'm a match for the whole lot of you?"

"We'll soon put that notion out of your head," cried their ringleader; and now they fell upon Owen more desperately than ever. He was already bleeding, and much weakened. A blow to the head felled him to the ground, and once down the force of numbers overpowered him. Every effort to rise and escape from his foes was in vain. They had so entirely lost all sense of manliness that they struck the poor fellow repeatedly as he lay. He soon became stunned and senseless. Then with a stout rope they bound his hands behind his back, and half-dragged, half-carried him along the shore, till they reached the mouth of the cave destined to be his prison.

Ben Pollard had not joined very heartily in this foul deed, for once or twice his conscience had smitten him. The action was such a thoroughly mean and cowardly one that he did not like being a party to it. On the other hand, his family were starving, and he did not wish to break altogether with his friend Nichols. Not a single blow did he level at Owen; he only hoped to hold him while the others bound him, and carried him to the cave. This was one of those low, narrow, winding caverns, to be found in most of the rocky cliffs round our shores, which were often the haunt of smugglers and thieves. In those days it was a favourite resort of the Cornish wreckers. Close by they burned their false lights to lure vessels on the rocks, and hither they dragged and concealed the property which, by their villainy, they had secured.

The entrance to the cave was concealed by a lofty mass of rock. It was barred by a strong wooden gate, well provided with iron bolts and padlocks. The place might, therefore, well be used for a prison. A more wretched dungeon could scarcely be conceived. Dark, even in brilliant noonday, damp and dripping with slimy seaweed, the ground full of pools of foul stagnant sea water, the air so chilly that it seemed to freeze one to the very bones – such was the place to which his dastardly enemies consigned the luckless Tresilian.

They dragged him, still unconscious, into a dark recess of the cave. Here, bound, bruised, and bleeding, they were about to leave him but this was too much for Ben, and he remonstrated with his companion.

"Surely you won't leave the fellow with his hands tied like that – and you said, John, you'd give him some food, too."

"Yes," replied Nichols, "I've got some dry bread and a bottle of water for him;

but you seem to be precious careful about the rascal all of a sudden, Ben."

"When we've got him safe and gained our object, I can't see what's the good of treating the man more cruelly than need be, John," said Ben; "why not unbind his hands?"

"Because he'll be trying to get out, and may succeed for all we know," said Nichols.

"But he can't get to his food like that, John; we don't want to starve him to death, I suppose."

Nichols uttered a horrible oath and glared fiercely at Ben, who, without saying another word, took out his knife and cut the cords round Owen's wrists. No one interfered, for most of the men sided with Pollard, and saw no reason why their captive should remain bound, as with the strong gate well bolted, there was no chance of his escape from this prison.

They turned away and left him. The bolts and bars of the gate were securely drawn, Nichols putting the key of the padlock in his pocket. Their victim was safe now, and could do them no further harm. Everything had favoured them, The sky was dark and overcast; the wind, already rising, would blow a gale before nightfall; rain was falling heavily; no lamps would shine from the lighthouse to-night, and as the sea was covered with shipping there was every chance that some vessel would be driven on shore.

Nichols was so pleased that he almost forget his ill-humour with Ben for unbinding Owen, as well as the wounds and bruises he had received in the struggle. Most of the men bore traces of the conflict, and agreed if any questions were asked, to say they had had a fight among themselves – not a very uncommon occurrence. They returned to the village to make every preparation for their dark night's work.

Let us meanwhile look at poor Owen in his prison. It was more than an hour after his cowardly foes had left him before he came thoroughly to his senses. He stretched himself, opened his eyes, and seemed at first to be in utter darkness; but as he became accustomed to the gloom, he saw a very faint light gleaming in the distance. He felt sick, sore, in terrible pain. Where was he? What could have happened to bring him into this state? Gradually he began to remember all that had occurred. He knew now why he felt such a terrible oppression in his head, why all his limbs ached so much. All the horror of his situation flashed across his mind. They had carried out their threat, then: he was a prisoner; and from the chilliness of his dungeon, the dampness of the ground, and the strong smell of seaweed, he felt sure that he was immured in some cave along the shore. He raised himself with difficulty – how stiff and bruised he was! – and staggered through the darkness towards the gleam of light, groping his way to the entrance of the cave; but here the strong gate barred all further progress. He shook it with all his strength, but it did not yield an inch; he was indeed a prisoner, and in what a dungeon. Like a madman he again put forth all his might, trying to wrench off the posts, or by the weight of his body break through the gate, but all to no avail. Weak from loss of blood and exhausted by these efforts, he sank down on the ground utterly wretched and hopeless.

And then a thought, which was far more terrible than his own sufferings, came into his agonised mind. His daughter, his darling Mary, what had become of her? She was left alone in the lighthouse, expecting him hour after hour; and in terrible suspense and grief, what would she do? She could never guess what had become of him. His absence would be enough to break her heart. She would die of fright at being left alone all night in the lighthouse. Bitterly did he reproach himself for ever landing on the shore. Had not the parson warned him to be careful when he went out fishing in his boat, not to go too far away and leave Mary long alone? To add to his anguish, too, he heard now the wind was rising, how the waves were roaring and dashing upon the shore. The rock which stood before the entrance of the cave hid the open sea from his view, but its sound told him of the coming gale. The sense of his utter powerlessness to help either his daughter or himself, seemed to drive him to the verge of madness. Again he shook the bars of his prison , and cried out, "Help! help! for God's sake help!" but the only answer he received was the shrill cries of the seabirds, as they sought among the rocks above a shelter from the coming storm!

Again, overcome by his exertions, he sank to the ground. The wind howled and whistled through the bars of the grate, and blew in so coldly upon him that it made him shiver But he had forgotten his own pain and trouble now, so entirely was his mind occupied by the terrible situation for his darling child. He pictured to himself how she would wait for his return – stand on the gallery and strain her eyes in the direction whence she might expect to see his boat – how frightened she would be when she heard the wind howling and saw the waves rising and dashing furiously against the lighthouse, and felt that, as there was now no hope of a landing being effected on the rock, she must pass the night there alone! He thought of Jordan's fate; if a strong man had been driven half mad by the horrors of one solitary night out on that storm-beaten rock, what would be the condition of a poor little child? He scarcely dared hope that she could survive it. And the lamps, too, would fail to shine to-night, for he knew that even if Mary were not rendered powerless by fear, she would not be able to reach them, or know how to trim and arrange them properly.

With his hands pressed against his aching brow, he sat crouched down in a corner of the cave. Not a ray of comfort fell upon his anguished soul. What a life of misfortune and trouble his had been! His wife dead, his son torn from him, and, for all he knew, dead too, and now his daughter, his only child, doomed to a horrible fate – himself a prisoner, powerless to aid her. In rapid succession these blows had fallen upon him, and for a time he gave way to utter despair.

Then, as he grew a little calmer, he began to think of all he had heard the parson say, and of what Mary had read to him, during their long evenings in the lighthouse out of the big Bible, about there being a Father in heaven who cares for all His children here on earth – One "Who does not afflict willingly, nor grieve the children of men." He remembered, too, that only last night Mary had been reading to him out of the Gospels the words of our Lord Himself, showing how he took care even of the sparrows, not one of them being forgotten before God; and then all the words of the text came into his mind – "Even the hairs of your head are numbered: fear not, therefore, ye are of more value than many sparrows." And this God was Almighty. He was able to overrule all the plots and designs of evil men, and make them work together for His own glory, and for the good of those who loved and feared Him. Could He not, then, if He willed, deliver him from this dungeon? Could He not watch over and protect is beloved child, exposed to the fury of the tempest on that lonely rock? He remembered, too, other words he had heard Mary read – "It is not the will of your Father Which is in heaven that one of these little ones should perish." And surely she was one of Christ's little ones. He could not, then, suffer her to perish. Oh! he would pray to Him, and entreat Him to protect her. The all-merciful One could not turn a deaf ear to a poor father's prayer for his only child; He could not be unfaithful to His promise, "Call upon Me in the day of trouble, and I will deliver thee, and thou shalt glorify Me." Owen knelt on the cold damp sand, and fervently prayed the Almighty to guard his dear Mary in her solitary watch, and make her feel that though deprived of the care of her earthly father, her heavenly Father was near her still, to protect and comfort her. When he rose from his knees he felt calmer, and more resigned to his hard fate. I was almost dark. He was faint with hunger, as well as from the rough treatment he had received. He wondered if his cruel enemies had left him any food; perhaps – terrible thought – they meant to starve him to death in that dungeon. Happily his tinder-box and matches were in his pocket, so he struck a light and speedily discovered the bread and water. The food refreshed him, but he was still so weak and exhausted that, in spite of his grief and anxiety, he soon sank into a heavy slumber.

19

The Little Watcher

"And the maiden clasped her hands and prayed
That saved she might be;
And she thought of Christ who stilled the wave
On the Lake of Galilee.
And ever the fitful gusts between
A sound came from the land;
It was the sound of the trampling surf
On the rocks and the hard sea sand."

- Longfellow

For some time poor Mary sat in her chair before the fire, and gave way to her grief. Her poor father, what could have happened to him? Why had he not returned? These questions occupied her mind even more than her own lonely situation, for if she could only feel sure that no evil had befallen him, she thought she might endure a night alone in the lighthouse, dreadful as it would be.

Rousing herself she perceived how dark it had become; she heard, too, how the tempest was rising and what a fearful night was in store for her. With trembling hands she tried to make up the fire, and presently, as its cheerful blazes lighted the little room, her eyes fell on the great Family bible. Ah! that was still left to her; could she not draw some comfort in her trouble from its sacred pages? Among the Methodists in those days was a well-meaning custom – which frequently, however, degenerated into superstition – of opening the Bible at random, putting the finger on the page, and reading the text on which it rested. This was supposed to give an answer to prayer, or to direct what course should be pursued in a matter of difficulty or perplexity. Mary had often seen her mother do this, and now she thought she would follow her example. She took down the Bible, and put it on the table, then praying God to guide and direct her, she opened the holy volume at the Book of Psalms; her finger rested on the text, "What time I am afraid I will trust in Thee. In God I will praise His word, in God I have put my trust, I will not fear what flesh can do unto me."

Here, indeed, was comfort! It seemed as if God Himself was speaking to her out of the sacred book. He was telling her not to fear; that He was at her side to protect her, lonely as she was, through that raging storm. The words of another Psalm she knew by heart came with fresh consolation into her soul: "Yea, though I walk through the valley of the shadow of death, I will fear no evil; for Thou art with me; Thy rod and Thy staff they comfort me." And her father? Would not the same Saviour be with him too; could she not trust him into the loving Hands of Him Whose tender mercies are over all His works. She knelt down, in simple childlike words she prayed to God, for His dear Son's sake, to watch over and protect her beloved father, and to bring him back to her at last in safety. And thus, not far off from each other, separated only by a narrow but impassable belt of raging sea, the hearts of father and daughter were as one, and their common prayers for each other's protection were mingled as they ascended to the ever-ready ear of Him Who never turneth away from the prayer of the poor, the needy, or the destitute.

When she rose from her knees she did not feel so frightened. She could trust God to protect her father, and watch over herself. The sun had set, it was getting dark, and already past the time when Owen was accustomed to light the lamps. She had heard him remark that morning how much shipping there was about, and that if squally weather came on in the evening, the warning light might save many vessels from destruction. And now a gale was blowing, and her father was not at his post. Here was a fresh misfortune, another cause for sorrow and regret. Then the thought struck her, could she light the lamps? She had often seen her father do it, but she knew the lamps were fixed very high up on the lantern, her father was a tall man and could easily reach them, but she was afraid she could not. She ran up to the lantern, rain and spray were both beating violently against the glass, the wind howling dismally, and the sea roaring louder than ever. She stood on tiptoe, and reached up her hand as high as possible, but the lamps were far far above her. If she stood on a chair she thought she might just reach them. She ran down stairs and quickly returned with one, upon which she mounted, but still she must be several inches higher before her object could be attained. She now fetched a large tin basin, this turned bottom upwards she placed upon the chair. It would be all right now she thought – she must be high enough to reach the lamps. But she had forgotten that she must be able to reach the top of the wick – and for this, even the basin added to the chair did not sufficiently raise her up. So now she fetched a pillow which she placed between the basin and the chair, but, alas! still the lamps were out of her reach, only a couple of inches more and she would succeed in her attempt.

She was a resolute little girl. The thought that on her exertions the lives of many depended, had made her for the time almost forget her own troubles, and nerved her to an energy beyond her years. She was determined that the lamps should be lighted. Nothing daunted by her want of success hitherto, she would persevere. How pleased her father would be when he knew that she had lighted the lamps, to find that she was able to perform his duty for him. How it would gladden his heart to see the light shedding its clear friendly rays over the wild rough seas, for by that he would know that she was safe and well, and that vessels were still being warned of the perils which awaited them on that dangerous coast.

Again she descended to the room below to look for some other articles to pile on the chair. She searched everywhere, but she could find nothing that would do. She began to despair. Because she could not raise herself a couple of inches higher it seemed as if the lamps would not be lit, and many brave men be doomed to a watery grave. Then her eye fell on the large Family Bible which still lay open on the table. She closed it. Ah! that, she said to herself, would make her just high enough. With it she could disperse with the pillow. But to stand upon the Bible! She could never do that. Her mother had always taught her to tread the sacred volume with extreme reverence. It was scrupulously dusted twice a day. No article, not even another book, was ever allowed to be placed upon it; to stand on it, therefore, seemed to her like sacrilege. For several minutes she reflected what course to pursue. Then she knelt down, and, resting her head upon the holy Book, prayed to God to direct her, and show her what He would have her to do. When she rose from her knees all hesitation had vanished. Her standing on the Book could do it no harm; she knew she did not mean to treat it with disrespect; she was sure God would forgive her, for by using it in this way she might save the lives of many poor sailors, as well as give a sign to her father and friends ashore that she was not only alive and well, but able, too, though alone and unassisted, to perform the most important of a lighthouse-keeper's duties.

The Bible was heavier to carry than either the chair or the basin had been, and the little maiden was quite out of breath when she reached the top of the staircase. Now she set bravely to work; confidence in her success gave her fresh energy. The Bible was placed on the chair, and over it the basin, upon which Mary climbed, not without some difficulty, and now she found to her great delight that she could easily light the lamps. They were all ready trimmed, as her father had done that earlier in the morning. She went down again and fetched the small lantern and matches kept to light the lamps, and then mounting again on the Bible she began her work. This took a long time to accomplish, for over and over again she had to get down from the chair and move it round, as one after the other she put her match to the different lamps. But she had the satisfaction of seeing how they all burned up brightly, and sent their cheerful beams over the mass of ranging waves which beat against the lighthouse on every side. And then her work being finished, she carefully took down the big Bible form the chair, and bore it to its accustomed place on the shelf below. Then she made up a bright fire, and sat down beside it weary and exhausted. Her anxiety about her father had made her forget her own wants; she had not tasted a morsel since the morning; but now the cravings of hunger made themselves felt. With tears trickling down her cheeks as she ate her supper, she thought how sad it was to be here all alone; the food she so greatly needed strengthened her; she seemed to gain fresh courage to perform the great and noble duty which God had confided to her, and felt more able to trust herself and her father to the tender care of the all-merciful Saviour.

The storm was increasing in violence every hour. The strong building shook and trembled as wave after wave broke over it. Mary went up again to the cupola; the lights were burning brightly,, but the spray had so dimmed the glass which surrounded the lanterns that she could scarcely see through them. Every now and then a huge wave would roll sheer over the lighthouse, completely covering it for several seconds. The wind, as it rose and fell in fitful gusts, howled and moaned fearfully, while rain and hail descended in pelting showers. What a night it was to be exposed to the pitiless raging of the elements! Her heart ached for the poor sailors in their ships; hard as her lot was, she was safer and better off than they were.

She went down again and sat before the fire – it was the only cheering object around her. She tried not to be afraid, but she could not help shuddering now and then when a wave, with a roar like thunder, came rolling up, and the whole weight of the Atlantic seemed to crash against the granite walls of the building. Then this terrible deafening noise from below; it was indeed enough to drive any one man who did not know what caused it. She thought that even Christian, in the "Pilgrim's Progress," couldn't have heard more dreadful sounds when he passed through the Valley of the Shadow of Death. Even the cat, now her only companion, generally so placid, had become restless, ran to and fro, and mewed as if frightened by the terrific noise. Mary took her on her lap, trying to soothe her by her caresses. There had not been such a storm as this since she and her father had come out to the lighthouse. She was very tired, not only from her unusual exertions, but from the anxious excitement she had suffered during the day. She determined to go to bed – in spite of all this noise she thought she must soon fall asleep. But, first, she took up the Bible again, and, with the winds and waves with deafening sound raging around her, she read from the ninety-third Psalm, "The floods have lifted up, O Lord, the flood have lifted up their voice; the floods lift up their waves. The Lord on high is mightier than the noise of many waters, yea, than the mighty waves of the sea." Yes, He, her Father in heaven, was mightier, stronger than even these huge billows, which every minute were dashing against her lonely prison house. And He Who had placed her there to do a work for Him, would certainly protect her from every danger. She knelt down and said her prayers, committing herself to God's care, and praying Him to bless and watch over her dear father, wherever he might be, and "to guard the sailors tossing on the deep blue sea," and, with the winds still howling in savage fury around her, with the wild waves lifting up their giant crests, and dashing in a thunder-like roar against the lighthouse walls, she sunk into quiet slumber, "pure and light," God's precious gift to the young and innocent.

There let us leave her, and return to the shore. When Nichols and his companions had safely secured their unhappy prisoner, they turned homeward to Sennen, and betook themselves to the alehouse, feeling that, after their struggles and exertions, they needed some refreshment. They had, moreover, to consult together as to the best measures which were to be taken to further their iniquitous designs. They felt sure that the lamps on the Longships would not burn to-night, and their plan was to display false lights on the shore, which, moving about from place to place, would appear as if they were the lights of vessels, and thus lure mariners on to the rocks.

"We have had a good luck," said Nichols, as he sat down at the table, and called for some grog, "though we'd trouble enough with the fellow. I'm sore and bruised too from the blows and kicks he gave me, yet we've secured him at last, and there'll be no lamps lighted to-night."

"And the weather, too, is just what we've wanted all along," said another man.

"It couldn't be better," said Nichols; "the wind's rising rapidly; it'll blow a tremendous gale from the south-west to-night."

"Yes, seldom have I seen so much shipping about as there is now," returned his nephew.

"We're sure of one prize, if not several," said another. "I believe even if the light did burn, some of 'em would be driven on shore."

"And as it won't, a great many will fall into our clutches," remarked Nichols.

They sat drinking and talking for about an hour, then their leader suggested they had better be on the look-out now. It was already quite dark.

"What a dirty night!" exclaimed the first man, who went to the door; "we've had nothing like it this winter!"

"All the better for us," replied the others.

"Get the horse ready, Bill," said Nichols, "and bring him here at once, but don't light the lantern till we get out on the cliffs, in case we should come across the parson or the coastguard."

Their plan was to fix the lantern on the animal's neck, he was then slowly led about along the coast, to imitate the motion of a ship on the water. .They waited a few minutes till Bill Nichols came back with the horse, then all started off in the direction of the Land's End, when they had the best view of the sea.

As soon as they reached the first rising ground whence the Longships could be seen, all suddenly started and stood still, as if thunderstruck. For a minute or two no one uttered a word. Then a volley of oaths and curses proceeded from Nichols, which were speedily re-echoed by his companions.

"Who would have thought it? That child has managed to light the lamps, and there they are burning as brightly as ever. Well, we're done after all," said one of the party.

"Who'd have thought it, indeed?" exclaimed Nichols. "If it had ever entered my head that the girl would have been up to those tricks, I'd have rowed out in Tresilian's boat, carried her off from the lighthouse, and locked her up with her father; and now here's all my fine plan spoiled by this wretched little brat."

"And there's no getting at her now," said one of the men.

"Of course not, Tom. This gale may last a week, and, as long as it does, no boat can get to the lighthouse. There's no doubt we're thoroughly floored, but we must make the best of it. On such a night as this, even with the lamps burning, it's likely enough some vessel will be driven on shore."

Ben was the only one of the party who was not altogether sorry at the turn events had taken. All the afternoon the fate of the poor little child, alone on the rock, cruelly robbed of her parent and protector, had haunted him. When, however, he saw the lights, he knew she was not frightened to death; to do such a deed she must possess spirit and courage beyond her years. This he hoped would sustain her. Not prepared altogether to break with his old associates, he still continued to follow the men as they wandered along the cliffs in search of plunder.

Arthur Pendrean had latterly been much occupied. Dick Evans' illness had taken up nearly all his time, and great was his joy when at last his care and watching, by God's mercy, seemed to be bearing fruit, and Dick, though still very weak, was beginning to get about a little.

Arthur often thought of his friends in the lighthouse, he rejoiced in the long spell of fine weather, which would make their sojourn there more endurable, and was cheered when he go good news of them occasionally.

When this afternoon such a sudden change came on, and he perceived every indication of a violent gale, he determined to ride down to the shore in the evening, for he always liked to satisfy himself on these occasions that the lights were burning, and if possible, to prevent the wreckers form any attempt to ply their old trade.

Through wind, storm, drifting rain, and sleet, he rode down to the Land's End. He saw the light burning as usual, though every now and then it would be completely hidden, as the waves swept over the building.

He breathed a silent prayer for the safety of its brave guardians, little thinking that one was a prisoner on shore, scarcely a stone's-throw from where he stood, and that the other was left alone, a solitary little watcher on that storm-buffetted rock. The lights which here and there might be seen tossing on the wild expanse of angry ocean showed him how many vessels were about that night – they indeed would profit by the friendly beacon on the Longships Rock. At last his scheme, to which he had devoted many anxious hours, bade fair to be a permanent success. He had much then to be thankful for. He felt that his work had not been altogether in vain among these people, for had he not seen some fruit of his labour. Dick Evans' return, his change of life, and, he trusted, of heart too, cheered him more than anything that had occurred since his ordination. Many of the men who formerly treated him churlishly and roughly had become more civil in their manner, and thus were more accessible to friendly admonitions or rebukes. Among these he reckoned Ben Pollard, whom he had accosted once or twice since Christmas Day, and with whose altered manner he had been so favourably impressed.

Much indeed still remained to be done, of this he was only too sadly reminded when he heard voices not far off from him; he could distinguish nothing but oaths and curses, levelled, as he could pretty well imagine, against those who had helped to build the lighthouse and kept the lamps burning. At some distance along the cliffs he perceived a glimmer of a moving light, indicating from whence the voices came. He knew now that wreckers were about; he would pursue them and if possible frustrate their plans. He turned his horse in the direction of the light, but it had disappeared . He rode someway along the cliffs in the darkness, but not a voice did he hear. The wreckers, ever cautious, had observed him, they had, therefore, extinguished their lamp, tied their horse up against a shrub, and scrambled themselves halfway down the cliffs, taking refuge in a safe hiding-place, known only to themselves.

Arthur was obliged to give up the pursuit and return home.

20

Homeward Bound

"Children of God! and each as he is straying
Lights on his fellow with a soft surprise,
Hearkens perchance, the whisper of his praying
Catches the human answer of his eyes."

- F.W. Myers

"'Courage!' he said, and pointed to the land,
'This mounting wave will roll us shoreward soon.'"

- Tennyson

Philip and his friend Marriot were detained as prisoners in the Island of Martinique. They were not harshly treated, and were allowed a certain amount of liberty; this captivity nevertheless was very irksome to both, they longed to be once more under their own flag, and often wondered if the wished-for day would ever dawn when they should again behold the white cliffs of dear old England.

The French authorities had hoped to effect an exchange of prisoners without sending the officers and crew of the "Redoubtable" back to Europe, but when, after the lapse of several months, no opportunity for this had offered itself, they decided to put the captives on board one of their own vessels bound for France. Once there all difficulty of arranging for an exchange of prisoners would be at an end.

Accordingly, early in the year, Philip, Tom, and the rest of the prisoners were conveyed on board a small frigate, which, immediately after, in the company with several other vessels of the French fleet, set sail for Europe. The Englishmen were all crowded together in the dark narrow hold, and very wretched was their conditions; none of them, however, complained, for they knew that the voyage once over, there was every prospect of regaining their liberty.

A very warm friendship had sprung up between Philip Tresilian and Tom Marriott. Already they were the marks for the sneers and mockery of the other prisoners, for they neither swore, gambled, nor got drunk, and more than once Philip had been overheard reading the Bible to his companion.

Crowded together as they now were, they had to listen to and endure much which caused them deep pain and sorrow; for many of the men would blaspheme against religion on purpose to annoy the two "Methodists," as they were called.

Once or twice, indeed, the two young men had remonstrated with their fellows and spoke out boldly in their Master's cause, but this had only drawn down upon them increased persecution and annoyance. They could do nothing then but meekly bear it, and rejoice that they were counted worthy to suffer shame for the sake of Him Whom they humbly endeavoured to serve and follow.

It was a long tedious voyage. For many days they lay becalmed, and then the wind that blew was so light it scarcely moved the sails.

"Are you not weary of this Phil?" said Tom one day. "We shall never get to Europe at this rate."

"It doesn't look like it, Tom, but we must make the best of it; we're on our way there, slow and sure perhaps, but we'll get there at last," replied Philip.

"I'm thinking," said Tom, "that after all this calm we shall have some dirty weather shortly, and bad as it is now, it'll be worse for us then. The vessel is overladen, I know; look how low she is in the water. We've not only all these prisoners on board but a number of invalided Frenchmen, both soldiers and sailors; and from the little I have observed of their goings on during this fine weather, I don't think the crew would be good for much in a storm."

"Neither do I," answered Philip; "they are as awkward a set of lubbers as ever I saw."

"And if a gale of wind came on we should all probably go to the bottom," remarked Tom, gravely.

"God preserve us from that!" said Philip. "After having guarded us in so many dangers He surely will not suffer us to perish now."

"Well, we're in His hands, Phil, and I hope we're neither of us afraid to die,, if He wills it, though I should like to see old England once more," Said Tom. "But come, don't let's be fretting over what hasn't happened yet, and perhaps never will; the weather's fine, and we'll hope it'll last so. I trust, when we get to France, we sha'n't be kept long in prison there, but exchanged soon."

"Oh, no fear of that, Tom," said Philip. "There are a great many more French prisoners in England than English prisoners in France,, and our country'll only be too glad to get us back again and be rid of the Frenchmen, who are only an expense to keep."

"True enough," said Tom; "oh! how glad I shall be when this voyage is over."

A couple of days after this conversation the weather did change, a strong and favourable breeze sprang up, and they now began to make rapid progress, but the English prisoners observed how heavily the vessel laboured, and were more and more convinced of the danger to which they must be exposed in case it came on to blow a gale of wind. Still, notwithstanding their fears, Philip and Tom were buoyed up with fresh hopes as each moment seemed to bring them nearer to their home. In three or four days now they surely would see the shores of France.

But the wind blew fiercer than ever from the west, and though it was a fair one, the frigate made a great deal of water; day and night the men had to work at the pumps. Of this the prisoners had more than their share, but hard as they laboured, there was no doubt that the water was gaining ground in the hold. Some of the more experienced seamen among the English captives asserted positively that the vessel was taking a wrong course, being too much to the northward, and that probably several days before they expected to sight the French coast they would find themselves among some of the dangers rocks or shoals which fringe the western shores of England. One man had been bold enough to make this representation to the captain, who went into a furious passion at an English prisoner presuming to question his knowledge and seamanship, and the course was pursued without alteration, while the English prisoners were made to work harder than ever at the pumps.

It had been a very stormy day. The wind was stronger and the waves higher than they had been during the whole voyage. The frigate rolled heavily from side to side, and incessant labour at the pumps was ineffectual to prevent the rapid rising of the water in the hold. The captain and officers were evidently anxious, the crew alarmed and excited, so that orders were not so punctually obeyed as hitherto, and discipline was becoming relaxed. Tom and Philip were working at the same pump,, they had had scarcely a moment's rest since dawn that morning.

"What do you think of it now, Tom?" said Philip

"Why, with a good ship, and well manned, there'd be no danger at all, but in this old tub, and with such a set of incapable fellows for sailors, there's little if any chance for us," replied Tom.

"I'm afraid you're about right there, Tom," said Philip. "Well, we must make the best of it, but it'll be hard and sad indeed for me not to see my father and sister once more, and when we seem so near home, too."

"We must try and keep our courage, Phil," said Tom in a more cheerful tone; "we won't give up all for lost yet. There's no telling what may happen after all. Meanwhile we'll work hard and do our duty, and leave the rest to God. He'll do what's best for both of us."

"Yes, Tom, I know He will," said Philip. "Ah! how often He has saved my life when there seemed but little chance for me. I won't despair even now, or give up my trust in Him."

"That's right, Phil," said Tom; then shading his eyes with his left hand he gazed intently over to the eastward, in which direction the vessel was sailing.

After a moment's silence he exclaimed – "It must be, I can't be wrong! look you, Phil, out yonder, that dark line on the horizon, isn't it land?"

Philip strained his eyes in the direction to which his companion pointed, and plainly enough he saw not only a line of coast, but black specks, too, which were evidently rocks or islands.

"Sure enough, Tom, there's no doubt about it, I can see the breakers now, but that's not the French coast surely. I believe Jim Cox was right when he told the captain the other day that he was altogether out of his reckoning, and that that's our own Cornish coast, and not far from the Land's End."

"I always thought Cox was right, Phil," said Tom, "and the captain wrong; and if that is the Cornish coast, with such a gale as we're likely to have to-night, there's not much hope for the ship or for any on board her."

"What's to be done, Tom?" asked Philip, "hadn't we better tell the captain?"

"He ought to have seen it himself ere this, and we shall get little thanks for our pains by giving him any information."

Tom now called the attention of the other English prisoners to the land ahead. All agreed that it must be the Cornish coast. Meanwhile it had been observed by the captain and officers, and had caused no little excitement among them. The captain hurried into his cabin, charts were spread out on the table, which where eagerly consulted. There was no doubt that this was neither the Norman nor the Breton coast; but must, therefore, be some region with which they were totally acquainted. With a gale rising, and a leaky, unmanageable, overloaded ship, their prospects were gloomy indeed. And now the crew had discovered the danger, and all came crowding round the captain's cabin, wildly gesticulating, loudly disputing with each other, and demanding to be told what coast this was, to which the strong wind was urging their vessel.

The captain seemed bewildered and nearly distracted. He gave orders for the vessel's course to be altered to bear more to the southward, but as the gale was blowing from the south-west, this was no easy matter. Then he ordered all the sails to be furled, but still the frigate was carried heavily and slowly on by the violence of the storm.

Complete anarchy reigned on board the frigate. The captain was at his wits' end. The English prisoners profited by the confusion to regain their liberty, and many ceased working at the pumps. One of the officers urged by the captain to consult the English sailors, who probably knew more about the coast than he did, and if they appeared capable of command to give them the complete management of the ship, promising their unconditional liberation if they succeeded in saving her. Humiliating as this proposal was, the captain felt that it was the only chance of saving their lives; as to the ship that must be given up, for if she weathered the storm, she would certainly run aground on the English shores, and become a fine prize for the enemy.

The Englishmen were all standing together gazing at the shores of their native land, and speculating as to their chance of reaching it when the captain came up to them. After hearing his proposal they consulted together for a while. They were too few in number to undertake the sole management of so large a vessel under such critical circumstances, and very little dependence could be placed on the French crew rendering them any material aid. However, as nothing could be worse than the present state of affairs, as liberty and large profit, too, would certainly be their reward if they succeeded in bringing the vessel safe into an English harbour, they promised to do their best. The captain ordered his own men to obey the Englishmen's orders, and the ablest and most experienced seamen among them was unanimously chosen to take the command, while all the rest promised him implicit obedience.

They first set to work thoroughly to examine the vessel; the leaks were larger and more numerous than they had expected, in fact, the most desperate and persistent work at the pumps would be necessary to prevent the ship from foundering. All the cargo, ammunition, and heavy guns were immediately thrown overboard. The masts were next cut down, and like a huge hulk the frigate rode on the foaming waves. Every effort was made to keep her head to the wind. Their only hope was in delay, for should the wind abate they might with difficulty get the vessel into some near port, but if the storm continued they must inevitably be driven on the rocks, or perhaps sink before they reached them. Night came on. The sailors now perceived ahead of them a bright and steady light, which seemed to be burning on the shore, though every now and then it would be hidden for a few moments. What could this light be? None of them knew. As they stood together on the poop debating about it, Philip exclaimed –

"I believe it is the lighthouse on the Longships Rock, just off the Land's End; it was just finished when I was pressed for the fleet at Sennen Cove last spring."

"You belong to Cornwall, then, do you?" said the man who had been chosen as captain.

"Yes, and I'm very much mistaken if we're not off the Land's End now."

"That's what I've thought all along, and there's no good anchorage about there, is there?"

"No; rocks bristle all round the coast, and in dark winter nights, and with heavy gales blowing, scores of ships are wrecked there."

"That doesn't look as if there was much hope for us, then," replied the man gravely; "are the people who live in the village on the shore likely to give us any assistance, think you?"

"I wish I could say so," replied Philip; "on the contrary, they will most likely do all they can to cause our destruction. Some of the worst wreckers on the coast dwell thereabouts, and though I belong to the place myself, I must confess that they're a terrible rough lot."

"This isn't very cheering news you give us, lad," said the man who had been chosen captain; "besides, it strikes me the wind is still rising, and a very dirty night we shall have of it. If we can only ride out the storm till daylight the gale may fall in the morning, but even then, with a ship in such a state as ours is, I don't see much hope for us."

"We're not drifting so fast towards the shore as we were before, and Bill Stokes has just told me the water is lower in the hold," said Tom hopefully.

"And we're still some way off from the shore, which is all in our favour," said the captain.

It was a terrific night. The fierce wind howled and roared, huge waves every now and then swept the decks, and the men, for self-preservation, had to lash themselves on to the capstans, to the remains of the masts, or to the gunwale, otherwise they would have been borne away into the foaming wilderness of waters which swirled in the pitchy darkness around them. The frigate's timbers creaked and groaned incessantly as she was beaten and buffeted by the furious billows. The French captain and his officers maintained their calmness and presence of mind, and did all in their power to assist the Englishmen, into whose hands they had entrusted their vessel, but many of the crew, overcome by fear, hid themselves between decks and in the cabins, where they crouched trembling together. They refused to work, and indeed they seemed incapable of doing anything. Some of them were blacks who had been hastily pressed into the service of the fleet at Martinique, and others were landsmen who had had no previous experience of a seafaring life.

The long-wished-for dawn appeared at last, but the wind did not fall as many had hoped. They were certainly nearer to the rock-bound coast than they were the night before. Notwithstanding all their efforts they were slowly but surely being driven to destruction.

Bravely and nobly had the Englishmen worked that night. Not one of them had even thought of taking an instant's repose. Pale and exhausted with all these exertions, and from exposure to this terrific gale, but still undaunted and determined to battle with the storm to the very last, morning found them resolutely standing at their several posts.

The French captain, full of admiration for their heroic efforts, ordered food – such as there was - to be liberally served out to them.

Tom and Philip were again standing side by side. "What do you think of it, Tom?" said the latter.

"Ah! lad, I can't see any chance at all for us. The Lord, of course, can deliver us if He wills, but it seems to me He must almost work a miracle to do it."

"It'll be hard to perish just within sight of my own home, Tom, won't it?" said Philip, in a choking voice: "with my father and sister so near me. Maybe they've given me up for dead already, but if my body should be washed on shore, close to my native village, it would indeed be a terrible blow for my poor father."   .

Tom couldn't speak for a minute or two. His heart ached for his poor friend.

"Cheer up, Philip," he said at last; "the Lord has delivered you from many dangers, and perhaps He'll save us after all. Whatever betide, we can thank Him for allowing us to be together; if He means us to sink together into a watery grave, it'll be some comfort to be side by side, to be able to say a word to cheer each other when the last dark hour comes."

"Ah! yes, Tom, indeed it will; however dark the cloud is, I've heard it said, there's some gleam of light in it, even though we mayn't see it."

A giant wave which came sweeping over the deck and made every plank and timber of the ship quiver, interrupted their conversation. Then their duties separated them. Tom was called to the helm and Philip went to work again at the pumps.

The water in the hold was rapidly rising now, and the English seaman who had taken the command ordered all hands, that could be spared, to the pumps – even the French officers, to set their men an example, took their turn at the work, but all these combined efforts were unavailing, for still the water gained ground.

That day, the dawn of which all on board had so ardently longed for, brought to them no ray of hope or comfort. Dark and gloomy clouds obscured the sky, fierce winds in violent gusts swept over the grey turbid mass of angry ocean; drenching showers of rain and hail ever and anon came pelting down and mingled themselves with the clouds of flying spray and foam, while before them frowned the dark rocky shores which bade them no welcome, and held out no hope of safety and rest after their toilsome and dangerous voyage, but rather threatened them with terrible destruction, with a cold and watery grave.

Hour after hour as they watched these cliffs and the rocks which studded the sea around, rendered more conspicuous by the white fringe of snowy foam which as each wave dashed against them rose and fell in clouds of feathery spray, they saw how surely they were, in spite of all their efforts, being driven on to this iron-bound and inhospitable coast. Nothing now but a change of wind could save them. There was no abatement in the violence of the gale, the most experienced and sanguine mariner could detect no sign of any probable alteration in the weather.

Such were their condition when the shades of evening again fell on the foaming wilderness of angry ocean around them, while the only cheering object which met their gaze was the light burning at the Longships. The building itself was now distinctly visible, though completely hidden every now and then by the large waves that swept over it.

Who was the watcher there? Philip often wondered if it was some one he knew, one of his fellow villagers; could it be his own father who had taken the post? Well, whoever it was, he must have a brave bold heart to live out there encircled by the fierce seas and roaring tempests, and a noble work he was doing in keeping the lamp burning. Even to the hearts of these buffeted despairing seamen it sent a faint gleam of hope. It told them that there was some one there on that lonely rock, one generous human heart, at all events, watching them, hoping – perhaps praying – for their deliverance.

Philip, who was well acquainted with every rock and shoal, creek and bay around the coast, was very useful in affording information to the sailor in command. As the vessel, unless the wind fell or changed within a very few hours; must inevitably be driven on shore, he wished if possible that this catastrophe should take place where there might be some chance of their lives being saved.

This Philip told him could only be close to Sennen Cove, but in such a gale as this, he added, and without any assistance from the land (for he could hold out no hope of that), he thought there was barely a chance of any of the crew getting safe to shore. They would under any circumstances go to pieces too far off for it to be possible, in such a surf, for any man to swim on shore, and even those who clung to pieces of the wreck would be almost certain to have the life beaten out of them before they reached the land.

"Had it not been for that light and what you have told me," said the man, "I should have let the ship now drive on straight ahead."

"Then we should have been dashed to pieces in an instant, far away from the shore," said Philip; "just here all the sea bristles with rocks; there isn't a worse place all round the coast."

"The further to the north we can keep her the better, then, I suppose," said the captain.

"Yes," replied Philip; "but even if we were to run aground near Sennen Cove I don't see much room for hope, though, as I said before, it's the best place."

"Bad's the best, then," said the sailor gloomily; "but we'll do what we can and work away to the last."

21

A Memorable Sunday

"Come Thou, O come,
Glorious and shadow free,
Star of the stormy sea,
Light of the tempest tost,
Harbour our souls to save
When hope upon the wave
Is lost."

- G. Moultrie

"The warrior from his armed tent,
The seaman from the tide,
Far as the Sabbath chimes are sent
In Christian nations wide;
Thousands and tens of thousands bring
Their sorrows to His shrine,
And taste the never-failing spring
Of Jesus' love divine."

- Lyra Sacra

It was long after dawn when Mary awoke next morning. Her ears were greeted with the howling of the wind, the dull thunder-like sound of the roaring waves, they mysterious noises from the cavern below; she rubbed her eyes and looked round her, expecting to see her father as usual moving about cleaning the lamps or getting his nets ready for a day's fishing. It was not till after the lapse of several minutes that the terrible events of yesterday flashed back through her memory, and she suddenly realised the utter loneliness, as well as the responsibility of her situation.

The uncertainty as to her father's fate weighed heavily on her mind. She burst into tears and lay sobbing for some time. Then the brave little lass got up and dressed herself, and after saying her morning prayer, she felt calmer and better able to bear the hard cross and burden which God in His infinite wisdom had seen fit to lay upon her.

It was her father who generally lighted the fire and got the breakfast ready, but to-day she must do it, and she set to work at once. She had to go down to the storeroom below to get some wood and coals, and there the noise from the hollow cavern beneath sounded louder and more terrible than she had ever hear it yet. She shuddered as she listened to it, and was glad enough when she found herself in the more cheerful room above. After breakfast she took down the big Bible. She read again the beautiful story in St. Mark's Gospel about the storm on the Sea of Galilee, and how Jesus came to His disciples walking on the sea, and said to them, "Be of good cheer, it is I, be not afraid." She too must try not to be afraid, for though she could not see Him walking on the sea as His disciples had done, she knew He was nevertheless as near to her now, as He then was to them. Afterwards she turned to the Psalms where last night she had found so much comfort, and opened at the sixty-second; to her present distress and trouble these words seemed to be specially suited, "He only is my rock and my salvation: He is my defence; I shall not be moved. In God is my salvation and my glory: the rock of my strength, and my refuge, is in God. Trust in Him at all times; ye people, pour out your heart before Him: God is a refuge for us." Cheered by these words, she put down the Bible. She felt she was not placed there to be idle. She must do the work her father would have done had he been in the lighthouse. The lamps would have to be taken out, cleaned, trimmed, and fresh oil put in. She had seen him do this every morning, for her it would be along and tiresome business, but she must do her best. She went up to the lantern; here she found that great quantity of water had come in, and one of the large strong panes of glass had been cracked by the violence of the waves.

Fortunately, no harm had been done to the lamps. Now she had to carry up the chair, the pillow, and the large Bible, so as to be able to reach the lamps, and take them out to clean them. One by one she removed them; and when she had got them all down stairs in the room below, she had no easy task to polish the reflectors and trim the wicks. Then she had to go to the store-room again to fetch the oil to replenish the lamps. This work so occupied her time that she paid little heed to the noise of the storm, which raged with continued vehemence around her, and seemed to shake the building to its very foundation. After she had put all the lamps back in their place, and had brought down the Bible gain, she sat down by the fire, feeling quite tired after this unusual exertion.

Suddenly, she remember it was Sunday. On the morning of that day she was accustomed to read a great part of the Church Service to her father, as well as the Psalms and Lessons. To be a Sunday all alone out here without him, was sad indeed. She took down the Prayer-book and Bible with a sigh, and began to read as usual. It was the ninth day of the month, and from the 46th Psalm she derived fresh comfort and strength to bear her solitary burden: "God is our hope and strength, a very present help in trouble: therefore will we not fear, though the earth be moved, and though the hills be carried into the midst of the sea. Though the waters thereof rage and swell, and though the mountains shake at the tempest of the same."

Truly, indeed, did the waters rage and swell around her, and the strong granite walls which protected her from them did shake and tremble at the tempest of the same; but with the Lord of Hosts to protect her, the God of Jacob as her refuge, she would trust and not be afraid. Were they not praying for her, too, in the church at home on shore? She wondered whether the parson knew where her father was, and realised her lonely position. But she was sure, at all events, he would not forget her and her father in his prayrs. When, too, in the Litany, she came to the petition: "That it may please Thee to succour, help, and comfort all that are in danger, necessity, and tribulation," she felt that she surely was included in those words. How many good people, then, who were that day using that prayer would, though unconsciously to themselves, be asking God to help and comfort her?

She was glad that it was Sunday now. These thoughts seemed to give her fresh strength and courage to bear whatever might be in store for her. The reading of the Service, too, occupied a great deal of time, and so absorbed her attention that she hardly noticed the sounds which accompanied the wild strife of the elements around her.

After dinner, before she sat down to read the Afternoon Service, she went up to the cupola to gaze over the storm-tossed waters, and to see if there were any signs of the tempest abating. But the sky was dark and cloudy as ever; the huge waves every now and then leaped over the lighthouse, burying it in foam and surf, while the rain and hail at intervals descended in torrents.

There were not so many vessels about to-day as yesterday, most of them had succeeded in reaching some port or sheltered anchorage; but she observed one large ship which certainly was not there on the previous afternoon. Its masts must have been carried away by the fury of the storm, or purposely cut down by the crew. It rolled and laboured heavily in the turbulent sea; sometimes it seemed almost buried in the waves, and Mary trembled when she thought it had really foundered; but then it appeared again, feebly trying to battle with the storm. Even she could see how unmanageable this huge ship was, and that unless the gale very suddenly fell, it must become a wreck. This was a sad sight indeed. Here she was powerless to help; for however brightly the lamps burned, they could not assist this large vessel to escape from that destruction which seemed to be certainly in store for it.

For a long time she watched the doomed ship. Then she went down again, sadder than ever, to read the Evening Service, and to pray for these poor men, who were struggling so bravely with the storm, and to whom death seemed very near. Their hard fate almost made her forget her own troubles; she could think now of nothing else. How she longed to be able to do something to help them in their sore distress.

She went up to her labour of love earlier than on the previous evening, hoping that the bright light might cheer them a little, for it must tell them that some one was near to sympathise with and pray for them. When she gazed out for the last time through the bloomy mist and blinding surf, she would just discern the vessel very much nearer than when she first saw it; it seemed to have been carried, too, more to the north. Perhaps it would be driven on shore near Sennen Cove.

Mary remembered, some years ago, that two vessels had been wrecked there, and how cruelly the men had behaved to the poor passengers and crew, whom they had refused to aid, so that all had perished I the waters. She thought that if her father were at the Cove now, he would do all he could to help save their lives. Perhaps that was the reason why God had kept him on shore; if so, she must not complain, but rather rejoice.

Wearied and exhausted she lay down to rest that night. Her heart ached at the thought of those poor fellows in that large ill-fated ship; she wondered how may there were, - probably passengers as well as crew, - perhaps women and children like herself on board. Again, before she closed her eyes, she commended them to the care and protection of the One great Father in heaven, and she thought that the winds were not howling quite so fiercely, nor the waves dashing quite so furiously against the lighthouse walls as they had done during the course of the day. Perhaps God was going to answer her prayer, and save that ship. With this gleam of hope in her heart she fell asleep.

The wreckers had been signally unsuccessful the previous night. They had gone along the coast for some distance, dragged their horse with his lantern backwards and forwards along the cliffs, but all to no avail. Although there was so much shipping about, and the gale continued to blow as fiercely as ever, not a single vessel – thanks chiefly to the Longships light, but partly, perhaps, to good seamanship – was lured by their false lights upon the sore.

It may be well imagined, therefore, with what feelings this lawless gang returned baffled and disappointed to the village. Nichols was furious. He swore he would be revenged some day on the hated young parson, and heaped curses on his head. Then he bitterly reproached himself for leaving little Mary Tresilian in the lighthouse; it was she who had done all the mischief by lighting the lamps. He only wished he had kidnapped her as well as her father.

The men tried to drown their ill-humour and disgust in a carouse at the alehouse, and agreed that, if the gale still continued, they would make another attempt that night; they had a faint hope that the child might be frightened or tired out, and not be able to light the lamps again.

"Where's Ben?" said Nichols suddenly, when he perceived he was no longer of the party.

"Oh, he turned into his cottage," replied one of the men.

"Sneaked off, has he?" observed Nichols angrily; "he's not been himself the last few days. He listens too much to what his wife says, or maybe the parson's got hold of him. I say, chaps, you must all look sharp, or he'll be playing us false; I don't trust him as I used to do, after several things he has said to me lately."

"He didn't half like our kidnapping Tresilian," said one of the men; "do you remember how he stood out against your plan, John?"

"Yes, of course I do," said Nichols; "if Ben proves a traitor, woe betide him!" and, uttering an oath, he struck his clenched fist upon the table with such a force that it made the whole room shake.

Of all the party who were out wrecking that night, Ben was the most wretched. Willing enough as he was to do a dishonest action, and bad as his past career had been, this last exploit of Nichols was too base and cruel even for him, sunk as he was in evil, to sanction. Then, too, strangely enough, the words which the parson had spoken to him on Christmas Eve had made a very deep impression on his mind, though he did not like to confess it, added to which were his wife's constant complaints and entreaties that he would lead a steadier life. When, therefore, as day was drawing on that Sunday morning, they returned, weary and out of heart, from their unsuccessful expedition, Ben, without saying a word to his companions, turned into his own dwelling, as he passed it. He paid no heed to his wife's reproaches, but sat down by the cold, empty hearth, silent and gloomy. A struggle was gong on within him almost as fierce as that of the raging elements outside his cottage. He had nearly made up his mind that Owen should not spend another night in that prison. Should he go and release him at once, or should he inform the parson of what had happened? In either case, when Nichols knew that Owen was at liberty he would naturally lay his release at his door; that would draw down his vengeance upon him, and with it the ill-will of all his former associates in the village. How would he be able to bear that? It would be hard enough, but not so bad as to feel that he had helped to murder a man who had never done him any harm, for if Owen were starved to death in that cave (which Nichols plainly had wished) Ben felt that he would have been an accessory to his death. Then, when he looked at his own children, he thought of the poor little girl left quite alone in the lighthouse in that fearful gale. A brave little lass, too, as the very fact of her having lighted the lamps last night testified! These latter considerations decided him. He would go and release Owen, but he must be cautions, choose his opportunity, and avoid Nichols. Not at present certainly, for when he looked out of the window he saw too many of his own set about, returning from the alehouse. He must wait.

That Sunday, which was ushered in with so fierce a tempest, was ever after looked back upon as a memorable day in the annals of the Cornish fishing village. A very dark day indeed it was in its calendar. Arthur Pendrean had ridden home the previous evening with somewhat mixed feelings; he had been cheered to see the lamps burning brightly, but was sad at heart when he thought that a gang of his parishioners were still plying their own wicked trade with too fatal success, he feared, on so dark a night, and during so fierce a gale. Before he retired to rest he had a long talk with Dick; he was better and stronger now, and hoped to go to church to-morrow, and there publicly return thanks to God for his preservation, safe return, and recovery from his late severe illness.

On Sunday morning, Arthur, anxious to learn what disasters might have been caused by the storm during the night, started rather earlier than usual for Sennen. On his way he met David Abbott coming to meet him. Stopping his horse he asked – "Any news, Abbott? Has the storm done much mischief?"

"There hasn't been such a gale, sir, since the lighthouse has been built. Poor Owen and his daughter must have felt it terribly, but the lights have burned just as usual notwithstanding, and the building stands firm and safe as ever. I've just been up to look at it."

"Thank God, Abbott, I'm glad indeed to hear it, but have you heard of any wrecks?"

"Not one, sir," he replied; "and those wrecker chaps, Nichols, Pollard, and all the rest of 'em, started off as soon as it got dark with a horse and a lantern after their old pranks, but they came back about four o'clock this morning, having got nothing for their pains, and putting it all down to you and the lighthouse. They were in a rage, there's no mistake."

"I think David, they're not far wrong about the lighthouse; by God's blessing it was, I trust, the means of saving many lives last night."

"And it'll save many more, I hope, sir," said Abbott; "but what I've come to tell you is, that we've seen a large vessel, dismasted, rolling very heavily, and evidently in distress, just off the Longships. We can't make out what she is; maybe a foreigner; it strikes me her crew can't manage her, and that she'll be a wreck afore nightfall."

"This is bad new, though, Abbott. Can't we render her any help?"

"Impossible, sir, no boat could put our in such a gale; the wind is blowing harder than ever. I am afraid she must go on shore and be a perfect wreck. The only hope is that when she does, we may save a few lives."

"We must all do our best in that case. You'll keep a sharp look-out, Abbott, all day; have the boats ready in case the wind should drop, and be sure to let me know when the vessel strikes, though God grant that she may be saved! After Morning Service I'll be down on the beach – meet me there."

"All right, sir," said Abbott, as he turned back to Sennen.

Before going to church Arthur had time to ride to Land's End to look at the ship in distress. He perceived at once that Abbott's report had by no means been exaggerated, and that she was in imminent peril if the gale did not very speedily abate. The chances of saving life depended, he knew, entirely on the spot where she struck the land; if any of the men on board were acquainted with the coast, it was possible that by skilful seamanship she might run on shore near Sennen Cove, and in that case efforts could be made to help the poor fellows struggling for their lives in the surf. He turned back towards the church, his heart aching for the crew and passengers of this evidently doomed ship.

All noticed the grave anxious look on his face when he commenced the service. Notwithstanding the rough weather, the church was well filled. The good folk round about were well seasoned to storm and rain, and were too much attached to their pastor and to the services of the church, to allow any but the most urgent cause to prevent them from coming to God's house on His day. Dick Evans was there, just under the reading desk, looking pale and thin and much muffled up; a neighbour had given him a lift in his cart, for the weather was too bad for him to walk in his present weak state.

Before the Litany, the parson asked the prayers of his congregation for the crew and passengers of a vessel in distress close to the shore, and after the petition "for all that travel by land or by water," he paused for a few moments, and there was a solemn silence throughout the building. Then, before the general thanksgiving, he gave out that "Richard Evans desires to offer up praise to Almighty God for great and special mercies received," and when he read the words, "particularly to him who desires now to offer up his praises and thanksgivings for Thy late mercies vouchsafed unto him," Dick could hardly restrain his tears, and when the 103rd Psalm, commencing

> "My soul inspired with sacred love,
> God's holy name for ever bless,
> Of all His favours mindful prove,
> And still thy grateful thanks express;
> 'Tis He that all Thy sins forgives,
> And after sickness makes thee sound
> From danger He thy life retrieves,
> By Him with grace and mercy crowned."

was given out, he was still more overcome, for he felt how exactly suitable the words were to his case.

The parson took for his text John xv. 13, "Greater love hath no man than this, that a man lay down his life for his friends."

Many then present afterwards asserted that never had their good parson spoke so earnestly and lovingly, as he did on that occasion. He preached to them in simple words of the great love of God the Father towards lost mankind, of the infinite condescension of the Divine Son in coming down from heaven to live, suffer, and at last to die for the sake of poor lost ruined men, whom He even condescended to call His friends, in spite of the ingratitude and hard-heartedness which so many of them showed towards Him. He spoke, as he was ever wont, of the willingness of our blessed Lord to receive and welcome sinners of even the darkest dye who with deep penitence implored His forgiveness. Then he urged them to endeavour to follow the example which their Saviour had set before them, by living a life of self-denial and self-sacrifice for the good of others. And he contrasted such a life as this, with that led by many people in the village, whose desire seemed to be rather to destroy life than to save it, who throve and prospered not by their honest labour, but by the sorrows and misfortunes of others. He thanked God that many of those now present had abandoned their evil ways, and he thanked Him too, for having in His mercy allowed the lighthouse to be built, which he felt sure had been instrumental in saving many a gallant ship during last night's tempest. He asked his flock to remember in their prayers the father and daughter who had left a comfortable home to go and live on the rock, that God might protect and bless them in the exercise of their lonely duty; but above all, he urged them to pray for the poor fellows on board the large ship buffeted by the merciless winds and waves so near to the shore. It seemed indeed, he said, as they listened to the winds howling round the church, and the hail and rain beating angrily against the window panes, and to the distant roar of the angry ocean, that there could be no hope for them; but God was all-powerful, He could deliver them, though all seemed lost to human eyes. He would not turn a deaf ear to the prayers they offered up for their poor perishing fellow-creatures. But to pray for them, he solemnly reminded his people, was not the only duty of strong men with an emergency like this, they must work for them too. Whether Englishmen or foreigners they were still their brothers, for "God has made of one blood all the nations of the earth," they all were children of the one great Father, redeemed by the same loving Saviour; let each man then present to do all in his power that day, to aid in saving the lives of the passengers and crew, boldly risking his own if need be in so noble a cause, battling like a hero with sea and surf, and proving himself worthy of the grand name of Englishman. If their country had won to itself an ill repute by these evil deeds of its inhabitants, let them now, for ever, retrieve its character, and show that Cornishmen were no longer backward in deeds of courage, pluck, and self-denial, and would never allow shipwrecked men to perish off their coast without hold out a brave and helping hand to save them.

The parson was pleased when he saw several of the fishermen remain to the Holy Communion which followed the sermon, and was struck by their reverent manner. Again, in the prayer for the Church militant, he paused after the words; "We most humbly beseech Thee of Thy goodness, O Lord, to comfort and succour all them, who in this transitory life are in trouble, sorrow, need, sickness, or any other adversity;" and all remembered in their prayers the storm-tossed ship hurrying to destruction. Little did Arthur think then how two of his flock very sorely needed the prayers of the church – both in solitude, separated from each other by the designs of cruel men, and both in much sorrow and adversity. Owen and Mary were indeed present to his mind, and included in his prayers, but he imagined them together as usual, trying to cheer each other during the raging tempest, and happy in the thought that they were aiding some tempest-tossed mariners to gain in safety the long-desired haven.

It was a very solemn service. All present seemed more deeply impressed than usual; there was indeed much to produce such an effect. Little did any of them, however, think that to one present it was the Last Communion, and that sorrow and bereavement were soon to fill all their hearts.

The parson found Abbott waiting in the porch after service was over. He told him the ship was still labouring heavily in the sea; she was making way rather to the northward, which made him think that there was some one on board acquainted with the coast, who, perceiving that shipwreck was inevitable, hoped to get the vessel to strike where there would be more chance of life being saved, if she went to pieces. He said that he and others were sure, from the building and general appearance of the ship, that she was a foreign, probably French, frigate. He informed Arthur that Nichols and the other wreckers who had been so bitterly disappointed the previous evening, were all now in high glee, hoping to profit by the impending disaster.

"We must do all in our power to defeat their evil designs," said Arthur. "How long do you think it will be before the vessel strikes?"

"I can't say I'm sure, sir; but it won't be yet a while. All depends on the wind and tide," said Abbott.

"Well, I've got to go over to service at St. Levan this afternoon; but I hope to be back here soon after four o'clock. I should be sorry not to be on the spot to give all the help I can," said Arthur.

"I don't think she'll run ashore before nightfall, sir; it's pretty certain you'll be in time," said Abbott, as Arthur galloped off in the direction of St. Levan.

We left Owen Tresilian overcome with fatigue and exhaustion, asleep in his dark, damp prison. He slept long and heavily. When he awoke and looked around on the grey dripping walls of his dungeon, he was a few minutes before he realised his situation – ere the events of the previous day flashed upon his memory. Then he uttered a groan of anguish, covered his face with his hands, his strong frame shook with emotion, and the tears trickled down his weather-beaten cheeks. Surely God must have utterly forsaken him, else why should he be left here to perish, while his darling child, his only treasure, was alone and unprotected in that storm-beaten lighthouse. Oh that he knew whether the light had burned last night! Were it not for the great rock which stood just before the entrance of the cavern, he would have been able to see. How long would it be the pleasure of his dastardly enemies to keep him here? Was it their intention really to starve him to death? He got up, but he was so stiff, both with the cold and from the bruises he had received yesterday, that he could scarcely stand erect. He staggered up to the gate, and putting forth all his strength, again shook it violently, but it yielded not an inch; it was firmly barred, bolted, and padlocked. He sat down again in despair.

The gale did not appear to have abated in the least; the winds were still howling round the shore, and whistling as they penetrated with chilly blast into his prison; the waves were roaring louder than ever, and dashing with fury against the rocks close by him. If the light had not burned, and he did not think that Mary would have the presence of mind to light the lamps, even if she could reach them, how many wrecks there must have been during the night! What would the parson think when he saw no beacon? Doubtless he would set to work at once to find out the reason of the calamity; and he was so clever, that perhaps he would guess the cause, and discover the wicked plot which had made him, the keeper, a prisoner, and cruelly condemned his daughter, to be left alone on that terrible rock. When he thought, too, how many were concerned in the conspiracy, he hoped that one among them might be touched and relent. So just a ray of hope, faint as it was, shone into his desolate heart, and he tried once more to trust in God, and when he lifted up his prayer to Him, words Mary had read a few days before came back to his memory: "Thou art about my path, and about my bed, and spiest out all my ways; the darkness is no darkness with Thee, but the night is as clear as the day; the darkness and light to

Thee are both alike." God was present with him, then, even in this dark dungeon. He would still trust Him, and surely He would deliver him.

Owen now took out his tinder-box, and lighted a match to explore his prison. He groped his way to the back part of the cavern, which grew narrower as he advanced. It seemed interminable, as he perceived, took, that he was rapidly ascending; the path was so steep that once or twice he had to climb with hands and knees. Every now and then his match would burn out, and he had to light a fresh one. Sometimes the winding passage became so low that he had to bend almost double to get through, and then it would grow wider again. The blasts of fresh air which met him occasionally filled him with hope that this long natural tunnel had an exit somewhere on top of the cliffs; yet if such were the case, the opening would surely be known to him, familiar as he was with every inch of ground in that neighbourhood. Nerved to fresh vigour by this hope, he scrambled on, and at last, to his intense joy, he saw in the distance the light of the day before him; and after a long struggle he found himself at the bottom of a lofty natural shaft, like a steep well, the sides jagged and rough, and closing in towards the narrow opening at the top. At a glance, Owen saw that there was no means of escape here; the pit was too deep, and its sides too precipitous for him to attempt to scramble up, still the means of communicating with the outer world were easier perhaps here, than at the gate of the cave on the sea-shore. He could call out, and he might be heard by some one passing. He sat down and gazed at the bit of grey sky, across which clouds were rapidly driven by the wind. That opening he reckoned could not be far off from the Land's End, where, on a stormy day, many came from Sennen to look-out over the sea and watched the homeward-bound vessels. The parson, he knew, frequently visited the spot; but when he suddenly remembered it was Sunday, he felt there was no much chance of rescue that day; and as the men who might be on the look-out would probably be the enemies to whom he owed his capture and imprisonment, his best policy would be silence. He groped his way back to the cave, where he refreshed himself with the dry bread and water which had been left him. Then he examined the gate again. With his strong knife, and by dint of perseverance, he thought it just possible he might cut a hole through it, by which to escape. But it would be a long job; he could hardly complete it in a day; perhaps, after all, he would not succeed. However, with God's help, eh would make every effort to get out of this dreary prison.

The wood was far harder than he expected, nevertheless he worked on with energy. About noon he finished the scanty food his captors had provided for him, and the dread of starvation urged him on to labour more vigorously. He had already cut two large perpendicular slits in the gate, and his next object was to cut two horizontal ones, thus making a hole in it large enough for him to crawl though. He was just beginning to do this when his knife broke off close to the handle, the blade remaining fixed in the gate. With a cry of despair he started back. But a moment before he had seemed to be so near success, and how all his hopes were shattered, and he, and perhaps his little daughter must miserably perish.

The gale blew as fiercely as ever; with a roar like thunder the mighty billows broke upon the shore. Owen perceived that another night of storm and tempest was in store for his poor child in that lonely lighthouse. The thought was intolerable. "O God, protect my dear child, my darling Mary," he exclaimed, as wringing his hands in an agony he fell on his knees in the centre of the cave. There for a few moments he knelt motionless, as if rooted to the spot. Suddenly he started to his feet. That could not be the wind which had shaken the gate and made the padlock outside rattle. Then he heard a low voice calling out, "Owen, are you there?"

"Yes," he replied; "who are you, friend or foe?"

"It's I, Ben Pollard," was the reply. "I'm come to let you out."

"You, Ben, come to let me out!" exclaimed Owen. "You're one of the last men I should have expected to do that. Ah! I fear it's only for some worse fate than this – are you going to murder me, then?"

"No, no, Owen," he replied quickly, but still in a subdued voice. "I was never in favour of Nichols' scheme for carrying you off in that cowardly way, and now they don't know that I've come to release you, though some of them suspect me, I think, of playing them false, but there's no time for taking about it now. Nichols's got the key of the padlock, and the only way I can get you out is to file through one of the links of this chain. I may have been watched and followed, so there's no time to lose."

"Thank God! thank God!" cried Owen, "that He has put this into your heart, Ben; but answer me one question – only one: did the light burn last night on the Longships?"

"Yes, as bright as ever, and didn't our chaps curse and swear when they saw it. Why, it was because they thought your daughter wouldn't be able to light it, that they kidnapped you, but we've got nothing for our pains. We were out all last night – and there wasn't a single wreck, and precious down in the mouth were the whole lot of us when we got back to Sennen this morning."

When Owen heard this good news he could scarcely utter a word, his heart was so full of joy and gratitude to God. He had heard his prayer then. He had not only protected his child, but given her strength and courage to light the lamps. How she managed it he could not think! And now, in a wonderful and unexpected way, by means of the man he looked up on as his enemy, the Lord was about to deliver him from this dungeon, just at the moment when all hope seemed to have vanished, and he was utterly overwhelmed with despair.

"Ah! you couldn't have brought me better news than this, Ben," said

Owen at last; "my poor child is safe, then, though she's left there all alone. God be praised for His mercy."

"It's a thick chain this, to file though," said Ben impatiently, "but so long as those chaps don't get scent of where I am, it'll be all right, though it's a longer job than I expected."

Ben had been watching all day for an opportunity to run down to the cave and release Owen, but it was not till late in the afternoon that he saw any chance of escaping unperceived.

The French frigate, which was evidently now being driven rapidly on the shore, had caused an intense excitement throughout the village; all the men had hurried down to the beach. When Ben saw them pass his cottage he guessed there must be wreck, and now, he reflected, was the time for him to carry out his intention. His absence from the shore would certainly be noticed by Nichols and his companions, but they were hardly likely to leave the chance of booty which a wreck afforded to follow him, even if they suspected the errand on which he had started.

He had left his cottage unperceived, and was already out of the village, when to his annoyance and disgust he met Nichols' hopeful nephew running along the road in the direction of the shore. As he passed him he called out, "Make haste, Bill, or you'll be too late."

The younger fellow, however, stopped, and said, "Ain't you coming too, Ben? wherever are you going off to?"

"No business of yours, Bill; I'll be down on the beach presently," said Ben and hastened on.

Young Nichols gazed suspiciously after him, He felt half inclined to follow Ben, for he knew his uncle's suspicions about him, but the immediate prospect of plunder outweighed in his mind any profit he might gain by obtaining proof positive that Pollard was a traitor, so he hurried on.

It was this meeting with Bill Nichols that made Ben so eager to effect Owen's immediate release. He filed on in silence as rapidly as he could, till at last the link was separated. The chain and padlock fell to the ground, and Owen Tresilian was once more a free man.

With deepest gratitude he warmly grasped Ben's hand. "You've been a true friend to me, Ben, I shall never be able to repay you for this," he said; and then he darted round the rock which stood at the entrance of the cave so that he might gaze out to sea, and behold the building which contained all he held most dear in the world.

It was quite dusk now, and the cheering light burned bright as ever on the Longships Rock. This was more than he had expected, for he had forgotten that the hour for lighting up had already arrived. Mary, then, was still safe, still intent on her duty. He fell on his knees on the sea-shore and once again poured out his heart in fervent thanksgiving to that gracious Father Who was so mercifully watching over his beloved child, and Who had just so wonderfully delivered him out of the dark cavern.

Ben, rough as he was, was touched when he witnessed Owen's deep gratitude to God and his tender attachment to the child from whom he had been so cruelly torn. He did not repent now of the action he had just performed. He felt misgivings about it all along. He had even been inclined to turn back after he met Bill Nichols, but now he was glad he had rescued Owen, and indifferent to what Nichols and the rest of them might say or do to him in consequence.

22

The Wreck - A Noble Self-Sacrifice

"Alone upon the leaping billows, lo!
What fearful image works its way? a ship!
Shapeless and wild …
Her sails dishevelled and her massy form
Disfigured, but tremendously sublime:
Prowless and helmless through the waves she rocks
And writhes as if in agony! like her
Who to the last avail o'er starving foes,
Sinks with a bloody struggle into death, -
The vessel combats with the battling waves
Then finally dives below! the thunders toll
Her requiem, and whirlwinds howl for joy."

- Crabbe

"Gave his pure soul unto his Captain, Christ,
Under Whose colours he had fought so long."

- Shakespeare

A long and weary day had that been for all on board the ill-fated French frigate. The English sailors had worked bravely and perseveringly, and the French officers had done their best to help them, but so far as any hope of saving the ship existed, their efforts, all saw, must be unavailing. The gale blew as fiercely as ever, the water was rising rapidly in the hold. The vessel must become a wreck, and the only hope was the bare possibility of reaching land by swimming or clinging to broken pieces of the wreck. When at evening the light again shone forth from the Longships, they were close to the shore, labouring heavily, the decks constantly swept by the huge billows. In a very short time their fate would be decided; and the frigate must strike soon, unless she foundered before they touched the land.

The French officers, brought up in the school of Voltaire and Rousseau, disciples of a philosophy which teaches that there is no future state, and that at the moment of death all is over and the soul ceases to exist, endeavoured to meet their fate with calm indifference, and glanced with a sneer of contempt at some of the crew, who, although they too had cast off their religion in days of prosperity, now, when death stared them in the face, began to remember the simple lessons taught them at their mothers' knees, and the solemn words of their parish priests, which they had heard in church before priests were proscribed, and churches shut, by order of the Republican Government. Many of these poor fellows were praying and crossing themselves devoutly, and repeating as far as they could remember, the Paternoster and the Ave Maria. With clasped hands some called on God to save them, imploring His pardon for their sins.

The English sailors continued for the most part to work at the pumps, but many, alas! as is so often the case on such occasions, when they saw that all hope of saving the ship had disappeared, obtained access to the spirit room and gave themselves up to a drunken carouse, defying the Almighty, and cursing the storm, which was hurrying them into eternity.

Tom Mariott and Philip Tresilian again stood together on the poop. They alone of all on board were able to meet the sad fate which threatened them, with composure.

"It can't last much longer, Tom," said the latter; "we're almost among the rocks now, it strikes me. If we're only driven round that point, and strike there, there's just a bare chance that the lives of some of us may be saved."

"You know all this coast well, then, Philip," said Tom.

"Know it, Tom! why I've lived here all my life. It's only that high cliff you see just there that hides the cottage where I was born, and where I hope my father and sister are still living and praying for me, too. Little do they think how near I am to them. Ah! Tom, it's hard indeed to die now; would I had fallen in the battle along with our good friend Forster."

"Don't say so, Phil," replied Tom; "God knows what's best for us, and chooses the right time and way for us to die. We mustn't repine at His will. Let's try and lift up our hearts to Him Whom we are so soon to see face to face, and ask Him to give us grace and strength to honour Him by dying bravely."

"You're right, Tom," said Philip, in a voice choked by emotion; "He's never forsaken me yet, and I'm sure He won't now; I'll try and trust Him still. 'Yea, though I walk through the valley of the shadow of death, I will fear no evil: for Thou art with me; Thy rod and Thy staff they comfort me.'"

"Yes, and with us through the dark river too, that you were telling me about last Sunday, Philip, out of the book called 'Pilgrim's Progress,' that you said you had read at home, and poor Forster used to be so fond of talking about."

At that moment a terrible wave, like a huge mountain of white surf, rolled over the frigate; every beam and timber creaked and shook; the awe-struck crew thought it was all over now, but again the vessel rose to the surface, driven some way nearer to the shore, and towards the point which Philip hoped they might gain.

"I didn't think the old ship would have stood that, Tom," said Philip, after the wave had passed.

"She won't survive another such," replied Tom; "she'll either go down or be dashed against the rocks."

"How close we are to the land now; don't you see the lights on the shore, Tom?"

"Yes, I expect there are plenty of folks on the look-out for us there."

"Most of 'em, I'm afraid, on the look-out for plunder, though, if our parson's there, I know he'll do all he can to try to save our lives."

"Well, lad," said Tom, "I've pretty well made up my mind there's little hope of any of our lives being saved, the waves are so big, and there's such a terrific swell along this coast – but I wish our poor fellows were better prepared to die. How sad it is to see how drunk many of them are, and to listen to their vile oaths at such a time as the present!"

"Ah! Tom, we must pray for them as well as for ourselves. God grant them time for repentance!"

"God bless you, lad!" said Tom, as he put his hand on Philip's shoulder; "how can we thank Him enough for bringing us together, and now it seems as if we were to go across that dark river side by side; doesn't it, Phil?"

Philip did not reply, for his eyes were fixed on the shore. There was a sudden lull in the storm just then, and the vessel, borne rapidly by the force of the waves, had rounded the point, and now the small white houses of Sennen Cove, clustering down to the beach, came into view. It was his own dear home Philip saw, and he was wondering if his father and sister were still there, and if at that moment they were thinking of him.

"There it is, Tom, there it is – the cottage where I was born – where my mother died – where" –

He could not finish the sentence. Another wave, more gigantic than the preceding one, rolled over the frigate, and carried her on with irresistible force towards the shore.

And now the sea demanded its first victims, for several of the crew, lashed as they were to the ship, were torn away by the violence of the wave and borne into the raging waters, beneath which they immediately disappeared.

Drenched, and almost blinded by the surf, Tom and Philip were some minutes before they could see each other; each thought his companion had perished.

"Thank God, Philip, you are still there!" said Tom.

He had scarcely uttered the words, when there was a terrible crash which sounded loudly even above the howling of the storm and the roar of the breakers.

The ship had struck at last. Then came crash after crash as wave succeeding wave rolled over the vessel; her timbers parted at once; the sea was strewn with planks, shrouds, cordage, together with hundreds of poor fellows struggling hard, but in vain, for dear life in that wild waste of waters.

The bows of the frigate, where Tom and Philip were stationed at the moment when she struck, remained raised some distance above the water, the forepart of the vessel having become firmly wedged in the rock. Hither, therefore, all who could escape crowded, many clinging to the bowsprit, as the highest portion, and least exposed to the waves, which, however, still continued to roll over them. All knew that it was only a matter of time. The frail remnant of the ship which was now their last refuge must speedily yield to the repeated shocks of the waves, and then they too must perish, - and yet they were so near the shore. Scarcely a man there but could have swam to land if the sea had been tolerably calm. In these days of life-boats and appliances for rescuing the shipwrecked, not one of those poor seamen need have been lost. They could see the lights on the shore, the figures hurrying along the beach. Would they make any effort to save them? Were they any brave hearts on that barren shore who would risk their lives for poor shipwrecked strangers?

Never perhaps had greater excitement reigned at Sennen village and cove than on that afternoon and evening. All who could – men, women, even children – had hurried down to the beach. Some, hard, cruel, unrelenting, were bent alone on plunder; they had not the slightest sympathy for the poor fellows on board the frigate; others, on the contrary, were filled with compassion for their unhappy fellow-creatures, and longed to be able to render them assistance, consulting to together as to what could be done, and determining to use every means in their power to save life. It was a motley group collected on the beach.

There were the rough fishermen of Sennen and the villages on the seaboard around; there were the uncouth miners from St. Just and Pendeen, some of whom had hastened thither from no good motive; others, whose lives had been changed by the preaching of the Gospel by John Wesley and his followers, had come to render what aid they could to the shipwrecked crew; there were farmers, too, and their labourers from inland; but he most conspicuous and energetic figure in the crowd, as he passed quickly from one to the other, here encouraging the brave workers, there warning those intent only on plunder, was Arthur Pendrean; his tall, manly figure now galloping on his horse along the road, now striding on foot up and down the beach, seemed to be everywhere at once. Nothing escaped him; he saw how Nichols and his companions at one end of the strand were plotting together how best to secure their booty. He was indifferent to the looks of defiance they cast at him. Since no words of kindness or persuasion could touch their hearts, he was determined to use every means to baffle their schemes. Strong ropes were at hand to throw to any drowning men who might be cast near enough to the shore to make use of them; and everything that could be thought of as likely to save life or restore consciousness, had been prepared by the brave young parson.

The frigate had been driven round the point. When the crowd on the beach saw the first huge wave roll over her they raised a half-suppressed cry of anguish, concluding that all was over with the ill-fated ship, but when again she emerged from the foaming surge, to renew her terrible but unequal conflict with the fierce seas, all breathed more freely, while exclamations of relief and thankfulness arose from many breasts. But at that moment a fresh excitement occurred, which for the time actually drew away from the attention of nearly all those assembled on the beach from the object which till then had so entirely absorbed it. Two men were pushing their way through the crowd up to the parson, whose eyes were so intently fixed upon the frigate that until one of them pulled him by the sleeve, and called him by name, he did not observe them. When, however, he turned round and looked at the man who addressed him in the face, he started back with a look of utter amazement, not unmingled with terror, his face became deadly pale, and exclaimed –

"Owen! Can it be you. What brought you here? and Mary – and the lighthouse? Am I dreaming?"

His astonishment was shared by the rest of the crowd, who regarded Owen as one risen from the dead. "How could he have come here?" was the question on every tongue; for there was the light burning, and it had burned last night too; and how, in such a tempest as this, could Tresilian, except by a miracle, have left the lighthouse? One group of watchers on the beach, of whom Nichols was the ringleader, could have solved this mystery; they, perceiving some fresh excitement, had approached the spot where the parson was standing, and had at once recognised Owen Tresilian and Ben Pollard.

"I told you how it would be, uncle," said Bill. "I was sure Ben would play us false; he was after no good when I met him on the road this afternoon."

Nichols, trembling in every limb with passion and resentment towards Ben Pollard, and uttering fearful oaths and curses, rushed through the crowd with the intention of levelling a terrible blow at the head of his former friend, when the parson, aware of his intention, seized him by the arm, and hurled him away with such force that he fell back on the ground. In a moment he was on his legs again; and this time, had he not been dragged away by his companions, would have aimed a blow at Arthur.

"you shall repent this day as long as you live, Ben," he said, as he cast a look of deadly hatred on Pollard; "and as to you, cursed parson, I'll be even with you yet."

Taking no further notice of him, Arthur now turned eagerly to Ben and Owen.

"What is all this, Owen?" he said. "Explain the mystery; I am quite unable to understand it."

In a few words, and as quickly as possible, Owen related to the parson the events of the last two days.

"Ah! sir," he said at the end, "If I had only listened to your advice, and not taken my boat with me to the lighthouse, this would never have happened. Oh! how my heart aches when I think of my dear little one all alone on that dreary rock in this terrible gale; and when will it ever abate? when shall I be able to see her again? She still lives, I know, for the light burns; but how long will she be able to bear that solitude? Oh God! O God! watch over her and protect her!"

"Bad and heartless as I knew your enemies were," said Arthur, "I did not think they would have gone so far as this. As for you, Pollard," he added, grasping Ben's hand, and shaking it warmly, "never mind the threats of evil men; God will bring all their plots to naught. You have acted bravely and rightly in this matter, and have nothing to fear."

Then turning to Owen, he said.

"Poor little Mary, I did indeed feel for her; but what a brave heart and what courage she has shown in lighting those lamps as she has done now for two nights! Never fear, Owen. God, who has given her strength so far, will surely continue to support her. It is her firm faith and trust in Him which has enabled her to bear up and do her duty in that lonely prison. The gale can't last much longer; and even if we are not able to land on the rock, we can get near enough to let Mary see us, so that she may feel we have not forgotten her."

"Ah! sir, if we could only do that to-morrow, how thankful I should be," sighed Owen.

"We shall see; but there's no more time for talking about it now, Owen. Look at the vessel yonder, how rapidly she is being driven in; she'll be a wreck in a few minutes, and all our thoughts and efforts must employed in trying to save the lives of those on board."

"Yes, indeed, sir," said Owen. "I'm only too glad that I should be here to help; and Ben, you won't join the wreckers any more, will you?"

"No, no, Owen; I mean to stick to you now. I don't think my old companions either would give me much of a welcome if I wished to join them."

But all further conversation was now arrested, for every eye was eagerly turned seaward, watching in the dim twilight the struggles of the ill-fated vessel as she writhed and quivered among the might breakers, whose plaything she had completely become. They could see the poor men on board, some clinging to the sides of the ship or lashed to the stumps of the masts, some running hither and thither, as if distracted, on the decks; while each great rolling wave swept fresh victims into the boiling surge, a cry of horror arose from almost every breast on the beach. In a few moments more the frigate went to pieces, becoming an utter wreck, before their eyes. They saw the poor fellows battling with the waves. Some few, however, remained clinging desperately to the bows, or huddled together on the forecastle, which still kept above water. Can nothing be done to save them? is the question which arises in every humane heart on the shore. In such a sea as this, is it possible for any to survive? The mighty billows are rolling in with majestic grandeur, dashing up their frothy crests to heaven – cold, merciless, and powerful – brave indeed would be he who dare venture an unequal combat with such foes, even when the lives of fellow-creatures are at stake. But "virtue is bold, and goodness never fearful."

"Men! brothers!" cried Arthur, "we mustn't stand here doing nothing, while these poor fellows are perishing before our eyes. We'll form a line, hold each others' hands, rope ourselves together, too, and, plunging into the sea, we may be able to seize and rescue a few of these unhappy men. What do you say to it, Owen?"

"I'm willing to try that, or any other way, sir, to help 'em; but I fear the life will be pretty nigh knocked out of 'em before they'll cast up near enough for us to get hold of them," replied Owen?

"Come! with God's help, let's set to work at once; not a moment's to be lost," said the parson.

Arthur's brave example and words of encouragement seemed to have an electrical effect on the men around him. Even a few who had before been his enemies were now eager to join the heroic band, of which he was the leader. The chain was soon formed; eight men firmly grasped others' hands, and now all gazed intently on the boiling, tumbling mass of surge before them: there, beaten about hither and thither by the waves, is a dark object almost within reach. There is a dash into the sea. Owen has insisted on being outermost, next to him is Ben, and then the parson. Owen, though up to his neck in water, has grasped the downing man. A ringing cheer bursts from the crowds; but the danger is not yet over. Before they have time to retreat, a huge billow rolls in, buries the whole party in the surf, and hurls them with violence upon the beach. Not one has relaxed his grasp. Those nearest the shore, less exposed than the rest of the force of the wave, pull sturdily, so that all are dragged in safely – Owen last, unconscious himself, but still clinging to the man he has saved. The rescued one, who is evidently a foreigner, and in whom life appears to be extinct, is at once taken to a neighbouring cottage, where every preparation has been made for the reception of the poor fellows, and where restoratives are at once administered.

Owen soon recovered his senses. Again the chain was formed. This time Arthur would not allow him to take the post of greatest danger, but insisted on assuming it himself; and when some of the men objected, he remarked that each must take his turn. Now another splendid dash into the sea, and another man saved! This time it was an Englishman, and, though stunned and unable to speak, there was little doubt but that life was still in him.

"Thank God!" exclaimed Arthur, as she emerged, exhausted and breathless, from the water. "I am proud of you, my lads; you're acting gallantly now; you'll retrieve the bad character we've got in these parts; but we must be at it again, as long as our strength holds out, and as long as there is a man left battling with the waves, we must do our best to save him."

Thus they continued their noble exertions, each taking it by turns to advance furthest into the sea, sometimes baffled indeed, but oftener cheered by well-earned success, till ten men had been wrested from the angry surf, and borne away to the cottages hard by.

Meanwhile, at the other end of the beach, Nichols and his party were almost as desperate battling with the sea, their object being to secure barrels, bales, stores of various kinds, with which, a soon as the frigate went to pieces, the sea was strewn, and which were every now and then driven in the direction of the shore.

After the tenth man had been rescued, Arthur and his gallant band were so utterly exhausted that they were reluctantly obliged to take a few minutes' rest, eagerly watching meanwhile the remnant of the wreck, which, though wave after wave rolled over it, had not yet broken up. They could perceive that many of the poor fellows who had been clinging to it had been washed away; cold and exposure had deprived them of strength sufficient to hold on.

Arthur's heart bled for these unfortunate men; fervently did he pray that they might be rescued yet. Oh that they had more strong arms to aid them! One thing he perceived with thankfulness and pleasure – that was, the wind had fallen. The sky was clearer, and the gale had evidently spend its fury; but for some time yet, after such a storm, little diminution could be expected in the size and force of the waves. How true is it that the most tender-hearted are often the most courageous! Arthur yearned so over these poor fellows, foreigners probably, and foes of his country, that he felt he could gladly sacrifice his own life, were it necessary, to save theirs. He thought of the text that he had preached from that morning – "Greater love hath no man than this, that a man lay down his life for his friends." The image of his dear Lord and Master, of His life of love and devotion, and of His noble death of self-sacrifice, was vividly present to his mind, nerving him with fresh courage and energy. These poor men, for whom Christ died, must not be allowed to perish, if he could save them.

When the gallant band were sufficiently refreshed to resume their generous but hazardous work, they could not perceive any more victims struggling in the waves; they must all have perished – the life beaten out of them by the cruel sea, and swallowed up in its depths; but there were still some men on the battered, quivering wreck, and to them all efforts must now be directed.

But an incident occurred which for a moment turned away their attention from the wreck. A yell of horror, piercing through the thundering roar of the breakers, arose from the group of wreakers at the other end of the beach. All eyes were immediately turned in the direction whence it proceeded.

Most of the men there, up to their waists in surf, had plainly been making a desperate effort to seize a large dark object with which a receding wave had just carried away from the shore. Dick Evans, who, too weak to join the gallant band of rescuers, was on the alert to make himself useful in other ways, now ran up to Arthur, and told him that one of the men who were employed in wrecking had evidently been borne off by a wave with the object that he was endeavouring to secure.

"Whoever he be, he richly deserve his fate," said one of the men standing near Arthur; "he ought to have been helping us to save the poor fellows' lives instead of trying to enrich himself."

"True enough, my friend," returned the parson; "but for all that we mustn't leave him to perish without an effort on our part;" and he hastened into the midst of the group of wreckers.

They seemed terror-struck; they had lost all presence of mind, and were making no attempt to rescue their companion who was clinging to a huge barrel, was being buffeted by the waves, and had already been carried some distance from the shore.

"Who is it?" said Arthur.

"John Nichols," replied one of the men; "he was just dragging in that barrel, when a wave came and washed him away with it."

"Nichols, indeed!" said Arthur, with a deep sigh, while an expression of sadness passed over his face. "I know no one here less prepared to meet his God that that man; at all risks let us try and save him. Why didn't you form a chain, men, at once, and dash in after him?" he asked, turning indignantly to the wreckers; "you don't exert yourselves as much to save one of your own fellows as we are doing to rescue these foreigners."

The men looked ashamed, but still they stood motionless, while Bill Nichols, the greatest coward of the lot, sneaked away behind the others.

"Come, Owen," said Arthur; "I see these cowardly fellows won't move; we must form a line again here, and try what we can do – we've no time to lose;" and he gazed anxiously at the wreck and the poor fellows hanging on to it.

The attempt was made, but proved unsuccessful.. The surf was too strong and the water too deep for them to advance far enough to grasp the drowning man.

"There is but one means left – a last chance – I will try it," said the heroic parson. "Dick, bring me my horse – quick – not a moment must be lost."

Arthur sprang upon the back of the faithful animal.

"What are you going to do, sir?" cried Owen and Ben together; "you're never going to ride into that boiling surf, your horse'll never stand it, sir – indeed you mustn't," and both seized his bridle.

"Let go both of you – I will be obeyed," cried Arthur, in such a tone of command that it compelled submission. "God helping me," he said in a calmer voice, "I will save him yet."

At first the horse refused to enter the water, but his master soon gave the intelligent beast to understand that he was to carry him whither he willed, even into the jaws of death if needful, and now he plunged into the raging breakers. A ringing cheer arose from every man on the sore as they beheld this act of bravery. All knew that Nichols was the parson's bitterest enemy; they remembered the intended blow, the cruel words he had spoken against him, and the threats of vengeance he had uttered but a few minutes before still rung in their ears.

Arthur had chosen a fitting moment to advance into the surf, when a wave had just receded, and a possibility occurred of securing the drowning man before another followed. Bravely did his faithful steed second his efforts. Though off his feet he swam in the direction to which he was guided by his master, and Arthur actually succeeded in clutching Nichols by the collar, and dragging him back apparently lifeless to the shore. It had been a fierce battle, and the rescuer, himself terribly exhausted, had to be helped off his horse, and laid on the shore for a few minutes to recover himself. So faint and spent was Arthur that he almost feared lest he should be unable to continue his noble work, of which much more remained to be accomplished. Meanwhile the men had gathered round Nichols. "Is he alive?" said Arthur, as summoning up his strength, he arose and bent over the form of his prostrate foe.

"He's alive, sir," said Owen,, "but it strikes me he isn't long for this world; he's been so battered about by the barrel that he would cling to as long as strength was in him, that I don't think he'll ever survive it."

It was quite dark now, but one of the men held a lantern close to Nichols' pale face. Arthur took his cold hand is his. "Poor fellow," he said. "I fear you're right, Owen. May God have mercy on his soul!"

At this moment the man opened his eyes. When he perceived that Arthur was bending over him a shudder passed through is frame, and he turned away his head and closed his eyes.

"Ah! he knows you, sir," said Ben, "or he wouldn't look like that."

Arthur bend down more closely over the dying man; he whispered a few words in his ear. Again his eyes opened, and he looked Arthur full in the face, but this time it was with an expression of wonder rather than hatred or fear. In a very low voice – almost a whisper – he gasped out the words –

"You, sir. Was it you ... who tried to save me? ...No; I can't believe it ... it must be a dream ... But do you forgive me, sir?"

"Forgive you – yes, Nichols; indeed I do. Oh! may God forgive you – pray to Him now. Even at the last moment He will hear you."

"Too late, sir ... too late," signed the dying man.

"Never too late to turn to Him, if you repent of your past wicked life. He died to save you. He will forgive you; only trust Him," said Arthur very earnestly.

Again he turned his eyes full upon Arthur with a sad, but almost grateful look. He feebly tried to press the parson's hand, which still held him. Then with a deep groan, he expired. No one spoke a word. Not a sound was heard but the roar of the ocean. Arthur turned away with tears in his eyes. God is long-suffering and merciful. "He willeth not that any should perish, but that all should come to repentance." He thought of the penitent thief on the cross, and hoped that the soul of even this hardened sinner might be cleansed in the blood of Jesus.

How thickly were the startling incidents of that eventful night crowded together! The parson and his brave band now returned to their former post. Still the fore part of the frigate remained fixed in the rock where it had struck; still the waves rolled over it, burying in surf the poor fellows who clung to the bulwarks; each succeeding billows causing the timbers to quiver and creak more violently. Tom and Philip were close together on the bowsprit. When the final crash came, they thought by holding on to this they had more chance of being buoyed up, and perhaps borne to the sore. As long as the twilight lasted they had watched the gallant efforts which had been made by the men on shore to save life; and Tom had remarked, "Ah, Philip, you gave the folks here a character they didn't deserve; they seem to be dong all they can to help our poor fellows. I'm sure they've dragged some of them on shore."

"Yes, I've been watching them, Tom,, and I've been greatly surprised; but it must be our parson who's at the bottom of it – it never used to be so – not when I lived here."

"I begin to hope God means to save us yet," said Tom; "there's not so much wind as there was, and it doesn't look very far to the shore."

"I don't despair either," said Philip; "life seems dearer to me than ever now I'm within a few yards of home. But God's will be done."

When the darkness came over then they were no longer able to watch the proceeding of those ashore, but they saw the lights passing backwards and forwards on the beach, and knew their friends were still as active as ever in their efforts to save them, And as the stars, one by one, came out they were not a little cheered by their friendly rays, which showed them that the dull leaden clouds that for so long had hidden the blue sky from their gaze, had at last passed away, and though the waves rolled as fiercely over them, and roared as loud as ever, the wind had altogether subsided.

Arthur perceived that more light had now become needful for them to keep watch over the remnant of the wreck. He knew, too, it would cheer those still on it, proving to them that they were not forgotten by their fellows on shore, who were determined at all hazards to save their lives if possible. He ordered, therefore, a great tar barrel to be fetched for a neighbouring store and set alight. When the bright red flames blazed up they shone upon a singularly weird scene of death, destruction and excitement. A lurid glare now fell upon the huge towering waves, and upon the mass of snowy foam which seethed along the shore. More distinctly than ever could they now discern the poor fellows hanging on to the wreck while the anxious faces on shore were so illuminated by the brilliant light that Philip and Tom could almost distinguish their features.

"Did you notice how she trembled when that last wave broke over her, Owen?" said Ben; "she'll never stand another."

"I wonder she hasn't parted before his," was the reply; "but surely I see two more men in the water; that wave must have swept them off. Come on, form a line at once."

The chain was soon ready. It was longer this time than before; the wreckers had been so terror-struck by Nichols' death that they had given up all further attempts to secure plunder, and joined the others in their efforts to save life.

Both men were rescued. One was a French officer, the other the Englishman who had acted as captain of the frigate during the last few days.

The former was unconscious, the latter in a very few moments revived sufficiently to be able to speak.

In a few words he told their sad story. When Arthur heard of the English prisoners on board, he felt still more anxious to save the lives of those who yet survived.

"There are two Englishmen, sir," said the man, "still hanging on to the bows, one belongs to these parts; if it hadn't been for his advice we should likely enough have gone ashore at a place where there'd have been no chance of saving any of us, he's quite a young fellow, too."

"Quite a young fellow ... belongs to these parts." The words struck Owen's ear and startled him for a moment. Could it be? ... he dared hardly hope, it was too unlikely; but the thought of Philip passed through is mind.

He looked seaward again, and saw a gigantic wave rolling in; a moment after, it had hidden the frail piece of wreck which had for so long been embedded in the rock. When it had passed over and dashed in a broad torrent of surf on the shore, not a morsel of the frigate was to be seen, but the sea was strewn afresh with timbers, spars, and rigging, the broken fragments of the ship.

The shriek of terror which arose from those who were thus torn from their one point of refuge, and hurled into the watery abyss, was heard in spite of the roar of the ocean. In all directions the poor fellows were seen floating hither and thither, making desperate efforts to battle with the waves, and they were met by as energetic and desperate attempts on the side of the brave men on shore. Three chains were now formed, success for most part crowned their efforts; some still conscious, some apparently lifeless, were wrested from the cold embrace of the angry waves and dragged in safely to land.

"Do you see those two fellows clinging to that broken piece of the bowsprit? One of them is he that belongs to these parts," said the captain to Owen. "They've been great chums all the voyage; they're terrible Methodists, and that's the worst that can be said of them."

Yes, there they were, distinctly visible by the lurid light of the blazing tar-barrel, but the next instant receding wave hid them for a moment from Owen's gaze, and when the broken spar again emerged from the surf – oh! horror – there was only one man on it; the other had released his hold, and was being tossed wildly about in the surge.

"Not a moment is to be lost," cried Owen, taking the lead. A chain was formed, the longest they had made yet. Owen, who felt nerved with a giant's strength, plunged into the thick of the boiling surf. Blinded, stifled, he battled with the waves till he had all but grasped the drowning man, when a mighty billow rolled in with irresistible force and hurled him and the whole chain back on the beach. He sank down senseless and stunned.

Arthur, who had yielded to the entreaties of the men to spare himself and rest for a while, had not formed one of the chain, but had eagerly and keenly watched the efforts of his brave friends. Now, when he perceived that their heroism had failed, and that not a second must be lost, he again sprang upon his horse, and; undaunted as before, urged the animal into the thick of the surf. He had this time to advance even farther than when he rescued Nichols. Twice the waves baffled him, and, just as he was about to grasp their victim, tore him from his hands; but the third time he succeeded, and Tom Marriott, pale and apparently dead, lay upon the beach.

A cheer broke from the crowd, in which none joined so heartily as the English captain, who observed to Arthur, "I've seen many brave men, sir, in my day, but you bead them all by a long way; you were cut out for a soldier or a sailor, and not for a parson, I'm sure. Ah! this is the elder of the two – not the one who belongs to Cornwall – I can see that chap still there, longing on to yonder spar."

Arthur was too exhausted to say more than "We must save him too;" and after a few moment's breathing time, he again sprang upon his faithful steed.

When the remnant of the ship on which they had taken refuge went to pieces, Tom and Philip continued to cling to the portion of the bowsprit, which had been snapped in two by the violence of the shock. As at first they sank into the cold water and felt themselves beaten about by the fury of the waves, both gave themselves up for lost. But they still kept their firm trust and confidence in Him Who holdest the sea in the hollow of His hand, Who stayeth its proud waves, and saith, "Hitherto shalt thou come and no farther." Philip now recalled the beautiful promise, "When thou passest through the waters, I will be with thee," and kept his mind fixed on his loving Saviour; he felt sure that He was close beside him in the midst of this cold, merciless ocean, and that He would soon take him from this wild strife to His blessed rest in the Paradise above, and poor Tom thought this must be indeed "the valley of the shadow of death," about which Bill Forster had read to him out of the "Pilgrim's Progress;" but commending himself unto the care of his Father in heaven, he clung as firmly as he could to the spar. A large piece of floating timber, however, coming in contact with it, struck Tom so violent a blow on the arm that he relaxed his hold. In a moment he was borne far away from the fragment of wreck. Philip clung to it alone.

A terrible blow was it to the poor lad when he perceived that his friend had been washed from his side. He was so faint and exhausted that he knew he could only hold on a few minutes longer. When now and then he was borne up on the crest of a wave, he could see by the light of the burning tar-barrel, all the cottages on the Cove, his own beloved home among them, and he thought, too, that he recognised the tall figure of the parson among the crowd which lined the water's edge. Ah, yes! it would be as he had pictured to himself; he must die within sight of his home; but at least his body would be washed up on the shore, and he would be buried by his mother's side in the little churchyard at St. Sennen.

Owen's consciousness had just returned when Tom Mariott had been rescued by the parson. As he staggered to his feet, he heard the men around him say that this was not the Cornish lad they had heard about, but his friend. "He must be saved," Owen cried, "where is he?"

"There, yonder on that spar," cried Ben, "don't you see him? – too far off for any chain we could make to reach him."

But Owen's gaze was now directed to the parson, whose horse was standing up to its knees in surf, as its rider eagerly watched for the opportunity to plunge again into the waves. He hurried up to him, "Sir," he cried, "let me go; I will ride in, I will try and save the poor lad. I can't help thinking – though perhaps it's foolish of me – that it may be Philip; let me go, sir; you're too done up already, sir, I can see by your face; you've worked harder than any of us; oh! sir, spare yourself, I entreat you."

"No, no Owen; even if I consented my horse would only obey his master's bidding on such an errand as this. Yes, I know I'm exhausted, but all the strength I've left, I'll use to save that poor young fellow, whoever he be; he's a good lad I know, or they wouldn't call him a Methodist. I may lose my life in the attempt, 'but the Good Shepherd giveth His life for the sheep,' and you know 'greater love hath no man than this, that a man lay down his life for his friends.'"

These were the last words Owen heard him speak. Ere they had passed from his lips, dauntless, heroic as ever, he had plunged into the foaming abyss. Eagerly, breathlessly did the crowd gather down to the water's edge and watch the brave rider as he battled with the waves, which were furiously opposing his advance. Now his horse was off its feet; he was swimming; they were close t the spar; the next moment, to their intense horror and disappointment, they perceived that the man was no longer on the spar – exhaustion, or perhaps death, had made him release his hold. But his brave deliverer had no thought of giving him up; his keen eye saw where he was still floating. Valiantly were horse and rider making their way towards him, when a huge wave, with a majestic roll and roar like thunder, in an instant enveloped spar, drowning man, horse and rider, in one mass of foam. It was a terrible moment of suspense to the watchers on the shore; but they were not idle; instantly two chains were formed to be ready to advance at once into the surge, to render help if needful. But the billow had spent its fury, as in clouds of spray it broke upon the beach. All eyes were strained towards the point of interest. They beheld a riderless horse struggling alone to reach the shore. Nothing else? Yes, two men who, though they clung to each other, seemed so completely exhausted that they were mere playthings of the waves. Not a second was lost; the parson was in danger; and eager desire to save him animated every heart; no on though of the risk to which his own life might be exposed. The two chains already formed dashed into the raging surf; blinded, breathless, half suffocated by the sea, they struggled nobly on. Owen is the foremost man of one, Ben of the other line. Each band emulated the other in heroism. Owen at last is within reach of the drowning men; he is already off his feet, and being obliged to swim, has let go his hold of the next man in the chain, but the rope still keeps him bound to his companions. He is too much blinded by the surf to see which of the two he has seized in his strong grip; but, though almost unconscious himself, he holds him tight, and a loud hurrah bursts from the throng on shore when his companions drag him up on the beach. A moment more and he looks on the pale inanimate features of the youth clasped in his arms. "Philip – my son – my long lost son!" he says; "but he is dead – he is dead!" and then he sinks down fainting by his son's side.

Ben, meantime, had plunged into the surf at the same moment as Owen, and he and Abbott together had fought their way onwards through the boiling waves. Twice they had all but seized the apparently lifeless form of the clergyman, but each time, carried away by their exertions that they had to call for help – they had not strength to bear their burden. Happily Philip's rescuers had now had time to reform their line, and rushed in to their aid, dragging the exhausted men up high and dry on the beach.

Their work was done now, they could rest from their heroic labours; but all the joy and satisfaction they might have felt in having by their valour been instrumental in saving so many lives was completely dampened, when they gazed on the pale lifeless form of their beloved pastor.

There he lay, stretched out on the beach, motionless, inanimate – not a sign to indicate that spark of life was still latent in that manly form. In their anxiety about him, every one else was for forgotten. They bore him at once to the nearest cottage, where he was laid on a bed beside a cheerful fire, and all those means used which are generally employed to restore animation to the apparently drowned. The village doctor, for whom Arthur himself had despatched a messenger about an hour ago, that he might be on the spot to give his help if required, arrived just at that moment. When he had examined the patient thoroughly, and felt his pulse and his heart, he turned very pale, looked grave, and shook his head. Still he ordered the men to continue rubbing his feet and hands.

At that instant Owen staggered into the room, pale, haggard, like one half dead. "The parson," he gasped; "Mr. Arthur – is he saved – does he still live?"

No one uttered a word, but despair was plainly written on every face. "He is dead, then – he is dead – and my son Philip is dead too," cried the agonised man. "O God! O God! this is more than I can bear."

Falling on his knees by the side of the bed, he seized Arthur's cold hand, and, in a paroxysm of grief, burst into tears. And now Dick Evans entered the room; his sorrow was quite as uncontrollable as Owen's. There was not a man present down whose weather-beaten cheeks the tears did not stream. Many of them indeed had been his enemies; but now, when too late, they realised how deeply they had wronged him – now noble had been his life- now glorious his death. He had won more friends, more devoted adherents, in his last hour than he had done during the years he had laboured among these rough Cove men. Even the surgeon, a stern, hard man, hostile to religion, and especially to anything like Methodism, was touched when he beheld how attached these rude, ignorant men – as he considered them – were to the parson. He turned away to hide his emotion, and asked if there were any more patients for him to visit.

Ben pulled him by the sleeve, and led him out. "Is there no hope, sir?" he said, with a stifled sob.

"Nothing but a miracle could restore that man to life," replied the surgeon, endeavouring to regain his ordinary composure.

"Come, then, and see the young fellow, to save whom he sacrificed his life," said Ben. He had heard that it was Philip, and he knew he was lying in Owen's cottage.

Pale and inanimate as Philip was, yet that deathlike pallor which was spread over Arthur Pendrean's face was absent from his countenance. When the doctor examined him, he said, cheerfully, "There's hope here; life is not extinct." He succeeded in pouring a few drops of stimulant down the lad's throat, who soon after sighed deeply, moved his head, and opened his eyes, but only to close them immediately.

"Ah! I wish his father could see that; it would cheer him up a bit," said Ben. "I'll go and tell him."

He found Owen in the same posture – still kneeling by Arthur's side, and holding his hand. Ben whispered something in his ear. He started. "Alive!" he cried; "ah, don't deceive me, Ben; he looked quite dead when I left him; but I'll go and see," and casting a look of deep sorrow and affection on Arthur's lifeless form, he followed Pollard into the next cottage.

The father's quick eye perceived the change in his son at once. Yes, he lived indeed. The good parson had not sacrificed his life in vain, then, as he had feared – he had saved Philip; but at what a price!

Owen bent over his son; he was changed indeed; how much older looking he had become during the comparatively short time of their separation; how worn and thin, too! Yet there was a look of peace on his face, which told of an inward calm, and made his father feel sure that he was ready to die, if such had been God's will.

Again the lad opened his eyes, and now he gazed full in Owen's face. "Father," he muttered; "is it you? – my father?"

"Yes, Philip; yes, thank God!" he said affectionately embracing him.

"But where am I? Surely this is a dream."

"No, no, Philip, no dream. You are at home in Sennen Cove," replied Owen, hardly able to speak for emotion, yet fearful of agitating the half-recovered lad.

Philip was silent and closed his eyes again, as if he were trying to gather his memory the events of the last few hours. Slowly, one by one, they dawned upon him.

"Tom – where is Tom?" he asked.

"If you mean your mate who was clinging with you to the bows, Philip, he's saved. I've seem him myself," said his father.

"And the parson – ah! the parson, Mr. Pendrean, father – where's he; is he safe?"

Owen hesitated; he did not like to tell him the whole truth in his present weak state. The surgeon, who was still standing by, and saw his embarrassment, interfered.

"You mustn't talk any more, my lad," he said, "or it may go badly with you yet. You're very weak; here, take this, and lie quiet. Sleep's what you want," and he motioned Owen to leave the room.

"The parson – tell me if he still lives, father, father!" he said in a faint voice, but there was no reply. Owen, perceiving from the doctor's manner how important it was that Philip should not be excited, had hurried out of the house.

With one exception – that of a poor Frenchman, who had been ill for several days before the wreck, and who died a few hours after he was brought on shore – all the rescued men were doing well. When Tom Mariott revived, his first question was whether Philip Tresilian had been saved. When he heard the good news, he fervently thanked God for all His mercies to them both. "What a brave set of fellows you are here!" he exclaimed; "how hard you worked to save our lives! You didn't spare yourselves; and what a noble gentleman your parson must be, about whom I've heard so much from my mate Philip! I'm longing to thank him for his endeavours to save us all."

"You'll be disappointed in that, my man, I'm sorry to say," said one of the Sennen fishermen who was standing beside him; "our good parson has lost his own life in his endeavours to save your crew. I could see he was dead beat when he plunged into the water the last time; he hadn't strength to bear all that battling with the waves."

"Your parson dead – drowned!" said Tom, as he started up from the bed on which he was lying. "This is sad news. Oh! what will poor Philip say?"

Slowly did the hours of that long night wear away. All hearts were sad and heavy; each one felt he had lost a friend – some the best friend they had; others were filled with remorse, for had they not turned a deaf ear to his earnest words and kindly warnings – too often slighted and mocked him while living among them? Arthur's noble, generous attempt to save the life of Nichols, his bitterest enemy, had caused every man there to honour and love him. Such a deed had more weight with them than a hundred sermons, however earnest and eloquent, on the duty of forgiveness. It proved to them the truth, the noble reality, of that religion which hitherto they had sneered at and despised. Christianity, which moulded heroes of such a stuff as this, could not be the mawkish, cowardly thing they had been led to consider it. After what they had witnessed that night, it would be long indeed before any man present would again venture to sue the words "saint" or "Methodist" as a term of reproach.

Morning dawned bright and cheerful; the sun rose in a cloudless sky; there was scarcely a breath of air. After the violent tempest which for well-nigh three days had been lashing the sea into fury, it was not to be expected that the heavy swell of the ocean would immediately subside; the waves, with a dull, melancholy roar, broke in long rolling curves of foam upon the beach, which was still strewn with the fragments of the wreck. Men and women, with sorrow deeply impressed upon their faces, stood in groups before the doors of the cottages. All felt that they had lost a friend. Though the sky overhead was bright, there was a dark cloud on the hearts of all – a burden of grief difficult to bear; none liked to speak of the terrible trial which had fallen upon them.

Late the preceding night, the sad tidings had reached the manor-house, and been broken to the old squire, who had just retired to rest. The servants told him first that a bad accident had happened to Mr. Arthur; but love is far-sighted, and the squire was keen enough to perceive from their manner that something was being kept back, and that the whole truth had not been told him.

The old man had been weak and ailing lately, but, feeble as he was, he sprang from his bed and began to dress.

"I will ride down to Sennen Cove at once," he said; "there is something wrong with my son, worse than you have said, I know from your manner."

"Sir," said Roger Barton, his oldest and most confidential servant,, "there's no use hiding the truth from you any longer. Master Arthur has lost his life in his brave efforts to save some poor fellows from a wreck down at the Cove, - alas! that I should have to tell you such news," and the old man burst into tears.

The squire stood motionless, as if petrified with grief and horror.

"Drowned – dead – my Arthur – my only boy – my brave son! No, Roger, it can't be true – that can never be – they would not have allowed him to perish – some one would have gone to rescue him, surely."

"It is too true, sir," sobbed Roger. "Dick Evans has just come up from the Cove with the news; the poor lad's almost out of his mind with grief. He says that the doctor gave no hope at all, and that Mr. Arthur must have died before they dragged him out of the water, which all the men most bravely did as soon as they were able."

The squire sank down upon a chair and covered his face with his hands; it was several minutes before he could speak.

"Ah! Roger," he said at last in a trembling voice, "this will break my heart; but go at once down to the Cove, and convince yourself that it is quite true, and then – and then, if it is – bring my son here."

"Yes, sir, I will go directly," said Roger; "but I pray you sir, don't indulge any false hopes that Master Arthur still lives. The other man who came up from the cove with Dick said just the same as he did; he is one of those who helped to pull Master Arthur out of the water."

"Go, Roger, go; I believe you," groaned the squire; "only let me look upon his face once more before I die."

Before daybreak Roger was back at the manor-house, having performed his sad and solemn errand. The body of the young parson was carried up to his own room and laid upon his bed. Then the faithful servant again stood before his crushed and afflicted master. He was sitting exactly in the same posture, in which he had left him some hours before.

"Sir," he said in a voice broken only by emotion, "I've been down to the Cove, as you wished me; and it's all true, I grieve to say; and we've brought Master Arthur back with us, and he's lying now in his own bed."

"True, is it? Ah, true," said the squire with a deep sigh; "and you've brought the dear boy here as I told you. Thank you, Roger. I will go and look upon his beloved face again."

The old man got up and tottered towards the door, but the shock had been too much for his already enfeebled heath; he would have fallen had not Roger seized him in time. Then, leaning heavily on the arm of the faithful servant, with trembling step, he proceeded to Arthur's room.

It looked to the east, and the rising sun was just sending his bright cheering rays in at the window; they fell upon the bed on which lay the lifeless form of his beloved son; and just as the bereaved father entered, the golden beams illuminated the pale face of the deceased, giving it such a look of life that the squire started and exclaimed –

"No, it's not true, Roger! he's still lives – look, look at his face; surely he has revived."

"No, no, sir; do not deceive yourself, I entreat you," said Roger; "it is only the sunlight falling on his dear face. Ah! how happy and peaceful he seems. Take comfort, sir, from that. He is at rest with the Saviour he loved so much and taught us all to love," and the tears flowed thick and fast down old Roger's face.

The squire bent over his son; he took his cold hand and kissed his pale face, and then turning to Roger, he said, "Yes, you speak the truth, Roger; there is no hope – he has gone from us – I shall never hear his voice again. He was the bravest of the brave; no man ever had so good a son – no man ever sustained such a loss as I have done. Oh! Arthur, Arthur! I cannot live without you," Overwhelmed with grief, he sank down on a chair by the bedside.

"My dear master," said Roger, trying to suppress his own sorrow, "try to think what Master Arthur would say to us if he could speak. He'd tell us not to fret and take on so about him, fur that he was quite happy, and gone to be with his Saviour – that he had entered into the joy of his Lord, and was resting from all his labours. And he's say, too, that we ought to look forward to the blessed day when we shall meet him again in Paradise above. Oh, sir! try and think of this, and take some comfort to your soul."

"Roger," said the squire, "I know what you say is true, and that he would say the same if he could speak, but oh! it's very hard."

23

At Home And In Peace

"They were –
But what avails it now to tell of what has been?
Fond-hearted, dear, and passing fair
As e'er on earth were seen!

" They are –
In safety with their God, secure from sin and care,
And the bright day cannot be far
When we shall meet them there."

- Monsell

"We doubt not that for one so true
There must be other, nobler work to do."

- Tennyson

Owen Tresilian watched all night by his son's side. Philip remained in a quiet peaceful slumber till the morning. Conflicting thoughts and feelings filled the father's breast. His heart swelled with gratitude tot he Giver of all good when he gazed on the calm tranquil face of his beloved son, who had been at last so graciously restored to his prayers But at what a cost! When he reflected on that, on the irreparable loss that not only he individually, but the whole country for miles around, had sustained, he was crushed with sorrow; he could not rejoice as he otherwise would have done over the recovery of his son whom he so often had given up for lost. Anxiety, too, about little Mary oppressed and troubled him. How long would she be able to endure that terrible solitude? when would it be possible for him to put out to the lighthouse and release her? The bright sunlight shining in at the little window, and the clear blue sky, inspired him with some hope. There was no wind, and though, in such a swell as for several days would range among the rocks, it would be impossible to land at the Longships, he might be able to approach sufficiently near for Mary to recognise him. He would have the satisfaction of knowing that she was alive and well, and she would feel that he had not forgotten her, and that as soon as the weather permitted he would hasten to release her. Many of the Cove men looked into the cottage that morning to inquire after Philip; there was grief and gloom on every face.

"They've carried him away to his father's, the squire's," said Ben; "the poor old gentleman is taking on dreadfully; they say he'll never get over it."

"I don't wonder at it, Ben," said Owen; "he might well be proud of such a son, and to lose him suddenly in the very pride of manhood must be a terrible blow to his father. If we all feel the loss so greatly, how much more must the poor squire?"

Tom Marriott, looking very pale and exhausted, now entered the cottage.

"They told me I oughtn't to get up so soon," he said to Owen in a whisper, "but I couldn't feel comfortable till I'd been to see how Phil was getting on; he's been a good friend to me, and for months now, we've kept very close to one another. I was afraid last night I'd lost him, but, thank God, I'm told he was saved after all, and now I see it with my own eyes. The Lord be praised! He's in a nice sleep, too."

"Sit down," said Owen, "and I'll give you some breakfast, and stay on here with me till Philip wakes, but don't say anything to him about our having lost our dear parson."

"Oh! that's a sad affair indeed," said Tom; "the good clergyman Philip told me so much about – only to think that he should have met his death in saving Phil's life!"

The two men sat down together by the fireside. Tom related to Owen the whole story of the voyage and its incidents, while Tresilian in return told the hardly less exciting story of the lighthouse.

"Philip didn't tell me very wrong, then, about the bad set of fellows you have here," said Tom, "but that daughter of yours must be a brave little lass indeed. She cheered us, I can assure you, by keeping that light burning so brightly; it was by it Philip made out whereabouts on the coast we were. If we hadn't seen it we should have gone on shore at a point where there'd have been no chance of saving our lives."

"Yes, thank God!" said Owen; "and many other vessels have been saved from shipwreck the last two nights by that light burning so brightly on the Longships."

Philip now began to stir, and in a few minutes he opened his eyes, and looked round the room with which since his infancy he had been so familiar. When he saw his father and Tom sitting before the fire, he raised himself up in the bed, asking confusedly, "Father, am I really at home? and where's Mary?"

Owen hastened to his son's side. "Mary is not here now, Philip," he replied, "but I hope you will see her tomorrow or the day after; yes, you are really at home now, thank God!"

"Ah! and there you are too, Tom! how good God has been in saving both of us," said Philip. "I should have been drowned if it had not been for our parson. I'd given up all for lost. I'd fought with the waves till I was dead beat, and had no more strength in me; then he came dashing through the foam on his good horse, catching hold of me just as I was sinking, and I heard him call out to me, 'Philip! Philip! thank God that I should be able to save you.' I remember no more, for just then a great wave came rolling over us both. I felt the parson's strong grasp round my waist, and then I lost all consciousness till I work up and saw you, father, last night standing beside me. And now I want to see our good Mr. Arthur, to thank him. Where is he, father? do you think he'll soon come to see me?"

Owen was silent; he did not know how to reply to his son's eager questions. There seemed no way of evading them; he feared he must tell the whole truth, now that Philip seemed sufficiently recovered to bear it. He knew that whenever his son heard the sad news it must cause him the bitterest grief.

"Ah, Philip!" he said, as the tears started to his eyes, "don't ask me about the parson."

"You don't mean, surely, father, that any harm has happened to Mr. Pendrean? Was he hurt last night? Tell me, what is it?" He seized his father's hand and gazed into his dad face, down which the tears were trickling.

"Philip! Philip!" said Owen, "there's no good hiding it any longer from you. Our dear good parson lost his life last night saving yours."

For a few moments Philip sat up in his bed motionless and silent, then covering his face with his hands, he burst into a paroxysm of grief.

"Oh! this is fearful news, father; would to God that I had perished before reaching the shore rather than that I should have been the cause of the death of our good, kind parson! Only to think that I, so unworthy, should be saved, while he, whose life has been so noble and so useful, and who will be missed by hundreds, should be lost – and for my sake, too. O father! I cannot bear to think of it!"

"I knew you'd take on bitterly, Philip, when you heard this bad news," said Tom; "but you must remember that though you and all the good folks here may well mourn the loss they have sustained, it's all gain to him that's gone. God's taken him away from all the cares and sorrows of this evil world, to be at rest and peace with Him. Try to take comfort from that, lad."

But Philip could not speak; he lay for some time on his bed sobbing bitterly.

To divert his thoughts from this sad subject, his father related to him his own adventures during the last few days, how he had been kidnapped and imprisoned, and how poor little Mary had been left alone in the lighthouse. "And now, Philip," he said, "I must go and get some of our fellows to join me and put out to the Longships, to cheer up our Molly by the sight of me. Your mate, Tom, here, will keep you company while I'm gone."

"Poor little Mary!" said Philip, sadly; "only to think of her being left in that lighthouse all alone. Ah! God has brought me home to hear many tales of sin and sorrow. Come back as soon as you can, father, and I hope you'll bring us good news of our dear Mary."

Owen hurried down to the beach. There was still a great deal of surf, but not a man now refused to help him when informed of the expedition he proposed. It was, however, with no little difficulty that they succeeded in launching a boat, in which Owen, and five brave companions, embarked for the Longships.

When Mary awoke on that Monday morning, she could perceive, by the light which streamed through the narrow window of the room, that the sun was shining, and at the terrible gale was over. The waves, indeed, still beat against the lighthouse, and the sea roared in the cave below, but she no longer heard the whistling and howling of the wind. She hastened up to the cupola. There was not a cloud in the clear blue sky, the sun was shining brightly; there was still a heavy swell and a broad fringe of snowy surf all along the shore, yet the waves were rolling in so slowly that she knew from experience that erelong it would be calm, and then she felt certain her father would come out to her once more, and she would learn the reason why they had been separated.

When she said her morning prayers, she thanked God for making the storm to cease, and causing the bright, cheerful sun nonce more to gladden her with its beams, and she prayed Him to grant that the calm weather might continue, and her dear father be restored to her. Then she thought of the great ship which she had seen labouring in the gale the previous evening, and she went up the staircase again and on to the gallery to look for it, but not a trace of it was to be seen. It must, then, have gone down, or be dashed upon the rocks during the fierce tempest which had raged through the night. She felt very sad, and her heart ached for those poor men who, she feared, had found a watery grave in the storm. Would that she could have saved them! She had done her best, indeed – she had kept the light burning; and she trusted that by God's mercy it had warned many mariners from the dangerous coast, and preserved their vessels from shipwreck.

And now, as she gazed over the sea, she perceived a small sail just turning round the point which hid Sennen Cove from her view. She knew at once that it was a Sennen boat, and felt sure that her father must be in it, and that he was coming back to the rock. But would he be able to land? When she looked at the wild waves tumbling in confused masses around, now leaping up the lighthouse walls, now rolling in long majestic sweep and breaking in cascades of foam on the rocks, she knew it would be utterly impossible. "Ah!" she thought, "my good, kind father is coming as near as he can, to let me feel he has not forgotten me." She never took her eyes off the smack bravely making its way over the waves, sometimes almost buried in them, so that nothing but the mast and sail could be seen, sometimes borne aloft on the top of a great wave. It had approached so near that Mary could see the men on board. She ran downstairs to fetch one of the signal flags by which they were accustomed to make known their wants when they could not otherwise communicate with the shore. The flag which Mary chose was that which signified "All right." The brave little maid felt sure her father – whatever might have been the cause of his own absence – must have been very anxious about her; and when he saw the "All right" flag waved from the gallery, how happy and relieved he would feel! And was it not "All right," too? She had been frightened, indeed, and suffered much in her solitude, but God had protected her; He had given her strength and courage to do her duty, and for two nights to keep the lamps burning as brightly as her father would have done. Yes, she felt indeed how true it was that "though the waves of the sea are mighty, and rage horribly, yet the Lord who dwelleth on high is mightier."

And now the boat had come so near to the rock that she could plainly see there were six men in it. She longed to make out her father's well-known figure, she would not feel quite easy at heart until she did. So violently did the little boat roll and pitch, that it was difficult to distinguish those on board; but when in a few minutes they lowered their sail, Mary saw a tall man stand up in the centre of the boat and wave a flag as an answer to hers. There was no doubt in her mind now. It was indeed her dear father. He was alive and well. This was all she cared for, all that was needful to set her mind at rest. Her heart swelled in gratitude to her Father above. He had answered her prayer. Whatever might have occurred during the last few days, she knew now that God had been with her father, and preserved his life.

When Owen returned to his cottage after his successful cruise, he found Philip and Tom sitting together before the fire. The former, who looked worn and sad, eagerly inquired what news he brought of Mary.

"Thank God, Philip," he replied, "she is safe; I saw her with my own eyes on the gallery of the lighthouse; there was such a heavy swell we couldn't get very near, but I think she made me out, for I stood up as high as I could in the boat, while two of the fellows held me tight lest I should be pitched overboard. I waved my flag, which she must have seen. There she stood, the dear child, holding up the 'All right' signal, which she knew would cheer me up – kind, thoughtful girl that she is. O Philip! if the weather only keeps fine like this, the swell'll be gone down enough by to-morrow for me to land on the rock and fetch her home to nurse you."

"Oh! that will be joy, to see her again, father; I never thought I should, especially the last few days. But who's going to keep the lights burning if you and Mary come on shore?"

"I shall go back again, Philip, before nightfall. We must never let those lamps out again. Nothing lay so near our dear parson's heart as that lighthouse. Trouble enough he's had in looking out for lighthouse keepers, and a bitter grief it was to him when for a time the beacon ceased to shine."

"When I get well, father, I'll be able to help you, and take my turn, I hope," said Philip.

"Perhaps I can lend a hand, too," said Tom. "I've some thoughts of settling down among you all."

"O Tom! I wish you would," said Philip. "We've been good friends, and I should be sorry indeed to lose you."

Mary felt quite happy and light-hearted all that day. She cleaned up the lamps, tidied the room, which she had not had the heart to do before, every now and then anxiously watching the appearance of the sky, fearful only lest another spell of bad weather might delay her father coming out to her. But as evening the sun set in a blaze of crimson and gold, the sea had become comparatively smooth; and when she lighted her lamps, it was with a firm hope that the morrow would terminate her solitary confinement. Early next morning she took up her post aloft to watch for the longed-for sail. She had not long to wait, and much more rapid progress did the boat make to-day than it had done yesterday, as, favoured by a light breeze, it danced gaily over the waters. And now it was close to the rock; she could see her father standing at the helm steering and giving his orders to the other men. She waved the flag as she had done before, and her father replied by a motion of his hand. And end had come to the long period of suspense for both father and daughter, but there was still so much swell that there was great difficulty in effecting a landing. Once or twice Owen thought it would have to be given up for that day. After several failures, however, he succeeded in springing on to the rock, but he was convinced of the impossibility of getting Mary into the boat with such a heavy swell as it was still running. He therefore told his companions to leave him and come out the next day should the weather be sufficiently favourable. Mary, alternately swayed by hope and fear, had eagerly watched from the gallery all the movements of the boat. When she saw her father safe on the rock, she hurried down the staircase to the door of the lighthouse, and in a moment was in his arms. The hearts of both were too full to speak for some time, as together they entered the gloomy little room, which had been their home for the last few months.

"Mary," said Owen at last, "this has been a terrible three days; thank God they are over and I see you again. Ah! child, how I have felt for you, and prayed for you too. You look pale and worn indeed, but blessed be God, He has watched over and preserved you. How brave you have been to keep the lights burning every night! I can't think how you managed it, my child!"

"O father! I've been all right and well," replied Mary, "except for fretting about you, because I didn't know what had become of you. And you look pale too, and sad, father. I'm sure something terrible has happened. You never looked like that before. Please, let me know what is the matter. Where have you been all this time? why didn't you come back on Friday?"

"Ah, Mary, dear! it's a long story I have to tell, and a sad one too, but there's joy mixed with sorrow. God has taken away from us, but He has restored too; first I'm sad, and then I'm happy; but I'm sure what He does must be all for the best."

"Tell me the worst first, father. I'm so glad to see you again, that I feel I could bear to hear the saddest news; but I hope no harm's come to Mr. Arthur."

"Alas! my child," said Owen, as his eyes filled with tears, "that's just what it is. God has taken our dear good parson from us. You'll never hear his voice again."

"O father, father! it can't be true. Mr. Arthur dead!" cried the poor child, in an agony of grief.

"Alas! too true," was the reply.

"O father! that you should have brought such news!" she exclaimed. "But tell me all about it; how did he die, and where?"

"He lost his life, Mary, in saving your brother Philip's who was wrecked off the Cove in that great French ship you must have seen pass by here last night," replied Owen.

"In saving Philip's life!" exclaimed Mary, in amazement, looking up into her father's face amid her tears; "has Philip, then, come back, and is he alive and well?"

"Thank God, he is," replied Owen.

Mary was too overcome by conflicting emotions to say a word more. To learn that her long-lost brother, whom she loved so intensely, was restored to her, was an unspeakable joy; but how was it damped by the terrible loss of the beloved parson, who had always taken so deep and affectionate interest in her father and her family!

When she had become a little more composed, her father related to her all that had occurred to him since they parted last Friday. He told her of his own capture and imprisonment in the case, of his release on Sunday afternoon, of the wreck at Sennen Cove, of the heroic exploits and noble death of their brave and generous clergyman.

Intently did she listen to Owen's thrilling narrative.

"O father!" she said when he had finished, "I wish I had been there, if only just to see our good parson for the last time, and say good-bye to him!"

"It's a heavy blow to us all, child," replied Owen; "there's not a soul for miles round that does not feel they have lost a true friend."

"But he's happy, father," she said, amid her tears; "God's taken him to His home above, where the wicked cease from troubling, and the weary are at rest; and then, how bravely he died!"

"Yes, Mary, it's a grand thing to meet death as nobly as he did – dying to save others; and wasn't it strange – they tell me that, on Sunday morning, he preached from the text 'Greater love hath no man than this, that a man lay down his life for his friends;' and they were his last words, too, he ever spoke to me."

"That was just like our good Mr. Arthur, always thinking about doing good to others, and never about himself," replied Mary.

They talked on till it was time for Owen to light the lamps. He found everything in perfect order.

"But tell me, Molly," he asked, "how did you manage to reach the lamps? They are far above your head."

"Why father, I got a chair, and when that wasn't high enough, I plied several things on top of it; and, last of all, when I could find nothing else, and still couldn't reach them, I took down our big Bible. At first I was afraid to stand upon the Holy Book – it didn't seem quite right; but when I thought that, unless I did so, the lamps couldn't be lighted, and ships might be wrecked, and poor fellows drowned, I felt that if there was any harm God would forgive me; and I was high enough then, and I managed it easily enough."

Owen smiled, and kissed his daughter.

"You are a brave lass, and clever, too, Mary. I'm proud of you, and so was Mr. Arthur. You should have seen how pleased he looked when he heard that, though you were left here all alone, you had lighted the lamps as usual."

Mary sighed, and the tears started to her eyes.

"O father! if I could have seen him once more!" she said.

Next morning the sun again shone from a cloudless sky, and the sea at last was quite calm. Soon after daybreak Mary and her father, who were eagerly on the watch, caught sight of the Sennen smack with a fair wind rapidly gliding over the short, crisp waves towards the Longships. This morning there was but little difficulty in landing. When the boat came alongside, Owen saw that there were seven men on board, among whom he recognised as his son and Tom Marrriott. The latter was the first to spring on the rock. Grasping Owen's hand, he said –

"Phil was determined to come off on this cruise; he said he felt much stronger to-day, and was so eager to see you and his sister, but I was not going to let him come without me; so we've both come, as you can see."

Immediately after, Philip, still very pale and rather weak, sprang on the rock.

"Here I am, father," he said, "all right again, and none the worse for the sail; but where's Mary?"

Owen led the way up into the little gloomy room of the lighthouse, and brother and sister were soon in each other's arms. It was a great surprise to Mary to see Philip. She had as little as her father expected that he would venture out to the lighthouse.

"This is a joy indeed, Phil, to see you again! Father'd given you up for lost long ago, but I never did, nor did Mr. Arthur. We always prayed for you; and I was sure, wherever you were, that God would bring you back to us safe and sound; but how pale and ill you look. You shouldn't have come out here this morning."

"O Mary dear, I couldn't wait, I longed to see you again, particularly after all I'd heard about you being shut up all alone in this dreary place. You must be a brave girl, I'm sure."

"Come, children," said Owen, "you'll have time enough to tell your adventures when you get on shore, and the sooner we start the better. Ben Pollard and Abbott have promised to remain here to-night to relieve me and Mary for a bit, so I'll just show them how to trim the lamps, and then we'll sail homewards."

Mary was not sorry at the prospect of a release from the lonely prison, where she had spent so many anxious hours. A short sail in the boat, sitting by her brother's side, and she was once more in the dear old cottage where she was born. Here the one dark shadow, the thought of him who had been so frequent and familiar a guest, and whom they would never welcome there again, cast a gloom over the complete happiness which father and children, once more united, would otherwise have enjoyed. Their thoughts and their conversation constantly reverted to the well-loved parson. None of them could speak of him without tears.

But it was Philip who felt Arthur Pendrean's death the most keenly of all. He had, during the whole of his absence, longed to see the parson again, to tell him how he had never forgotten the last words and admonitions he heard from his lips on that Sunday afternoon when he was carried off by the pressgang, - how he had treasured the little Testament he had given him, reading it whenever he had a chance, and drawing comfort from it, not only for himself, but also for his mates. He wanted to tell him, too, how in the midst of sin and temptation, he had striven to lead a pure and upright life, and how God had helped him to do so by giving him strength and patience, and by raising up friends who encouraged him to persevere in a Christian course. All this, and much more, he had hoped to pour into Mr. Arthur's ear if God ever answered his prayers, and brought him back to Old England again. And now he was once more in his dear home, by his own fireside, with his father and sister; but Mr. Arthur, his beloved friend and pastor, was no more. He had sacrificed his own life in saving his. The one was taken, and the other left.

He told his father and sister all this, adding, "I am unworthy indeed of such a sacrifice, that a life so noble as his was should be given up to save mine; but I'll try, father, from henceforth, if God gives me health and strength, to make it as worthy as possible of the price that has been paid for it. I hope I'll never shrink from doing my duty, however hard it may be. I will try, God helping me, to save as many lives as I can, not only from shipwreck, but from other evils too, - I mean those which destroy the soul. If Mr. Arthur can see me from the happy place where I know he is, he shan't feel that he gave up his life for nothing. Oh that God may give me His Holy Spirit, that I may have the grace and strength to follow the parson's noble example!"

The events of that memorable Sunday night spread rapidly through the country. There was not a village or hamlet within a circuit of six or eight miles to which the tidings of the death of the good young clergyman did not bring bitter grief and sorrow. All mourned the loss of one who, by a life of self-sacrifice, generosity, and true piety, had won the hearts of all, except the most utterly depraved.

Upon the old squire the blow had fallen most heavily. His son had been all in all to him. Very gradually, and by slow degrees, he was beginning to see that Arthur was right, that religion was the one thing needful to make a man happy in this world and the next. From that son's noble, pure, Christ-like life, he had learned that one who fears God, and whose earnest aim is to serve and glorify Him, is not necessarily a milksop or a coward; and now that he had died as a true hero, by giving up his life to save that of another, his father was thoroughly convinced of the truth of that Christianity of which his beloved Arthur had been so devoted and zealous a disciple.

Henceforth, for a few short and weary years which he might be permitted to spend in this world, he would endeavour to serve that blessed Master, Whom his son had so loved and followed, humbly trusting that God would accept his service – late, alas! as it was offered Him – and bring him at last to that eternal kingdom of rest and peace whither Arthur had already entered, and where he hoped one day to meet him. Henceforth his one object in life should be to continue his son's work as far as he was able.

They laid the young pastor to rest among his own people – in the midst of the flock he had so carefully and lovingly tended – in the little bleak churchyard of St. Sennen. His father had at first directed that Arthur should be interred in the family vault in the large church of St. Burian, but the fishermen of Sennen begged very hard that their beloved parson might lie in the churchyard of the village where he had laboured. In that church, Sunday after Sunday, they had listened to his voice – now silent for ever in the grave – therein burning words he had told them of the love of God to their souls, and how earnestly He longed that they might all be saved – there he had warned them of the evil consequence of sin, and directed them to the Cross, where peace and happiness could alone be found. The old squire was touched by their loving and natural request; he felt, too, that Arthur himself would have desired it, and therefore, he readily gave his consent.

The funeral was a plain and simple one. The day was cold and cheerless, and a cutting east wind swept over the barren moorland as the faithful pastor was borne by the rough fishermen, to whom his short life had been devoted, to his last long home. A college friend, like-minded with himself, had, at the squire's request, come to perform the ceremony, and for the present to remain at Sennen and carry on Arthur's work. The whole population from the villages and hamlets around had assembled in and about the little churchyard. Not a dry eye was to be seen among them, and the voice of the clergyman who read the service was repeatedly drowned by their sobs. Weighed down by the intensity of his grief, the old squire stood beside his son's coffin, resting on the arm of his devoted servant; but with the eye of faith he was ever and anon able to pierce the gloom of sadness which surrounded him, and take some comfort to his soul. The beautiful words of the service telling of the sure and certain hope of resurrection to eternal life through our Lord Jesus Christ, helped to cheer the bereaved father, and to enable him to bear the heavy burden which God had seen fit to lay upon him.

Owen, with Philip and Mary at his side, stood beside the open grave;

they indeed were overwhelmed by the bitterness of their sorrow, still they tried to take heart for they all knew the truth of the words then spoken, "Blessed are the dead which die in the Lord, even so saith the Spirit, for they rest from their labours." Their loss, then, was his infinite gain; he, now delivered from the burden of the flesh, was in joy and felicity. They prayed God to give them grace and strength to follow the good parson, as he had followed Christ.

All the men who had been rescued from the wreck were present at the grave; the English sailors, most of whom had led wild, dissolute lives, never giving a thought to religion, were so touched by the events of the last few days and the solemn words of the burial service, that many among them resolved to turn over a new leaf and try to lead a better life; while the French crew, with the susceptibility of their race, wept like children when they saw the coffin of their brave preserver lowered into the ground. Their officers, who were never tired of praising the generosity and heroism of the young English clergyman, confessed that after all there might be some truth in the Christianity they had hitherto despised – for a religion which inspired such noble deeds could hardly be based on an utterly false foundation.

On the headstone that marked the young clergyman's grave two texts were inscribed, one was the last from which he preached, and which he had so nobly illustrated in his death, "Greater love hath no man than this, that he lay down his life for his friends;" and to this was added the verse from the Psalms, "He asked life of Thee, and Thou gavest him a long life, even for ever and ever."

Philip, as soon as he had a little recovered from the effects of the shock, and of the long exposure on the wreck, went to see Bob Harris's mother, to break to her the sad tidings of her son's death, and to give her his last message. To learn that he died bravely fighting for his country, penitent for his sins, and humbly trusting in the merits of his Saviour, was a great comfort to the poor woman, who, having heard nothing of her son since the day he was pressed, and torn from her, had already given him up for dead.

Dick became a frequent visitor at Tresilian's cottage; he and Philip had very much to tell each other, and they were never tired of talking about the good parson. God's providence had indeed watched over those three lads, who on that Sunday afternoon had been dragged from their homes. One the Good Shepherd had taken to Himself, the other two He had guarded and preserved in terrible dangers, that they might glorify Him by continuing His faithful soldiers and servants until their lives' end.

Tom made up his mind to remain at Sennen, and soon after he married a young woman belonging to the place.

The wicked custom of wrecking now almost ceased to exist in those parts. If undertaken at all, it was only secretly, and by a very few of the worst and most depraved characters.

The improvement and reform among the fishermen which Arthur Pendrean had with such perseverance and self-denial worked for during his life, became after his death an accomplished fact. So steady and well-conducted were the majority of the villagers now, that the very few who clung to their old manner of life found it best to leave for other parts of the coast. Among these was Bill Nichols, upon whose hard heart as yet no impression had been made.

Mary never again lived at the lighthouse, though she frequently went there to visit her father and brother, and sometimes even to stay a night or two when they were acting as lighthouse keepers.

The light on the Longships rock never went out again. Ever since that day it has burned on "steadfast, serene, immovable, the same." Neither has there been any difficulty in finding watchers.

In love and reverence for the memory of their dear pastor, who had taken so deep an interest in the lighthouse, it became with the Sennen men a point of honour that the beacon on the Longships should never cease to shine. The noble work of saving life from shipwreck, which he began, they determined to carry on. Henceforth the lighthouse should never be untenanted. All the Cove men made a compact to watch thereby turns, two always, and sometimes three, being on the rock at once. Owen and Philip occasionally occupied the post, as did Tom Marriott and Dick Evans. However violent might be the gale, though the winds howled and the waves dashed with terrible fury against the strong walls, while the roar from the cavern beneath was awful and deafening, no lighthouse keeper ever murmured, none shirked his duty when his turn came round. Each thought of the little child who had once been left there all alone, how bravely she had performed her duty, undaunted by the fearful solitude and by the roar and tumult of the elements as they raged around her. From her example they took courage, cheering each other to bear patiently the short period of exile and privation, which, however irksome to them, was of such infinite benefit to humanity; and remembering that by the regular and quiet exercise of their humble duty many lives were constantly preserved to their families and their country.

Within the last few years a new lighthouse has been erected on the Longships. The old building, the scene of our tale, which for eighty years had battled with the wild Atlantic storms, was not considered sufficiently high, and a noble lighthouse, with a lighting apparatus fitted according to the improvements and engineering of the present day, now stands on the Longships rock. The light shines at an elevation of 110 feet above high-water mark, and is visible at a distance of 18 miles. Brighter, clearer, more cheering by their glorious rays do the lamps now burn in the new lighthouse, warning the mariner of the treacherous rocks, and guiding him to his desired haven.

"Steadfast, serene, immovable, the same
Year after year, through all the silent night,
Burns on for evermore that quenchless flame,
Shines on that inextinguishable light.

"Like the great giant Christopher, it stands
Upon the brink of the tempestuous wave;
Wading far out among the rocks and sands,
The night-o'ertaken mariner to save.

"And the great ships sail outward and return,
Bending and bowing o'er the billowy swells,
And ever joyful as they see it burn,
They wave their silent welcomes and farewells."

Note

The new lighthouse which was erected on the Longships some three years ago has not been free from accidents. The Western Morning News of Nov. 1, 1877, states: "It will be remembered that for several days signals of distress and a flag half-mast high were flying at the lighthouse, which was unable to communicate with the shore in consequence of the fact that the signals long in use at the Longships had been taken away, and a new code substituted, the rough sea making boat communication impossible. It seems that the accident occurred on 25th October. Just after dinner the house keepers (Steer, Cutting, and Boyle) went down on the rock to stretch their legs, the weather having prevented their leaving the tower for more than a week. It was low water, and the weather was fine. Boyle was full of spirits and fun, and was cautioned by Steer, the principal keeper, to mind what he was about, or he would get into mischief. No sooner had this been said than the other keeper, Cutting, called out 'He is gone over;' and both rushed to the other side of the rock to try to rescue him. They got a rope under his right arm, and at the imminent risk of their own lives got him close up to the rock, but he seemed to be stunned and powerless, and was carried away by the strong tide form under their very hands, and of course they saw him no more. This is the fifth mishap which has occurred at the Longships, and confirms the opinion that in highly dangerous lighthouses none but staid and experienced men should be employed, young keepers being altogether unfit. In fine weather they take liberties with the sea, not knowing its treacherous character, and in heavy gales they are terror-stricken at the frightful waves which break over the tower. The first cause hurried poor Boyle to his doom; and it is upon record that in more than one instance, notably, in the case of the Longships, more than one untrained keeper has been driven insane from sheer terror.